THE WIG, THE BITCH &
# the meltdown

# THE WIG, THE BITCH & the meltdown

## A NOVEL
## JAY MANUEL

THE WIG, THE BITCH & THE MELTDOWN

First paperback edition July 2020

ISBN: 978-1-946274-43-4 (paperback)
ISBN: 978-1-946274-44-1 (ebook)

{1 2 3 4 5 6 7 8 9 10}

Cataloging-in Publication number: 2020935691

Cover Design by Aaron Favaloro and Litsa Vintzileou
Book Layout by Amit Dey

Published by Wordeee in the United States, Beacon, New York 2020
Website: www.wordeee.com
Twitter: wordeeeupdates
Facebook: wordeee
e-Mail: contact@wordeee.com

# ACKNOWLEDGMENTS

We all have a story to tell. And we all hope there is someone to listen when that time comes. It's my sincere hope that this story resonates for many people and it finds its intended audience. Sharing our pain through comedy provides us with a divine pursuit of humanness, prompting us to be more humane to each other. If not Shakespearean, are we not all court jesters?

To all seeking authentic selves, may it be so. Thank you to all the people who have been instrumental in guiding and encouraging me to tell this story. To the handful of die-hard friends and family who hung in with me through every rewrite, you are saints. Special thanks to Marva Allen who, before I wrote a word, encouraged me to find my own voice in telling this story. Hundreds of calls later, I'm sure she could argue the Devil writes books too!

# CONTENTS

CHAPTER ONE – AMUSIN' PERIL . . . . . . . . . . . . . . . . . . . . . . . . . . . . . 1

CHAPTER TWO – THE HONEYMOON . . . . . . . . . . . . . . . . . . . . . . . 8

CHAPTER THREE – A SHOW IS BORN . . . . . . . . . . . . . . . . . . . . . . 20

CHAPTER FOUR – STYLE HIM FAMOUS . . . . . . . . . . . . . . . . . . . . 29

CHAPTER FIVE – CATTLE CALL . . . . . . . . . . . . . . . . . . . . . . . . . . . . 45

CHAPTER SIX – MAKEOVER MUSINGS . . . . . . . . . . . . . . . . . . . . . 55

CHAPTER SEVEN – FIERCE CREATURES . . . . . . . . . . . . . . . . . . . . 67

CHAPTER EIGHT – LOOK WHO'S JUDGING . . . . . . . . . . . . . . . . . 77

CHAPTER NINE – TERRIBLE TWOS . . . . . . . . . . . . . . . . . . . . . . . . 92

CHAPTER TEN – KEISHAVISION . . . . . . . . . . . . . . . . . . . . . . . . . . . 102

CHAPTER ELEVEN – COPY THAT . . . . . . . . . . . . . . . . . . . . . . . . . . 120

CHAPTER TWELVE – REALITY CHECK . . . . . . . . . . . . . . . . . . . . . 142

CHAPTER THIRTEEN – THE MADNESS UNFOLDS . . . . . . . . . . . . 152

CHAPTER FOURTEEN – MR. FIX-IT . . . . . . . . . . . . . . . . . . . . . . . . 162

CHAPTER FIFTEEN – MELTDOWN . . . . . . . . . . . . . . . . . . . . . . . . . 171

CHAPTER SIXTEEN – LIGHTS OUT . . . . . . . . . . . . . . . . . . . . . . . . . 179

CHAPTER SEVENTEEN – KIMORU . . . . . . . . . . . . . . . . . . . . . . . . . 191

CHAPTER EIGHTEEN – TWISTED VANITY . . . . . . . . . . . . . . . . . . 205

CHAPTER NINETEEN – REVELATIONS . . . . . . . . . . . . . . . . . . . . . 215

CHAPTER TWENTY – SCRIPT CHANGE. . . . . . . . . . . . . . . . . . . . . 226

CHAPTER TWENTY-ONE – DUCK FACE . . . . . . . . . . . . . . . . . . . . . 235

CHAPTER TWENTY-TWO – RELIABLE SOURCES. . . . . . . . . . . . . . 242

CHAPTER TWENTY-THREE – LIVE TV'S THE BITCH. . . . . . . . . . . 247

CHAPTER TWENTY- FOUR – IT'S A WRAP . . . . . . . . . . . . . . . . . . . 263

CHAPTER TWENTY-FIVE – A NEW DAY . . . . . . . . . . . . . . . . . . . . . 279

CHAPTER TWENTY-SIX – EVENING THE SCORE. . . . . . . . . . . . . . 287

CHAPTER TWENTY-SEVEN – TRUTH BE TOLD. . . . . . . . . . . . . . . 299

CHAPTER TWENTY-EIGHT – DAMAGE CONTROL. . . . . . . . . . . . . 306

CHAPTER TWENTY-NINE – SHITSTORM . . . . . . . . . . . . . . . . . . . . 315

CHAPTER THIRTY – I SEE YOU . . . . . . . . . . . . . . . . . . . . . . . . . . . . 324

CHAPTER THIRTY-ONE – THE JOURNEY HOME. . . . . . . . . . . . . . 333

The world of Reality TV is not real, and yet reality television has morphed into *reality*. I've worked in this world of smoke and mirrors. And when the smoke dissipates, the mirror reflects the truth.

—*Jay Manuel*

# AMUSIN' PERIL

**Lincoln Center, New York City**
**8:36 p.m.**

ETAL CATERING RACKS crashed into each other as the ebony-skinned model—hair set in pin-curls, face in full glam—fell out the doorway and into the deserted back alley outside the illustrious fashion week venue. Two plates and three champagne glasses teetered dangerously on the edge but stopped short of toppling to the frozen pavement. Squeezing her eyes, she raised her face to the heavens and blinked back the tears that threatened to ruin the makeup her personal glam guru had spent over an hour perfecting. Out front, entertainment news vans crowded the massive tents that housed the glitz and bling of the latest trends, designers, and, of course, Supermodels. She looked left. Then right. Coast clear, she shuddered away the horror of a few moments ago. "Asshole," she snuffled.

A diminutive assistant multitasking on two iPhones burst through the same door. She looked left. Then right. "Keisha?" she called, squinting into the murky night.

"Where the hell's my driver?"

"*Ohmigod.* You scared me," the girl blurted, having no idea how scared she really should be. "I texted him twice. Shit, how do I not have service out here?"

The five-foot, eleven-inch model—towering like a cat over a little bird—grabbed one of her iPhones, smashing it to the ground. "Just get me my damn car!"

"Yes, Keisha. Right away, Keisha." The assistant ran back into the tent.

Noticing two heroin-chic models, winter coats drawn tight over their white bathrobes, walking in her direction, the Supermodel ducked behind the catering racks. She watched as they expertly navigated their way up the icy ramp, holding on to each other's arms for balance, their slippery pedicure flip-flops making them look more like waddling ducks than mighty catwalkers of the runway. Plumes of white smoke billowed from their vapes.

"It was bound to happen," the blonde girl quipped. "At the Veronika's Privates fitting, she had to wear a size eight, and that barely fit."

The brunette shivered. "Donatella won't even look at anyone over a size zero."

Keisha dropped to her knees behind the carts of empty champagne glasses. The fashion industry that insisted it no longer encouraged models to starve themselves was all lip service. The duck-walking cats simultaneously nodded their heads like dashboard bobblehead dolls. "I hear she's not booked for any shows in Europe either. She's getting too old anyway."

Blondie took another drag on her vape and choked. "I don't care how big a bitch she is, Michael Kors going on like that tonight was way rough."

"Did he fire her or did she fire him?"

The metal stage door flew open again, and this time a strikingly handsome, racially ambiguous man in black leather skinny jeans burst into the alley holding on to his headset. The caterer's racks could stand no more. The teetering glasses that had been barely clinging to their perch toppled to the ground, shattering over the crouching model's hidden head.

"Shit," the show coordinator for Michael Kors screeched, grabbing two of the racks to steady them. "What are you guys doing out here?" He saw the anorexic models, hurrying toward the tent door. "We're starting the show in five minutes. I need you inside and in your first looks," he yelled at the smokers. "Have either of you seen Keisha?"

"Didn't you get the memo, Pablo?" the sickly Nordic-type sniped. "Michael told Keisha she was getting too big for his britches. We figured that was good for another smoke," she sassed.

Pablo sneered at the girls. "Clearly, it's *you* who didn't get my memo. Beyoncé and JLo started the booty revolution. It's all about loving your curves now, girl." He looked the rail skinny models up and down. "Michael just needed to be reminded. Keisha's in, and we're on in five." He looked left. Then right. "As soon as I fucking find her," he mumbled under his breath. If Pablo were a firefighter, he'd be the one holding the hose. His job was to put out fires. Quickly. Efficiently. Permanently.

The girls waddled toward the door in their pedi-flip flops.

"Better hurry; Ashley Graham is probably replacing you for a major campaign as we speak."

The starving models gasped in horror, now skating toward the door.

"Ashley will never get the *real money* gigs," Blondie whispered to her cohort.

"Don't count on that," Pablo, who'd overheard the snide comment, retorted. "Michael Kors needs a big headline this season, and I just reminded him—big is beautiful. Keisha's opening *and* closing the show tonight, booty curves and all."

"Shit, she'll get an extra fifty grand for that stunt," Blondie said, stepping through the threshold.

"Honey, she gets twenty grand per turn. She'll get two-fifty tonight." Pablo slammed the door shut on the girls' stunned faces.

"Hell, that's more than I make in a year," he heard one of the models say. Their muffled voices faded away.

Pablo enjoyed putting the little ingrates in their place, but right now he had a seriously urgent matter to attend to. "Does anyone have a twenty on Keisha Kash," he yelled into his mic. "I need a twenty on Keisha Kash. Now."

Like a black Venus rising, the Amazonian Supermodel uncurled to her full majestic height from behind the catering racks. A few shards of glass twinkled in her pin curls like glitter. Pablo's mouth gaped open as he looked up at the black goddess herself. "*Ohmigod.* Miss Kash, I...I'm so sorry you heard that. If I offended you in any way...I mean, you're not fat or anything, those skinny girls are just...ah shit, I mean, you're stunning, you're real...most women would kill to be you."

"I know." Keisha's gold-tinted lips curled into the smile that had made her millions.

"Pablo, come in, Pablo," his headset blared. "She's left already. I heard her assistant calling an Uber."

"I've got her."

"You've got her?"

He nodded, as though the stage manager could see him, then repeated, "Yeah, I got her."

"And you are?" Keisha asked, looking him up and down, pursing her lips as she judged his merit and his looks.

"Aside from being an inarticulate dumbass?"

"Aside from that."

"The show coordinator, Pablo Michaels."

She reached over and tapped the end of Pablo's nose. "And you convinced Kors to let me open *and* close the show?"

Pablo nodded slowly.

"You're my new BFF, Mr. Pablo." She blinked her false eyelashes at him, twice.

Pablo's heart thumped in his chest. He'd loved Keisha Kash since she'd made the cover of *Vogue* at the age of sixteen, single-handedly redefining beauty as a young woman. Very few black models had that honor at the time. And now, he hoped, she might get to do it again in her 30s, representing the full-figured woman.

Keisha's smile faded into a churlish grin that was a little creepy, like one of those toy clowns in a horror film. "Do you know what I can do for you?" She fixed him with a gimlet gaze and stared into his eyes with such intensity that Pablo wondered if she was trying to hypnotize him.

"An Uber is two minutes away." The errant assistant rushed through the door, waving her now only iPhone.

Keisha's eyes shot daggers at the girl. "An Uber? I have my own driver paid for by Kors. How useless can you be?"

The girl stammered her way through trying to explain her reasoning to her irate boss. "I'm sorry. I'm—"

"Fired." Keisha grabbed her cell phone, dropped it on the ground and smashed it with her heel.

"That was my phone."

"It still is." Keisha turned away as her now former assistant dropped to her knees and tried to pick up the pieces of her shattered device.

Pablo stooped down to help the stunned assistant, when the saccharine voice floated toward him.

"You coming, Mr. Pablo?" Keisha purred. "Pablo Michaels. I like that. It's a name people are gonna remember, if I have anything to say about it." Keisha walked over to the backstage door. "Your show begins in two minutes, and I still need to get to wardrobe."

Leaving the assistant to solve her own phone problems, Pablo found himself walking behind the sinewy sway of the Supermodel like her personal consort. He was having a 'pinch himself' moment, but it was too soon interrupted by the stage manager's panicky squeal into his earpiece. "*Merde*...Anyone got a twenty on Pablo or Keisha?"

Pablo pressed his mic. "She's flying in. Cue the music."

Five minutes later, Keisha Kash was figure eighting her curvaceous way down the runway in seven-inch spikey heels and a bandage dress. Cameras flashed. Seventies disco thumped. She vogued. Posed. The crowd erupted.

New York Fashion Week's Fall/Winter shows always land in February, amid the dreary skies and frozen slush of Manhattan's icy sidewalks. Still, its *bright lights, big city* drew A-list celebs, fashionistas and fans to the prominent bi-annual gathering of everybody who's anybody.

Backstage was a typhoon of naked or half-naked models racing back and forth in between the runway and wardrobe, stopping by for first, second and third looks, touch-ups from makeup and hair artists. Pablo couldn't believe that twenty minutes earlier, this top designer had been having a hissy fit, followed by an even bigger temper tantrum from his Supermodel who was now garnering a standing ovation. He peered through a crack in the curtains and sighed. There were Ariana Grande and JLo, tragically sitting in the front row alongside bloggers of the moment and teenage social media stars.

It used to be that fashion week was the place to be discovered. Now, the overhyped runway presentations were reduced to spotlighting viral influencers. For the most part, fashion editors were forced to sit, or worse, stand in back, while the popular yet uninformed posse, who now inhabited the coveted front line, spoke in sound bites and hashtags. Pablo looked over at Anna Wintour, who seemed unbothered by her surroundings, as she remained the only recognizable editor with a front-row seat.

Kors came up and patted his shoulder. "I'm glad we didn't get Kendall Jenner. I'm obsessed with Keisha now."

Pablo's heart stuck in his throat. "Thank you," he whispered.

As Keisha strutted off the catwalk for the last time, she winked at Kors and said, "He's mine."

And he was in that instant—sign, sealed, delivered—hers.

# THE HONEYMOON

THE KORS SHOW wrapped with stars falling from the ceiling, as even bigger stars—literally and figuratively, like Keisha Kash—strutted down the catwalk, hand in hand, with the famous designer. Backstage, champagne flowed like kisses, and everyone congratulated each other and themselves for being fabulous as well as putting on a fabulous show. No one seemed to recall that it was Pablo who'd rescued the show from the brink of disaster and made it fabulous. Keisha and Kors got the accolades, but Pablo didn't expect more. With others, he graciously toasted the designer and the model, promising himself to sleep in the next morning now that the revelry was over. Finally, he could recover from the hectic month of prep work that was needed to pull off the show. He was beyond exhausted.

"Let's bounce," Keisha whispered in Pablo's ear. "I can't stand wrap parties."

Pablo looked regrettably around the room. He'd been looking forward to getting to know Kors more intimately, and to networking the after-show soiree at TAO Downtown. He really should be putting himself out there and working on securing jobs that would move him toward his own dreams, not just others, but Keisha's invitation was too tempting to ignore. "Me neither," he said, following her into the night.

Stripped of all her dramatic makeup, baseball cap perched, Pablo couldn't believe his luck to be the one selected from the crowd to escort lady-fabulous out the door to where her over-sized blacked-out Escalade was waiting. He wondered briefly who'd ordered the car, as this was clearly not an Uber. When the SUV door was opened by a drop-dead gorgeous hunk of a chauffeur, Pablo stopped caring, though.

"Where to, Ms. Kash?" It seemed the driver could find her just fine without her assistant.

"Home, James," she giggled, stretching out like a feline across the back seat of her souped-up ride. She patted the empty space beside her. "Sit." She kicked off her shoes and plopped her feet into his lap. "My feet are killing me."

Pablo had seen models' feet bleed after walking in shoes that cramped their toes and cut into their flesh. Callouses were standard fare in the industry, but Keisha's feet were pristine and perfect. Just like the rest of her. He began massaging her arches and toes.

"How does Chinese sound?"

"Great."

"Shit, my assistant has the number to my favorite place."

"No big deal. I'll check Grubhub. What's it called?"

"I dunno."

"Where do you live?"

"565 Broome. The big glass towers."

With deft efficiency, Pablo typed the word "Chinese" into his food delivery app and began to read out the list of names of restaurants in the area. "Jade Garden. The Big Wong. Lo Hung Cock. OMG, they're next to each other."

"It's somebody's name."

"Joe's Shanghai?"

"That's it! Crab dumplings. Get seven orders."

"Seven?"

"I'm starving! Oh, and order the delivery under the name *Crystal Lite*. My doormen know what to do."

After adding the new delivery address to his profile, Pablo processed the order with his Apple Pay. "All done."

An hour later, they'd devoured three platters of dumplings and were staring down the last one when Keisha shook her chopsticks at Pablo and said, "I think we were meant to meet."

"I was just thinking the same thing."

"It's like serendipity. And don't think I dunno what you did for me tonight." She stared down the plate. "So, what's your story? How did you end up my knight in shining armor?"

"Well, you know, Midwest boys love to rescue damsels in distress."

"Midwest to Manhattan? Come on, tell Mama."

He smiled shyly. Was Keisha Kash really interested in lowly Pablo Michaels? "Well, I studied photography and marketing at Parsons, and my senior project was to produce the entire concept for the fashion class's runway spectacle."

Keisha twizzled her chopsticks. "Short version."

*He was boring her.* "Anyway, Fern Mallis herself was in the audience," he blurted.

"Wow."

Fern Mallis was none other than the woman who had created 7th on Sixth Productions—or New York Fashion Week, as it was now known.

"Fast forward, Fern recruited me. I became her assistant and then she recommended me to Michael Kors. And here we are." He popped a cold dumpling into his mouth. "Ta-dah."

Keisha squealed with delight. "I love rags-to-riches stories! This calls for ice cream and more champagne." She pointed to the double door Sub-Zero refrigerator.

Pablo got up and opened the unit's doors. Her fridge was bigger than the bathroom in his apartment. Hell, it was bigger than his bedroom. And there was room enough to sleep in it. There was nothing but champagne and leftovers on one side, and quarts of ice cream on the other.

"My KonMari consultant organized it by flavor." She was now behind him, peeking over his shoulders.

Pablo couldn't believe Keisha had a certified tidying specialist organizing her frozen treats. It was a rainbow of flavors: coconut, blue moon, green tea, mint, limoncello, tangerine, raspberry, red bean, cookie dough, chocolate, caramel, latte, coffee…Pablo had never seen so much ice cream in one person's freezer.

"What's your poison?" She giggled like a little girl, pulling out a tub of Häagen-Dazs Dulce de Leche, and headed back to the sofa.

"That looks good to me." He followed, champagne in hand.

She sat the tub between them, stabbing it with two spoons, as he popped the champagne cork and poured.

Scoring the top of the ice cream until she had a mound on her spoon, she began to lick it like an icicle pop. "I've been feeling really low, ever since Veronika's Privates made a big deal about bringing me in to model plus sizes," she confided.

"And then when Kors started in on me tonight, I just wanted to die. You have no idea how hard it is to be me."

Pablo nodded empathetically.

"When you came along and told those skinny bitches off…" She bit into her ice cream. "You made me feel so much better about myself."

"How could you feel anything but? You're wonderful and—"

"I'm actually very insecure."

"You're an icon!"

Keisha stared into the ice cream carton.

"Seriously. Come on." Pablo flicked her spoon, trying to get a reaction. "I'm not joking around. Why are you looking all sad?"

Keisha paused, sucking on her ice cream. "I was bullied by my brother."

"No."

"Whenever I didn't have my weave in, he used to call me Gollum, like in *Lord of the Rings*."

"That's horrible."

"I know. But hashtag truth? Every time I step out of the shower after my braids are taken out, I look in the mirror and see a bug-eyed Mantis with a potbelly who's not accepted in *real* fashion circles anymore." Tears were slipping down her million-dollar face and into the carton, making it salted caramel ice cream.

"You gotta stop that old childhood shit. First, it's not true. At all. You are not some pasty creature hanging out in a cave. And you have almond eyes, not bug eyes. Your skin is flawless. Where's your brother now? Huh?"

"In a psych ward."

Pablo bluffed the shock by making his I-told-you-so face. "Hashtag, just saying." He crossed his fingers in the air.

Keisha's eyes squinted at the gesture and then she stabbed the ice cream, twice.

It was one of those moments where one secret divulged deserves another. Pablo inhaled and prepared to spill his own beans. "I'm adopted."

"My mama's in prison."

They both burst into tears.

"I've always had to fend for myself," she whimpered. Her crying seemed somewhat manufactured. Rehearsed perhaps? "So, I armored up. I've never had my feelings truly heard before. I don't even think I like any of my family."

"I didn't know much about my birth mother. Only that she was a teenager and white. My biological father was young and black. A mistake in so many ways. My adoptive parents were the answer to any child's prayers, but I was also an answer to theirs. As devout Catholics, my mom told me she'd prayed to get pregnant until she was forced to have a hysterectomy at the age of twenty-seven. 'Then, God told me he had a special soul for me in heaven,' she'd say. 'I just had to be patient and wait for my blessing to come into the light. And then one day, here you were.'" Pablo had spent much of his childhood experiencing the empty feeling of depression, and it always set in when he talked about his past. Zoloft, however, had become his savior at twenty-two, and it kept his unhealed trauma in check.

"OMG, that's beautiful." Keisha scooped more Dulce de Leche into her mouth. "My fucked-up, cheating dad left my mom when my brother and I were little kids. I barely remember him. Then, when I was thirteen, my mama got locked up. We had no real family growing up."

"That's horrible."

"I have PTSD from it."

"I have PTSD just from hearing about it. How'd you manage then?"

"We lived with distant cousins. My real name is Kiki Grimes."

"Mine is David...*something*. I don't even know." Pablo felt his eyes get hot again. There was a lot more to his adoption story, but something deep down told him it wasn't time to spill *all* the beans. Plus, he wasn't even ready to face it. The tears leaking from his eyes, however, betrayed his stoic expression.

"We're gonna need more ice cream." Keisha jumped up and ran to the freezer. Moving from size zero to plus had its advantages. "You wanna watch a movie or something?"

"Sure," he said, wiping his eyes and trying to act normal.

Moments later, they'd settled on the couches in the living room, each holding their own quart of ice cream. Pablo dug into his Rainbow Swirl. An old black-and-white movie flickered across her supersized screen.

Keisha had a curious look in her eye. "You know, I don't think I've ever known somebody who was adopted. Isn't that so weird?"

Pablo didn't think it was that weird, but they'd been drinking champagne and eating a lot of sugar.

"I don't think I could handle the rejection. I mean, your own mother abandoned you."

"I wasn't left in a basket like Moses," Pablo said as he sat back, trying not to feel offended. Keisha was clearly abandoned, but he didn't dare bring that up. He chirped, "Besides, she gave me great parents. My mom is supportive about me finding my birth mother if I want to, but I'm not interested." He dabbled with his ice cream. "She was just a carrying case for nine months, you know? I don't even wanna know about my birth family. What would I do after I meet the woman who gave birth to me? Send Christmas cards and chat on the phone once a month?"

Keisha shook her head. "That's all I get to do with my mom, and she birthed me."

Pablo felt like one of the bulimic models on a binge. Keisha had probably been one, once. "Life is so hard," he murmured. "I feel like all I do is fight people who are trying to take me down." Keisha finally shifted her gaze from the ice cream to look Pablo in the eye.

"Hey, you fought your way to the top and had to challenge the powers that be. That doesn't mean you're ugly or a bad person. It's hard for women. Hell, it's even harder for black women."

"Truth." She zeroed in on him. "I need someone like you. Someone I can trust. Someone who gets me." Pablo mashed the ice cream beneath his spoon and nodded. He was loyal, empathetic, hardworking and besotted. *Could she be...*

"I used to be full of dreams. I used to think the entertainment world was all about everyone getting along, helping each other, *supporting* each other." She stared into the second empty tub of Dulce de Leche. It was all soupy at the bottom, and she was stirring and sipping it from her spoon now. "But it's so cutthroat and superficial, you've gotta have someone you can trust to stay sane. You were meant to come into my life, I know it."

Pablo didn't know what to say. They barely knew each other, yet Keisha was so earnest in her affections towards him. Strange. It made him feel a little uncomfortable. This friendship was clearly going to develop fast. Superfast. Did all Supermodels operate in the fast lane? Pablo certainly didn't know. Nonetheless, she was the dream BFF he'd always wanted. That was the blessing. And no one is so rich as to throw away a friend.

On the giant flat-screen TV that reigned supreme over the living room fireplace, Pablo recognized the black-and-white Turner Classic film. A young Judy Garland and Mickey Rooney were hugging each other and running toward a barn. "*Babes in Arms*," he whispered. "Ever watch it?"

Keisha looked at the screen and turned up the sound.

"Let's put on a show!" Judy was saying to Mickey.

"It's so much easier when you're a white girl," Keisha scoffed.

"Who can sing," Pablo added. They both burst out laughing.

"Mr. Pablo, you wanna know a secret?" Keisha's voice suddenly sounded like that of a five-year-old girl's.

Pablo tilted his head away from the screen to glance at her. *Of course, he wanted to know a secret.*

"I used to watch the Oscars when I was a little girl and I knew I would be there one day."

"Me too," he blurted.

"OMG."

"And the Emmys too," Pablo said. "But, you know what I've always secretly wanted?" Pablo paused for a moment. He'd never told anyone his dream job, but he felt like he could tell Keisha anything. "I wanna have a talk show and really help people."

"You are such a good person. I can totally tell."

Tears sprang back into Pablo's eyes. He'd never found a reason for so many tears as he had this night. He was so moved that she really did see him. And for the first time, he felt like he was on the path his life was meant to follow. "What about you?" he asked. "Do you have any dreams other than being who you are right now?"

"Now? This is a nightmare, not a dream. I'm just this *objet d'art* that gets picked apart every chance they get. Nothing I ever do is good enough." Keisha's voice cracked. "I've never heard anyone tell me I'm beautiful other than my mama."

"What are you talking about? I hear people say it at least twenty times a day. You're stunning. Believe that."

"No, Pablo. *Keisha Kash,* the celebrity, is beautiful, not me. They see the hair, the makeup, and the clothes. They see the fantasy. That's all a lie." She wiped her face and stared at his chin. "I wish that people would see me for a change, the *real* me. Maybe then I could love myself more. Who am I really when I'm not Keisha Kash, Supermodel?"

Pablo could not believe what he was hearing. How could someone so stunning be so insecure, so vulnerable, and so fragile? So much like him? He wanted to protect her and help her. "But you *are* you." His voice was soft and reassuring.

"Oh," she gasped, her lips quivering. "That's so profound." She looked at Pablo with those amber eyes that had inspired contact lens companies to create a new color in her honor. "I love you."

"OMG, I love you too." Pablo blurted. And that was the clenching moment. Their relationship was a narcissist's dream come true.

*　　*　　*

Fashion Week was a polar vortex of revelry amid hard work and fawning fans. Now, everywhere that Keisha went, Pablo was sure to go. He didn't have much choice. She wouldn't let her new BFF out of her sight. She bragged about him to the press, touted him at after-parties, and munched on French fries in his ears during one-on-one tête-à-têtes at Buddakan and *Per Se.* Since she'd fired her assistant, it seemed only natural for Pablo to step into that role. He was *free* too. Swept up in the Supermodel's wake, it took him a few days to realize that he was actually working for Keisha. It was quite a wake.

Pablo was the perfect foil for the temperamental trade winds of Keisha's erratic personality, but he didn't take any of it personally. Deep down, he knew how vulnerable she was, and to his surprise, sensitive. They swanned around town like two lovebirds. Keisha posted a selfie of the two of them smiling and crossing their pinky fingers with *#BestFriendsForever* written across it. It went viral. His Instagram account blew up with new followers. People began to recognize him on the street, even when he wasn't with the Supermodel, which wasn't often. Most of the nights during fashion week, they'd collapse in her loft, streaming Judy Garland and Mickey Rooney singing and dancing their way through the 1940s.

"Which one are you?" Keisha asked one night.

"Dunno. Which one are *you?*"

"I can't sing," she confessed.

"Can you dance?"

"Not really."

They giggled, and she rested her head on his shoulder. Pablo loved the affection Keisha gave him. *Maybe she's my soulmate?* he thought. He was in bliss.

In the afternoons, a change of clothes and a shower later, Keisha would be back in the hallways and on the staged runways of Lincoln Center, swishing, a perpetual smile on her face for the best designers and fashionistas in the world. The cameras never stopped flashing. Pablo, himself always smiling now, finally understood why models frown and pout. Smiling used too many muscle groups. It hurt.

By the end of Fashion Week, Pablo and Keisha were an item on *Page Six, US Weekly* and *Women's Wear Daily*. Vinny, Keisha's stockbroker boyfriend, finally showed up for her last standing ovation and together, they attended the big bash ending the season. It was the most grueling fashion week Pablo had ever lived through. With Vinny by her side, he knocked back one too many drinks and slipped away unnoticed. Pablo was dog-tired and just wanted to go home for a change.

An Uber later, he was in his tiny Hell's Kitchen apartment, happily falling into his very own bed for the first time in six days. He was ecstatic. Sprawling atop the down comforter covering rumpled flannel sheets, he stared up at the ceiling. Musing about his whirlwind friendship with none other than Supermodel Keisha Kash and how it could possibly change the trajectory of his career, he wondered what was in store for him now that fashion week was over. "I had no idea being a celebrity was so exhausting," he mumbled into his pillow. *You're definitely not the same person you were a week ago.* This was the last thought he had before sinking into well-deserved slumber.

# A SHOW IS BORN

THE ANNOYING BACK-UP beep of the early morning garbage truck shrieked below his window. Hungover and tormented by a dream, Pablo moaned. After the past week's gypsy lifestyle of sleeping on couches and beds in Keisha's apartment, it took him a moment to recall where he was.

Beep. Beep. Beep.

He threw a pillow over his head and fell back on the bed. His cubby wasn't the dream apartment Keisha had manifested for herself, but it was his. The second-floor walkup did not offer soundproof walls or a private elevator, but he'd long gotten used to bouncing up the stairs. The reality of life in New York hadn't entered his mind when he'd begged his parents to let him move to Manhattan. He'd made all sorts of promises to get their support: "No, I won't do drugs. Yes, I'll wear a condom. Yes, Mom, always. No, I won't go home with strangers. Yes, I'll floss twice a day." Finally, they had agreed to help with the steep deposit—first and last month's rent, and the promise of the first-born grandchild required by Manhattan landlords.

"You'd think you'd at least have an elevator for this price," his mother had said after huffing and puffing up the narrow stairs of the brownstone. She was even more distressed to discover that Pablo had lost a coin toss with his roommate, Malaki, and ended up in the front room of the small, dusty, overheated box he now called home. At least he had the fire escape for a balcony.

Amid the beeping of garbage collection outside, his iPhone was now buzzing around on his nightstand. Pablo fumbled for the device and squinted at the screen. The selfie of Keisha and him illuminated his phone. It was 5:16 a.m. He'd only been asleep for three hours!

"Hello?"

"*Ohmigod.* I got it. It *just* came to me, and I couldn't wait to tell you."

"Do you know what time it is?" Pablo croaked as he sat up in bed, pulling his comforter over his head.

"This is your destiny wakeup call. You ready?"

Never a morning person, Pablo mumbled something unintelligible.

"What is everyone really obsessed with on Reality TV? Supermodels. Not fashion. The problem with most model competition shows is, they're looking for the next *real* Supermodel.

Silence.

"Hello?" She sounded annoyed. "You awake?"

"Uh huh." He did have eyes open, at least.

"I got the idea last night when I was making Vinny watch that movie we watched."

"*Babes in Arms?*"

"That's the one. You and I are gonna pitch a show that allows real girls–like the ones on Instagram–to have someone like *me* support their dreams. Do you know how much I wish someone had helped me? Now I can be the guru of Supermodels in the making."

It didn't sound at all like the movie they watched, but Pablo didn't say anything.

"Of course, we'll push their viral antics all over social. It'll give us a *huge* platform."

"How exactly is that any different from *America's Next Top Model* or *The Face?*"

She chortled so loud he had to hold the phone away from his ear. "Hellooo? *Keisha Kash!*" She reiterated her name, in case he'd forgotten who she was. "I'm the one who's relevant with the kids today. And I repost potential models on my social accounts *all the time*. That's like an endorsement. Plus, I'm *constantly* being begged for advice and mentoring. I should be paid to do that, and on camera."

He'd stopped nodding in the dark and was sitting upright. "Well, you're gonna need some kinda hook." Pablo was definitely listening now. "*Especially* if you're gonna sell this to a network in today's crowded streaming landscape." He jumped out of bed and pulled up the blackout blinds covering his window. This idea needed light, and he was getting more and more excited as the conversation continued.

"I knew you were the person to call. What are you doin' later today?"

Sleeping, he thought. "Meeting you?" he said. He looked out at the grey light of a winter, New York morning. A rat, the size of a small Rottweiler, scurried down an alleyway across the street. The muffled beep of the garbage truck had moved down the block, beckoning like his destiny.

Their first unofficial production meeting was held in Pablo's second-floor walkup. Keisha arrived with more Chinese takeout. This time, she paid for it, though. Pablo had taken a cocktail of Aspirin, Tylenol and protein to counteract his hangover from the night before. The last thing he needed was more MSG, but Keisha was so excited to work on her new TV idea that he couldn't tell her he needed another night to recover. When Pablo's roommate came home from work, he did a double-take at the incognito Supermodel spread sumptuously across their couch. Malaki was so tickled by the whole situation that he popped popcorn and sat crossed-legged on the floor at her feet like an acolyte. They stayed up into the wee hours of the morning, brainstorming format, idea, pitch.

Keisha tossed some popcorn at Pablo's head. "Why don't you be on the show?"

"Gee, Judy. I dunno. You're the one with all the talent." Pablo tried to sound as much like Mickey Rooney as possible.

Keisha squealed with laughter. "I'm serious! You're hot. Smart. Talented. You'll be our Creative Director. People love to feel like they're behind the scenes. You'll be the backstage guy." She looked like a queen bestowing a knighthood. "You follow my lead and play your cards right. Give it a couple of years, and I'll get you that talk show you've always wanted."

"For real? A talk show?" Pablo squealed with excitement.

"It's like Christmas, only better." Malaki joined in the excitement, the two of them leaping around in the apartment, hugging each other. Grabbing ahold of Keisha, the threesome were popping up and down like the popcorn they'd already eaten three bowls of.

It was all too much excitement. Yawning, Keisha sinuated her way through their twelve-foot-long apartment and peeked into Pablo's bedroom. "Is this your cave?" She didn't wait for an answer. Minutes later, they could hear her snoring like a buzz saw from his room.

Pablo lay awake on the couch, his body twitching with excitement. His flesh felt like it was humming with electricity. Hook, line, and sinker. Pablo was in! Keisha was his champion. His family. His muse. His brain churned with excitement until he finally fell into the deep sleep of the emotionally drained.

While most models were at spas recovering from fashion week, Keisha was pushing Pablo to help formulate her idea into a full-fledged television show. She loved every idea he threw at her, and for the first time in his life, he felt genuinely accepted and applauded. Nourished by the confidence that she could bring anything he could imagine to fruition, he let his ingenuity run completely unbridled. If Judy Garland and Mickey Rooney could put on a show in three days, so could Pablo and Keisha. Nothing was getting in their way.

Like her secretary, Pablo scribbled notes on napkins as Keisha's brain worked overtime on the idea. While she was napping, he honed the concept and polished it so when he gave the pages back to her, it looked better, more professional, and like a real TV show. Flipping through the pitch deck he'd drafted, complete with images to illustrate the show's concept, Keisha leaned back on the sofa in her loft and sighed. "I think we're ready."

"Ready for what?"

"To pitch."

Pablo felt the strength in his legs drain out of him. They couldn't possibly be ready.

"Here's my phone, call this executive and pretend to be my assistant."

Pablo rolled his eyes but did what he was told. Seconds later, Keisha was chatting with the President of the network on speakerphone and, within minutes, they had a meeting set with the head of development.

"How'd you do that?" Pablo asked as she hung up.

"I'm Keisha Kash, baby, and don't you forget it."

He genuflected in her direction.

Planning a show in three days had been tough, preparing to pitch a show in less time was even worse. Nerve-racking didn't begin to describe the level of stress Pablo fell under. Organizing concept boards, teaches and challenges, photoshoot creative, sketches of sample set designs and putting together a list of potential fashion icons they could bring on the show, Pablo forgot what sleep felt like. Every night was an all-nighter. Keisha ordered take-out and helped by being encouraging when she wasn't being distracting or distracted. While Pablo worked on complex renderings to create a slick-looking presentation—she Instagrammed and Tweeted with her fans.

"I don't think you need to work so hard."

"It needs to be love at first sight, Keisha."

"It always is." She looked at him and raised an eyebrow.

"We're only going to get one shot at this. It can't just ride on your name."

"Why not?"

He wasn't sure, but he wanted to make sure that she looked like a serious television show producer, not just a Supermodel, and that was his job. They took an Uber to the network. By the time they walked into the TN Network building, Pablo was semi-delirious, had lost five pounds, and looked like one of those heroin-chic runway models he so despised. In the lobby, they received name tags from security and, with clearance, headed to the elevator.

In the elevator, Pablo jiggled his portfolio against his thigh.

"Don't fidget," Keisha whispered.

"I've never done anything like this."

"Act as if you have."

The elevator flew up to the twenty-third floor, revealing an open concept, studio style office. Staff, dressed in everything from casual jeans and sneakers to designer suits and Louboutins, milled about the water cooler and communal printer. As they walked in, heads turned, and hushed whispers of awe followed Keisha as they beelined to the receptionist.

"Keisha Kash is here for her three o'clock," Pablo said.

"And you are?"

"Pablo Michaels."

"Her assistant?"

He bristled but didn't know what else to call himself, so he nodded. The receptionist picked up her phone and listened for a moment. Seconds later, a well-turned-out executive in a pencil skirt and the new Bottega Veneta pumps came through the door.

"Dawn Gately, head of development. It's an honor to meet you, Miss Kash." She shook Keisha's hand and nodded to Pablo. "And you are?"

"My assistant," Keisha said brightly. "Pablo Michaels."

They walked into an airy office with couches and comfortable chairs. "Would either of you like some water?"

"I only drink Bling H2O or Fillico," Keisha told her.

The exec snapped her fingers and an assistant disappeared. "The others will be here in a sec," Dawn informed.

Pablo, too nervous to drink anything, began pulling out concept boards and setting them up on the easels. He was ready and waiting in the room when the full team entered. Two execs introduced themselves. One was VP of Development and the other, the network's Original Programming Coordinator. Pablo was impressed. He knew Keisha had clout on the runway, but to have garnered top brass at a major network was impressive.

"We're not in Kansas anymore," Pablo whispered to Keisha. As water bottles were poured into glasses, someone pressed a remote control and black screens drew across the windows. "Privacy," Dawn mouthed to Pablo. His mouth went dry. Keisha crossed her famous legs and nodded at Pablo with the model's signature *petit pomme* smile.

He unrolled the concept with finesse and forgot his anxiety. "Imagine a young girl, working a cash register in Walmart, selling magazines with Keisha Kash on the cover—wishing she could be her. Now, Keisha's offering them the opportunity to become a brand—like herself. Think *Project Runway*, but for models. We're looking at a one-hour episodic competition show where we plan on selecting a group of wannabe models from social media to live in a model's apartment—like in the old days—and compete for the chance of becoming a real fashion icon. Each week's episode will start off with a *teach* segment so they learn what it's like to be a real model."

Pablo paused to gauge the executives' enthusiasm. They all sat with blank faces as if he were telling them about his grocery list. A lump formed in his throat. He swallowed hard and continued as if nothing was amiss. "We'll follow with a *challenge* segment based on the lesson they received. Girls can win immunity from elimination that week, or prizes. A big part of *every* episode will be the photoshoot, and in some cases, a TV commercial or other motion capture. This exciting all-access, backstage, insider look will give viewers a sense of weekly themes, crazy model antics, and set the contestants up for the last segment of each episode, *judging!*" He'd practiced the pitch enough that when his part was done, all he had to do was turn to the star of the show.

Now cued, Keisha rose above the executives so their chins followed her skyward. She smiled down at them, then did a slow seductive walk, drawing her index finger along the backs of their chairs. "That's right. Judging is where we'll eliminate the weakest contestant each week with a panel of fashion experts—led by me, of course—until we find our winner." Stopped at Pablo, who now revealed the last board with the logo he'd designed for the show, she did her twenty-grand Supermodel spin and said, "I'm Keisha Kash, and this is *Model Muse*."

The show was greenlit on the spot.

*     *     *

"Mom! I have a job! On TV!" Pablo shouted into his phone.

"On TV?"

"I'm gonna be the Creative Director on a new model show with Keisha Kash."

"Is she famous?"

He laughed at how provincial his parents were. "She's only, like, the biggest model in the world, Mom."

"That's nice, dear."

"I'm gonna be in charge of all the photoshoots, the runway shows. And I'll be directing the contestants."

"It's a game show?"

"Noooo…it's a reality TV show."

"Honey, how can anything on TV be reality?"

He gave up trying to explain more. "I just wanted you to know that your faith in me has paid off. I'm living the dream, Mom. Thank you."

"Oh, sweetheart, you don't have to thank us. We've always been proud of you."

Pablo thought of all the times he hadn't felt like enough; times he felt like he had to prove to his parents that he was worthy of being adopted. His eyes smarted. "I love you, Mom."

"I love you too. Even though I don't understand what it is you're doing, I'm very proud of you, dear."

# 4

# STYLE HIM FAMOUS

THE IRONY WAS that Pablo hated reality shows. They lacked empathy for people's feelings, and social media made the humiliation all the more public. Mockery and bullying against wannabe stars almost always went viral. Of course, society loved to snoop into the lives of others and reality TV was like the village busybody on steroids. Pablo called and texted friends about his good fortune and received loads of support. Even his childhood idol, whom Pablo had stalked on social and who in turn became his mentor, texted back with a "Congrats," followed by a second and more cryptic text a few seconds later.

**I.C.E. TEXT:** Warning…working on a Reality show is the modern day version of the Roman gladiator, without the blood! Trust me, I know. ☺ I'll be here if you need me.

Pablo took the message under advisement. He and Keisha were going to make reality television a better place, though. Something that really helped young people make a career out of their gifts. The thing that really bothered him on these kinds of shows was seeing someone in pain, or worse, seeing someone rejected. There had to be an element of that in their show, but Pablo hoped to approach everything from a positive standpoint. That's what would give the show its real edge. Pablo's golden rule—*Never quit people; Everyone deserves a chance*—would be his standard.

And what a chance it would be for him too. From an unwanted baby, adopted by loving and supportive parents, and backstage handler to being a part of a new television show. Keisha had single-handedly validated Pablo's belief that anyone can work in the fashion industry if given a chance. *Model Muse* was going to be all-inclusive. It was going to represent all the areas of the business: photographers, designers, creative directors, hair/makeup artists, stylists, set designers, and fashion journalists, as well as models. This was definitely a win.

The soundstage for the fledgling show was to be at Silvercup Studios in Queens. The raw space was pretty raw. It needed a fresh coat of paint and a clean floor. Wires dangled from the rigging where lights would be hung when production started. Keisha and Pablo did a walk through, figuring out where the models would be held, and what the judging set might look like. "It doesn't look like much," Keisha murmured. Her voice reverberated through the empty space.

"It's like Cinderella before the ball," he said.

"More like, we need to turn this frog into a princess."

Outside on the street, they stared up at the large red-lettered sign arching over the rooftops of Long Island City.

"We did it."

She smiled down at him in a strange, almost pained way.

"You feeling okay?" he asked, slightly concerned.

Just then, a teenager with braces and horne-rimmed glasses walked past them, then turned around and stared up at the Supermodel.

"Excuse me, my mama loves you. Can I get a selfie?"

"I don't do selfies." Keisha turned away from the child, dismissively. Pablo was shocked. She always took selfies. Why was she being so rude to the poor kid, who clearly needed a self-esteem boost? He watched the girl's stooped shoulders as she slumped away.

"Why'd you do that?"

"Her mama," she scoffed. "And she was butt ugly."

"I seem to recall you were too, once."

"Not *that* ugly." Keisha made Gollum eyes at Pablo and slapped his arm, teasingly. "So, listen, before our production meeting I wanna give you a makeover."

"A makeover?"

"If you're gonna be on TV next to me, we have to get you gorgeous. Besides, don't you think you should have the same kind of makeover our models are gonna have? That way, you can empathize with their experience."

Pablo thought empathy was the one thing he had loads of, but he didn't say anything.

"De La Renta, my miracle man, will see you in the morning."

"What's he gonna do to me?"

"Whatever he likes."

The studio's car pulled up to the curb and the driver got out to open the door. "Hashtag I got this." Pablo gestured and winked at the handsome chauffeur, holding the door open for his BFF. He was about to crawl into the backseat when Keisha pushed him away.

"I'm headed up to Vinny's and traffic's gonna be more of a bitch than *I am!*" Keisha laughed and kissed the air. "See you tomorrow, 10 a.m. sharp. Don't keep him waiting, Mr. Pablo, or he'll make you look like the Bride of Frankenstein." She slammed the door shut and tapped the window, smiling up at him.

Pablo forced a smile and waved. He couldn't shake the sense of rejection. Butch up, he chided himself. You're about to get everything you've ever dreamed of.

*   *   *

Ringlets of Pablo's black tresses drifted through the air to land in a hairy crop circle beneath De La Renta's chair. Pablo felt like he was being shorn like a sheep. Would slaughter be far behind?

"Can I look?" he asked the hair master, who sported perfectly braided cornrows.

"Nope."

"Oh, I see how this works now."

De La Renta slapped him and chuckled. "You the new kid on the block and Mother wants you to look the part, as well as play it." He had a soft southern lilt to his voice that made Pablo feel calmer.

"I thought I looked pretty good."

"You and me both. But what Mother wants, Mother gets."

Pablo relaxed into the leather chair and let De La Renta get on with it. If Keisha trusted her own personal hair/makeup artist, why shouldn't he? De La Renta coated all Pablo's hair with some color and set him in the corner with no mirrors. "Fifty-five minutes," he told him, "and no peeking."

An assistant brought him a latte and two *People* magazines. The British Royal family were making babies. His favorite section of *People* was the red-carpet gowns and the fashion dos and don'ts. There was Keisha in a 'fashion don't.' He held it up for De La Renta. "She really shouldn't be allowed to dress herself."

The glam guru guffawed. "Don't I know it? Mother has terrible taste."

When the bell buzzed, Pablo had to cover his eyes to walk across the studio and get his hair washed and scalp massaged. It was the full treatment today and he wondered if he had enough cash in his pocket for a tip. When he got back to De La Renta's chair, the mirror was covered with a black hairdressing gown. "I don't trust you not to peek," De La Renta teased. He fluffed some product into Pablo's hair and pulled out the hairdryer. The sculpting took as long as the cut.

They both got texts from Keisha at the same time.

**Keisha TEXT:** B there in ten.

"Almost done. You go slip in the back for the reveal." De La Renta handed Pablo a small plastic case. "Mother wants a complete overhaul, so pop these in as well."

Pablo looked down at the contact lenses he was supposed to slip into his virgin eyes and almost panicked. "How do you put them in?"

"Girl," De La Renta giggled. "You brand new."

It took a few tries and a lot of eye drops, but the lenses finally floated where they belonged.

"Where's my creative director?" They could hear Keisha calling from the front room.

"You ready, Mommy?" De La Renta shouted from the back room and bustled out to greet her. Pablo waited for a second, then slipped out the door as De La Renta announced, "I present the first *Model Muse* makeover!"

Pablo thrust his hips forward and pouted as he strutted his

stuff into the salon and did a three-point turn, his head tilted over one shoulder.

Keisha shrieked and applauded. "Bring it on. Yes. You're genius, De La Renta. Pure genius."

"True dat." De La Renta preened himself.

Surrounded by mirrors, Pablo looked at the stranger standing before his ecstatic friends. Close cropped hair, no curls. Silver grey instead of black. Grey eyes.

"Oh, my, God. I look fucking amazing."

"You look fucking *fierce*," Keisha praised.

Something about having his eyes a different color made him feel different inside, more confident, and sexy. He leaned in closer to the mirror to look into the windows of his soul. He almost didn't look biracial anymore—he looked *other*, except for his nose. It was just broad enough to speak to his ethnicity. He turned his face right and then left. The cut swept up over his ears, revealing his own fine chin and cheekbones. He was almost perfect. Almost. "Do you think I should get a nose job?"

That afternoon, a much-needed rain poured down on a dusty Manhattan as Keisha and her new creative director rode in the chauffeured Escalade traveling north on the FDR. Staring at his new reflection in the tinted windows, transfixed by his grey eyes and the grey New York City rain that was sheeting down the street, Pablo tried to remember if he'd taken his antidepressant that morning. If he hadn't, that could explain the sudden sense of detachment and loneliness. Perhaps it was just the weather...

The pressure of starting a new show had worn on both of them over the past few weeks, and tempers had flared—hers. Today, it was a relief to see Keisha finally lightening up. She had every reason to be in a good mood. He did too, for that matter. So why did he feel the low pressure of depression coming on? He had to snap out of it. They were about to do something really big together. He had to be in top form like his partner, who was always in top form.

Keisha snapped her fingers in front of his face. "Earth to Pablo."

"Sorry?"

"What's going on in that brain of yours?"

"I can't get over how I look now."

She laughed.

"Well, I was just saying this first production meeting is really important. We have to set the stage for how we work with everyone." She paused and looked at him, meaningfully. "It's you and me in control, no matter what anyone else thinks."

"It's all about you, Mommy," he quipped.

"Awe, my little porcelain prince," she teased. "I'm gonna tell you a secret."

He turned to her expectantly.

"*Model Muse* is gonna blow up. It's gonna build my empire. *Kashing In Productions*."

"Ummmm. You might wanna rethink that name. Hashtag keeping it real."

"Ya think? Well, some ghetto kid in Compton owns the URL and is tryin' to make me pay him a thousand dollars for it."

"Hello, hashtag queen of cheap?" He used his trademark gesture, crossing his fingers in the air as he laughed out loud. "Cut the kid a break and throw him some coins. Didn't you and your brother have it hard growing up on the west coast in Compton? Hell, buy the URL and hire him to do your website."

Keisha shifted in her seat as she tightened her upper lip. "I dunno."

"Generosity makes you feel like a million dollars, rather than just being worth a million dollars."

"I'm worth a lot more than a million." For a second,

he thought she was going to snap his head off. Instead, she laughed.

"Which reminds me. I found you an assistant. Finally."

"That took long enough."

"You keep me pretty busy."

She had too. And Pablo hadn't minded until she snapped her fingers at him to pick her panties up off the floor. Finding someone for her to flog was no easy task, though. He called his alma mater Parsons, the Fashion Institute of Technology, and all of the other art colleges in New York City to see if there were any soon-to-be-graduates desperate for work—someone smart enough to foresee problems and solve them, but not so smart she (or he) didn't want to be verbally abused. The assistant didn't need to understand Keisha—that was Pablo's still-to-be determined job description.

Pulling up outside of the network, the driver hopped out to hold an umbrella over her head as he opened the door to the Escalade and they jumped out to rush into the lobby. Inside, shaking the wet from their shoes, Keisha looked at him. "Are you ready for this?"

It was such a rhetorical question Pablo didn't even bother to answer. As they came off the elevator, Pablo could hear the receptionist speaking into the intercom. "Miss Keisha Kash is here."

"Send them in," a boisterous voice crackled over the speaker.

They were ushered into a conference room made of glass walls, where a small group of people sat around a large metal table that could've easily sat twenty, comfortably. Their new colleagues. Pablo paused and let Keisha walk past him with a dramatic swish.

Tall, dark and handsome did not begin to describe the man standing up to greet his new star. "Keisha Kash. We're so honored to have you as the host and EP of *Model Muse*. I'm Broyce Miller, Network Exec in charge of the show. We spoke on the phone."

Keisha smiled broadly at him. "Finally, we meet."

Broyce looked delighted. "So, let me introduce everybody to you." He pulled out a chair for the Supermodel to sit in. Pablo grabbed a seat on the fringe. "This is Joe Vong, formerly EP of our hit docu-reality show, *OFFICERZ*."

Pablo wondered what EP stood for. As if reading his mind, Broyce added, "Executive producer. He's our showrunner, overseeing all production."

"*OFFICERZ*?" Keisha paused and looked over at Vong. "That just got canceled, didn't it?"

Vong had the paunch of a man who spent too many hours sitting in his office, and the face of a man who yelled a lot. The petite and oddly boyish-looking Korean didn't look happy. "It got moved to a bad time slot. That killed the show."

"I'm sure it did, Mr. Joe," she said as she slipped into her creepy child's voice.

Pablo knew from the moment she said Mr. Joe something was wrong, but what or why, he had no idea.

"Rachel Simpleton, your supervising producer," Broyce continued.

Rachel had the earnest and gaunt look of a vegan, and Pablo wondered if she'd purposely dressed down for the meeting. He also wondered if he stooped down and looked under the table if she would be wearing Birkenstocks on her feet.

"And we're extremely lucky to have Luciana Velásquez casting for us. She just left IMG as head of their women's division."

Pablo was impressed at how Broyce Miller kept deferring to Keisha throughout the introductions.

Keisha looked over at Luciana, a tight fake smile curling the side of her lips. "Shanna, is it? I thought I knew everyone over at IMG." She shrugged. "Hmm, nice to meet you."

"Luciana." The casting director smiled back and started to flip through her papers. "I actually booked you on the Swarovski Christmas campaign. But that was years ago. You were a new face then."

Pablo cringed at the ageist comment. Was the woman an idiot?

Like a mythical harpy about to eat its kill, Keisha didn't blink.

Broyce jumped into the potential fray. "I just want to say that the network feels *Model Muse* is going to be a huge hit with someone of your caliber at the helm."

"And it will be." Keisha gestured in Pablo's direction. "I want you all to meet Pablo Michaels, my creative director and right-hand man."

Overcome by a wave of bashful shyness, Pablo simply waved. Keisha moved like a cresting wave toward the front of the room and leaned on the table. "Pablo worked for Fern Mallis and made his mark art directing and co-producing the Michael Kors show last winter. I'm sure you all heard about it. It got enormous press because of his innovative stylings. Everyone who works with Pablo, loves Pablo. He's gonna *werk* his fashion connections with stylists and photographers for us, so we have real cred, as well as ratings. And he's ours—exclusively. The *only* real fashion insider we have, other than me, of course."

Pablo could hear the rippling of hair standing on the back of the casting director's neck. "Well, as a seasoned booker at *the* biggest modeling agency in the world for eight years," Luciana fired back without missing a beat—Snarl! Hiss. Cat-fight—"I think I have a little experience in fashion."

With the grace of a *maître d'*, Broyce Miller diffused the friction in the room by quickly announcing, "Now that everybody knows each other, Luciana, why don't you bring in this season's models?"

"Happy to." She jumped up and opened the conference room door to a parade of stunning young female specimens. They snaked across the room in a crooked line, then turned to face the team, posing awkwardly with one leg bent and toe pointed. It felt suspiciously like a Miss America pageant, without the tits and ass. "First, we have Angela." Luciana gestured for a stick of a girl to step forward.

Keisha stood up. The girls sighed in collective awe at their muse. "Thank you. You can all leave now."

The models looked at Luciana and then at each other.

"We're good." Keisha flicked her perfectly manicured fingernails at them.

They wiggled back out of the room.

"I'm sorry. Did you want them to wait in the hall?" Luciana closed the door firmly behind the last contestant.

Keisha walked around the conference room table. Her *I'm gonna eat your liver* smile slowly spread over her face. Pablo wondered if Luciana would have any flesh left after the altercation that was about to ensue. The casting director looked completely unaware that she was about to become Keisha's lunch.

"I'm sorry, Lucia." Keisha leaned on the table and looked at the rest of the team. "You have it all wrong. *My* show is all about the Cinderella story. I need to build girls from the ground up. I need a little more broken bird. You feel me?"

"Yeah, I feel you. And it's Luciana! Lou…See…Anna."

Keisha ignored her. "I need girls that are odd-looking, fragile. Girls who have never walked a runway or posed in front of a real camera before. Girls who come from poor backgrounds and are struggling to be seen by modeling agents on social media. Real girls." She looked at Pablo as if making sure she'd explained the idea he'd given her. "Girls like me."

He nodded and added, "Keisha was thinking we could have an open call where we'd choose twenty girls with popular Instagram accounts to appear on the first episode. From that group, we'll select ten finalists who'd live together in the apartment where we'd film and follow them day-by-day."

"Of the ones selected from the larger group, get me at least four black girls. Three chocolate and one mocha-skinned—but she can't look like me." Keisha turned to Pablo. "Was there anything else we discussed that Lucy should know?"

"A redhead, a brunette, two blondes and one plus-sized girl."

"What would I do without you?" Her eyes twinkled merrily at the havoc she was creating around them.

"What about an Asian girl?" Joe hissed.

"And we'll need a Latina," Luciana added. She was about to explode.

"Brilliant. Your Cinderella idea is fantastic." Broyce swooped into the fray like a soldier disarming a bomb, without the protective garments. "So, let's make the finalist count a lucky number thirteen by adding one Asian girl and two Latinas. The network loves inclusivity. We're all here to support your vision, Keisha. You're the star." He turned to the irate casting director, his voice soft and kind. "Luciana, I'm sure you can find us girls who are a little more pedestrian but have the potential of becoming swans?"

"Broken birds flying in," the fiery Latina muttered. "Lemme figure out how to pull off an open call on such short notice. I'll email the details later today."

Broyce tilted his head toward Keisha in a silent query— was that okay with her? She pursed her lips and gave him a flirty smile, then shrugged as if she didn't care. She didn't.

She had won the first round, and that was all that mattered. Everyone in the room now knew who was really in charge. Pablo was surprised at her business acumen but even more astonished by her ruthlessness.

"Now, should we discuss the judges?" Broyce took the stack of folders sitting in front of Luciana and began to hand them out. Pablo found the gesture reassuring. The guy was a true diplomat; he knew how to give Keisha her due while protecting Luciana from further animosity. "In the interest of saving everyone's time," he introduced the next item on the agenda, "Luciana and I have whittled our selection of judges to four minor or formerly major celebrities. Let me add here that budget is a concern. All of these people fall within our budget and are aware they're under consideration."

A projection screen lowered behind them, and they all turned to see the first face.

"Miss Thing," Luciana began, "has coached almost every great Supermodel on her walk, including Keisha, and continues to have a semi-lucrative career teaching top models all over the world how to own the runway."

Pablo knew instantly why Miss Thing was chosen. Controversy. He was known for his twitter account profile: *For all my LGBTQXYZ rainbow-colored friends of the alphabet. I am not bisexual, transsexual, or a transvestite. I'm a gay man who parades around in women's couture to confuse white, straight America.* He was inappropriate, flamboyant, wickedly witty, and had been a runway coach since the dawn of time. He was going to be a handful.

"A six-foot five-inch man in heels teaching *the walk* can make for some humorous moments," Broyce added. "We're also counting on a gay audience tuning in, as well as young women and—"

"Dirty old men," Joe Vong said under his breath.

Luciana flicked the next judge's photograph onto the big screen. "Sasha Berenson."

Pablo nearly swooned. The undisputed, highest paid Supermodel of the world, whose nine-year Estée Lauder cosmetic contract had been unprecedented, and who he'd loved since he was thirteen was right before him! As a teenager, he'd plastered her *Vogue* covers on his bedroom walls. Sadly, she was the casualty of numerous botched plastic surgery attempts. As Broyce flicked another image of her onto the screen, Pablo realized it looked as if she'd had another frankenlift. Still, she would give the show credibility where Miss Thing gave it edge.

"Since Sasha can be very outspoken, we expect some great soundbites out of her," Broyce said. "She'll be our Simon Cowell for *Model Muse*."

Pablo liked both decisions and nodded, glancing over at Keisha to see if she agreed. Her eyes were narrow slits of gold glaring at the face of the first lady of Supermodels. She noticeably relaxed when she saw Pablo's approval, though.

"And because the American public are anglophiles, and we need a hot straight guy on the panel," Luciana added, "fashion photographer, Mason Hughes is our uber-blonde Brit."

The homophobic prick. Now it was Pablo's turn to narrow his eyes. He was definitely handsome, but Pablo had always thought that Mason Hughes had all the sex appeal of a smooth parts Ken Doll.

"Ooh, I love me some eye candy." Keisha smiled broadly at Pablo and giggled.

"Exactly," Broyce said.

The last photo on the giant screen was none other than Keisha Kash, herself.

"Our model's muse." Luciana and Broyce cooed together. Had they rehearsed the moment, or were they just psychically attuned to sucking up?

Keisha stood up, letting the image project on her body. As she moved back and forth, the photograph of her younger, svelter physique undulated across her chest. "I've created a *fierce* show, and with talent like this, I think we're looking at an exciting first season."

"And hopefully many more." Broyce stood up, joining the shimmering model's flickering light. "We have a top-notch executive team and with you at the helm, I think we can have a hit TV show. Thank you, everybody."

Keisha glared at Broyce Miller's presence in her spotlight. "I look forward to meeting my cast at the open call. Whenever you can get that organized, Lucie."

In the backseat of the Escalade, Keisha was almost chirping with delight. "That went well, don't ya think?"

"They seem like a highly professional team."

"But you're the only person I trust."

"Oh, I dunno. Broyce Miller seems really dependable."

"You can't trust anyone in this business. Don't let their superficial politeness fool you–it's all fake love. You and me," she pointed to his heart and then to hers, "we have to make sure you always directly loop me on everything, Pablo. We're running this show. No one else."

Pablo nodded in agreement. "You didn't like Joe Vong. And I have a bad feeling about him."

She looked surprised that he'd noticed. "You don't miss a beat, do ya? He's a real bastard."

"How could you possibly know the EP of a cop show?"

She sighed and stretched her back, looking at her friend. "He shot the arrest of my mama on the side of the 405 in LA— with that bullshit *OFFICERZ* show."

"No way."

"Way. Probably looking to win an Emmy."

"Shit. We gotta get rid of him. There's no way you should have to bear that burden."

"Clearly, he doesn't recognize me. My brother and I were in the car." She looked out the tinted windows.

"You were there, Keisha? How come you never told me this?"

"It's not something I want bragging rights to. He thrust a camera in my face as I screamed and cried and had snot dripping on my shirt."

"What a fucking scumbag." Pablo hated Joe even more.

"My agent bought the tape of the arrest and buried it, so I could have my career. How do you think I got discovered?"

"I thought you walked into an agency when you were sixteen and they signed you."

"That's the official version. Unofficially, my brother and I were in the backseat sobbing as our mother was dragged away in handcuffs for stealing jewels outta the safe at the morgue where she worked. She got thirty years. You know how they do us black folk."

"She worked in a morgue?"

"She photographed corpses."

Pablo felt queasy. He wasn't sure he wanted to know more. "We have to get rid of him. I don't want you traumatized by this guy."

"Don't' worry about me." She patted his leg. "Payback's a bitch. And I'm gonna make his life hell."

# CATTLE CALL

**B**Y THE TIME Pablo and Keisha got into the souped-up Escalade—the network now provided for their star—headed for Highline Stages, they were already running late. Keisha had made sure of that. "Always be fashionably late," she reminded her *protége.* "It drives Miss Thing nuts!"

"If we were any more fashionable, we'd get there tomorrow." Pablo was trying his best not to chew his nails, but his nerves were already frayed. In the past week, he hadn't slept more than four hours a night and eaten nothing but protein bars and almonds. To make matters worse, Keisha liked slumming it in Hell's Kitchen and thought his apartment was really "cute." She kept crashing in his bed, so he was stuck on the old couch, while Vinny and Keisha were doing the nasty in his bedroom. He couldn't even bear to look at the sheets. If it wasn't for his makeover, he would've looked like shit. And now they were stuck in traffic.

"What's going on?" Keisha yelled at the driver.

"Gridlock."

"Try another avenue."

"Gridlocked too."

She huffed and tapped her foot. If Keisha had one pet peeve, it was New York City traffic. It brought out the drama queen in her.

"We should walk," Pablo said.

"I'm not walking to the open call I'm hosting!"

"Then you might wanna call a helicopter," the driver said.

"How 'bout I run ahead and make sure everything's going smoothly." Pablo stepped out of the car.

"Text me the 411," she yelled as he hurried up Hudson Street. Pushing past pedestrians and tourists, his Gucci satchel thumping against his butt, Pablo power-walked toward the casting site. At the corner of Tenth Avenue and Fifteenth Street, he stopped cold. The line, no, the *lines* of young women wrapped around the block two, three, four times?

"Is this for us?" Pablo asked Luciana, who was standing by the door clipboard in hand.

"Ten thousand girls." Luciana rolled her eyes.

Sasha Berenson came stumbling up the sidewalk. "I know I'm fucking late, but I had to walk all the way from Fifth Avenue." She leaned on Pablo's shoulder and took off one of her high heels. "God, how did I wear these twelve hours a day? Give me Uggs or give me death."

"Where's Keisha?" Luciana asked.

"Coming from a meeting just around the corner," Pablo lied, while quickly texting his boss.

**Pablo TEXT:** Utter chaos! Traffic is because of our casting.

Just then, the Channel 5 News van pulled up outside the front entrance.

"Looks like we're gonna make News at Noon," Luciana said, clearly enjoying the chaos Keisha's request for an open call had caused.

Right behind the news van, Miss Thing exited his Uber wearing a crisp white shirt, skinny black tie and monstrous black tulle skirt with a six-foot train. He power stalked a bee-line for Pablo. "Oh, HELL no. Miss Thing is not sitting here all day looking for a *gold tooth* in this mouth full of decay–no, ma'am."

Manic Mason stepped out of the building and tapped his watch. "There is no way we are going to get through all these girls in one day. I have a shoot in four hours. I was told this was simply a press op and I did not have to do anything but show up. This looks like work here."

The judges looked at Pablo expectantly. Luciana raised a single eyebrow.

"What time is Joe Vong getting here?" Pablo asked.

"Not coming."

"What's more important than a new show?"

"He has a doctor's appointment."

"A testicle lift?" Miss Thing asked. The men looked at him in horror. "It's new plasma technology, tightens the scrotum."

"I am going to be sick," Mason blurted.

He did look a little queer.

*What the fuck.* Pablo almost blurted in desperation. The EP/Showrunner wasn't going to help oversee the first stage of the show? "We should have our cameras shooting this, not just the news networks. Where are our PR people?" Pablo was pissed. He didn't even know what or if he was on salary, and now the on-camera talent was looking at him to put out the fire. They didn't call him Mr. Fix-It for nothing, though. He closed his eyes for a moment, then opened them. "We'll have to divide up," Pablo told his colleagues. "Luciana, divide the girls into alphabetical groups of 100 each. The girls will carry numbers as they walk across the stage. We each get to pick twenty."

"That's one hundred," Miss Thing squeaked.

"It's less than ten thousand."

"So, you can do math," Miss Thing sniped back. "Who the hell has time to look at that many girls?"

"You do!" Pablo barked. "You signed on for this gig, not me. The twenty girls we all choose will come back and give us their life stories and headshots. Everybody gets seen. We don't go home until we're done. Mason, you'll have to postpone your shoot."

"You sound like an EP," Luciana said.

"I'm not paid like one."

At that moment, Keisha's blacked-out Escalade pulled up alongside the curb. Her driver got out and opened her door.

"There's Keisha Kash," rippled over the heads of the crowd.

"Oooooo. Upstaged again," Miss Thing muttered.

A news reporter made a mad dash across the sidewalk, microphone in hand. "Keisha, Keisha! Did you know that all of lower Manhattan is in gridlock because of this audition for your show?"

Keisha looked at the chubby blonde with baby doll cheeks. "That's what happens when you use my name." She smiled and waved to the girls standing ten deep in line. "Now, let's find my models." Girls screamed and waved. Miss Thing swept in beside Keisha, matching her stride step for step—he hadn't taught her how to walk for nothing.

Sasha sighed, but rather than following ten paces, she looped her arm into Pablo's and said, "What's a nice boy like you doing in a place like this?"

Behind them, Mason was using his most posh, British prep school accent as he argued on his phone. "I have *absolutely* no idea when we shall finish here. Bloody hell, it's a fashion show, what do you think?" He paused and held the phone away from his ear. "*You're* putting up with? My old nanny could handle this better than you are. Just make it work." He turned and sighed dramatically. "The problem with Americans is that no one has a butler in this country."

"As if you ever did." Miss Thing snorted and tossed his train in the air, as he swished away.

It was mayhem inside. Almost. Pablo could tell by the way Luciana was pacing back and forth that she must've been as shocked by the turn out as he was. He also guessed that she'd hoped the open call would backfire on Keisha and no one would show up. Her plan had backfired on everyone but Keisha. The Supermodel goddess sat through the first hour of casting before excusing herself with a wink and a nod. "I'll be back when you've gotten through the slush pile," she whispered in Pablo's ear.

"Am I getting paid for this?" he asked.

Miss Thing and Mason snuck out soon after. Sasha happily nursed her bottle of water, dutifully picking two girls per every thousand that came in. Though by the second hour Pablo feared she was doing eeny, meeny, miny, moe. When he suggested a coffee break, she toddled off to the ladies' room and he took a swig from her bottle—straight vodka. At least she was there.

Standing outside for a breath of fresh-ish air, Pablo saw the news anchor interviewing a sobbing contestant. "It was awful. I stood in line all night and by the time I got inside I didn't have any makeup on, my clothes were wrinkled and I had to walk past the judges with like a million other girls—the ones who got chosen were ugly nobodies. It was terrible. I was Miss Jersey Shore last year. I haven't seen this many young girls line up since my junior high went to an R. Kelly concert."

"R. Kelly?" the reporter asked.

"Yeah, but at least *there* I got one-on-one time with Kells!"

"You heard it here first, from WNYW, I'm Bonnie Pruitt at the Highline Stages casting call for TN Network's new TV show, *Model Muse*, the brainchild of Supermodel Keisha Kash."

Pablo had a feeling that he was watching a hurricane hurl itself toward the coastline at 200mph and only he and Keisha were in the eye of the storm, sweeping everything and everyone out of the way. She'd been right—the show was going to blow up.

By eight o'clock that evening, Luciana and Pablo alone finished winnowing through the finalists, listening to sob stories and picking one hundred headshots that they could submit to Keisha and Broyce.

Luciana leaned back in her chair. "I need a drink."

"I need two."

"You buying?"

"The network is. Dinner too." He stood up and held out his hand to the handsomely beautiful and fatigued Latina.

"I love a good expense account." She looped her arm around his. "Remind me next time I try to bring Keisha down to size that she really *is* huge—literally and figuratively."

Pablo had to laugh.

Late that night, he dropped Luciana off at her apartment and Ubered back downtown to Keisha's flat with the headshots of one hundred girls, and their stories stapled on the back. It was going to be an ice cream orgy and, after the long day, Pablo was ready to match Keisha pint for pint. He started with Green Tea. She had Coffee Almond Crunch. They both needed caffeine.

Luciana and Pablo had organized the images over dinner, arranging them by ethnicity. Keisha flipped through the black girls first, placing her first glance choices to one side. Then Pablo held up the image and read the story out loud.

"Oh, gimme a break. There's no way she was a homeless teenager. Borderline personality disorder, maybe," she would blurt, or "Boring!" or "Come to Mama." Those were all the categories Keisha had. By three in the morning, they had twelve sob stories, six former beauty or prom queens, four rags to hopeful riches, and three borings but too pretty to ignore.

*       *       *

With the twenty-five semi-finalists finally chosen, *Model Muse* was ready to begin filming its first casting special. Broyce Miller had the brilliant idea of filming the reveal of the thirteen finalists live at Silvercup Studios. In an effort to capitalize on the explosive national news cycle calling attention to the new show, this one-time live event was expected to garner massive media attention and cement *Model Muse* for the network's fall lineup. It had been a smart move on Broyce's part, feeding Keisha's own flair for live drama.

The warm-up comedian had finished with the audience, and the people in the studio bleachers quieted for a moment, as an anonymous voice announced, "Ladies and gentlemen, welcome to the live broadcast of TN Network's Casting Special for our new model competition show. So, give a big round of applause for our judging panel, Miss Thing."

From behind the curtain, Miss Thing did his signature walk, while waving and tossing kisses to the crowd, wearing a gown with green crinoline and lace.

"The highest paid Supermodel of the world, Sasha Berenson."

Sasha had done something new to her face, but at least it was symmetrical now. She looked like a silver slinky slithering across the stage, gorgeous as ever.

"And famed fashion photographer, Mason Hughes."

Mason was the only one not wearing a dress. His suit was shimmer blue and his eyes were ice. He held his hands up as he walked to his seat, mock shooting the audience.

"And now, the star of our show, Keisha Kash."

Strutting across the Silvercup soundstage on a custom-built, fuchsia pink, glitter runway, the multi-million-dollar model's muse swept onto the set. The audience went wild, cheering. She swirled and sparkled in a form-fitting, nude illusion, flesh-toned gown, encrusted with thousands of Swarovski crystals. She tossed a three-foot-long ponytail over her shoulder, so it cascaded past her butt, and gazed at her fans through black glittering smoky eyes. Pablo watched from the sideline in awe. She was amazing, and he was proud to be part of her dream.

"I'm Keisha Kash, and welcome to *Model Muse*." She held out her arms as if to embrace the world. There were whistles and cheers. "Thank you! Oh, wow! Thank you." She touched her heart dramatically. Her eyes glistened with tears. Rachel gestured to the PAs to wrap it up. The PA gestured to the audience for quiet. Keisha smiled sweetly.

"You've met our judges, but now you have to meet our creative director, Pablo Michaels, my right-hand man." She gestured across the stage to where Pablo was standing and beckoned for him to join her. The cameraman swung the long telescopic jib in Pablo's direction. His grey eyes lit up as he ran out on stage to join his BFF. She beamed at him. He beamed back. "Thank you, Keisha."

From where he was standing, everything looked different—the crowd was a group of dark, faceless bobbleheads behind the bright lights beaming down on him.

"Every week, Pablo's gonna shepherd our models through the tasks they need to master to become Supermodels. He'll coach them in the *fierce* photoshoots he's created and help them become the best they can be."

Joe Vong was fuming and texting. Broyce had stepped into a nearby wing, no doubt about to call the network about Pablo's sudden inclusion in the show.

"So, Pablo, why don't you call our semi-finalists out so we can meet them. Let the judging begin." She clapped her hands, and the audience cheered.

Pablo had the eeriest feeling that he was suddenly in a real-life *The Hunger Games*, without the murder, yet. He ran over to the curtain and pulled it back. Music blared and a herd of scrawny young women pranced like giraffes into their future as reality TV fodder.

"That's a commercial break. Back in three minutes," the AD shouted.

"Reset camera 2 for cue #105," Rachel called.

Joe Vong ran over to where Keisha was leaning back in her Director's chair. "What are you doing?"

"Getting my makeup touched up." De La Renta puffed on his brush so powder floated in Joe Vong's face.

"You can't have Pablo on the show. He didn't do a screen test."

"This is his screen test. They love him."

"He doesn't have a fucking on camera contract!"

"Are you *fucking on camera*?" Keisha asked Pablo.

"I'd need to be paid more."

"You know what I mean," Joe screamed.

"You'd better get him a contract then."

"We don't have a budget for him."

"Oh, you don't have to pay him," Keisha laughed. "He'll do it for me."

Pablo was close enough to hear his bargain-basement price. "Keisha, I can't work for free."

She shrugged. "Broyce will figure it out."

"You did this on purpose." Joe was hysterical.

Her amber eyes took one long look at Joe Vong. "You bet I did." She stood up and walked away from the showrunner.

"Kash: one. Vong: zero," Pablo whispered as he followed behind her.

"We're back in five," the Assistant Director shouted, "four." He held up his fingers for silence: three, two, one. Cameras rolled as the votes were tallied onscreen. It was quick and painful—thirteen contestants, like the apostles, were selected out of the original ten thousand hopefuls, and twenty-five semi-finalists. The chosen girls leaped up and down and hugged each other, celebrating their good fortune.

It would be mostly Steadicam shots now, portable cameras strapped to operators who would follow the girls behind the scenes, down the street and into their lives. In a few hours, after their confidentiality agreements were signed and all basic rights were given up, they would be swept away in a giant Hummer to The Chelsea Hotel, where they would live together for the next several weeks while being transformed into swans. Hopefully.

In their own ostentatious stretched Escalade, Keisha and Pablo collapsed back in the soft leather seats and stared at each other in shocked silence. Then they started laughing. They laughed so hard tears rolled down their faces. They laughed as Pablo popped the champagne and it sprayed their faces. They laughed as they toasted their success, their show, the world. They laughed until they couldn't laugh anymore.

# MAKEOVER MUSINGS

THE FIRST DAY of shooting had covered the models moving into The Chelsea Hotel and filmed Keisha, alone, welcoming them to their new abode. The second day of filming focused on the makeover. The first stop was the Plaza Hotel on Fifth Avenue, overlooking Central Park. The network's model mobile was a twenty-foot-long super-stretched black Hummer, fully loaded with a giant TV, colorful LED mood lighting, hidden cameras, bottles of water and snacks. It pulled up outside the Plaza, where Queen Keisha and Pablo waited on the red-carpeted steps, under the large flags and the green-gold awning of Manhattan's most illustrious hotel. A rainbow of ethnically diverse models piled out onto the sidewalks of New York, gaping up at the fashion dignitaries.

"New models need to be versatile. And you can't always

depend on your natural beauty," Keisha told her young cast. "So today, I'm bringing you to the Warren-Tricomi Salon, one of New York's *most* prestigious salons, and giving you makeovers."

The rock-star of hair, Edward Tricomi, stepped up next to Keisha and introduced himself. Tricomi's own long tresses swept under his chin as he pursed his lips and looked at the disheveled girls standing before him. "We have a lot of work to do."

Keisha nodded. "We sure do."

"Right this way." Tricomi gestured toward the steps leading up into the famed hotel.

Upstairs on the second floor, and inside the salon, were a collection of assistants who stood at attention, with black capes to adorn the models. Two Steadicam operators, wearing body harnesses to secure the cameras firmly to their chests, danced around the models and stars as Keisha and Pablo discussed bone structure, hair, assets and weaknesses with the stylist. Moving down the line of guinea pigs, Keisha was loud and brutally honest. Here, Keisha reigned supreme with her ideas on how to transform the girls with new looks that would give them an edge in the fashion world. Pablo found he didn't always agree with her, though, and tried to only play up assets. But he was playing second fiddle to Keisha's first. Tricomi narrowed his eyes and snapped the scissors in his hands, impatient to start cutting.

"Hannah, you're next," Pablo said.

A charming girl-next-door blonde with ice-blue eyes stepped up and smiled. She had one of those smiles that was so genuine that Pablo found himself smiling back.

Keisha looked over at him and tilted her head. "Hannah needs more edge to be a model," she began. "Rebecca of Sunny Brook Farm isn't high fashion."

Pablo disagreed but didn't say anything.

"I'd like to see a pixie cut and her bangs chopped right here." She gestured up high on her own forehead, above her eyebrows. "And dyed black. Blue-black."

Tricomi raised one eyebrow. It was all Pablo needed to see to gather his courage and disagree with Keisha. "She'll look way too harsh on camera," he said. Tricomi nodded affirmatively. The camera swerved to close in on Pablo's face. "And her structure is all wrong for short bangs. She has a fleshy face and needs hair to shape it. I love the white blonde, but I'd like to see some depth and give her a bit more volume. Some darker blonde to help her face stand out. What do you think, Edward?"

Tricomi stepped forward. "I would give her lots of layers. Color, a 7G and 7NG, just a bit beneath the layers to create color volume. It will shrink her face and we can work the hair into a variety of styles."

Keisha pouted her gorgeous lips but shrugged. She'd clearly been overruled by both men. "I guess that could work."

"Great!" Pablo surprised himself by saying, "Who's next?"

The hair transformations were going really well. Pablo sighed with relief. He'd saved Hannah, and now...

"Ahh!" Heather, the ebony beauty ran past them, screaming her head off.

"What's wrong?" Pablo ran after her.

"Follow them," Rachel shouted at one of the Steadicam operators.

"My expensive weave. It's all gone." She threw herself into Pablo's arms and sobbed. "I look like a boy."

"You look beautiful." Pablo tilted her head back and looked directly into her terrified eyes. "You couldn't look anything but beautiful. Keisha's given you an edge. You have to look deep inside yourself and have the courage to believe that and work it to your advantage."

She snuffled. "How?"

"That's what we're here to teach you."

"Great stuff," Rachel whispered.

The full makeovers were going to take all day. The girls' only break, per SAG-AFTRA regulations, was a thirty-minute meal break every six hours, but the cameras kept rolling. Soggy tuna fish sandwiches with cans of Diet Coke were handed to the model contestants as they got back into their Hummer limo to be driven to their next appointment.

In the crew van, Pablo looked down at their cold, damp cardboard lunch boxes from The Little Beet and looked over at Rachel. "Can't we get some food sponsors to cater us?"

"Not my job, but if you want to try, my stomach would love you."

Pablo was now starving and somewhat annoyed that Keisha had taken off in her Escalade with De La Renta, ahead of the production team, and didn't bother to ask him to join her. He hated the feeling of being left behind.

After driving around in circles to kill time, the contestant's Hummer finally arrived at Laura Mercier's NYC offices on the Upper East Side. The young models with their new looks piled out of the metal beast, tripping over themselves and each other to get into the bright lights of the makeup artist's salon. The sharp modernist décor and high ceilings stunned the girls into semi-silence.

"So, girls, this is gonna be your first, of weekly, teach sessions," Keisha told the wide-eyed models, "where you will learn the art of being a model muse."

"What's that mean, anyway?" Hannah whispered to Heather.

"Got me."

They didn't have time to think more.

"To accomplish that, I wanna introduce you all to none other than Kim Kardashian's makeup artist, Mario Dedivanovic." Keisha gestured toward the drop-dead gorgeous, yet bashful, Albanian.

"Makeup By Mario," the girls squealed like little piglets. It was not at all attractive. It was, however, understandable. Mario was hot, and his brushes had touched the faces of many A-list stars.

"So today, models, your muse is gonna make sure you know how to work your new look for castings, fashion parties," she paused dramatically, "and, of course, Instagram."

When the cameras turned toward Pablo, no one squealed. "A team of artists will do half your face, teaching you the art of applying makeup." He got the boring lines. "Afterwards, you'll make up the other half of your face. We'll look at how well you did. Keisha and Mario will make suggestions, and we'll move on to the next look they're gonna teach you."

"Before I forget, I'm giving you all a white tank top and skinny jeans, regulation model attire for all castings. You know Mama's always looking out. Hashtag I got you." Keisha crossed her fingers like Pablo always did and stamped the air. The PR on-set photographer snapped her hashtag gesture. "Send that to me," she told him. "ASAP."

Mario pointed at a tall, lanky brunette, pulled her out of the lineup, and started applying light makeup, a fresh look for casting. Pablo walked around to check in and start dialogue. The cameras followed close behind, capturing every moment.

"What's the difference between casting and Instagram makeup?" the brunette asked. Half of her tinted moisturizer had already been applied.

"On Instagram, it's all about heavy foundation, baking under the eyes, over contouring, and exaggerating your features. You can't go to castings like that. You'll be laughed out of the room," Pablo told her.

Mario looked irritated. "But you need to keep up with the *social media* style of makeup we use on IG if you wanna become an influencer/model."

"I think we got *that* beat down. We already a big deal on the gram. That's why we're here," one of the nearby girls quipped.

"Don't be so sure." Pablo wasn't having her know-it-all attitude. "Just because you were Miss Soy Milk back in your hometown—"

"Soybean...Miss Soybean," she interrupted and chuckled.

"Soybean...Soy Latte, whatever. If you think you know it all, *you* don't need to be here." Pablo looked like an authority, but on the inside, his heart was beating so hard he could barely breathe.

From the side of the room and out of camera view, Rachel gave Pablo the thumbs up. Joe nodded his huge head in approval. Behind them, a second camera had moved in on the drama.

Grazing at the craft service table and sensing the tension building from across the room, Keisha swooped in quickly, as if a fresh tub of Häagen-Dazs had been opened. She blinked her innocent eyes at the unsuspecting model.

"Hey, you know one of the first lessons I learned as a young model?" Keisha said in her creepy little girl's voice. "Sometimes, you only get one chance to make an impression. And you made yours. Pack your bags. You're going home. Now!"

Mario froze. Pablo didn't know where to look. Miss Soybean looked terrified. Keisha leaned over her and pointed her finger. "Move it."

Her face half made up, she turned to face the camera.

"Zoom in," Rachel whispered. "Go super tight."

The farm girl who was a big name in Wisconsin didn't know what had hit her. She may have been a big deal in the cheese capital of the Midwest, but she stumbled away in tears. The other models reached out to touch her arm as she fled the scene, sobbing her sorry heart out.

"Make sure to follow her and get an exit OTF," Joe bellowed at Rachel, who was standing in complete shock.

"Get her OTF," Rachel mumbled into her IFB. A segment producer ran off the set.

"What the fuck are we gonna do now?" Joe cursed at Keisha.

Keisha narrowed her eyes. "Calm down, Joe. And secondly, watch your tone. It was great TV for our first episode."

"Well, I hope your Boy Friday here can come up with a solution because we still have to eliminate a girl at judging this week, and one *every* week till the last episode. You wanna fire other contestants outside our format, you see me."

Rachel walked up to where the trio was standing.

"What's an exit OTF?" Pablo asked.

If Keisha could have sent Joe Vong off the set, she would have.

"OTF stands for *on the fly* interviews." Rachel's voice was gentle, the tone condescending. "An *exit OTF* is the last interview a girl does before she's sent to the hotel."

"Shh...we can't let that out," Joe hissed.

"I thought you sent them home?"

Rachel shook her head. "We can't give them their cell phones back and let them go home. It would be all over social before our first episode aired."

"Our audience would know who was sent home and no one would watch. We use the eliminated girls with the active cast, whenever we go out in public, to maintain secrecy." Joe knew the reality TV Bible. "Welcome to Reality 101, kid."

Keisha's brow had rumpled up into a vast wrinkle, something Pablo had never seen before. "We need a code name for them."

"Have the crew call them *bogies*. They'll never catch on," Pablo gleamed.

"Exactly." Keisha snapped her fingers in their faces.

"Bogie it is." Joe and Rachel walked back to their makeshift video set up.

He always seemed to know exactly what Keisha wanted to hear, Pablo thought to himself, smugly. They were such a great team. He couldn't help but feel sad for the ultimate fate of the bogies to come, though. Stuck in some network sponsored hotel under lock and key, but there were worse places in the world to be locked up. Look at Keisha's mother.

The afternoon dragged on, but finally, all the models had their fashion party looks applied. Smoky eyes, contouring around the cheekbone, shimmery highlighter on the nose and chin. Like a proud Mama bird inspecting her chicks, Keisha walked up and down, scrutinizing the group.

"You all look *fiiiiiiiierce*." She wagged her finger as if she was judging a drag ball in Harlem.

Dropping his face into his tiny childlike hands, Joe cringed.

"I've got another surprise." Keisha seemed devilish. "You've all been invited to a swanky New York fashion party with noted editors and bigwigs from the rag trade. *Dress to impress*," she emphasized. "Hurry back to your digs, because your ride will pick you up in two hours!"

As if on cue, the girls squealed. Pablo refrained from covering his ears but made a mental note to buy some earplugs. He couldn't shake the image of squealing piglets going to slaughter, now stuck in his mind. The models grabbed their overstuffed bags and new wardrobe and raced for the freight elevator. Down on the street, they piled into their stretched Hummer. A producer loaded in the front seat while a cameraman jumped in the back with the girls.

The hidden Nest camera rotated from the spot where it was clipped in the air vent. Keisha had access to the girls day and night, and while standing in Laura Mercier's office, she pulled out her iPhone and logged into the private server set up just for her. Pablo leaned in and watched as the girls dished.

"Oh, my, God...I *just* wanna have a hot bath and go to sleep! Hannah kept me up with her snoring last night."

"I don't snore."

"Then you were sawing wood."

"Hello? What about Keisha sending Natalie home like that? That was *so* mean." They cackled like Macbeth's witches.

"They can only pull that stunt once. They wouldn't have a show without us."

"My feet are fucking killing me. Do we have to go to some BS party? We just worked like a twelve-hour day."

"Do you think *real* Supermodels stay home when they have a chance to get their face out there?"

Keisha looked at Pablo and pointed to Adrianna, who had spoken such wise words. "She'll be our winner."

"You don't know that."

Keisha smiled at him and raised an eyebrow. "I don't?"

Two hours later, the models, in their swankiest glam—super high heels, super tight skirts, push-up bras, party touched up and perfected, if that were possible—climbed back into their flamboyant Hummer. Once inside the limo, their constant complaining of tiredness turned to excitement. The driver pulled away from their temporary home, the infamous Chelsea Hotel, and turned off 23rd Street and headed south on

Seventh Avenue. The TV screen in the Hummer flipped on, and a taped message from Keisha began to play.

"As a new model in town, you should sport your natural casting glow. You never know when you're gonna be discovered. You've got this ten-minute ride to tone down your looks and show up at your destination looking model fresh. *This* is this week's challenge. The judges will be waiting on the red carpet to choose the winner of this first challenge. Good luck!"

"Why didn't you say so beforehand?" Hannah yelled at the screen.

Standing on the red carpet all gussied up, Pablo and Keisha watched the girls on her iPhone live feed and they couldn't help but laugh. "What fun would that be," she said to him.

It was a madhouse inside the Hummer. Two girls began to strip their gold Lamé off their frocks. One of the models began wiping her face with her sleeve. They peeled their eyelashes off and blotted their red lips. Adrianna, who'd worn her skinny blue jeans, pulled off her sheer black blouse to reveal the white tank top Keisha had given them earlier that day.

"Aren't you the *fucking* teacher's pet?"

"I'm no dummy. She gave us this wardrobe for a reason."

"Well, fuck you, Goody Two-shoes."

"Hey, it's a competition."

Another model pulled antibacterial wipes out of her purse.

"You a germaphobe?" one of the girls asked, as she began to take all of her makeup off, rubbing her skin pink and fresh.

"I'll pay you forty bucks for one of those," Hannah begged.

"Not a chance."

Things were starting to get ugly now. Girls started pushing and shoving each other so vigorously that Adrianna got elbowed in the nose. Blood gushed all over her clean, white tank top. The lone cameraman pushed in for a closeup.

"Bitch."

"Cunt."

"You broke my nose!"

"It was too big, anyway."

By the time the limo pulled upfront of Buddakan on Ninth Avenue, only a few models looked fresh. Most looked like they'd been run over by the massive Hummer they arrived in. Two Steadicams met the bedraggled contestants as they tumbled out onto the curb. Pablo and Keisha looked at their protégées and shook their heads, disappointed.

"I'm gonna give Adrianna points for dressing the part, but blood *really* creeps me out. What do you think, Pablo?" Keisha turned her head away and tucked herself behind her silver-coifed fixer.

"She looks the part–aside from the blood. I can only assume—"

"This business doesn't make room for assumptions," Keisha interrupted, pointing to the Iman copycat model, Heather. "You look the most like a model this evening, and I'm glad to see you owning your black version Mia Farrow haircut. You get immunity this week, will be safe at our very first judging, and free from elimination."

"Congrats on winning this week's challenge," Pablo added.

The remaining girls clapped half-heartedly, heading off to the party. By the time Keisha and Pablo made their entrance, Sasha had already parked herself by the bar, Mason was deep in conversation with a handsome Indian editor from the *New York Times* and Miss Thing was showing off, parading up and down the long communal table in the famous oak room, like it were his personal runway.

Watching the deprived model coach's need for attention, they were ready to go home. "He wishes he were me," Keisha whispered to Pablo.

"Who wouldn't?"

She giggled. "The problem is, he has a face made for radio."

# FIERCE CREATURES

I T WAS ANOTHER sleepless night for Pablo. Anxious about the morning's photoshoot, the first time doing what he was *actually* hired to do, he rolled back and forth in bed, fretting away any chance of REM sleep. Looking up at the ceiling, counting Supermodels instead of sheep backward from one-hundred didn't work, so he began singing a Tibetan mantra—*Om Ma Tri Mu Ye Sa Le Du.*

His call time was 6:30 a.m. Every time he did doze off, he'd wake with what felt like an electrical jolt and jerk awake. What if the alarm didn't go off? What if he set it wrong? What time was it anyway? Fumbling in the dark, he tapped his iPhone at irregular intervals, double-checking: Alarm alert. Sound. The time: 12:05; 1:43; 2:31; 3:26 a.m. It was pointless. At least if he got up, he'd be doing something besides ruining his beauty sleep.

Pablo dragged himself to the bathroom and looked at his insomniac grey-haired self in the mirror. "Might as well be early." There was a moment of disassociation. The reflection looking back at him did not look like a person he knew. The overhead bathroom light flickered, exposing his natural black roots beginning to sprout beneath his faux silver locks. He looked peaked and washed out. *Model Muse* was going to take a toll on his own good looks, and they hadn't finished the first episode yet. *Shit, how old will I look by the time we wrap season one?* he wondered.

He shook his finger at the mirrored face. "Don't go there, Pablo." Turning the water on in the shower, he filled the chipped porcelain mug sitting atop the apartment's original, pre-war bathroom sink. Everything in the apartment was original, Malaki liked to say, including the roaches. Pablo popped his antidepressant and, in a tribute to Bob Fosse, splayed his hands out like he was about to start a tap dance number and said, "Showtime." And indeed, he was about to dance, for it was time to transform into his new persona Pablo Michaels, Creative Director of *Model Muse*. He jumped into the shower.

Before they'd even selected the models for season one, Pablo had worked hard to negotiate venues and secure fashion industry creative talent to support the show. It had been a game-changing deal to get Highline Stages. Their sponsorship included the gold standard of studio space coveted by the industry; the be-all and end-all of trendy. By getting them to host all the fledgling show's photoshoots, *Model Muse* would reap all the benefits of working one day a week in the pre-eminent photo studio in Manhattan, the epicenter of the biz. Pablo was able to convince celebrated photographers to shoot for the show just because of Highline Stages' prestige.

A few hours later, looking like a picture-perfect mannequin, Pablo was standing in Studio A and in front of the camera on his own for the first time. The grips were still fixing the lighting. Pablo tried not to feel anxious and practiced some deep breathing.

"You look great, Pabs," Rachel told him. She nodded to the assistant director.

"Places," the AD yelled. "Rolling!"

From where Pablo was standing, he could see Joe and Rachel looking at the video screen on a stand. Broyce was holding a cup of coffee in his hands. Vong was chewing on a pencil. Everyone's eyes were peeled on him.

"Action."

The models entered the studio in a line-up formation. Flanked by posters attached to easels on either side of him, Pablo couldn't shake the sense of being in front of a firing squad. His. He took a deep breath and said, "Hey, girls." His voice sounded a little high and tense to his ears. He inhaled. Held his breath for a moment and then exhaled. "As you can see by these amazing archival images next to me, shot for *Vogue's* Spring 1999 issue by the late great Irving Penn, models back then were asked to pose through all the extensive hair, makeup and cumbersome wardrobe that completely camouflaged who they were."

A surge of positive energy coursed through his veins as he began to own his solo moment. "This famous editorial hit stands and created major buzz for the *Star Wars* prequels featuring Natalie Portman as Queen Amidala." He paused dramatically. "Let these characters be your *muse*. Today we're gonna create new versions of these iconic shots."

On cue, four major fashion celebrities stepped out from behind each of the four posters. There was a gasp and a few whispers. The Steadicam operators skirted the girls, to catch the moment of surprise on the first take.

"Your A-list team today. Legendary photographer Annie Leibovitz will be shooting; JLo's personal style team, Mariel Haenn and Rob Zangardi, are on wardrobe; and hair/makeup illusion master, Raja, will whip you into shape."

Jumping up and down uncontrollably, the girls over-exaggerated their reactions for what felt like five minutes. Rachel twirled her finger in the air, signaling the contestants to move on.

"But there's a twist. Models are often asked to work with co-stars." Pablo gestured to the white photo backdrop at the back of the studio. "Today, you're working with these guys."

"I bet they're naked male models," one of the models muttered. "These shows *always* pull this stunt to get sex stories going." An A-1 eavesdropper, the sound man's boom had swung over their heads and captured the hot mic moment.

"Shit...I'm game! Bring me a naked hot guy with a cute ass and I'm *all* good!"

"I *really* hope you're game girls," Pablo said, as a man wearing a safari hat and jungle shorts appeared carrying an enormous python wrapped around him. Following behind him was a crew of similarly dressed animal trainers leading or carrying everything from nature's offering: a cheetah, a Dalmatian, a parrot, a sloth, a camel...

"It like Noah's fucking Ark," one of the girls said.

It was true. They just kept coming.

"A sloth!" There was a screech, followed by hysterical crying from one of the girls. Rachel pointed and a cameraman ran over to the emotional breakdown. "I love sloths. *Ohmigod,* I love sloths. Please, Pablo, please...can I...*Ohmigod!*"

"Caitlin, everyone's already assigned," he looked down at his sheet of paper. "Oh, psychic me." He smiled. "You're already assigned to Eli, the sloth."

She ran over and hugged Pablo. "*Ohmigod,* this is the best moment of my life. I don't care if nothing else happens."

"Okay, calm down." Pablo turned toward Rachel, who was laughing so hard she could barely contain herself. "Should I go back to my script?"

She nodded while wiping her tears and blowing her nose. "We'll edit in post."

Pablo gestured toward the collection of creatures. "Meet the furry, feathered and scaly celebs of Noah's Ark." Pablo was really enjoying the shocked faces of the girls. "We've already assigned each of you an animal friend. So, let's take a few minutes to get to know your co-stars before we get you into hair and makeup."

Pablo paired them up. Steadicams wove in and out of the bonding session. A kiss from a camel. A hug from a sloth. A lick from the Dalmatian. A nervous touch of the snake. A lot of oohing and ahhing.

"Okay, ladies, it's time to leave your co-stars, as they're already dressed in their natural costumes, and you need to head off to be transformed."

"Alright, everybody," Rachel shouted, "I want—"

Across the room, there was a huge thud and a scream.

"*Ohmigod.* Is she dead?"

Adrianna had fainted. Out cold.

"Keep rolling, but get me the fucking medics. NOW!" Joe ran in, screaming.

"Medic," the AD shouted.

"Medic." A PA ran toward the craft service table where the trained nurse was chowing down on brioche and croissants.

"*Ohmigod!* She just went grey!" Pablo was completely freaked out. "I should've asked if she was okay." He rushed to Adrianna's side.

"Never," Joe hissed. "This is how we're all getting an Emmy out of this."

"Move aside. Give her air." The medic pushed through the group gathered around the model. "What's her name?"

"Adrianna."

"Adrianna?" the medic repeated. She blinked up at them. A lump was beginning to form on her forehead. Pablo's heart pounded in his chest. He was mortified. They'd already lost one contestant this week with Keisha's impromptu firing. Was Adrianna out for the count as well? Who was going to face the judges at the first elimination this week? If girls kept dropping like flies, they'd have to start adding them instead of taking them away each week.

The medic was helping the lumpy-headed model wannabe to her wobbly feet. "She's okay. She's suffering from ornithophobia."

They looked at him blankly.

"She's deathly afraid of birds."

The parrot squawked.

"Okay, we'll switch you with the…" Pablo looked desperately around at the girls, "the Cheetah!"

"Could I have the Dalmatian instead," she looked plaintively up at him and rubbed her forehead.

"Okay, the Dalmatian."

Pablo swore Adrianna's smile had a wicked twist and wondered if she hadn't planned the whole fiasco so she could get the dog, who was almost as gorgeous as Keisha.

The studio transformed into a flurry of chaotic excitement as the artists whirled their subjects into hair and makeup, the stylists selected couture for the models and the animal handlers ran around keeping the co-stars occupied. It was mayhem of the best kind. Pablo bustled about checking on the progress of the girls, while the Steadicam operators wielded their hefty cameras amid the chaos. Rachel seemed to be everywhere at once, beckoning for a camera here then over there. "Catch this. Got that?" It was stupendous.

Working with animals is never quick or easy and it was

well after 2 p.m. when they finally began the photoshoot—twelve girls to shoot.

"Parrot first," Pablo announced. The medic had suggested they wrap the parrot before Adrianna had to come back on set.

"It's a blue and yellow Macaw," the handler said.

"And already causing me too much drama." Pablo turned to Annie Liebovitz. "How would you like the bird?"

"Let's try something traditional and on the shoulder first. There's so much costume that I don't think we need to be overtly original."

The model had a hairpiece with glittery gold ribbon and tiny reflective mirrors. Sitting quietly on her shoulder, the blue and yellow Macaw began to bob up and down. Then he reached up and pecked her head.

"What's he doing?" the model asked.

"Do you have lice?" Pablo asked.

"Of course, I don't have lice! Ouch."

The handler pointed out that the Macaw was reacting to the mirrors. "He's flirting."

They moved the parrot to her hand and got a fabulous kissing shot, profile bird and model.

"Next up, Cheetah," Pablo announced, sighing heavily into his mic. One down, eleven to go. He was a nervous wreck and had been up since 3 a.m. *Note to self: get a prescription for Lunesta—you need to sleep.*

The Cheetah rippled across the room over to a velvet couch, where the handler instructed the oversized cat to stand statuesquely beside the ebony beauty of Heather—its noble head and tail erect, ready to chase a gazelle to the ground. "Annie, she's all yours." Pablo backed away.

"You look great with the cat." Annie smiled at the girl. "Place your hand on his back. That's it. Let the wildness of this magnificent creature come out of you. You are two of a kind. Wild."

Heather turned her head, her profile matching the cheetah's.

"Nice. Now turn slowly toward me. You're unfettered. Nothing can stop—"

"*Achoo*," she sneezed.

"Stop. Her hair got mussed." The hairstylist ran in to fix the wig that had flopped to one side.

"Give me the Canon." Annie Leibovitz held out her hand for the assistant to switch cameras. "Where were we?"

"I'm wild. Unfettered...*Achoo*."

Raja stood up and threw his hands in the air. "Her eyes are all red, suddenly."

"I think I'm allergic to cats."

"Adrianna, you're with the Cheetah," Pablo yelled across the studio floor.

"I wanted to be with the dog," she whined.

Pablo raised an eyebrow at her.

"Sorry, Pablo. I just felt like we bonded." Adrianna walked away from the dog and replaced Heather on the couch. The Cheetah was her new co-star.

"Even better," Annie said. "Your wardrobe coloring and the cat's are one and the same. And Heather will look great with the Dalmatian."

By the time they were on the last model, Pablo was leaning on the digital tech station, beyond exhausted reviewing the photos so far. He'd been up for sixteen hours and looked twice his age. "Whose idea was it to use animals?" It was a rhetorical question.

"Yours." Rachel shook her head at him.

"Remind me to never do that again." He called for the last setup.

"It's gonna make a great episode, though."

As the camel strode out onto the set, the Steadicam guys worked the room.

The white-blonde Hannah was last. "Have you ever ridden a camel before?" Pablo asked.

"No."

"Are you allergic to them?"

"I don't think so."

The animal handler was dressed as an Arab sheik and motioned for the camel to kneel. As he helped her get astride, Liebovitz reached for her Hasselblad. "Slow down. I want to get this action."

Hannah worked the movement of the camel as it swayed forward then back. Unfolding its long legs from beneath her, Hannah rose toward the ceiling. She looked like a female *Lawrence of Arabia,* with the same ice blue O'Toole eyes. The handler was dark and swarthy. The camel was pale cream, Hannah luminescent.

"She looks great," Pablo murmured.

Then the camel belched.

After all the tension of the day, the studio erupted into laughter. Atop the camel, Hannah laughed so hard her head tilted back, opened mouthed, turning toward Annie, who was the only one not laughing. Focus. Shutter frame. Clicks captured the entire moment in less than 10 seconds.

"Got it." Annie turned to Pablo. "I'm all good."

Cameras pushed into Pablo's face for a closeup. "That's a wrap!" he yelled.

"Annnnd, cut!" the AD shouted.

Pablo sighed and sat down.

"Can't handle the pressure, blondie?" Joe cracked.

"Of course, I can. Just like you've effortlessly executed this Steve Jobs, black, mock neck get-up with sneakers," he fired back. "And P.S. I'm not blonde. I'm silver grey."

"Watch yourself." The pissed off Korean stomped away, looking like Napoleon in Converse.

Rachel applauded. "Don't mind Joe. He was *forced* to be the Showrunner here." She plopped herself next to Pablo and put her arm around his shoulders. "He wanted an EP position on another show, and he's arrogant enough to believe that his film school side job as the *guy with camera* taught him all he needs to know."

"He needs to stay outta my lane. I know what I'm doing here," he added, "almost always."

"You were a rock star today, Pablo. A natural, and he's jealous. All he's ever done is that testosterone-fueled, *COPS* knockoff show."

"Well, he should've been arrested for the fashion crime he committed on this set today." Pablo liked Rachel and sensed a friendship blossoming between them.

"Touché," she whispered. "But let's be real, where *Model Muse* is concerned, Joe couldn't produce his way out of a Gucci, printed paper bag."

# LOOK WHO'S JUDGING

THE MASSIVE JUDGING set was still getting final touches when the crew loaded into Silvercup Studios in Queens the next day for the first model elimination—well, the first *official* elimination anyway. Judging days were going to be thrilling, and seeing which contestant got sent packing was exciting for the entire crew. It would've been more thrilling if the studio didn't smell of dusty insulation, and the faint whiff of mold wasn't blowing through the air-conditioning ducts. It was freezing too. There was simply no warmth in the oversized space except near the giant studio lights and, even then, it was cold. Keisha liked the A/C on max, which meant the crew had to come dressed for a polar vortex.

Pablo was learning how reality shows were made. He wasn't on camera, for once, so he sat with De La Renta, Joe and a small team of producers in what everyone referred to as "video village" along the "fourth wall." It was the one angle that all cameras shot from, covering the three-sided set where Keisha and the judges would interview and evaluate each model while looking at the images from their photoshoots. In truth, video village was nothing more than a makeshift area full of monitor screens and folding tables, but it offered a front-row seat to the in-person drama of the judging soundstage.

Rachel was lucky enough to sit upstairs with the directors in the warmth of the control room, with all the soundboards, large screens—with every camera view—and snacks. She would remain in communication with Joe and the team via IFB—also known as *interruptible feedback* or *interrupt for broadcast*. This was a monitoring and cueing system used in television and video production for one-way communication from the director to other producers or on-air talent.

Kim K's makeup artist, Mario, was their first guest judge. One of Pablo's additional responsibilities was to find a different fashion insider every week to inhabit the open seat, thereby completing the panel with five arbiters of style. He was quite sure he wasn't being paid for his contacts and held his private list of names close to his chest.

"Here." Rachel handed him his own headset and radio pack before they began filming. "You might as well be on the same wavelength as the rest of us." She winked at him.

"Thanks." He fit the headset over his ears and instantly could hear all the audio coming from the judges, already sitting on set, and models waiting backstage. It was a voyeur's paradise.

"Sasha, let me have a sip of your water," Miss Thing said.

"I don't share my germs with anyone."

"Or your hooch."

"I was really comfortable with the python," one of the models said.

"My feet are killing me."

The soundman walked up to video village. "*She* won't wear the concealed earpiece," he sighed.

Rachel rolled her eyes. Joe Vong went ballistic. "What!?" he shouted. The soundman winced. "She has to. How are we supposed to give her directions during the shoot?"

"She says she's intuitive."

Pablo jumped up. "Lemme talk to her."

"Would you? Please," Rachel begged. "It allows us to communicate with her easier, so we can all be more efficient with time when we're taping the lengthy sequences."

Pablo was about to stand up when Keisha seemed to magically materialize before them.

"There's no way," Keisha said. "I'll *never* be able to focus on what I'm saying—you all chatting in my head. There'll be too many voices."

She had a point.

De La Renta looked at Pablo and mouthed, "She's already got too many voices in there."

"That's the way it's going to be then." Broyce jumped into the fray. "You can make it work, Rachel. I know you can. The important thing is that Keisha is happy and able to do her job. Period."

The slated judging scene was supposed to take five hours to shoot. Opening words from Keisha, 15-minute evaluations per contestant, deliberations with the judges, meal break, and then the elimination moment followed by the exit OTF from the unlucky model sent packing. Keisha turned it into ten.

There was Keisha's long monologue welcoming the girls, then her six takes at attempting to set up the competition and the prizes—that would be fixed in post—then the introduction of the judges, the meal break, and finally Keisha leading the panel in a long, rambling evaluation for each of the twelve contestants.

"How are we going to edit ten hours of footage into the last 15 minutes of this episode?" Joe Vong gasped. Pablo actually felt a little sorry for him.

During the first camera *"stop down"*—to swap out batteries and digital recording cards—Rachel and Joe had a sidebar with Keisha. "We need to move things along," Joe said bluntly. Never a good way to get Keisha to do what you want.

"Everything we're doing here is important."

"That may be, but only a very small portion of it is going into the show."

Keisha narrowed her eyes. Her voice ratcheted up an octave. "Mr. Joe, I don't think you know anything about fashion and even less about my show. If you wanna hurry up, get the batteries back in those cameras and start shooting." Her creepy child's voice was enough to scare everyone from saying another word.

Rachel turned away, clearly relieved she'd kept her mouth shut, and retreated upstairs to the safety of her control room.

It was almost midnight by the time the judges reached the last model's evaluation—Adrianna. Everyone looked tired and no amount of makeup was going to change that; they had started filming judging at 2 p.m.—as in, the afternoon! The crew's call time had been 11 a.m. How were they all going to keep up their stamina through the entire season if every day was fifteen hours long? Pablo was starting to see that his life was going to be on set. There wasn't going to be room for anything else. *Model Muse* had become *Model Deluge.*

"Last, but certainly not least, Adrianna, you're next up for evaluation," Keisha chirped.

Adrianna stepped down from the second row where she'd been standing in silence throughout the entire judging, and walked along the expanse of the fuchsia runway, landing in front of the judges' desk. Pablo knew Keisha would save her for last.

"Miss Adrianna," Keisha used her most charming voice. "First, we need to talk about that walk. When you enter any room as a model, we need to feel your presence. Go back and start all over."

Doing what she was told, Adrianna slumped back towards her spot on the risers with the other contestants.

"We can still see you," Keisha bellowed. "Look *fierce!*"

Adrianna changed her walk to a strut and turned, maintaining her composure.

"Yaaaassssss. Now come back to Mama."

The model then stomped down the runway, landed on her final mark with attitude, and stared down each judge.

"Now, there is a model," Mason chimed in.

"Remember, baby," Miss Thing cooed, "you need to walk with your hips forward like *the rent is due tonight.*" He snapped his fingers.

Keisha shot Miss Thing a dirty look.

"Let's see the photo *you* shot this week where you had massive wardrobe, heavy hair and makeup, and posed with an animal." Keisha gestured towards the giant LED wall that hung above the runway and filled the space between the judge's table and the model's risers. The photo of Adrianna posing with the Cheetah appeared, filling the digital screen.

"I thought you were with the Dalmatian?" Keisha blurted. "I wanted you with the Dalmatian."

Keisha looked confused.

"We already saw the Dalmatian." Sasha's voice was slurred and her lipstick was looking more distributed on her water bottle than her lips.

Keisha was fuming mad. "I should've been consulted."

Pablo was pissed now. She hadn't even shown up for the

photoshoot but she knew he had Adrianna with the parrot. Suddenly, he found himself wondering if Keisha herself had put Adrianna up to her fainting episode. Was Keisha fixing the *Model Muse* deck?

"Whatever," the Supermodel said flippantly. "You look really great with the Cheetah. Your wardrobe coloring and the Cheetah's were made for each other."

"You really owned the makeup so it doesn't consume you," Mario stated, firmly. "I think you look amazing here."

"The Cheetah is the only thing I'm looking at," Sasha blurted. "I don't even see the model."

"Sasha, dah-ling, it might be late in the day for you grandma, but if you can't see that hand-beaded, crinoline-caged Dior masterpiece, we might need a medic to check you out," Miss Thing quipped.

"Oh, I know you're not coming for me sitting there in reams of chiffon, like a reject from Big Apple Circus."

"Hellooo. This is about Adrianna," Keisha interrupted. "Speaking of medics, though, you had a bit of a hard week, Miss Adrianna. First, it was that unsightly bloody nose you arrived with at the fashion party in Buddakan. And Pablo's notes say," she fumbled through papers on the desk, "'Adrianna displayed great range on set, but that was after passing out and forcing me to change my creative, and several wigs, to accommodate for her fainting incident.'"

"It was a zoo in there," Miss Thing laughed.

De La Renta leaned over to Pablo, slid his headset off one ear and whispered, "This is what Mother does best. She likes to eat girls for lunch."

Pablo chuckled, but he was glued to the monitor in anticipation of what would happen next.

"I'm like, *so* afraid of Parrots that I saw white and passed out."

Keisha looked back down at the notes. "But, he adds that you were swapped again from the dog to the Cheetah because Heather was allergic to cats."

"I pass out *when* I see pussy…"

"That's enough out of you, Miss Thing!" Keisha snapped her fingers and glared over at Joe. He nodded. Code for *edit that out*, Pablo figured.

Keisha looked lovingly at the young model now. "With all you had going on, I love you in this photo. Your pose looks like fashion, you carry the garment with grace and you're handling the Cheetah with ease."

Adrianna clapped and looked excited. "Oh, thank God."

"But," Keisha wasn't finished, "in the *real* world of fashion, you would've been sent home the moment you fainted because you're not serving the client. And I feel the judges need to take that into account as we begin our deliberations."

Adrianna's face turned to horror and she quickly made her way back to her spot among the contestants.

Raising her voice, Keisha pointed her grim reaper finger at the group of models. "It's time for you to go backstage to our soundproof booth—"

"Closet," De La Renta whispered to Pablo.

"—so we can deliberate your merits and make a decision." She was now standing, donning the innocent face of the Virgin Mary herself. "When we bring you back in, one of you will be going home."

The models slowly turned and exited through an opening behind them. Their feet clunked on the stairs, sounding like cattle being shoved into a trailer.

"That's a cut folks," Bill, the 1st AD yelled.

Pablo took a deep breath. "I'm not sure I can deal with the pressure of this moment every week."

"Baby, you're the one who wanted to be *Pablo Michaels.*

Did you think it was gonna be all roses?" De La Renta shook his head. "Speaking of, those roots need some attention."

"So soon? The bleach burns my scalp."

"As I saaaaid, *you're* the one who wanted to be Pablo Michaels."

On the stroke of midnight, Hannah ran from the judging set in tears like Cinderella running from the ball. She was eliminated for some reason Pablo couldn't figure out. Something was said about her open mouth in the camel shot. An amazing image that had stunned every one of the judges, except Keisha. A shot that Annie Liebovitz told Pablo was one of her best—ever. Things weren't adding up. Personally, he didn't think they'd seen the last of the white-blonde farm girl, but he had more pressing worries. He had to get to sleep. One full episode in the can. Episode Two would begin filming early the next morning. He didn't even know what day it was. Shooting seven days a week—with four days to shoot an episode—was going to be relentless.

*　　*　　*

Six weeks and several meltdowns later, Keisha came out of wardrobe wearing a custom Pamella Roland, dusty rose-colored feather gown, ready to begin filming the final judging scene of season one. Sinuously maneuvering down the catwalk toward the judges, she swiveled her statuesque curves to reveal a completely bare back and a little more than a half-inch of her derriere. The gown was breathtaking, and so was the Muse.

Pablo was seated on camera for the final elimination panel with all the regular judges—no *guest* judge needed tonight. Since he'd mentored and coached the girls week after week, Keisha felt he deserved this special moment on screen—when victory for one was announced, and the others' dreams were dashed. "It'll build your brand," she'd told him.

Standing on the runway, the final two models stood waiting to be crowned.

"This is a big moment in your lives and mine." Keisha's voice sounded about 12 years old. "I'm really proud of everything you've accomplished over the past weeks, and you both have shown that you have talent, drive and willingness to learn." She named each girl and discussed their strengths and weaknesses. Adrianna, the fainter, got a six-minute monologue that post-production would have to cut down to thirty seconds. Heather, the ebony Mia Farrow, got three minutes. Pablo wondered if the length of the monologue was Keisha's tell for the winner.

"And our first-ever *Model Muse* is..." Keisha dragged the moment out, "Adrianna!"

Adrianna jumped up and down and squealed—big surprise. Heather cried but was gracious and congratulatory. In that moment, Adrianna's photoshoot images for the season began filling the giant LED wall: there was the Cheetah image, a photo of Adrianna seemingly nude with body paint and male models all around her, a photo of her on the top of the Empire State Building wearing a bikini, and a beauty shot that looked like a cosmetic ad. Keisha continued talking, a little speech about Adrianna's future that no one paid any attention to because Sasha was pouring champagne into their coffee cups.

On the digital screen above the models and in front of the judges and the crew, the past several weeks of their lives appeared in the glossy high-fashion images from every episode Pablo had worked so tirelessly to create and manage. The *Model Muse* logo that he created floated at the top of the tightly cropped beauty image of Adrianna, and it sealed the deal as the title of a make-believe magazine for the reality show. Pablo had laid it out to appear like a real magazine cover.

"That looks great!" Mason said, sitting to Pablo's right.

"It should, I was up half the night laying it out."

"Overtime?"

"Sucker time."

"Some babies never learn." Mason smiled. "Never tell anyone about all the shit you can do, or they will expect you to do it for free."

"That's not news."

"You have to start lying, Pablo. When they say they need something, keep your mouth shut."

"Easier said than done."

"This business is all about *fake it till you make it*. And in your case, just fake it."

"That's a wrap on season one folks," Rachel bellowed across the ostentatious judging set. Everyone cheered. Some more relieved than others.

As the house lights powered up, the glossy scenery looked like nothing more than the cardboard it was; the set walls were scuffed, exposing chipped paint. It was here, on this flawed set, episode after episode, that the young model hopefuls had been eliminated like unwanted Factions in the dystopian movie trilogy *Divergent*, without the blood. Well, just a little.

Grips and electric crew started winding up cables and taking down rigging, as they sipped from paper cups. Production had splurged on cheap champagne and beer to celebrate the wrap of the fledgling show.

Under the cruelty of fluorescent lights, the tired Supermodel, even with slight bags sagging beneath her amber eyes, still looked like a million—a few million. Shielding his eyes from the harshness of the house lights, Pablo looked over to see Sasha and Miss Thing on the opposite side of the judging table; courtiers at the queen's table, flanking Keisha in twos.

De La Renta came running in waving at Keisha and pointing to the ceiling. It didn't matter that the cameras had stopped rolling, he wasn't letting his boss look unflattering under those blue fluorescent hues. "When da lights go on at da club, it's time to bounce," he scoffed as he escorted Keisha down the runway and right past the first winner of *her* show. The Supermodel paid no attention to the new *Model Muse* now that the cameras had stopped rolling.

Pablo was shocked by her callous disregard.

"She bounces all right," Miss Thing muttered under his breath.

"Ha," Sasha guffawed. "I'm sixty-two and *still* wear a size four. Keisha better get a diet and stick to it if there's a season two."

Mason leaned over and whispered in Pablo's ear. "Size four or not, Sasha smells like my Uncle Abbott–denture cream and scotch."

Pablo chuckled. Over the course of shooting the season, he'd developed a fond liking to the handsome Brit, which surprised him. Maybe Mason wasn't as homophobic as he thought.

"We should really get together and work on some shoots of our own, while we're on hiatus that is. You are quite the talented chap."

"I'd love that. I could use a break from working on shoots that involve suntan lotion sponsors. If I gotta come up with editorial content around one more toiletry essential, I'll barf."

"Well, you do sport a natural tan every day." Mason winked his right eye.

Was Pablo seeing things? Was Mason flirting? Nah. He was happily married to an Indian woman from New Delhi.

Broyce Miller ascended the stage and introduced himself to the two models, congratulating Adrianna first and shaking her hand. "Young lady, you've epitomized the absolute journey from disenfranchised, poor, young, middle-American oddball to say-it-like-it-is stunner who's ready to take on the fashion world." Broyce was glowing. "Your transformation was epic."

Adrianna giggled and appeared as if she were flirting with the handsome exec.

Always the diplomat, he praised Heather, as well. "You two really gave the judges a hard time deciding. And the network is thrilled that you both worked so hard to help make the show a success."

Like a heat-seeking missile, Keisha turned back to where Broyce was congratulating her models, instead of her. She ran back onto the stage and hugged Adrianna. "I knew she would win the moment she came to the first party in her white t-shirt and skinny jeans."

"You did?" Adrianna said.

"Well, don't you worry about a thing," Keisha was all syrupy charm, "I'm gonna do everything to make sure we keep in touch. *Anything* you need, just reach out. Hashtag I got you."

Adrianna broke down some more. Her tear-soaked face was blackened with mascara lines down to her chin.

"And *hashtag I got news* for you too, Keisha," Broyce said. Pablo winced. Broyce sounded so corny. "After all the news buzz around the show from the open call to the live casting, we've greenlit *season two* and are moving ahead with pre-production!"

"That's *fierce*," Keisha quipped. "I'm not surprised."

"Of course, we'll still need to do a full PR campaign for the launch of season one, but get ready, we're taking off!"

The entire room erupted in cheers. The crew hugged each other. Sasha held up her water bottle, toasting the room. Miss Thing opened a bottle of champagne, let the fizz explode all over the other judges, and then got up to strut himself offstage with his own bottle tucked under his arm. Why not? No one was paying attention to him anyway.

Mason patted Pablo on the back and then wiped some champagne fizz off his cheek. "Looks like you are going to have your hands full for a while."

"You have four weeks off!" Joe yelled at the crew. "Don't spend it all on wine and women!"

"That's exactly what I was planning on doing!" Rachel yelled back, sarcastically.

Pablo felt like a mother who'd just given birth and had been told she was pregnant again but wasn't going to get nine months to recover. He hadn't had any free time to himself since the show was greenlit. When his life wasn't Keisha's, it was the show's and Keisha. He sat in his judging chair trying to figure out how he could slip away from the wrap party and have a quiet night at home. Maybe read a good book? But the thought went out the window when Keisha beckoned her BFF with *the look*. Virgil's was her new favorite barbecue joint on West 44th Street near Times Square; it had become her new obsession. If she was in a good mood, they'd go to Virgil's. If she was in a bad mood, they'd go to Virgil's. If there was drama that needed an emergency discussion, they'd go to Virgil's. Pablo could only imagine the amount of sodium infused pork he'd been forced to ingest while holed up in Virgil's corner booth reserved for VIPs.

"Tonight?" he mouthed at her. "It's the wrap party."

The crew was already dancing and drinking. After an intense two months of work and no sleep, there was nothing like a good wrap party. This was the night everybody got lucky because they got to go home and get some sleep; a fortunate few had sex first.

Joe Vong looked more like a toddler from a Baby Gap commercial than a high fashion model, as he stomped his way down the runway toward Keisha. How the hell he ever got a gig producing *Model Muse* was a mystery Pablo feared he'd never solve.

"Keisha. We gotta talk. Season renewal changes everything."

Keisha smiled at him so seductively that Pablo thought he was hallucinating. "We *do* need to talk." She cut him off. "Meet me in my trailer in ten minutes."

Joe looked confused. The poor guy still thought he was in charge of the production. Pablo chuckled to himself.

"Pablo?" Keisha shouted behind her. Pablo followed.

Exactly ten minutes later, comfortably seated in her trailer's makeup area, where the lighting was more flattering, Keisha looked radiant in her crisp white robe and slippers. There was a knock at the door. She crossed her leg, arranged the slit of her robe so her thigh was mostly revealed, and cued Pablo.

Joe Vong didn't stand a chance. He entered without waiting for a reply. "I'm sure you're tired, but we have to change some protocols. For one thing, you need to wear an earpiece."

"Tell me about *OFFICERZ.*"

"Huh?" He stopped and looked at her leg. "What's to know?"

She drew her finger along the line of the robe, up her thigh. Pablo wondered what she was playing at, and wished he'd paid more attention in Psych 101.

"I'm just curious. What attracted you to making *that* particular show?"

"It was a job."

"And?"

"It got amazing ratings."

"And?"

"The thrill? Cops arresting a bunch of low-life losers, what's not to like?"

"And *that's* where you fucked up, Mr. Joe." Keisha's voice lowered an octave and reminded Pablo of something out of the *Exorcist* or *Poltergeist*. Was there really such a thing as demonic possession?

"You don't recognize me, do you?" Keisha stood up, a real-life Super Barbie doll intimidating the short man.

Pablo made a mental note. Keisha Barbie—huge profits there.

"I don't suppose you would. I was only thirteen."

Joe's skin flushed. He looked like a gazelle being clawed to death by a very beautiful, very deadly, big cat.

She leaned in close to Joe, her creepy child's voice rising into an irritating screech. "Think, Mr. Joe. The 405 highway in Los Angeles."

"We did several shows there."

"Mother. Two kids in the back seat." She sounded like a shrill prosecutor hammering a witness. "You thrust a camera into my face as police officers cop-dropped my mama into a cruiser."

The color immediately drained out of Joe's face. He closed his eyes and dropped his head back. There was a hollow thump as it hit the wall.

"*Egg-zackly.*" Keisha sneered. "Payback's a bitch, *bitch!*"

"Are you going to fire me?" He looked truly frightened.

"Oh, that would be too easy. Mr. Pablo, show Mr. Joe out." She exited with the finesse of Betty Davis into her dressing area. "Hang onto your seats, it's gonna be a bumpy season two."

# TERRIBLE TWOS

"I'M SORRY, I *just* can't do that again."

"It won't be as bad this year," Keisha reassured Pablo. "Everyone will be there this time to help out."

"My eyes were bleeding by the end of the day. Sasha was literally doing *eeny, meeny, miny, moe*," Pablo sighed, settling into the pillowy, soft leather seat of the Bombardier Learjet. They were 45,000 feet over North Carolina, headed to Florida. He wondered if there was a parachute included in the cost of the private jet they were sitting in.

"Season one's open call was *fierce* publicity and our fans now expect us to have another one," Keisha said.

Pablo frowned. Another grueling open call was his idea of hell. "Only if you promise to be there."

"Of course, I'll be there! I'm the star *and* EP. All the execs will be there this time."

"This year," he mumbled under his breath and waved at the flight attendant. "Do you have Advil on the plane?"

"Just champagne and snacks."

Pablo's head felt like it was being squeezed by a massive steel C-clamp.

Ever since the first season of *Model Muse* had wrapped, he'd become Keisha's sidekick and beard, an emasculating position that paid nothing and provided zero fringe benefits. Shortly after she'd ordered him to book the venue for her charity ball, *"Smile With Your Soul,"* she began telling him it was time to move out of Hell's Kitchen. Just how much could he do, he asked? So, like an overbearing mother, she called in a real estate agent and instructed them to scout for something trendy, spacious, and close to Broome Street for her sidekick. "We work together all the time," she'd chirped like an excited bird. "If we lived closer together, we could see each other all the time."

Pablo was beginning to think anything in the outer boroughs was too close. Especially since poor Vinny— literally and figuratively poor—the gorgeous stockbroker was jettisoned. He hadn't stood a chance once the show was a slam dunk. Falling in love with a Supermodel had its downsides.

"If you only knew," Keisha had confided in one of their now rare tête-à-têtes. "He calls me his own 'Personal Super-model.' I have to sleep with mascara and concealer on. And I *never* let him touch my hair 'cause he doesn't know I wear wigs." She shuddered.

"I didn't know he was like that." Pablo was a little shocked. He thought Vinny was really in love with her, but maybe it was just infatuation or, worse, arm candy. "You're a powerful woman, Keisha. You just have to be yourself. He'd be crazy not to accept you as you are."

"Well, there's NO way I can seriously date a guy who only earns two hundred and fifty thousand dollars a year. I mean, that's just embarrassing."

"You broke up with him because he only makes 250 grand?" Pablo couldn't believe his ears.

"He may have been hot in bed, but I can't bankroll a charity case."

Poor Vinny. Now she was dating one of the Uber-Rich. She was still arm candy, but at least he was a billionaire—or was it a trillionaire? Pablo couldn't make sense of all those zeroes. He was bad at math.

"T-Rex," that was Keisha's pet name for him, "doesn't trust me, Pablo. So I need you to come with me. I'm so horny I could die. I need a *real* man." She was now having an affair with the tight end for the Tampa Bay Buccaneers. "You should see his tight end."

Pablo, now on a Learjet to South Beach, came along for the ride so Keisha could have her little, or rather big, "dick date." And she didn't understand why "T-Rex" didn't trust her? He wondered who was bankrolling this impromptu trip to South Beach at $8,500.00 per hour. The "queen of cheap" certainly wouldn't spring for this booty call in Florida.

"So, if T-Rex asks, we're scouting a venue. And this is a tax write-off."

"A venue, for what?"

"For our four-city open call." She squealed like one of her contestants. "We're adding Chicago, Miami, and LA to the list!"

"What?" Pablo was taken aback.

"Joe and I discussed the idea the other night."

"Wait, what? Joe's your new BFF now?"

She waved at the flight attendant. "I need another bowl of those honey-glazed pecans." She blithely babbled as if she hadn't said anything unusual. "Don't act like you don't love it. Besides, what do you care about Joe Vong? You're a trending topic on Twitter these days—more than me." She sounded snarky and jealous.

He looked over at his beautiful friend. Was that what this was all about? Was she punishing him for having his own hashtag? She'd probably been one of those kids in kindergarten who came home with the grade card that said, "Kiki Grimes doesn't know how to share." After everything he'd done to help make their show a success: retouching contestants' photos on his laptop, editing footage for her Instagram account, putting out fires that Joe should've been hosing himself, painstakingly creating the *Model Muse* logo and taping way more scenes than he was responsible for producing and executing on camera, she was jealous of three minutes on Twitter?

There is silence and there is *silence*. Quietly fuming, Pablo turned his head and shut his eyes. The word *bitch* came to mind. He erased it. Others might use that word to describe her, but he was *not* one of them. He was her loyal friend. Foot soldier. Confidante. Family. Down below the Atlantic Seaboard, they were passing by. We must be near Savannah, he thought.

It was a long weekend. Pablo signed the venue for the open call and spent the rest of it lying on the beach waiting for Keisha to text him. She hadn't even planned a hotel room for him or an expense account. All she cared about was being able to write off the trip while he did her work and she got laid.

The idea that the on-camera talent was going to have a four-week holiday evaporated when open calls for season two were announced and all the new cities that had been added were preposterous. Sasha flew to LA. Miss Thing wouldn't leave NY. Mason got Chicago. Keisha, surprise, surprise, flew to Miami. Like Mary's little lamb, everywhere that Mary went, Pablo was sure to go. Keisha showed up for the casting but, yet again, she didn't stay. So here he was in Miami with Luciana, both of them again left to work through ten thousand hopefuls until their eyes bled. At least this trip was on expenses.

\*     \*     \*

The show's wardrobe supervisor couldn't contain herself with excitement. "I have a box of next season's Dior samples waiting at the front gate that you *must* wear," she blurted the moment she saw Pablo. "Can you believe it? It's only season two of *Model Muse* and we're getting fucking Dior."

It was only their second day of pre-production and the designers were practically beating down the doors, trying to reach him. Pablo was going to need an assistant to help with all the sucking up going on.

"Who knew that when I became Keisha's personal stylist that I'd end up styling a TV show." Dionne bubbled with excitement.

Who knew? Pablo knew. It was Broyce who'd told him.

At the end of season one, Broyce called Pablo in a panic. "*She* says she has no plans of leveraging herself to lure other fashion icons and design houses to the show."

"No one will work with her, Broyce." Pablo sounded remarkably calm, breaking the news to the one man involved with the show who'd stuck up for Keisha in the past.

"She's Keisha Kash," he said, startled at his revelation.

Pablo burst out laughing. Over the nearly two years they'd been "BFFs," it had become abundantly clear that Keisha's slash and burn approach to business had left her industry connections in tatters.

"I'm the one who set up all of last season's creative talent, Broyce. Not Keisha."

"She said she did it."

"Welcome to *Keishavision*." Pablo shook his head. "Don't worry, I got it covered. I'm not gonna let the show down."

"Silent and steady," Broyce sighed. "That's rare in this business."

"Silent? You *know* how much I can talk." The men chuckled.

"Well, it's a good thing we renewed your contract, or we'd be sunk. I owe you dinner."

Pablo wondered if Broyce was a man of his word, but had a feeling that good intentions didn't always make the exec's calendar.

"Try this on." Dionne tossed a suit over the chair and scampered out of the wardrobe room to grab another box of Dior samples. Alone in nothing but a pair of white Y-front Calvin Klein briefs, Pablo caught his reflection in the mirror. He flexed his muscles. Turned sideways to suck in his washboard abs. Not bad for a kid who'd been stumpy and short-waisted. Now on the eve of turning thirty, he was hot. No wonder his fans loved him. OMG. He had fans now. His heart swelled. A wave of euphoria and excitement pulsed through his entire being—he was living the dream, *his* dream. It was going to happen. All he needed to do was hang on, and he'd be more than a talk show host, he'd be *the* male Oprah.

"You should model BVDs, mate." Mason leaned on the door jamb and, if Pablo hadn't known better, he'd swear he was checking him out.

"Are all Brits metrosexuals?"

"Pretty much." Mason strode into the room and looked around. "Dionne said there was wardrobe to try on. Looks like there's more than wardrobe."

Pablo felt somewhat shy all of a sudden.

"Why haven't we talked about doing a test shoot with you, yet?" Mason framed his face, looking through his hands like they were a camera lens and made some mock shots of Pablo's nearly naked body. "I am positive we would create magic together. Wrap that body in my seductive light."

*Corny British humor?*

"Extreme Close Up!" Mason moved in close now. Pablo could smell his easily recognizable Extreme Noir Tom Ford cologne.

He did a little voguing. Twisting his shoulders, his hips. All in good fun. Suddenly, Mason slapped Pablo's nipples like they were frat boys and grabbed his ass.

"Hey." Pablo turned away. Mason raised an eyebrow, as if to say, *"You game?"*

*Was he? Mason was handsome. Sexy. Straight?*

A strange detachment between the present and the past skipped across Pablo's mind. Half of him was still the ugly, awkward kid. The biracial boy in a sea of white faces. "Don't let them get you down," his mother used to tell him while wiping the tears from his eyes. "You're more than your outside. They just can't see beyond their own skin and narrow minds. You've got to be better than them and show them you're their equal." Pablo could hear her voice as if it were yesterday.

Like a predator about to pounce on his prey, Mason moved closer. "No one has to know."

"Know what?" Pablo was confused.

Mason grabbed Pablo by the chest and threw him to the floor. And like a seasoned initiator, dropped his own pants all in one quick gesture.

"What are you doing?" Pablo pushed back.

"Don't be a cock tease. You've been coming onto me for months."

Mason slammed his hard body on top of him and thrust his tongue down Pablo's throat. His saliva tasted sweet, but Pablo was still disgusted.

"I know how *your people* like it."

In a boa constrictor hold, they rolled across the wardrobe room, Mason's legs clamped around Pablo's. "You make me so hard."

Thrusting his pelvis against Pablo's, Mason dry humped and heaved a hard and ribbed erection against the trapped creative director.

Pablo forced himself to relax. Mason eased his grip on him. "That's how he likes it."

Pablo punched him. Slam. "Get off me." He scampered to his feet. "You arrogant fuck."

"What?" Mason was agog.

Pablo grabbed his clothes and bolted for the door. "Why don't you go on Pornhub and jerk off." He exited the dressing room and roared behind him, "Better yet, go fuck yourself!"

Pulling on his clothes in the elevator, Pablo ran onto the street barefoot. His heart pounded in his chest. His ears were ringing. He waved his hand in the air for a yellow cab and jumped into the back.

"Soho. 565 Broome."

From the rear window, he could see Mason racing out of the building, waving. "Pablo, come back."

Sinking into the back seat of the cracked vinyl in the old cab, he stared at the meter already running. Then and only then did he burst into tears.

By the time he'd crossed the Queensborough Bridge into Manhattan, he'd calmed down. It wasn't that bad. Just a misunderstanding. Maybe he'd given off the wrong signals. It wasn't rape, just a fondle and fumble. A pass. An incomplete pass, in fact. What was his problem? He was shaking. His lip wouldn't stop trembling. He felt like a little boy, vulnerable and innocent. He needed assurance. A friend. Someone who'd understand being treated like an object. If anyone would get it, Keisha would. "Mama will make it right." That's what she'd say.

"What's wrong?" Keisha said as she opened the door to her loft and ushered Pablo in. "I thought you were supposed to be in fittings this afternoon?"

The haphazardness of her ill-conceived, multi-million-dollar designer disaster seemed like a metaphor for the chaos in his mind at that moment. He kicked off his shoes, walked past the open space kitchen, and plopped onto the purple velvet fainting couch that looked more like an oversized dildo. Keisha's taste in furniture was about as bad as her taste in clothing, but he loved her and didn't care.

Grabbing a pint of *Dulce de Leche* Häagen-Dazs from her fridge, Keisha settled next to Pablo and began to eat. She didn't offer him any but that wasn't unusual. "Tell Mama what's wrong?"

Pablo spilled his guts. He even cried. "It was disgusting. I feel dirty. You know?"

He turned to look at her. She was not nodding empathetically.

"I don't know if I can work with him on the show anymore. How can I hide how I feel about him on camera? I'll just wanna wrap my hands around his neck and throttle him every time he opens his condescending mouth! He said something like, 'I know how *your people* like it.' What the *fuck* does that mean?"

She bit her spoon and looked at him, hard. Her brown/green eyes burned. "*Model Muse* has taken off, Mr. Pablo. This is what you wanted. It's what I want. We can't let anything happen to the show." She licked her spoon and tapped him on the nose. "Besides, Mason *is* kinda hot. Think of it as a compliment. I mean, it's kinda flattering. No one's manhandled me in years."

He looked at her incredulously. Gobsmacked, he stammered, "I can't believe *you*, a woman who's been objectified your entire career, continues to stand up for equal pay and publicly endorses the *Me Too* movement—you are telling *me* that this is not a serious offense? If I was one of the female staff, you'd have his fucking head."

"But you're not." She stood up and walked away. End of subject. "You can't tell anyone, Pablo. No one can know. You'll ruin his reputation *and* the show's." She put her ice cream back into the freezer. "Now, you'd better get back to the studio and finish your fittings. I have to call my new manager." She'd dropped Pablo's drama and picked up her own. "I just got Andy Levenkron to sign me. That's right, *the* Andy Levenkron—he's a beast. He's gonna make sure I have the biggest second act of my career."

Pablo felt like he was walking through a desert of sand, his legs heavy, and his feet unstable. He ordered an Uber and left her apartment. She hadn't fixed it, nor made things right. Instead, she had officially flipped the script on male supremacy and reminded him that she was *"The Boss."*

# 10

# KEISHAVISION

"**I** THINK I SHOULD record an album," Keisha blurted out of the clear blue.

Pablo nearly spit out his protein shake. "What?"

"Come on, let's be real. JLo was really created by glam gurus, auto-tune, and Benny Medina. Who's really the brain behind the beauty? All you need these days is a brilliant producer to become a star."

"P.S. She can *actually* sing."

"Madonna can't and look at her. With Andy Levenkron behind me, I can do whatever I want. He'll make sure of it. He's made oodles of popstars."

"Isn't it enough to have a hit television show and be one of the world's most gorgeous women?" Pablo tried not to roll his eyes. "Far more beautiful than JLo, Beyoncé and Madonna combined, I might add."

"I wanna be more than my looks, Mr. Pablo." He cringed as her voice shifted into what he now thought of as, scary child's voice. "You know that."

"But you can't sing."

"Details, details. Did you even hear what I'm saying? Andy will take care of everything."

Season two was already gearing up. They'd just finished four open calls and assessed thousands of models, picked the semi-finalists, planned the creatives, and were about to start filming. Pablo was already tired and he knew that no matter what, he was going to get sucked into the *Keishavision* vortex and have to help her become a popstar—on top of his regular workload. De La Renta wasn't going to have to dye his hair grey for much longer; he'd be natural grey if this pace kept up.

The Supermodel had already given the go-ahead to her new—I can do no wrong—talent manager to pull together the ultimate dream team to make Keisha Kash *America's next top recording artist*. Andy hired the best songwriters, the hottest Hip-Hop record producer, and Celine Dion's own voice coach, a Cherokee dude with a long ponytail and pained expression on his formerly kind face. He only lasted one day before having a Celine Dion emergency and flying to Canada. Clearly, he could only feel safe from Keisha's voice if he was in another country. As an A-list celebrity, no one dared tell Keisha that her voice sucked, especially when she was trying to become a musical popstar.

Keisha didn't care. "He taught me so much that first day, I don't need any more lessons." She smiled at her BFF. "Besides, you can sing. You can coach me if I need it."

Pablo tried to look pleased with the idea.

At the first recording session, Keisha wailed into the microphone so loudly that the sound engineer had to remove his headphones. He looked over at Pablo and whispered, "Are you kidding me?"

Pablo headed into the sound booth.

"How was that?" She smiled gleefully at him. "I'm digging this whole set up. It's so dark and cool."

"Keisha, *fiercest* icon of the world..." Pablo began.

"Did we get it in one take, or should I go again?"

"Keisha." Pablo swallowed hard. "You *can't* sing."

"I just did."

"No, what I mean is, you can't carry a tune. You're *just* a touch tone-deaf."

"I'm black! We can all sing."

"Well, evidently, you're not black enough. And I say this with love, my goddess of the catwalk, you're no Beyoncé. You'll be a laughingstock if you release this track."

"Excuse me?" She hissed at him. "You used to be so supportive, but lately, you've gotten really difficult and petty."

"I'm trying to help you avoid embarrassment," Pablo said earnestly.

"You're just jealous."

He looked at her in shock.

"Why don't you try singing something?" she dared him.

Nothing got by that Venus flytrap of a brain of hers. From the glint in her million-dollar eyes, Pablo suddenly realized that every little detail of his life scooped out over those all-night ice cream binging orgies had been filed away for her use later. He hadn't known back then that his confides would be the fodder used against him at some random later date. Now, he wondered what else he'd told her over the past two years when they were just *Babes in Arms*. Though his dream of being a singer when he was a spotty faced, awkward teenager shouldn't have been ammunition—what teenager hadn't wanted to be a singer in a band? He turned toward the mic and called her bluff.

Swaying his hips back and forth, he did a little salsa and serenaded the most beautiful woman in the world. "Yo, soy el cantante…" He sang in Spanish as Keisha frolicked around him, pretending to be a flamenco dancer. Of course, the song had a salsa beat. He watched her and smiled sweetly. She so wanted to be more than her looks. But she couldn't sing, though. She couldn't dance either.

Was that why they were in this recording studio now? Pablo felt a strange coolness sweep through his body. It hadn't occurred to him before that she was usurping his own talents and claiming them as her own. She'd adopted his hashtag gesture and made it her own, borrowed almost all of his catchphrases and made them famous on *Model Muse,* and now she was trying to sing.

He returned to the engineer's studio and shrugged. "You'll have to fix it in the mix."

*　*　*

"So, Andy had a great idea, Mr. Joe." They were in their last pre-production meeting before filming began on season two, planning the teaches, challenges, and photoshoot themes. "We're gonna release my new single with a music video and use the models as back-up dancers. Mr. Pablo will come up with the treatment and direct, and maybe get someone from *Dancing With The Stars* to choreograph."

Pablo nodded obediently, knowing better than to object to anything his BFF says publicly.

"This is not part of our production schedule, Miss Kash." Joe Vong politely argued. "I don't see how we have time for this, and there's no budget for a choreographer or an expensive location shoot."

"Mr. Joe, I think you're gonna have to make it happen." She aimed her finger at him and pressed an imaginary trigger with her thumb a few times. "Don't you?"

"Broyce will have to okay it."

"You'll have to make sure he does. Remember, you're mine now, Mr. Joe. And you *don't* wanna learn what I'm really capable of—you owe me." She blew on her finger and turned to Pablo. "Make him go away now, Mr. Pablo."

Pablo opened the door for Vong and shut it behind him.

Keisha had gotten a pair of brass balls—Andy Levenkron's, to be exact. Her new talent manager was working overtime to give his *Model Muse* star a branding makeover. What Keisha wanted, Andy got. Period. No one crossed him. And with his power behind her, she knew she could place Vong's testicles in a vise and squeeze until he was her pawn. It may be cliché to say that Hollywood managers are all crooked and unethical but in the case of Andy Levenkron, that was an understatement. Slimy and devious were Andy's most positive attributes. He shrewdly used his high-powered connections to keep his more debaucherous escapades out of the press and himself out of hot water, but Andy was always on the cusp of another public sex scandal. He was the *"golden child"* of managers because he was ruthless. "I'm the best in the business because no one dares fuck with me," he often spouted. True enough, Hollywood can be a pretty shitty place, especially for those who find themselves in a position where powerful people like slimy Andy don't think twice about asserting control over them to get what they need. Thinking about his incident with cocky Mason, Pablo wondered, *Why do abusers always win the power struggle...while the abused fall into silent defeat?*

*Girls Are The World*, Keisha's debut single was to be released to coincide with the airing of the 5th episode of season two's *Model Muse*. On top of everything else Pablo had on his plate, he now had to produce the music video–a task which normally took months. It was to be used in the judging elimination segment. He would have forty-eight hours to shoot the video and have it perfected for the judges to evaluate. Keisha refused to have them review a rough-cut, even though production could easily edit in a polished final version for the episodic airing months later. Nope. Keisha wanted everyone to see the final product at the judging, which only gave Pablo two days to shoot the contestants with Keisha and turn around a *perfect* product. When had his Supermodel boss become so unreasonable, or had she always been this way and he'd just never noticed?

*   *   *

A burned-out Pablo leaned his head on De La Renta's shoulder. Next to them, sitting in video village watching Keisha introduce her music video, were Joe and Andy. Keisha had given strict orders for none of the judges, or crew, to hear the song or see the video before her onscreen moment. Always the teacher's pet, Mason had a pleasant look on his face. For once, Miss Thing and Sasha sat patiently waiting; of course, Sasha was drunk. The guest judge for the episode was Derek Hough from *DWTS*–who'd choreographed the video. Though a complete professional who embodied cool, Derek was nibbling on the quicks of his fingernails.

"Who knew he had an oral fixation," De La Renta quipped.

"I cannot tell you how nervous I am right now. My legs are literally shaking because this is the most vulnerable thing I've ever done." Keisha addressed the eight contestants who'd participated in her music video. "This week you had a very special photoshoot. You performed in my first ever music video."

Sasha turned to Miss Thing, silently opened her mouth and stuck her finger down her throat in a mock gag. Pablo wondered if any of the cameras had caught her and hoped for her sake they hadn't. Keisha wouldn't like being made fun of, even if it was going on the cutting room floor.

"After nine years of secretly working in music studios around the globe, it's time to present the world premiere of my first music single, *Girls Are The World!*"

"She means nine minutes," De La Renta cracked.

The jib swung across the soundstage and pulled out to a wide shot revealing Keisha, the judges and all the contestants directing their attention to the huge LED wall above the runway. Per Keisha's direction, an old-fashioned white circle with black numbers doing a silent countdown and the background sound effect of crackling static filled the room.

3...2...1...

FADE FROM BLACK: Keisha in an all-white catsuit is riding a black horse past barrel drums on fire. A post-apocalyptic vibe à la *Mad Max*.

Joe instantly snatched Pablo from his seat and dragged him through the nearby soundstage door, where Andy was already standing in the hall. "OK, Keisha didn't want me on set while she shot her video–*fine*." Joe was more ballistic than normal. "But explain to me why the word 'girls' is being repeated every four beats—this all sounds and looks very familiar. Even to me. If Beyoncé sues us, it's on your heads. Not the network's."

"Calm down, Vong." Andy shook his head. "Artists are always getting inspiration from other artists–look at Taylor Swift, she totally knocked off Beyoncé's *Homecoming* performance once. They *all* hail the queen."

"Fuck! I knew it," Joe screamed. "This is a blatant rip off of Beyoncé, isn't it?"

"Listen, Kim *Vong*-un..."

"What the fuck did you just call me?"

Unbothered, Andy continued without addressing the racist slur. "Beyoncé's *Run The World (Girls)* isn't even close to Keisha's *Girls Are The World*."

"Can I just jump in here and say..." Pablo was saying, as both irate men ignored him and continued yelling.

"Pablo worked with Keisha on this. We've changed enough details to avoid any first glance comparisons."

"What are you talking about?" Joe's face was solid red now, "I don't know fucking shit about these pop singers and even I noticed. Beyoncé fans are gonna crucify us when this airs."

"You're overreacting, Joe."

Pablo was too tired to jump in and didn't understand why he was dragged into the hall in the first place, if they were just going to ignore him. He was just a soldier, not a general, and certainly not the President of this shitshow. He'd had enough and slipped back into the soundstage.

"If we get a Cease and Desist letter from Beyoncé's team, I'm gonna make sure—"

The soundproof door clicked shut.

Pablo now watched as the scenes on the LED screen continued to play out exactly as Keisha had requested, with the model contestants acting as her army of power women taking on the masculine world. Keisha had several wardrobe changes that were all carefully designed to look just like all of Beyoncé's outfits. Her wheat gold hair flowed long with a tasseled wave, expertly styled.

"You know how long that wig took me to make?" De La Renta leaned into Pablo and asked. "Too fucking long. That's how long. That piece was a bitch to color! She had me match highlights and lowlights so her *Queen Bey* wig looked authentic." De La Renta, whose hairstyle changed almost daily, began playing with his now short Senegalese twists in frustration. "But I'm hitting production with overtime. Trust." Being the youngest child of seven, the hair guru was raised by his grandmother in Atlanta. She was a loud, say-it-like-it-is kind of woman, and he inherited her mouth.

Pablo had used bright beauty ring lighting and only noticed now that he inadvertently made Keisha's complexion appear lighter than usual. She really *did* look like Beyoncé in a few of the wide shots. The similarities were worrying. What would the fans on social media say when the episode finally aired?

The video ended with Keisha gyrating in a green sequin and chiffon dress, with a dangerously revealing diagonal slit over her breasts. She punched a male dancer standing in front of her on the last downbeat, and with the whip of De La Renta's custom sewn wig, she turned her back on the camera and sashayed away.

FADE TO BLACK.

Mason, Miss Thing and Sasha sat frozen in time. The *Model Muse* cameras pushed in for closeups. Keisha had tears in her eyes. The others? Well, they had tears of a different sort.

"Before we evaluate all your individual performances, I just wanna say, I'll never forget the eight of you who will forever be a part of my dream. Hashtag," she crossed her fingers, "bonded for life." The Supermodel dabbed the corners of her eyes as the camera pushed tight.

"And, that's a cut everybody," Bill yelled. "Quick change on batteries and let's repos for evaluations. This isn't a break people. Keep comments for the cameras. No talking."

"Bravo, Keisha," Mason proffered while politely clapping. "You sounded fantastic."

"Oh, you're so sweet," Keisha bashfully sat down next to the handsome Brit, "but no talking. Wait till we're back up."

"Are you fucking kidding me?" Miss Thing fired across Mason's bow. "Canines in *New Jersey* could hear that auto-tune. *Beyon-say-you-Betta-don't.*"

Keisha turned towards her model coach, the man who'd given her, her signature walk and in essence made her who she was today. If her eyes could shoot bullets, he'd have been a dead man.

Pablo didn't dare get up from the safety of his seat on the sidelines.

"I bet Beyoncé wished she had that beat Keisha." Sasha jumped in.

"Why, thank you, Sasha," Keisha interrupted and smiled. "Us *girls* need to stick together." She stuck her tongue out at Miss Thing and closed her eyes as De La Renta stepped in to touch up her makeup.

Sasha whispered in Miss Thing's ear, but her audio was still being transmitted to all the production crew's headsets— including Pablo's. "She gotta *certain* beat all right. Did you see her ass jiggling in those outfits? Looked like two pigs fighting under a blanket."

Hearing them on their mics, Pablo accidentally swallowed the mint Mentos he was sucking on and began to sputter and choke.

"God don't like ugly," Keisha said, her eyes still shut as De La Renta applied more liner. Maybe she did possess magical powers?

"Places everyone," the AD yelled. "We're back in 3, 2, 1."

"What's our criteria for judging the models?" Miss Thing asked. "I mean they were barely onscreen. It was all Keisha."

The silence in the studio was deadly. By now Pablo had figured out how most things worked on the show and in post— the hours of footage that they'd shot were organized into some semblance of order, and the real story was crafted. It didn't matter what the cameras shot; the show was made in editing. Flipping coverage between the different camera angles the editors created the "moments" Keisha *wanted* on TV. The rest was garbage. No gag reel. Nothing.

When season one hit the airwaves, a harsh lesson was

learned. Keisha had hoovered up all of Pablo's good lines, adopted his hashtag gesture, and he noticed that she now tilted her head like he did when he was talking to the models. The most talented person on the show, full of hilarious impersonations and witty one-liners, Miss Thing got slashed and burned in the editing room. Keisha degraded the cross-dressing runway coach to a babbling buffoon and ensured nothing of real substance came out of his mouth. There was only one star of *Model Muse*, and that star was Keisha Kash. No one else.

*     *     *

Keisha got an evil little glint in her amber eyes that spelled trouble. The kind of trouble the network would love. "Get some male models to surprise the girls," she told Pablo.

"What do you have up your sleeve?"

"I thought we could stir things up. Models aren't nuns, you know."

That was for sure, Pablo thought. He'd spent his entire 24-hours in South Beach looking at venues for the open call, while she got her "toes" tickled.

"And tell The Wine Barn to send over a case of red and white."

"How about I get us some product placement, and fund this party for free?" He called the marketing department of Interboro, an alcoholic drink that packed a punch. By the time he'd gotten off the phone, they were committed to delivering four cases—two to the models' apartment on Canal street and two to Silvercup for the wrap party in a few weeks.

"That's what I like about you, Pablo—you're so thoughtful and always thinking ahead."

"A drunk crew is a happy crew." He hoped she'd heard him.

"Oh, and make sure the boys are willing to get naked too," she added.

Season two's models were housed in an actual apartment rather than a hotel like they'd been in season one. It was thoroughly rigged with cameras and microphones—like the CIA, only more fun. Almost every night after work, Keisha and Pablo would retire to Keisha's couch, with a pint of ice cream apiece, and watch their own private reality show—unedited. So they could see the live feed from the apartment as five gorgeous hunks arrived carrying two cases of Interboro, followed by two Steadicam operators.

"Hey, girls!" Sexy Guy #1 said, "Keisha's really proud of all the hard work you've done over the past few weeks and sent some refreshments."

"OMG. Party!" the models' screeched.

"Why do girls squeal?" Pablo plugged his ears and turned to Keisha. "It's really annoying."

Sexy Dude #2 opened a can and handed it to one of the girls. Keisha smiled and leaned back to watch the shenanigans she'd set up. And there were shenanigans. One of the girls put on Spotify as their hunks—permission to strip approved—began handing out instant mixed drinks. Music blared. Another girl began dancing and the rest joined in, showing off their back-up moves from the music video. "OMG, we had to listen to Keisha's track over and over. It was the worst song ever," someone blurted. Another girl caught her eye. She shut up.

Pablo looked over at Keisha to see if she had heard the reproach. She stabbed her ice cream.

"What's wrong with you?" Sexy Guy #4 asked the one girl who seemed to be holding back.

"I'm just homesick."

"You're not from New York?"

"I haven't even seen the city. All we do is go back and forth to different studios where we may have to sit in a closet and not speak to each other, or we're locked in here or driving around Manhattan in a stretched Hummer."

"Shit." He drank some of his Interboro Gin & Tonic. "I love your accent. Where're you from?"

"North Carolina, where *thanks* is a three-syllable word. You from here?"

"Chicago."

"What do you do for a living?"

He looked at her and puffed up his chest. "I mostly work fancy catered events where they want model type waiters, but I've been shot for GQ and recently did a spread in *Vogue* with Gisele Bündchen."

"You model?"

"Don't sound so shocked." He handed her another G&T. "Erik."

"Mandy."

"Come on, Mandy. Let's go out on the balcony. It's too loud in here."

As they trailed away from the camera, Keisha looked over at Pablo and winked. "Love at first sight."

The party was getting raucous now and most of the guys had pulled off their shirts. The girls were stripping off their layers too.

"What a bunch of sluts." Keisha laughed hysterically.

"Hey, where'd Mandy go?" one of the girls shouted as she grabbed Sexy Guy #1's belt buckle and pulled him toward her. "She's missing all the fun!"

The Steadicam began moving down the hallway to the rooms of the girls. One or two were making out, but no Mandy. He turned left down the hall.

"Ohh…Baabeee," a southern voice moaned.

"Fuck, you're hot," Erik said.

The bathroom door was slightly ajar. The cameraman

pushed it open and there in the shower, behind a steamy clear vinyl curtain, were some very fine male buttocks thrusting between some very pale, long legs wrapped around his waist.

Pablo burst out laughing.

"Mandy?" Keisha dropped her ice cream and screamed. "She wasn't supposed to fuck the guy."

"They aren't nuns! You said so yourself."

"They shouldn't be sluts."

"Since when?" Pablo rolled across the couch, laughing so hard tears squirted out of his eyes. "Models shouldn't be sluts?" He roared. "You're the queen of the booty call."

"Stop laughing," she ordered.

Of course, that didn't work. He couldn't. The more she glared at him and threatened him if he didn't stop, the worse it got. He laughed so hard he snorted. Waves of laughter cascaded through his body—he hadn't laughed so hard since he was a kid.

"What do I do?" the camera operator said into his IFB.

"Bust them up," Keisha screamed.

"Poor kid. She just needs to let off some steam." Pablo burst out laughing again. "And that shower is certainly steamy." It took five minutes to get himself under control and even then, all Keisha had to do was look at him and he would start laughing all over again.

Over the live feed, Mandy's southern charm vanished and she sounded Hillbilly distinctly. "What the hell?"

"Hey, that's not cool, dude." Erik grabbed a towel and, like a true gentleman, wrapped it around himself, leaving naked Mandy to fend for herself.

"I gotta hand it to you, Keisha, this is gonna make great television," Joe Vong said over his IFB.

Keisha made a little told-you-so face at Pablo, who'd finally recovered some composure. His sides ached.

Keisha looked like a stern housemother. "I'm gonna teach that girl and all girls on my show a lesson they will never forget."

"Be afraid. Be very afraid." Pablo wiped his eyes.

The next morning, Keisha ordered the Steadicams to follow her into the girls' apartment at 8 a.m. The contestants had an afternoon call time and looked not entirely *Model Muse* worthy. They welcomed their Supermodel with a little less glee than they had on the first episode.

"Where's Mandy?"

Mandy came out of her bedroom in her bathrobe. Her eyes had dark circles under them.

"You went to sleep with your makeup on?" Keisha sounded more horrified at that than the indiscriminate sex. "Models always take their makeup off at the end of the day. True beauty is not skin deep."

Pablo thought of Vinny and the makeup Keisha had slept in every night to make him happy.

"But that's not why I'm here. We need to talk." Keisha pointed to the rest of the girls. "This is between Mandy and me. Go to your rooms." Like a flock of chickens, the models scurried away. Keisha sat down on the couch and patted the spot next to her. "As I said, we need to talk." The camera zoomed in on Keisha's perfect face. "About being sexually responsible." Mandy's face was crimson red. "Did he wear a condom last night?"

Mandy began crying and shaking her head; she whimpered a "No."

"Are you on the pill?"

"No."

Keisha shook her head back and forth. "What were you thinking, girl?"

"I dunno."

"I do. You *weren't* thinking. We don't know anything about that guy. He could've had any number of STDs, Syphilis or Gonorrhea perhaps. This is New York City, Mandy, you can't just get laid by any old random stranger."

"You sent him over."

"Cut that." Keisha looked at the cameraman and slashed her throat. "Let's be clear—I sent some refreshments to you girls after a hard day's work. That's it."

Hanging in the back, behind the camera, Pablo nearly choked. It was so not true.

"I've made an appointment for you to go see a gynecologist. You're gonna get a blood test and pap smear, and test for STDs. You're also getting the Morning-After pill."

Mandy began sobbing. "I'm sorry. I was just so lonely."

"How else are you gonna learn? As a Supermodel, your body is a temple. You have to take care of it." Keisha was on a Mother Teresa roll now. "That means eating the right food. Never eating sugar. *And* make sure you're healthy."

"What if I test positive?"

"I'll have to send you home."

Mandy bawled.

Keisha looked at her coldly. "I thought you were homesick." She signaled to the camera crew. "To the doctor's office."

Joe Vong leaned over to Pablo and whispered, "The ratings are gonna explode from this episode."

"You can't follow her to the doctor for a gynecological exam," Pablo said.

"Watch me."

Of course, most of the saga was cut by the Network censors—*Model Muse* wasn't supposed to be more than soft porn, and it was certainly not a doctor show. But Keisha and Joe got enough of the story in the final edit so that Mandy and her nice Baptist family in Morganton, North Carolina, were embarrassed on national television. It was the ratings spike that solidified *Model Muse* as the reality show to watch.

\*   \*   \*

At around 3 a.m. Pablo's phone started buzzing on his bedside table. The new screenshot that lit up his screen featured Pablo and Keisha posing against some rocks and sand in South Beach–he looked buff in his Tom Ford swim trunks and she looked like an overstuffed mango in a strapless, orange one-piece. Pablo was proud of how he looked though, and that's why he chose this new pic of them for her contact photo.

"What." His voice was hoarse from long days on the set and lack of sleep.

"I'm late."

"For what? It's 3 a.m."

"My period."

His head fell back on his pillow with a thump. "You couldn't tell me that at breakfast?"

"I need you to get me a pregnancy test."

"Me?"

"Get a couple. Different brands."

"In the morning."

"Now."

"Keisha, I'm not gonna get up and try to find an all-night pharmacy so you can do something now that you can do just as easily in a few hours. Go to sleep." And then for the first time in his life, he hung up on her.

His phone buzzed. He groaned. Answered. "No."

"Please." Her tone slipped up a few octaves into her high pitched little girl voice. "Please, Mr. Pablo."

"Ugh, are you worried about T-Rex or South Beach?"

"South Beach."

"You're telling me you didn't use a condom?"

"No," she whimpered.

"And you're not on birth control?"

"No."

"What were you thinking?" He repeated the lines she'd used on Mandy. "I know, you *weren't* thinking."

"You don't tell a star football player to wear a condom, Pablo."

"I wouldn't know. I was looking at venues for an open casting call—for your show."

"Will you go now?"

"No. I'm going to sleep. Tomorrow morning I'll swing by Rite Aid and grab you a couple brands and bring them by. It's a few hours, just try to relax."

"I can't..."

"I'm turning my phone off, Keisha. Good night." And then, he did exactly what he said he was going to do. He turned off his iPhone and fell back on his mattress. For a moment, he thought he would never get back to sleep. A few hours later, he woke to sunlight on his face. *If I left my phone off every night,* he thought, *I might actually achieve some REM sleep.* He hadn't dreamt in so long. He'd forgotten how good it felt to be swept away and truly slumber.

# COPY THAT

**W**ITH TWO SUCCESSFUL and lucrative seasons of *Model Muse* on the air, Pablo was finally able to purchase his first apartment in New York City. Keisha helped him look for something and advised on how to negotiate with realtors. Ultimately, he'd done it by himself. After living in a cramped Hell's Kitchen railroad flat, Pablo hungered for a room with a view. It was the fourteen-foot ceilings and wall of glass overlooking Seventh Avenue that sold him on the apartment. The moment he walked inside, he knew he'd come home. Now the fun began.

Like any good designer, Pablo spent hours planning the renovations down to the smallest detail, so by the time season two wrapped, he was ready to decorate. "I'm gonna visit my parents in Illinois," he lied to Keisha. He needed a serious holiday from Keishavision and needed to use the show's hiatus to create a safe haven from the chaos of the celebrity world—not playing her beard for booty calls. It was bliss. Peace and serenity reigned supreme in his life and he began to feel like a real human being, again. And a real artist. Every bit of his apartment was an expression of Pablo's creativity, and his eye for design and beauty elevated the decor. He'd taken a page from Philippe Starck's modern white loft suites at The Sanderson Hotel in London, but his apartment was all Pablo Michaels.

Coming through the front door, Pablo wanted his guests' eyes to be drawn to the ultimate focal wall opposite his bedroom. At first glance, it looked like an architectural detail, but it concealed the components to his Bang & Olufsen home theater system, which revealed with the press of a button—or a request from Siri. In front of that was a light grey Minotti sectional sofa and one of the last famous *Script Rugs* with illegible black writing scribbled across the white fabric. A white lacquer desktop appeared to be floating in space, above clear Lucite legs that had been fashioned to look like cut crystal stemmed champagne glasses. He'd actually splurged on having a custom made Eames Executive chair created for his desk. White, of course. Like the clean palette of a painter, Pablo had created a modern neoclassical vibe to help him keep a clear mind when he wasn't on the chaotic set of *Model Muse*.

With meticulous care and precision, his bedroom was measured and fitted with wrap around, floor-to-ceiling, white ripple fold drapes. Their dramatic flair gave a sense of texture and comfort that he adored. A Lucite framed Ghost Mirror hung over his king-sized bed, creating the illusion of greater space. It was sexy too.

To his delight, the one-bedroom loft resembled the film set from the movie *Oblivion* with Tom Cruise. The modernity of the space might've been intimidating to some, but Pablo loved it. Pablo savored the feeling of living in what he called an "art installation." A couple of select artisan-crafted chairs, uphol-stered in warm orange and grey hues, offset the all-white.

The evening before they were to return from break, the intercom buzzed.

"A very lively De La Renta to see you, sir," Sean, the Irish doorman, announced.

"Is he dressed to kill?" Pablo asked.

"I hope not, sir."

"Send him up." As much as Pablo loved his apartment and the location, the old Irishman on the door may have clinched the deal. He loved Sean's brogue and sass.

Fluffing the Missoni Home pillows in his living room, Pablo looked around one last time. There was a *badda bop rap* on the door.

"Hey *Siri*, play my chill mix," Pablo said, dancing toward the door.

The robotic Siri voice confirmed, "Playlist *chill mix* now playing." The silken voice of Cynthia Erivo floated down from the ceiling, emanated from the walls and filled the room.

Pablo flung open the door.

"Yaaaassssss. Come on new apartment," De La Renta shouted and handed his buddy a bottle of pink Veuve Clicquot Champagne.

"Get in here, fool." Pablo hugged the man.

Always the nosey queen, De La Renta peeked into the half bath as he walked through the foyer. "You got a half bath? *S-hi-t*," he made it a three-syllable word, "I'm lucky I got one sink to spit in when I brush my two back teeth."

Pablo laughed and slapped his friend on the back. "I'm so glad you're here."

"Vacation has done you good." De La Renta walked in, kicked his boots off as Pablo placed the bottle of Champagne on the nearby kitchen counter. "Lord, you look ten years younger."

"You mean, I look my age?" Pablo chuckled.

"*Egg-zackly.*" He looked around the space. "It's *on and poppin'* now with this new pad."

"Check this out. Hey *Siri*, make it sexy." Blackout blinds descended over the windows as soft accent lights illuminated the base of the sofa, the under lip on the baseboards and decorative notches cut into the walls. "I went for the futuristic vibe, LED tape hidden everywhere, and the whole place is controlled by Apple Home. Surround sound, lights, entertainment."

"Only you, Pablo," De La Renta laughed. "All you need is someone to seduce."

"I'll work on that after we wrap next season." Pablo rolled his eyes.

"Don't tell Mother you gonna take another vacay. She'll flip her wig."

"Okaaaay. But she's not the only one who needs booty calls."

"True dat," De La Renta chuffed. "So, what's Malaki doin' with your old place?"

"He popped the question to his girlfriend and *Mrs. Malaki to be* moved in." Pablo tapped his iPhone to open the blinds.

De La Renta stood in awe, looking out the enormous corner window that wrapped the far side of the living room. Pablo's view used to be a tenement block and overweight hookers hanging out on fire escapes. Now he had Seventh Avenue and the reflective grace of the Freedom Tower at One World Trade. Pablo was in the kitchen, enjoying De La Renta enjoying the view. Pressing the cork on the champagne bottle, he said, "Get the glasses."

De La Renta made his way over to the kitchen and looked at the walls. "Where?"

Pablo tapped a flush inset button next to the cabinet above

his kitchen sink. The door slowly opened up to reveal a collection of crystal glasses.

"Oooooo, fancy you."

"Where else would one keep champagne flutes?"

"Bitch, in a normal cabinet. That is if you're lucky enough to have a kitchen in this city."

The cork popped, and foam erupted.

"Whoo," De La Renta squealed. Pablo hadn't heard anyone squeal in weeks and thought how nice it had been.

He poured the bubbly into the Moya handmade and mouthblown, tapered waist flutes and handed one of the special glasses to De La Renta.

"Girl, do you have *anything* that's normal now?"

"Not even my friends."

"*Touché.*" They clinked their glasses and moved back into the living room where De La Renta took a seat on the kitten grey Minotti sofa. Running his hands over the textured fabric, he cooed. "She's lovely. So chic."

"And expensive. A whole episode's salary for me." Pablo looked down at his friend's holey dark blue jeans. "Those aren't indigo dyed, are they?"

"You think I'm gonna stain your precious sectional? Don't get your panties in a wad. They've been washed more than your hair and your hands in one lifetime."

Pablo sipped the champagne and relaxed. "You're my first guest."

"Don't let Mother know. She'll have my head if she thinks I beat her to the unveiling." There was a framed photo of Keisha and Pablo sitting on a set of floating shelves. "It all started with her." He raised his glass.

Pablo did too. "To Keisha. Long may she reign."

"At least, until you can pay off your mortgage."

"I hear that." They clinked their glasses again.

"I've so enjoyed having the last three weeks alone to finish decorating," Pablo sighed. "Being *Keisha-free* was my real vacation. I really don't know how I got away with it."

"T-Rex problems," De La Renta spouted.

"Really?"

"Yup. That's why I have the day off. She canceled her *InStyle* cover shoot because she was up all night arguing with him." The glam guru sounded annoyed now. "Of course, I only found out when her doorman told me this morning–at 6:30 a.m. The bitch couldn't text me beforehand?"

"Well, that was bound to end soon."

"I told her last week, if you want another *New York City douche*, I can go to CVS on West 23rd Street and get you one."

Pablo nearly spit out his champagne. "Where the fuck do you come up with all these one-liners? You need your own show."

"Oh, no. I'm not goin' down like that? No, ma'am." De La Renta wagged his finger. "Okay, time to snoop more." He stood up and strode over to the bedroom. He peered into the large white en-suite bathroom. "You have an egg tub? Oh! Please, pretty please, can I come over and take a bath some night?"

"Sure. Just bring your own bubbles."

"OOH. I can't wait. I've always wanted to bathe in an egg!"

Pablo looked at their reflections in the mirror. It was encased with soft-focus LED ring light, the best light to do makeup in.

De La Renta approved. "You should do your makeup here instead of those shitty trailers at work." They walked back through the bedroom to settle on either side of the kitchen island that divided the open-concept space. "Everything here is the exact opposite of Keisha's place."

"Yeah, I'm not really into the whole *mix-and-match mansion* thing," Pablo sniped.

"*Ohmigod*, every time I go over there, I feel like I'm in Starbucks."

"Huh?"

"Oh *puh-lease*." De La Renta loved to dish on bad taste, especially celebrity's bad taste. "That ceiling in the living room painted with those muted earth tone circles and gold leaf accents?" De La Renta closed his eyes and tilted his head like a confused dog. "And that odd-looking furniture with those geometric shaped pillows? Starbucks." He snapped his fingers.

"Got it. I told her to pick a theme and stick to it," Pablo scoffed. "It's like she tries to throw in every motif she's ever seen or liked."

"Sort of like what she does on the show," De La Renta pointed out. "Last season she was a popstar. This season she's a novelist."

"What?" It was Pablo's turn to snort.

"You didn't know?" De La Renta had clearly been waiting for the right moment to drop this tidbit. "You should've seen her the other day. While I was relaxing her hair and braiding it all up, she was two-finger pounding the whole time. Mavis Beacon, she is not." De La Renta leaned in as if someone could hear them speaking. "She says you were there when she got the inspiration and now that she's on hiatus and you begged off for Springfield—or so she thinks—she's clacking away at her computer, becoming an author."

"Oh, that," Pablo chuckled then took a sip of champagne. "She got some idea when we were flying down to Florida for her dirty weekend with *Mr. Tampa Bay Buccaneers,* something about alien models."

"Child, I can't!"

Pablo searched his memory. "I think they come to Earth under the guise of being Supermodels and basically save the planet."

De La Renta spewed his champagne across Pablo's spotless kitchen.

Thank God they weren't sitting on the sofa. Pablo stood up to wipe the floor. "Now that I think about it, it does sound a lot like that bestseller *Star Planet*."

"*Ohmigod.* She had that book next to her while she was typing!"

"Well, I guess plagiarism isn't an issue when you're a Supermodel."

"Or a Super Alien." They roared with laughter again and gave each other a high five.

\*      \*      \*

Season Three started with an eight major city tour, including London, Sydney, Tokyo and Paris. Each of the judges had taken on an international city, but everyone showed up in Miami, LA, NYC and Chicago. As Keisha had predicted, her show had truly blown up. If Pablo had worried about his mortgage, his latest residual check from sales to countries all over the world eased his anxiety. At least, in terms of money. He had other things to worry about, though. For one thing, Keisha's burgeoning writing career. De La Renta had been 'write' (Pablo was thinking in puns). Keisha had been absent during the international model selection—showing up for the cameras and press and then skiving off to her hotel room, where she was evidently "working" on her book. Back in America, she spent most of the first episode's filming in her dressing room, while the twenty-five semi-finalists sat in their cramped closet sweating and forbidden to speak to each other.

"Anyone have a twenty on Keisha?" had become the season's refrain. More than once, Pablo thought to himself, *Isn't this where I came in?*

At least she wasn't hiding behind a catering cart. She was always in her dressing room. Typing. De La Renta had been right about her technique. This was not the elegant Mavis Beacon—all five fingers on the QWERTY keyboard, never look down at your hands—method. This was the two-finger hustle, clippity-clop. Stooped over the keyboard of her portable MacBook Air, she pounded the poor little keys with the emphatic beat of a rock-n-roll drummer. She typed while De La Renta did her hair. Typed while he did her makeup, except the eyes. Typed while they changed camera positions. Typed when they called for places on the set.

"I'm busy," she'd yell at the PAs who'd come to gather her. Pablo had seen them pulling straws to avoid having to bring her to the set, which was bound to bring a verbal lashing and possible job loss.

"Do Not Disturb. Artist At Work" was always hung under the star on her dressing room door. It was hard to follow those instructions when you were on a shooting schedule and the entire cast and crew were waiting for the host to make an appearance.

Strolling down the upstairs hallway of Silvercup Studios, Pablo watched a young production assistant dodging TV equipment like a soldier going into battle; his life probably did depend on it. The anxious-looking kid was safeguarding a USB thumb drive close to his chest. Pablo held open the big metal door leading to the control room and without even a *thank you*, the kid shoved past the creative director to Rachel Simpleton. Like Pablo, Rachel had looked refreshed and happy when she came back to work. Now she was slumped over her computer, coffee cup in hand and a bottle of Xanax lying in front of her. If anyone needed a makeover, it was Rachel. She'd aged beyond her years in just two weeks of filming season three.

"Already on the Benzos?" Pablo asked lightheartedly.

Rachel didn't even register. She was hopelessly muttering into her IFB.

"What do you mean she's not in the building!?" she screamed, slamming her fist on the table.

The production assistant slipped his cargo onto her desk and backed away. Rachel snatched it up and popped the USB drive into another computer, downloaded the file and opened it up on the main screen in front of her, and hit the space bar for Play.

An animated flash of light sounded off with a faux hip-hop theme song. Then, Keisha's nasal television voice joined in, sing-song like, over a montage of model contestants and seductive footage of Keisha, herself posing in a heavily jeweled corset creation by designers, The Blonds.

"I wanna show everyone what I learned in becoming a fashion boss. I'm gonna make a *new* breed of Supermodel. And I'm gonna take someone from utter obscurity to fame. I'm Keisha Kash, and this is *Model Muse*."

Pablo had not seen the new edited show open before. It was *somewhat* better than the main titles they'd used for the first two seasons–but still not nearly as chic as he would've wanted. That wasn't his department though and he didn't need any more work. Halfway through the final montage of model contestants, Rachel froze the screen on an unflattering close-up of Keisha. She had the eyes of a hawk. She grabbed the studio phone and dialed an extension.

"Brad? You missed the circles under Keisha's eyes in the ECU! People expect her to look like the model superstar–she *is* the face of Veronika's Privates for fucks sake." Rachel listened for a brief moment. "I don't care if her eyes were puffy on the day we shot. It's your job to fix them in post. Hurry up. I have bigger fires to put out right now."

She slammed the phone down so hard her clipboard fell off the table.

"Girl. What's wrong?" Pablo said with a soothing voice.

"Wrong? HR is on my case. Keisha's gone rogue. We're over budget. I'm on the verge of a nervous breakdown. Nothing's wrong. It's just a regular Monday around here." She sounded a little bit hysterical.

"I'm tired too."

"You don't know what the fuck tired is, Pablo."

"You know, Rachel, being a celebrity is exhausting," he shouted, with a little giggle.

She looked at him and burst out laughing. "I love you, Pablo." It was the kind of hilarity that overexertion and exhaustion creates. "And your BFF? She's driving me crazy."

"She's driving everyone crazy."

"It's like she isn't even here when she is here."

"She *isn't* here," Pablo stated the obvious. "She's on *Planet Fierce.*"

"Great, here comes *America's next top author.*"

Pablo had no idea Rachel could be so funny.

"It's a real problem, Pablo. We haven't wrapped a single shoot on time and the overtime is killing the budget, which means the bobbleheads upstairs are on Joe's case, which means he's on my case. We're up for renewal for God's sake."

"They're not really in charge."

"No one's in charge."

"Keisha is."

Rachel rolled her eyes. "You sure about that?"

"Oh, she's in charge of the show. She's just not in charge of herself."

"You have to talk to her. Broyce and I both agree that you're the magic bullet to take our monster down."

"That sounds dangerous."

"It is."

"You're sending me in to tame a hot ego run wild, without back up?"

"Try barbecue," she giggled. "We're talking job security, Pablo. If the network decides she's too unreliable, they'll find another model who isn't and re-launch a copycat without either of you."

He felt ill. He didn't even hashtag the air when he said, "I'm on it."

Sitting in the VIP back corner of her favorite eatery, the checkered tablecloth was already spattered with barbecue sauce, Keisha's lips were telltale orange. She didn't even pause to stop chewing as she told Pablo how happy she was he'd invited her to lunch.

"Being an author is so hard," she confided over a platter of ribs at Virgil's. "I had no idea. And De La Renta is such a pain in my ass. He insists on doing my hair while I'm creating."

Pablo didn't dare respond for fear of laughing. "Do you have a publisher, yet?"

"Andy's sure he can get one but says I'll be lucky to get more than a six-figure advance." She shook her head disgustedly. "If I'd known how hard it was to write a novel and how little they'd pay me, I never would've started."

"Well, your name alone will sell books."

"My name is not what this is about. You, of all people, should know that. I'm trying to inspire young girls. I'm trying to do something here that's important, Pablo."

"On another planet," he said softly.

"My aliens save earth."

"Do they recycle?" he smirked.

"Are you making fun of me?"

"Keisha, you used to have a sense of humor. You're so wrapped up in this book that you're stressing yourself out too much. Look at yourself. You're starting to look like an author."

"I can't stop the muse, Mr. Pablo. She won't just turn off like a faucet."

"Thank God for De La Renta is all I can say. Someone has to save that hair of yours."

"This is my number one priority."

"Shouldn't the show be our number one priority? We don't want to piss the executives off." He used the royal we.

"They don't want to piss me off."

"Well, that's the truth. But we're up for renewal. That means new contracts. They might try to take more control if you keep holding up the shoot."

Her eyes narrowed at him.

"Don't shoot the messenger, Keisha!"

She stopped chewing and spit out a piece of gristle. "They sent you?"

"They begged me to talk to you."

"I don't like that." Her nostrils flared. "Whose side are you on, anyway?"

"Yours! The show's."

She tore the flesh off a bone and sucked it hard. "Mr. Pablo, remember you're a nobody without me. You work for me. I made you."

He nodded obediently.

She shook the bone at him. "What happened to Judy and Mickey?"

"A TV network."

"Uh huh." She waggled the bone back and forth. "No one can come between us, Pablo, or it all goes to shit."

"It's a small ask from the execs. They just want you to come to the set when the camera is ready. That's all."

She pursed her lips and licked her fingers.

"And not fire every PA that comes to bring you to the set."
He felt like Alex Honnold free soloing up El Capitan, except
Pablo had vertigo. "How about we create a code? Instead of
yelling 'Camera's ready,' they tap softly on the door and wait.
Then tap again. Wait. And whisper, 'Miss Kash, are you ready
to come to the set now?'"

She nodded. Sighed. "Please."

Pablo nodded. "Please."

"That would be less disruptive."

"And I'll make sure Rachel knows to give you at least five
minutes."

"Ten."

"Five is a lot. There is a budget. We're overtime every night."

"The show can afford it."

"Not according to Broyce. Over budget is a red flag to
accounting and that influences renewal decisions."

She made a face. "It was so much easier back when I used
to be just a Supermodel on the catwalk."

"This is your dream, though. You have a brand. And now
you're gonna have a book. There's nothing you can't do."
Egos are like swans; you have to feed them carefully, or you
get bit.

"Tapping, whispering, please."

"You're the best." He touched her arm tenderly.

"I am."

Back on the set, Pablo gave Rachel the lowdown. She then
instructed the PAs on the *new* Keisha protocol and prepped
the camera crew. "Make sure you give me a ten-minute warning, so the PAs have plenty of time to tap," she deadpanned.
Pablo knew all this was a bit risky as their star hated arriving to set before the cameras were ready. Keisha, unlike the
other judges, did not like sitting around. Sasha loved sitting
in her director's chair chatting up the grips, nursing her water

bottle and being part of the chaos. Miss Thing, who took his cues from Keisha, kept running to his trailer where he could be alone and superior in his solitude. Mason, on the other hand, would generally go outside for a walk. Leave it to the Brits; they did love to walk—rain or shine.

The next few weeks smoothed out and even Keisha seemed happier. On the final day of shooting, Keisha arrived on set with a doorstop of a manuscript and plopped it down on the production desk in video village. "Done!" she exclaimed. Everyone dutifully applauded.

De La Renta whispered, "Thank God, that's over."

Rachel looked over at the tome. "*Ohmigod,* Keisha, how many pages it that?"

"One thousand. I have callouses on my fingers!"

"Quite an achievement," Broyce said, diplomatically. His eyes were on Pablo.

"It is." She turned toward the finalists, who were waiting to begin filming. "In a few moments, one of you will be named *Model Muse,* but I want both of you to know that whoever wins, you can both do anything you want because you've made it this far, and like me, you are *fierce.* You are unstoppable."

"Save it for camera," Rachel begged.

"Don't worry, I have that memorized. I wrote it."

Pablo thought it sounded a bit too much like one of Michelle Obama's graduation speeches.

They wrapped season three with the threat of unannounced renewal. Broyce was at the wrap party with the champagne but no news of renewal. Pablo worried at his silence.

"Anything I should know?" he asked quietly.

"They haven't decided on how many to renew for," Broyce assured him. "But I've been told to keep quiet. They want Keisha to be worried and feel threatened. She walked a thin line this season."

Relieved, Pablo sighed.

"I never thanked you for helping us get Keisha back and focused," Broyce said.

"You're welcome."

As Broyce walked away, Pablo realized that he still hadn't thanked him. That was show biz for you.

Keisha sauntered up to her BFF. "I have a prezy for you. A little housewarming gift." Behind her two of the PAs were carrying a huge six by three-foot package.

Pablo was unabashedly thrilled. "OMG, what did you do?"

"Open it," Keisha chortled.

He ripped through the length of the brown paper packaging. Sweeping letters in blue and red, gold rays like a sun (but really a curtain) radiated up underneath the words: THE BIG FUN AND MUSIC FILM SENSATION. And there was Judy Garland's colorized face pressed against Mickey Rooney's. It was a movie poster for *Babes in Arms*, 1942. He hated it. "WOW. I love it."

"I have the same one in my apartment."

He hugged his BFF. "You're so thoughtful."

"Don't ever think I don't know everything you've done to get my show off the ground and keep it going."

He almost believed her.

\*　　\*　　\*

Oh, how she *loved* an announcement. Any announcement, and there were many. The pre-launch for her book was the longest of any teen novel the literary world had ever seen. There was going to be a review in *The New York Times*— every writer's dream. *People* magazine—every publicist's dream—had promised to make it a starred read before they read it. After five-and-a-half months of promising the world that *Planet Fierce* was going to change their lives and rushing production of the mammoth book, it finally hit the shelves of Barnes & Noble. Any excuse to be the center of attention, and to appease the insatiable ego that yearned for constant approval from the world, was met in the pre-launch promotion of *Planet Fierce*. "JK who?" Keisha liked to tease. The only problem was, it was not flying off the shelves. Sales numbers didn't worry Keisha, thinking they'd pick up when she hit the airwaves. "I'm all about the interview." Sales didn't go up but she certainly knew how to strut her stuff. For all her desire to be more than a Supermodel, entrepreneur, business goddess, Keisha was no intellectual and that became painfully obvious to viewers. When she told the press that her book was going to change young women's lives, she believed that to be true.

When the big question was asked, "How?" her answer was, "You'll have to read the book to find out!"

"What Keisha Kash wants Keisha Kash gets," the oracle of *Model Muse*, De La Renta, repeated time and again. With the added media attention expected around the run-up to the book's release, the network had decided to renew and this time, the commitment was serious. *Model Muse* was locked in for another three seasons. Thanks to Pablo, Rachel, and the rest of the crew's hard work, they were secured till season six. God help them. But the world didn't always subscribe to Keishavision.

FICTION

# The Catwalk Launches, but Fizzles Out in Space:

## A Galactic Supernova For Black Women Implodes Into A Black Hole

**By Dr. Baraka C. Karenga**

**PLANET FIERCE**                    August 14, 2020
By Keisha Kash

One critique of science fiction is its faithfulness to white supremacy. White males are the swashbuckling heroes who conquer unknown galaxies and species with the occasional interruption of sexual relief from white female shipmates or nubile aliens. Readers are so accustomed to this de rigueur narrative because it mirrors the colonization we have come to accept on this planet; the erasure of people of color and women is yet another dystopian iteration of the racism that has triumphed for the past several hundred years on planet Earth. So few

know the work of the preeminent Afro-Futurist author and MacArthur recipient Octavia Butler, that there seems to be no literary imagination in the vastness of space (unless you're Gene Rodenberry, who through Nichelle Nichols as Lieutenant Uhura gave us the first Black woman to explore the cosmos). Indeed, our hunger for a diverse sci-fi future compelled us to dance in the aisles of theatres across the globe, greeting each other with salutations from a nonexistent country. "Wakanda, forever!" we shouted.

"Planet Fierce," a sci-fi adventure about alien models with superpowers who save Earth, aims to meet this literary and cultural gap in a market starving for representative fiction. As the self-proclaimed spokeswoman of fierceness, Ms. Keisha Kash has stomped her stilettoed feminism into the hearts of young women of color who have voraciously consumed pages of the Veronika's Privates catalog for a satiety of racial equity. Her presence satisfied the hunger to see women of color as "fierce" in a world where

beauty is not even worthy of a future in Andromeda–where Ms. Kash's novel is mostly set. Despite the solipsistic nature of her feminism (remember the "Smile With Your Soul" campaign?), we believed that Ms. Kash's enthusiasm was sufficient enough to translate a complex, powerful set of theories. In common parlance, her "wokeness" was real because the one soundbite from Black political theorist Julia Jordan-Zachery that boomed from her televised catwalk felt like authenticity. If models could strut to Jordan-Zachery's exhortation to challenge the oppressive nature of intersectionality, surely "Planet Fierce" would be that culmination. Ms. Kash would unleash a sci-fi manifesto of our beautiful future. The glamour of the runway would resurrect women of color from a futuristic dystopia.

Instead, Ms. Kash's space odyssey has managed to epically crash and face plant across 830 some odd pages.

Unlike her fashion spreads that are brief and tasteful, this tome is replete with literary clichés. The reader is subjected to a visual blitzkrieg of repetitive scenes where we are to be amazed at the Amazonian beauties who have weapons that, "fiercely kill, fiercely maim, fiercely decimate, fiercely torture, fiercely conquer" (Did I say fierce?). As someone who regularly works with words, I was rendered apoplectic at the basic disregard for variation in language structure and the simple need for a thesaurus. But I fiercely digress…

It is not the silliness of the premise of her novel, nor the turpitude of out-right plagiarism and story structure theft (why do the weapons seem reminiscent of Suzanne Collins' "Hunger Games" and the narrative a blatant rip-off of "Star Planet"?)–these are minor infractions. Most egregiously, the woman who proclaims herself as the savior for women of color has managed to commit every sexist trope and patriarchal sin. I would rather readers subject themselves to endless reruns of "Buck Rogers." At least with Rogers we know that he is Mr. White Boy Wonder and expect his racism. But the same thoughts through the pen of a Black woman feel outright psychotic. Read "Planet Fierce" and mire your mind in a weaponized goo of self-hate.

Clearly, Ms. Kash is using her reality TV show, "Model Muse," as a personal platform to hawk outrageously dimwitted projects. While I, personally, do not watch reality TV—generally, I prefer to read books, or I did. As part of my research for this review, I perused last week's premiere episode of Season Four–conveniently airing the day of the "Planet Fierce" book launch. The aspiring model contestants were used as part of a faux "Planet Fierce" movie trailer. Did someone from production actually read this behemoth? If Ms. Kash is anticipating a movie deal by showing what her novel would look like as a feature film, she'd better think again.

Perhaps in order to continue the myth of fierceness for her public, Ms. Kash, who is clearly suffering an existential crisis, must have pain from the revulsion of propagating a lie; the illusion of inclusive glamour that only celebrates white aesthetic is a profound contradiction. This psychological trauma is the wardrobe of her writing which ironically–though cloaked in the dazzle of spaceships, raunchy sexual tropes and exceptional weaponry–reveals a fierce self-loathing. If there is to be any redeeming quality of Ms. Kash's hulking wreck of a literary debut, it is that her existential crisis serves as a wonderful psychological case study for explaining theories of internalized racism. Perhaps this is the greatest literary contribution "Planet Fierce" could make.

PLANET FIERCE
By Keisha Kash
836 pp. Skinning & Grinning. $26.95.

# One Year Later

· · · · · · · · · · · · · · · · · · ·

## SEASON SIX

# REALITY CHECK

## 7 DAYS TILL WRAP, SEASON SIX

THE "LAST MODELS STANDING" arrived at Silver-cup and walked demurely past where Pablo was sitting nursing his morning coffee. Slumped in his director's chair, he watched the handful of run-down contestants—the four that were left—drag themselves backstage to what Pablo thought of as "the cupboard." He wasn't too far off. The cubbyhole where the girls had to wait was small, airless, had no windows, and barely had any furniture. How the girls managed to sit there and not lose their minds was a mystery to him, especially when so many other minds were going AWOL on the show. Still, when the time came, the model contestants smiled like circus animals, prancing their way down the runway for judging, in hopes of grabbing the brass ring and becoming a finalist for season six. It was hard to believe that just weeks before, these wide-eyed hopefuls had arrived brimfull of excitement and ambition, only to have their aspirations destroyed by what *Model Muse* had become—a show that humiliated them to entertain the masses. By the time they'd realize this truth—if they did—it was too late. They'd signed on the dotted line and had become slaves to production and a network whose legal team was tougher than the US Supreme Court Justices.

God, he sounded cynical. It was a good thing his brain didn't have a mic because it would be saying, "This is your brain."—Pablo remembered the anti-drug commercial breaking an egg onto a hot griddle—"This is your brain on *reality TV*. Fried."

Maybe he was overreacting. For all he knew, the girls were happy. Maybe they didn't feel misused and abused, but he didn't dare ask. Maybe they were living their dream and would dine out on their celebrity for the rest of their lives when they went back home to Podunk, wherever. Maybe he had it all wrong and didn't know shit. Maybe he was just overwhelmed by exhaustion. Maybe he was depressed.

Making TV was like waging war. A fierce and exhausting campaign. A constant uphill battle against the relentless enemies of deadlines, stingy budgets and colossal egos. Making a *successful* TV show required a lot more than talent; it required herculean stamina and dedication, despite the collateral damage. Keisha went through stylists and assistants as quickly as she ate a platter of pork ribs. She left behind a spectacular body count. Only De La Renta and Pablo seemed impervious, and sometimes he wished he wasn't. By season six, the show's jack-of-all-trades, Pablo did more off-camera than on and seemed to be running just about everything behind the scenes. Why? Because Keisha trusted him and no one else.

"Mr. Pablo, can you UPS the box of autographed *Model Muse* swag I have sitting in my dressing suite? Send it to Mama. No one else can know. Use your home address and my fake name on the shipping label."

"Pablo, I've just had *such* a hard day of taping. I'm gonna take some quiet time and chill in my dressing room. Meet with Joe for me to run down details for tomorrow?"

"Pablo, ugh, can you come over to my place? Horrible date at Soho House. No chemistry. The dude just talked about himself the entire time, with horrible breath. Need to vent with ice cream and back rub, ASAP."

"Pablo…"

Pablo felt compelled to do whatever she asked in exchange for all she'd done for him. They worked in an industry that normally forged friendships of convenience and proximity, not real friendship. Pablo was lucky to have found so much more with Keisha. She'd gotten him on TV, after all. Four years later, he was now a household name. She'd handed him the career and the life he now had. Even his mother understood what he was doing for a living, and that was really saying something.

Had it really been four years since he'd met Keisha at the Michael Kors show and they'd shared their first pint of ice cream? Unfathomable. How many gallons had passed between them since then? She hid it well. The thing about being five foot eleven is that she really could sock it away. Almost. Over-indulgence, however, was now starting to catch up behind her.

It was one thing for Keisha to run him ragged. She deserved his loyalty. But Joe Vong and the rest of the senior producers were now equally demanding. "Pablo, book that venue. Pablo, get that designer. Pablo, retouch these images. Edit this music video. Get a stylist for wardrobe…"

"I don't know what's wrong with me," he'd confided in De La Renta.

"Oh, I do. You're just fucking overused and abused—like the toilets in Port Authority. Join da club."

Like always, De La Renta preached the truth. Pablo was emotionally drained and was suffering the deep exhaustion of the exploited and disenfranchised. They were now nearing completion of their sixth season, with hiatus just a week away. Their ratings were higher than anyone had predicted, and there was talk of a three-year contract renewal. Churning out two seasons of *Model Muse* a year was brutal. Pablo wasn't sure he could survive another three years. The rose-colored glasses—or in his case the silver-grey contact lenses—had been peeled away and unveiled a rough reality. What started as a creative step to career salvation had turned into a dizzying psychological pattern of bewildering emotional, personal, and spiritual challenges. Everything in Pablo's life was dangling on gossamer thread: his devotion to Keisha, the show, and his values.

Overworked or not, Keisha relied on Pablo to save the day. Failure was not an option. And while he might not always have the most ethical approach to problem-solving, he was the show's fixer, as well as Keisha's.

Was it worth it? Sometimes he wasn't sure. He was also beginning to doubt whether Keisha actually cared about him, or if she was simply using him the same way she used everybody. Worse, he now doubted himself—who was he without his connection to Keisha? Was he really a fraud, incapable of achieving the heights of the fashion industry on his own? Was he using her? He was close to spiraling into a morass of serious self-doubt. His loyalty to Keisha had become so twisted and strange, that it left him wondering if it would soon vanish like last summer's fashions.

The associate producer who typically babysat the models when they were off-camera wandered off to the craft service table. Contestants were not supposed to speak unless the cameras were rolling and they were mic'd up with sound. If they dared to speak to each other, someone would hiss, *"On ice."* Off-camera conversations were contractually forbidden and a sure way to be dismissed immediately.

The last four survivors of one harrowing fashion trial by fire after another were backstage, huddled together like best friends in 'the cupboard.' Over the weeks, they'd forged a bond, but Pablo knew firsthand they didn't feel anything like gladiators in the fierce fashion competition. A stray audio headset that someone had left on his chair still had some battery power and Pablo could hear the girls whispering to each other. It was a rare moment to slip into their world, a world that he had no part in, except when he was one of their on-camera mentors and sometimes one of their comforters.

They had a lot to talk about. Keisha had sprung a surprise "branding" makeover on the girls, who'd already undergone one makeover earlier in the season. The reason? Well, the real reason was that Keisha's ringer needed help to win. The competition was too *fierce*. The problem was the Irish girl, Nichole; her thick red hair reached down to her very slim waist and she was *slaying* almost every photoshoot. The solution? Keisha ordered Nichole's head shaved. It had been a moment of open-mouthed horror for all of the girls. Nichole looked hard at the Supermodel host and then acquiesced. "Under one condition."

"Condition? You comply or you leave." Keisha pointed to the exit.

"That my hair be donated to Locks of Love."

"What's that?" Keisha's eyes were hard and mean, despite the girl's willingness to be shorn.

"It's a non-profit," Pablo answered. "They make wigs for children who have lost their hair due to medical procedures, like chemo."

"That's so…" Keisha didn't seem to know what to say.

"Generous," Pablo chimed in. "We can certainly do that," he assured the young model.

"Thank you." Nichole bit her lips and nodded bravely. Her hair was bound in three sections before it was cut close to the nape of the neck. Then it was cut shorter. Then it was shaved. The cameras stayed on Nichole's face. She didn't drop a single tear. Keisha was furious.

Kayla's makeover had also been radical. Like many young aspiring model wannabes, Kayla—an alluring Greek girl with doe-like brown eyes—idealized the Supermodel host. "I just wanna be like Keisha one day," she had said during casting. Kayla had applied every season for five seasons in a row until she had finally made the semi-finals. She was also pushing the ringer off her rigged throne. Unfortunately for Keisha, Kayla had come out of her makeover looking hotter than ever and even more confident than usual.

Elyssa was an illustrated girl, tattooed with cursive ink that made her a colorful canvas the photographers loved. She was the quirky girl, but highly intelligent. Pablo liked her a lot, and Keisha loved her story—the smart girl who'd had it all and then lost it all and ended up living on the streets. Elyssa's makeover utilized the art on her body to create a hairstyle that was equally interesting and set off some of her neck tats. But make no mistake, Keisha had predestined Elyssa to be eliminated during the last episode for some manufactured reason that the production team had yet to discover or fabricate. Pablo felt a little sick about it, but Keisha had a research team working on drumming up some reveal for the last show that would embarrass Elyssa and cause her demise.

"The Ringer" was Beth, the first plus-sized winner *Model Muse* would ever announce. She loved raiding the craft service table and hoarded bags of Cheetos in her room, which explained why her right index finger and thumb were permanently stained orange. If the other contestants had known that "Miss Flaming Cheetos" had already been hand-selected by Keisha, herself, they all would've lost their little minds. Beth's makeover had been specially designed to help her win. The problem was that Kayla's makeover turned out better than Beth's. At least Nichole's botch job gave Keisha an easy way to exit the model from the show without anyone guessing the fix.

"She did it on purpose," Pablo overheard Nichole whispering to the others. "I feel like she scalped me before chopping my head off. I'll be cut tonight, for sure."

"I just don't understand why she did it. It *was* your best asset," Beth said. "I wish I had red hair like you have."

"Had."

"At least you didn't freak out," Kayla said. "You were so brave."

"Stoic," Elyssa added.

"She just wanted me to freak out, so they could film me having a meltdown. It's all about ratings. I wish I'd never done this stupid show."

"Nichole, you are beyond beautiful—inside and out." Elyssa jumped in. "Even if you don't win, people will be following you. You'll get a contract."

"I don't even know if I wanna model anymore." Nichole sounded like she was crying now. "If it means you have to be a bitch in this biz, what's the point?"

"Keisha *always* picks some odd-looking girl to be the winner," Elyssa added. "It makes sense she shaved your head bald. She's just trying to ugly you up, for the win!"

"Fucking bitch!"

"Look at you. Your skin is flawless, your face is perfectly symmetrical. You photograph better than any of us." Elyssa was being so supportive.

They all chimed in to support and encourage her. It really was sweet. Pablo wondered if lambs going to slaughter felt the same way about each other?

"You're the obvious *Model Muse*."

"Elyssa's right, you're probably gonna win," Beth told Nichole, then looked pointedly over at Kayla, their resident slut. "And if you don't, at least you didn't fuck your way to the crown."

"I just sucked him off. We never had sex."

"Who are we talking about?" Elyssa asked.

"The hot DP."

"Fine. She's as innocent as Monica Lewinsky then."

Listening to the girls, Pablo had walked over to the control room to let Rachel know the girls were chatting alone. As he walked in, he noticed the entire production crew were eavesdropping on the girls' conversation too. En masse, they turned to glare at Bill, accusingly.

"Why does everyone *always* think it's me?" Bill bellowed, defensively.

"Because it's *always* you." Rachel was fuming. "Damnit Bill, why can't you keep your dick in your pants? You're a hashtag Me Too nightmare."

The crew looked at their Mr. Fix-It. The last thing *Model Muse* needed was a scandal that could shut down production.

"Bill, we could get shut down because of this, and you know it," Pablo blurted. "And if Keisha finds out, you'll be out of a job."

"If *she* finds out," Rachel's voice raised an octave, "I should fire you now."

"We have to do everything we can to protect the show," Pablo said. "If you fire him, he could go to the press about how the show is fixed. Beth has to win."

"The show is fixed?" the newest producer hire, Harper Phibbs, screeched.

So much for innocence. "You didn't hear me say that," Pablo told her.

"Oh, for God's sake, grow up, Harper." Bill added.

Harper was one of those annoyingly chipper types who was always overly positive—she got on everyone's nerves. "It would be great to have a plus-sized champion, though." She now seemed all too easily relieved of her ethics, though she feigned a stricken face. Harper was the Pollyanna producer who believed the show could bring a positive message about body image to young women. Pablo cringed at her high-pitched shriek. "She'll be an amazing role model for big girls, like me."

"Mr. Bill," Pablo turned to the offending DP and used Keisha's creepy voice trick, "yes, Kayla's probably the best model of the bunch, but you can't go promising girls a win in exchange for sexual favors."

Bill looked uncomfortable.

"Now, we're all gonna have to work double-time to dig up dirt to keep her quiet. She can't come back and bite us in the ass when we ax her," Pablo continued.

No one moved. No one said anything. "She just looks media hungry—we need something to keep her mouth shut."

The producers looked at him with nothing but blank faces. "So, get research on it," Pablo yelled at them. They jumped up and began scurrying around the room. Shit, he'd never yelled at the crew. "Sorry, guys." He really was losing it.

Everyone began talking at once about what they should do. Pablo's phone rang and vibrated. He looked down at the screen: the face of Faye Dunaway as Joan Crawford from *Mommy Dearest* glared up at him. He held up his hand for quiet.

"Hey, Keisha." He wondered what it would be this time—another pregnancy test? A dirty weekend playing her beard? Did she need a pedicure or pint of Dulce de Leche?

"Meet me at Virgil's."

"We're shooting in 90 minutes."

"Now." She hung up the phone.

Feeling castrated, Pablo turned to Rachel. "Hold down the fort, I've gotta go."

"She was supposed to be in hair and makeup 30 minutes ago," Rachel shouted after him as he bolted out the door.

# THE MADNESS UNFOLDS

I T WAS AN UNSEASONABLY warm March evening and Pablo let the windows down to smell the faintest tinge of spring in the air amid the exhaust fumes on the Queensborough Bridge. It hadn't taken long to get into Manhattan from Silvercup Studios, but getting back to Queens was going to be a nightmare—traffic out of the city after 4 p.m. was like getting caught in a whirlpool with no way out. Why couldn't Keisha have a refuge that was in Williamsburg instead of Times Square?

The dimly lit, mesquite smelling and smoke-filled restaurant was bustling with a pre-theatre crowd. Of course, Keisha never waited for a table; she practically had rent control on her regular table, she was there so much. The food was great, but Pablo had started to think the Supermodel ate there just to be seen sneaking incognito into her VIP back corner booth. She loved to hear the ripple effect of her passing. *Isn't that Keisha Kash? I think I just saw the star of Model Muse. Look, there's Pablo too.* Well, she almost liked the comments.

He entered the throne room of self-proclaimed Queen Keisha, who was holding court with three platters of pork ribs. Half-eaten sides of mac and cheese and collard greens littered the table like a crime scene.

"Here, eat something." She shoved a cold platter under his nose while gnawing on a rib.

"I'm fine." Pablo pushed the plate away as his iPhone binged at him from his lap. It was Miss Thing. Keisha was eating and explaining some drama in her life. Pablo knew the drill: listen, agree with her, express opinion (preferably outrage), offer support, and get her back to the set. He didn't need to hear what she was actually saying to know how to respond. He looked down at the text.

**Miss Thing TEXT:** Where the fuck is she? We're stranded on set!

Pablo discretely snapped a photo of Keisha sucking on a rib bone and texted the image back with a few words.

**Pablo TEXT:** Crisis in Keishaland.

He immediately regretted it, but text regret was a common millennial phenomenon. What had possessed him—his therapist would ask—to send that pic of Keisha chowing comfort food to her biggest frenemy on the show? He would say he didn't know. He did, though. He did it because he could and he was too tired to care about not doing it.

Miss Thing binged back.

**<u>Miss Thing TEXT:</u>** Tell her to come suck on this meat!

Attached was a dick pic. Miss Thing's. What little appetite Pablo might have had was now gone for good.

"I'm completely freaked out," Keisha was saying. Pablo had missed most of her monologue, but since she generally repeated herself, he didn't worry. He'd catch up on the next cycle. Then she reached into her purse and pulled out a luxurious red Cartier box. Her hand trembled as she placed it in front of Pablo.

"Did T-Rex propose?" This was one plot twist he hadn't foreseen.

"Just open it." She was not in a joking mood.

He dropped the jewelry box on the table. "Is that blood?"

It was indeed. Between them, a vial of blood lay in Cartier's velvety cushions, capped with a purple stopper. Pablo looked at Keisha in disbelief.

"It gets worse."

She had his full attention now and just as his phone binged at him. He placed it on Airplane mode—there were some situations that nothing should interrupt and this was one of them. He took the scrap of folded paper that was grasped in her hand.

"What are you gonna do with it?" She sounded frightened.

He unfolded the note. "Read it."

She watched every move on his face. Squeezed his hand when he reached and took hers. Closed her eyes as he sighed.

"What's a Kimoru?" Pablo asked.

"I dunno."

"Hmmmm…"

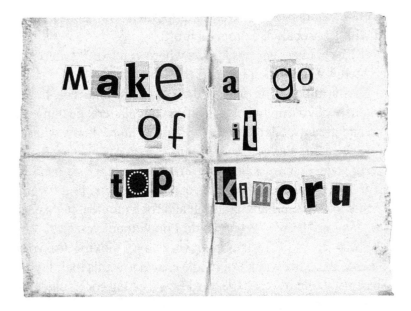

"Please, Pablo, I'm scared." He could see the fear in her huge eyes the way she scanned the immediate vicinity, as if looking for the first sign of danger.

"Do you think you have a stalker?" he finally asked.

She grabbed his wrist and dug her nails into his flesh. "That's why you're here? I have no clue!"

"I'm gonna hang onto this." He folded the note up and put it inside his jacket pocket. "Put the box in your purse. And don't let anyone else see it." Pablo's mind was whirling. "I think we should go to the police."

"No," she blurted.

"Do you know who sent it at least?"

"No."

"How'd you get it? I mean, this is some freaky shit, Keisha!"

"It was left with the overnight doorman. Some messenger kid with a baseball cap dropped it off."

"So, whoever sent this knows where you live?" Pablo was horrified. "What in hell is going on?"

Keisha nibbled on one of the cold ribs, and then began nervously devouring what was left on the platters, pushing the cold and greasy collards towards Pablo. "I *don't* know what to do. I'm scared, Pablo. *Really* scared."

He nodded and reached forward again, putting his hand on top of hers. "I'm gonna figure this out. No one's gonna hurt you."

She looked eternally grateful, and for a moment it was just them, again—BFFs. "What would I do without you?"

From across the restaurant, a very angry looking Joe Vong power-walked his way through the crowd towards their booth. Clearly, not one of those die-hard fans looking for a selfie, the bouncer let him pass.

"I've been to six places looking for you guys," he yelled at Pablo. "When the EP of the hottest show on TV calls, you pick up your fucking phone."

"I had my phone on do not distur—"

"Back off, Joe," Keisha snapped back. "I have an emergency situation and I needed Pablo to help me."

Joe leaned towards Keisha. "I don't care if your apartment is on fire. You're supposed to be in the studio, on set. Filming. Now."

"How dare you speak to me like I'm some flunky? I'm your boss. And I own you."

"Do you really think I'm the only one who wants to know why you aren't on set?" he hissed at her. "The network brass sent me."

Pablo flipped his phone off airplane mode. Six messages from Vong binged at him. Joe Vong glared over at him. "Oh, *now* you're receiving messages?"

Keisha slurped one last sip of her vanilla milkshake as Joe waved to the waiter to bring the check. Her signature was an aggressive slash that nearly tore the receipt. She stood up and looked at the two men. "Well, come on. We gotta go." She turned and left them hurrying to catch up.

The traffic back to Long Island City was more like a parking lot. Joe sat up front in the Escalade. Keisha wouldn't sit with him in the back, ever. When Pablo's phone binged, twice, she complained that the high-pitched bell gave her a headache. It was going to be one of those nights. Pablo quickly flipped his device to vibrate, but it wasn't Miss Thing texting now, it was Rachel.

**Rachel TEXT:** 911…damage control STAT!
Judges going to walk!

Pablo didn't bother with a response. What could he do stuck in traffic? Miss Thing would blow a head gasket at the smallest inconvenience. He'd once lost his cool when the DP called for a *"battery change"* in the middle of one of his runway lessons. The problem with being a Mr. Fix-It was that Pablo couldn't help feeling that he was somehow responsible after texting that photo of Keisha. For once, the Supermodel's tardiness was justified, but it was a pattern. The more successful the show became, the later she got. They were two and a half hours behind schedule and she *still* had to go through hair and makeup—which was easily a two-hour process on its own. If he was one of the judges, he'd go ballistic.

The evening clouds hung heavily over the enormous red Silvercup Studios sign, etched across the New York City skyline. There was a PA waiting for them on the sidewalk ready to usher Keisha to her dressing suite, while Pablo and Joe hurried to the main soundstage. In his head, Pablo went over the order of fires he was going to have to put out because Joe was better at pouring gasoline onto problems than dousing them with water. First up, was Miss Thing. He had to make sure the photo he texted of Keisha at Virgil's didn't fall into the wrong hands, or worse, end up on social media.

Rachel looked up at Pablo as he stepped into the control room. A wide shot of the judging room was on screen. Three of the *Model Muse* resident judges and guest judge, Christian Siriano—the youngest designer to win *Project Runway*—were sitting uncomfortably under the blaring lights, using small battery-operated fans to keep themselves from sweating.

"Thank God, you're back." Rachel looked relieved. "The fucking A/C is down."

"That, I cannot help you with. What else can I do?"

"Hold on a sec," Rachel barked over at three producers working at a long collapsible table. "Uh, excuse me, people. How about doing reaction shots, while we're waiting for her highness?"

"I've already taken care of that," the perpetually perky Harper chirped. She had one of those cheerful *customer service* voices that made Pablo want to strangle her. "Seeing as we always take so much time at the end of the night shooting reaction shots, I took it upon myself to shoot them now. Especially since Sasha is sober-*ish*, or was. She hasn't had her evening bottle of Chardonnay with Adderall chaser yet."

Harper was a fashion train wreck who wore saggy jeans that fell halfway down her butt, ugly sneakers and a nylon fanny pack that solidified her spot as the least fashionable person on the crew, after Joe Vong. But no one cared how she dressed because she was the kind of person who never seemed to have a bad day and never said anything nasty about anyone, which said a lot in their business. Getting a warm hug from her on a bad day was enough to change any-one's mood; she gave good back rubs too. In a boot camp of drudgery, she infused such positive energy Pablo appreciated but often wondered what anti-depressant she was on. Or was it Lithium?

"I also told the judges Keisha was recording voiceovers," Harper said. "They seemed to buy it."

Rachel looked at Pablo. "That girl is going places."

Pablo had to agree. She may act like the Pollyanna of Pri-metime TV but she was inventive, efficient and a good liar. All excellent character traits for a producer.

"Well, De La Renta is gonna need some Febreze. When Miss Thing catches one whiff of smoked pork ribs coming off Keisha's wig, there'll be hell to pay," Pablo quipped. "I gotta ask him why good human hair wigs hold so much odor."

"Great. Why don't you go over to Keisha's dressing suite and ask him now?" Rachel mocked. "And while you're there, tell them to hurry the FUCK UP. I need her like, yesterday."

"I was just trying to have a little fun, jeez. Take my head off why don't you."

Rachel pointed to a close-up of Miss Thing on a different monitor while she struggled to utter the appropriate politically correct term. "You can't sneak much past her. I mean him, them, *whatever!* Just get me Keisha, please. Miss Thing is gonna start throwing a tantrum, if we don't do something fast."

Sure enough, down in the judging room, while the studio buzzed with crew members setting up lights, taping marks on the floor and producers frantically running around trying to look busy, Miss Thing was perched in his chair, looking not just annoyed but like trouble in the making.

Mike, the goofy looking sound engineer, all legs and arms and very little torso, walked up to Miss Thing with his sound rig, holding a wireless microphone pack.

"If we're just shooting *God damn* reaction shots, with no audio, why do I need a mic, Mike?" Miss Thing screamed at the top of his lungs.

Completely unphased by the outburst, Mike smiled. "Ah, come on, Miss Thing. After six seasons, you know the rules. Plus, I'm the only person you actually like on this set."

"It's true. I love to be mic'd by Mike. But it's just because you gotta juicy ass and your girlfriend doesn't mind me flirting with you."

Mason coughed and cleared his throat. "Do all the boys you like have girlfriends?" Winding up Miss Thing was one of Mason Hughes' favorite past times.

"Lemme make one thing very clear. I don't like boys." Miss Thing stopped him mid statement. "I like men. Your arrogant ass might wanna examine why your '*wife*'–who does way too much yoga, I might add–looks like a prepubescent teenage boy, herself."

Mason's face flushed red. "Your rude and insinuating comments about my wife are—"

"Is there something you're not telling us about Sukhdeep?" the model coach interrupted, glaring at the Brit. "She don't *pass* to a trained eye like mine, ya know. And P.S. she might wanna stay outta harsh daylight. Hashtag just saying."

"What are you implying?" Mason sputtered.

"Zip it, King Arthur." Miss Thing flipped his hand up in Mason's face and dismissed him. "Queer fear is so last century."

Chin in her hand, her elbow on the table, her words slurred together, Sasha leaned over toward Mason. "I heard you saved your wife from a sex trafficking ring in India."

Simultaneously, Mason stood up as Miss Thing pushed back his chair.

"Annnnnd they're off," Sasha mocked.

"Tell Rachel, I'll be in my trailer." Mason stormed off the set like he had a cricket bat and two balls stuck up his arse.

"Tell Rachel, I'll be in my trailer too." Miss Thing grabbed his makeup purse, a miniature reproduction of a doctor's bag. It was a race between Mason and Miss Thing to see who could leave the set first and most dramatically.

Sasha's head spun around to watch them flounce away, then passed out with a loud thud, her head on the table.

# MR. FIX-IT

LEAVING THE COMPARATIVELY calm sanctuary of the control room, Pablo walked down the three flights of stairs and onto the soundstage dedicated for elimination scenes. Rolling his eyes, he entered the hot and oddly humid space, annoyed. The judging set had been redesigned for the start of the new season, and Pablo couldn't get used to how similar it was to his apartment. Keisha had loved his new pad, called it *"super modern fierce."* Did she really need to steal *every* idea he had? Of course, this was a woman who plagiarized an entire book. Why was he even surprised anymore?

Pablo zeroed in on crew members—including Rachel, who'd taken the elevator ahead of him—gathering around Sasha passed out on the judging table. Joe Vong, of course, was screaming and making his way through the crowd.

"Wake her the fuck up. And where the *hell* is Miss Thing and Hughes Junior?"

Rachel pulled Joe aside trying to diffuse the situation. "She's beyond coffee, and Miss Thing has locked himself in his trailer." She sounded relieved now. "At least Mason's walking back to set with a PA."

"How could you let this happen?" he hissed.

As if on cue, celebrity guest judge Christian Siriano interrupted the two by tapping Joe on the shoulder. "I know I'm just here doing a cameo, but this is running really late. And I have to fit Christina Hendricks in an hour."

Joe Vong's face lit up at the thought of the buxom redhead. "I wouldn't mind holding that measuring tape. You need my help?"

Siriano looked disgusted. "I'm leaving. It's been, well, interesting."

"Are you fucking kidding me?" Joe went apoplectic. "You can't just leave."

Christian didn't respond and proceeded to walk out. Pablo raced after him. "Christian, I'm so sorry."

The designer looked Pablo up and down. "And I thought fashion shows were crazy. This is totally insane. I don't know how you do it."

"Neither do I, sometimes. If there's anything I can do to make it up to you, just call me. Maybe Sunday brunch?" Christian shrugged and shook his head. That was a 'no'. Another fashion star bit the dust. Pablo watched the studio door slowly shut in his face. If this continued, he was going to lose his reputation with the designers the show dissed. He would never be taken seriously by Christian Siriano, again. And if word got around that the set was a cluster fuck of incompetence and Keisha delays, no one would agree to come on the show as a celebrity guest judge, ever.

Joe Vong didn't even care. He acted like everyone was replaceable. "Get me another guest judge now," he yelled at Pablo.

"Get your own," Pablo yelled back at him. "I'm not putting my contacts and reputation in jeopardy of your temper."

Across the studio floor a gaggle of producers were trying to revive Sasha.

"I'll get a judge," Harper responded with cheery excitement. "Who are you thinking of?" When there was no reply, she opened her mouth to repeat the question.

"Some Fashion Fuck! I DON'T CARE," Joe exploded.

Sprinting over to the producer's table, Harper scrolled down a list on the computer screen and then dialed a number. "Hi. This is Harper Phibbs, segment producer on *Model Muse*. I was wondering if Anna Wintour was free this evening to come and...Hello? Hello?" she looked dumfounded. "Well, that was rude!"

Pablo shook his head in disbelief. Did she really think she could simply call up and get the editor-in-chief of *Vogue* magazine to pop round for a quick cameo? Wintour was like the Fort Knox of fashion—no one got through her security wall of personal assistants. Clearly, Harper hadn't seen or read *The Devil Wears Prada*.

Pablo pushed the studio door open and made his way out to the parking lot, where the talent trailers were hooked up, in hopes of manipulating Miss Thing back to set. Pablo's first order of business was to delete the incriminating text and photo he'd sent from Virgil's—before it came back to haunt him. Stroking egos was not part of his job description, but then, most of what he did on the show wasn't. When he wasn't caressing Keisha's ego, he was soothing Miss Thing's. The best way to keep Miss Thing complaisant was to listen to all of the model coach's tall tales and never confront the gossip he spread like manure, in hopes of creating a stink. As long as the runway diva felt he was operating in stealth mode, he was happy as a pig in shit. Well, almost.

Outside the catering truck, "Switzerland"—as the crew now lovingly referred to De La Renta—was carrying a blue slushie and a bag of pretzels. The hair/makeup guru made an effort to stay out of any and all drama on the set because, as he often said, "I got one lane, and I stay in it. No one is fucking with my check."

Clearly, his grandmamma's teaching.

"Heading into Mother?" Pablo asked De La Renta.

"What da fuck Pablo? You had to take her to Virgil's before shooting today? Her piece smells like you two were rolling around in a platter of pork ribs."

"You think I dragged her to Virgil's? I was here two hours early when she ordered me back into the city."

De La Renta rolled his eyes. "I shudda known. I tell you, I'm so sick and tired of being *sick and tired*. Making her a new wig every other week is not what I signed up for. It's like she eats them."

"Put some barbecue sauce on that wig and I'd agree with you."

"And now she's insisting I stitch up some new locks she just *threw* at me the other day—by tomorrow. She's tired of wheat/blonde and wants to go red. Tell me, Pablo, do I look like a wig machine? Do I?"

Pablo knew the routine all too well, but they had to be careful speaking about Keisha's *"lid"* in public. She professed to the world that she was *"proud of wearing a weave,"* but the truth was that she wore a full custom-made lace-front wig over thinning cornrows and a receding hairline.

"You don't deserve to be treated that way."

De La Renta took one long slurp of his slushie and crossed his eyes from the brain freeze. *"Egg-zackly.* And she's in there talking about how she's gonna launch her own makeup line. I told her you ain't no makeup artist. Girl can barely draw her own eyebrows on straight."

*What new branding strategy was she cooking up now?*

"Just watch your back," De La Renta hugged Pablo and whispered in his ear. "When Broyce Miller called to reprimand her for being so late to set, she said that *you* made her go to Virgil's, not the other way around. Don't be a fool. She'll throw you under the bus to save herself. It's always about her. Always has been. Always will be."

De La Renta's words hit him like a sucker punch. He felt nauseous. Broyce was the one person left he really wanted to respect him, and the one man who could help him with his own career goals. Had his servitude served him, at all, or left him vulnerable to whatever whim struck Keisha's fancy? The fact was, the entertainment industry lived in a perpetual state of adolescence. No one wanted to take responsibly for anything they said or did, unless it was a success. There were no consequences and as such, the industry bred these power-hungry monsters. Pablo was starting to learn Keisha Kash was no exception. Reality TV was spawning and unleashing these demon-like people, and like a virus they had jumped species, now populating Washington, Wall Street and the world over. Pablo had to move on. Giving his friend a tight squeeze back, as if to say *"thanks,"* he darted over to the talent trailers.

The Queens traffic hummed like annoying, never-ending tinnitus. Pablo peered in through the half-drawn curtain of Miss Thing's Double Banger trailer to see what the miserable model coach was up to. Perched in front of his makeup vanity, he grimaced at the stubble on his chin and his reflection in the mirror.

"There're only so many dick pics you can take," Pablo teased. He entered the trailer and sat himself on one of Miss Thing's vanity stools.

"I don't know how you stand it, Myrna," Miss Thing said to Pablo's reflection. It was the pet name he'd given Pablo, who affectionately hated it. "You clean up her messes like a maid, and when she says, *'jump'* you're the first to say, *'how high?'*"

"First of all—"

"Oh. Hold on. Lemme check my box of Altoids. I'm sure your tiny balls are rattling around in there somewhere."

"Well, with that breath, I'm surprised you even know where your Altoid mints are."

"Okay, bitch, two points for that clapback," Miss Thing roared. "So, is she here yet?"

"Yup. De La Renta's just finishing her up," Pablo lied.

"Then she can sit on set and wait for *me* for a change."

"You can't sit here all night and keep everyone on punishment."

"Da fuck I can't."

"Tyreeq Levern Jackson."

"Myrna, if *anyone* finds out my real name, I'm comin' for you." Miss Thing's eyes bulged out of their eye sockets. Pablo picked up the model coach's phone and snapped a photo of him.

"Look at yourself, fool."

The runway diva unlocked his device and scrolled through to the camera roll. "So what? I make stupid faces and post them on the gram, all the time."

"Can I see it, again?"

Miss Thing handed over his phone. With the iPhone now unlocked, the quick-thinking creative director flipped over to iMessage and deleted the unflattering image of Keisha that he'd sent earlier. He handed the device back to the dimwit. "Yeah, it's not that bad. So, can we count on you coming to set at some point tonight?"

"Lemme know when you raise Sasha from the dead and I'm there." Miss Thing reached into his makeup purse, pulled out a bottle of pills and rattled them in front of Pablo's face. The prescription label clearly read: Sasha Berenson, Adderall. "This is all that stands between shooting tonight and wrap. The only thing that will wake that drunk bitch up, after her dinner bottle of Chardonnay."

"Klepto."

"Annnnnnd what? I took it from *Bride of Chucky's* purse." He smiled wickedly at Pablo, rattling the container loosely in his hand.

Miss Thing stole the weirdest stuff. Pablo had once caught him sneaking around in Keisha's dressing suite pocketing mini bottles of Scope, travel toothpaste, toilet paper and Zip-lock bags of cold cuts. "Do you spend every waking second of your life trying to find ways to bring misery to the lives of others?"

"Only those who pose a threat to my own celebrity."

"Did it ever occur to you that sabotaging this show could thwart your own career?"

"Nothing can take an old bitch like me down." He was still playing with the prescription bottle.

Pablo did what any good creative director would do—he snatched it and dashed for the door. "You really wanna be here all night? Let's get this shit done. One of us needs beauty sleep tonight, and it isn't me. Grab your makeup purse and let's go."

"It's not a purse. It's an antique doctor's bag!"

"Whatever." Pablo shoved the bottle of Adderall in his pocket and headed out the door.

Vanquished, Miss Thing followed mumbling, "I guess you do have a big set of balls after all."

Halfway across the parking lot to the soundstage, Joe Vong yelled at Pablo, "I see you've solved *the thing* problem."

"Problem?" Miss Thing shrieked. "I'll give you problems

all night long. Problems you can't even reach with your little step ladder."

Joe ignored the hyped-up star and glared at Pablo. "I need you to get one of your overrated *fashion friends* here now to be our guest judge."

"I thought your genius producers were on it."

"You're the one who took her to Virgil's. You fucking fix it." He scuttled off looking like an angry elf in Nikes.

"Ouch. You just got Vonged," Miss Thing snickered.

Kashed and Vonged, Pablo thought. Then yelled, "I didn't take her to Virgil's, FYI."

"Little turd." Miss Thing screamed across the parking lot at Joe Vong's retreating back. "We're not overrated."

Dragging his feet now, Pablo headed back to the soundstage, Miss Thing in tow. Finding a major fashion celebrity to be a guest judge *and* have them show up to shoot within the hour was next to impossible. Pablo flipped through his iPhone and scrolled Instagram. One photo caught his eye. He slipped over to iMessage.

Seconds later, he punched the air like he'd just scored the winning goal in the World Cup Final. "Yaaaassss!" Pablo screamed. "Celeb guest judge flying in."

Miss Thing made a sucking sound with his lips.

"Now. Please, pretty please, go sit on set and powder your makeup down. You're starting to steal everybody's shine with that forehead and nose."

Miss Thing wagged his abnormally long finger in Pablo's face. "Oh, you gettin' *real* brave." He sashayed away with his famous runway sweep, stepping toward the soundstage. Pablo flagged a harried looking PA running from craft service with a cup of coffee.

"I need you to crush these up into a Diet Coke." Pablo shook the bottle of Adderall in the dazed kid's face. "And get

Sasha to drink the entire can. Then put the bottle back in her purse and zip it up. Do *NOT* let Miss Thing near it."

And that was that. Mr. Fix-It had done it again. He'd deleted the photo of Keisha sucking on a rib bone, freeing himself of the damning evidence. Miss Thing was back at the judging table. Sasha would be awake in twenty minutes. And Coco Rocha was on her way to fill in as the guest judge. Pablo stretched his back and took a deep, well deserved breath. What else could possibly go wrong?

# MELTDOWN

IT HAD BEEN a long day and it was about to get even longer. Officially in overtime, Joe Vong paced the back of the studio like a caged panther. At least there were five judges, including Pablo's surprise guest, Coco Rocha, seated in their assigned spots. Sasha was still passed out, face down. But she was there.

Bill yelled over at Joe. "Are we gonna shoot her like that?"

"Just fucking roll on a four shot. When she wakes up, we can get the full wide shot and hopefully some usable close-ups of what's left of her face."

"I got a few reaction shots of her, earlier," Harper chirped.

Joe grabbed a handful of Twizzlers from a nearby jar and began tearing them apart ferociously.

"It's hotter than hell in here today, and I love it!" De La Renta whispered to Pablo.

"Mother's pissed," Pablo whispered back. "She told Rachel to get the A/C fixed ASAP or there'll be no judging next episode."

"Oooooo. Rachel must be poppin' major Xanax upstairs in the control room," he giggled. "As long as Mother's makeup don't melt, I could give two shits. I'm so *sick and tired* of freezing in here."

"I just need this judging over with before Keisha has a meltdown and I'm forced to fix the A/C myself."

"Settle," Bill yelled across the studio floor. "Quiet on set."

"Quiet on set," the 2nd AD echoed.

"Rolling."

The lights rose, changing the doldrums of the cardboard looking set into a fantasyland of glitz and glamor. Under the full intensity of the camera lights, the on-camera talent became doll-like versions of themselves. Safely tucked away in his usual spot next to De La Renta, Joe and a few producers in video village along the "fourth wall" of the judging set, Pablo sighed with relief as Bill began his countdown. "Models walking in on three, two, one."

The four remaining contestants strutted out trying to look saucy and brave. If the delay had worn on anyone it was them. No one had told them what was going on, and, unlike the judges, they didn't have a private trailer to escape to. Lining up in two rows on the multi-level platform across the runway, they looked to Keisha, standing solo center in front of the judging table flanked by the other judges—two on each side.

"Welcome ladies," Keisha began her usual introduction with all the charm and charisma of a *Stepford Wife*. "This week we're joined by the *'Queen of Pose'* and the founder of her own Model Camp, Miss Coco Rocha."

Coco's beautiful heart shaped smile spread across her face as she waved encouragingly to the girls. They fawned appropriately and waved back excitedly. Even Pablo had to smile—Coco was one of the sweetest women he'd ever met. In or out of the fashion industry.

Keisha squinted her eyes at the "model media darling's" enthusiastic reception. She had that fake tight smile pasted on her face. Trouble was afoot. What now? Pablo fretted.

"This week, you all had *surprise* branding makeovers and your photoshoot was all about adopting your new *Kash-branded* look. But, before we begin evaluations, I have an announcement to make."

Joe ripped his headset off. "What fucking announcement?" He glared at Pablo.

"I have *absolutely* no idea what she's talking about," Pablo snapped back. He was so fed up with the way Vong treated him.

Keisha gestured to the seat where the celebrity guest was always seated. "You ever notice how the really *famous* models have interesting names? Different names like Coco?" She paused and stared down each of the contestants. "She wasn't born Coco Rocha you know."

Sweat sprouted on Pablo's forehead. He saw the betrayal on the wall in BIG LETTERS. On the fateful night he met Keisha, talking about their real names—his was David *unknown*, hers, Kiki Grimes—and then in a Chinese dumpling, ice cream and champagne induced haze, he'd told her, "Coco's mother nicknamed her *'Mon petit Coco'*–and from kindergarten on, it became her name." That Venus Fly Trap of a brain of hers had grabbed that little tidbit and filed it away to pull out and use later.

Coco's eyes darted over to video village alongside the judging set and gave Pablo an ice cold high-fashion stare.

"Oooooo, you gettin' a *certain* stink eye now, Pablo," De La Renta scolded. "What'd I tell you about fucking with these bitches?"

Pablo went cold.

"Born Mikhaila Rocha, she *borrowed* the beloved Coco Chanel's legendary name, to elevate her *own* brand," Keisha scoffed. Obviously, the jealous Supermodel host had Googled Coco's legal birth name.

As the *"Queen of Pose,"* Coco's expression remained stoic and sophisticated. She didn't blink an eye. Pablo could feel the psychic dressing down she was giving him, though. Especially since she'd filled in at the last minute as a favor to him. For a brief moment, he could only hear the hum of the A/C units struggling to cool down the soundstage. The studio was that still. And it was hot as fuck now.

"So, in the spirit of Coco honoring us with her *celestial* presence, I'm changing *my* name to a metaphor. Keisha Ka$h—with the *'s'* in my last name becoming a *dollar sign.*"

Unilaterally, the models, judges, producers and crew stared at their narcissistic host in dumfounded shock.

"Hashtag Flashback Friday." Miss Thing sounded boisterous and bossy. "Didn't the singer *Ke$ha* already rock that look, *Keisha?* And why not swap out the *'s'* in both your names?"

Keisha ignored him. "As much as we've progressed with equal pay for women in this business, there's still a long way to go. My *dollar sign* will serve as a reminder that *Keisha Ka$h* is now bankable and here to help young girls—like yourselves—become empresses of their own empire brands."

"That's it. She's lost her mind. *Officially,*" De La Renta quipped. "And clearly the bitch is bad at math. Everyone knows female models earn thirty times *more* than male models. Equal pay for who?"

Bill looked over at Joe with a confused expression. The flustered EP simply twirled his stubby index finger signaling, *keep rolling.* But Pablo was pretty sure what he meant to say was, *"Fuck my life, fuck Keisha and FUCK Model Muse."*

"So remember girls, we are all *brands* and we need to redefine who we are to stay relevant in this, sometimes, *spiteful* world of fashion." Standing with the air of a deity, Keisha's multi-million dollar smile beamed. "Ok then. Nichole, you're first up for evaluation."

The newly bald model hesitantly stepped down from the second row and walked across the long runway directly toward the boastful host. Her porcelain skin and chiseled features looked radiant under the lights.

"Nichole, I challenged you with your new *Ka$h-branded* look, but by the disturbed expression on your face, I don't think you handled it very well."

Nichole smiled and interrupted the star. "Actually, I'm extremely proud to rock my bald head because," she paused for a moment, swallowed, "my mom fought a long and painful battle with breast cancer." Droplets of tears formed along her lower lash line. "Listening to what you just said, reminded me of *true* inner strength and integrity that my mother instilled in me…"

Keisha tried to cut the teary-eyed model off. "Oh, that's sweet but—"

"And," Nichole cut the Supermodel off, a second time, "having my long, red hair shaved off, gives me a far more noble cause than *your* TV ratings. *'Bald is beautiful'* will be my new identifier—my brand. So, I thank you for freeing me from wanting to model myself after you." Nichole's smile was radiant. Victorious. Lethal.

Pablo's body levitated into the air. The judges, everyone, even Joe Vong was gobsmacked. No one could believe that a model contestant was *actually* standing up to Keisha and calling her out—on camera. It was a bit like watching a giant cyclone building onstage. There was a reason her brother used to call her Gollum—Keisha's eyes bugged so far out of her head that she looked like she was about to blow her lid—literally.

Over the headsets, Pablo could hear the low-pitched rumble of Keisha's *don't fuck with me* demonic possession voice. "Do you know who I am? Do you know where I've come from and what I've gone through? Who do you think you are?"

"I'm a proud bald woman, who's going to raise breast cancer awareness and raise money to stop this awful disease." Nichole's eyes blazed with defiance.

"Brilliant," Harper accidentally chirped out loud.

Pablo had never seen Keisha like this, but the scene felt like a déjà vu. This would undoubtedly haunt her for the rest of her career.

"Stop talking," Keisha screamed. "When I speak, you listen. Everybody listens."

The shouting woke Sasha up. She swiveled her head toward Miss Thing. "What's going on?"

"Meltdown alert."

Like a gunslinger, Sasha reached between her recently plumped breasts, pulled out her iPhone and from her comatose vantage point, aimed.

"How dare you challenge me? You were nothing before you came here. You think you're better than all the other girls who fought like hell to get here? You're nothing. A no one. And you're done. You can leave. Now. Go back to Grandmama's house and sleep on that ratty-ass mattress with your brother Davey and his club foot."

"Well, I..."

Keisha pointed at Nichole's body with a look of disgust. "You think this is gonna last? Men are gonna tire of you and find the next hot, young thing. Designers will turn on you too. Everyone will leave you in the end. Everyone."

"Wait a min," Nichole yelled.

"BE QUIET," Keisha shrieked. Her voice echoed throughout the soundstage.

Pablo was terrified now. He could feel Keisha's energy pummeling him from across the room.

"You know what's wrong with you?" With an air of superiority, Keisha ran her hands up and down her own curvy body. "You don't have what I have. We thought you had what it takes, and I actually wanted you to win." She shook her finger in the girl's face. The veins on her neck were pronounced and distended like a weightlifter's. "Supermodels have to be strong. Swallow whatever's done to them and come out on top. You couldn't do that. And you just proved to us that you don't have what it takes. If I went around feeling sorry for myself, I wouldn't be where I am today. Learn from this."

"Is this normal?" Coco looked around the room, confused by what was happening. "I was going to vote for her," she said to Mason.

"Look." De La Renta shoved his iPhone in Pablo's face, distracting him from the meltdown drama playing out in front of his eyes. Pablo tried to make sense of what he was looking at on the bright screen. WTF? Oh God. No. Instantly, his body experienced the horror of sinking on the Titanic—with no lifeboats left.

Now upstairs in the control room, Pablo and De La Renta burst in waving an iPhone. Rachel and the group of directors looked like dazed deer caught in a semi-truck's headlights.

"Hello?" De La Renta shouted, "Tell me this shit ain't really Live on Instagram! Somebody better fucking get Keisha outta there."

Pablo looked at the wide shot of the judges. Sasha's head was still lying on the table, but her position had changed and her eyes were now wide open. She had a slew of fake Instagram accounts too.

Rachel switched her walkie talkie to the producer only

channel. "Joe, you gotta get her outta there. Someone on set is Live streaming this."

"What?" Joe's voice cracked over the walkie. "Who?"

"I can't see. Just get her off stage."

"Fuck," he yelled as he stood up in video village, down on the studio floor. "This is why I need her wearing a God damn earpiece." Joe Vong dove onto the stage and grabbed Keisha by her waist, dragging her off the set, kicking and screaming.

"You have no idea. I've put up with them all. I've suffered through all the bullshit. I did whatever it took…" The sound-stage door shut with a bang, cutting Keisha's voice off.

From the judging table, Coco began to applaud.

# 16

## LIGHTS OUT

THE EXHAUSTION HE felt earlier had vanished, and Pablo was now wide awake. He couldn't help but feel sorry for Keisha, but he was also freaked out by what he'd just witnessed. He'd never seen anything like the vitriol spewing from her mouth. She scared him.

The night was not young, when the Supermodel host had her viral meltdown, but when anything significant goes down on any reality show's set, the senior producers assemble with military precision. Pablo peered around the oddly silent control room, waiting for the rest of the team to come flying in. Everyone in the room was transfixed, staring at the screens of their own cell phones. He had to go check on Keisha. Hovering in the doorway, he was trying to catch Rachel's eye. She looked more bedraggled than ever.

Just then, Joe Vong arrived huffing and puffing. He pushed Pablo back into the control room.

"Is she okay?"

"She locked herself in her bathroom."

"I should go see her then."

"She doesn't want to see anyone."

"But—"

"Not even you," Joe barked. He turned to De La Renta. "Switzerland, go wait outside her door in case she comes out."

"You don't have to ask me twice. I'm out."

A cadence of heavy footsteps approaching the room reverberated from the hall. Broyce Miller came through the doorway, shaking his head. "What are you guys doing here? How did something like this get out?" He held up his iPhone. The headline read:

*Keisha Crash explodes on the set of Model Muse.*

No one dared make a sound.

"Don't we strictly enforce no cell phones on the set?"

"Yes."

"First of all, I want to know who's responsible. Whoever it is—and I mean whoever, is fired. I want their contract."

"It wasn't any of the crew," Joe blurted. "No one would dare..."

"Second of all, the network is putting *Model Muse* on hiatus, indefinitely." Broyce ignored him. "You're dark, as of now."

Joe scrambled after the exec. "Wait. No. I'm sorry, Broyce, you can't do this. Please."

"Oh, yes I can, and I just did. Go home. All of you."

On his way out the door, Broyce flipped the light switch, plunging them into blackness.

"Fuck my life," Rachel muttered in the dark.

Silence.

"I've got it." Harper was like a babbling brook even at the worst of times. "Let's get Mason to recreate that cover he did for the *Time Magazine* Body Image Issue, only this *time*—pun intended—he'll use our semi-finalists. They can be naked, covered only by Nichole's beautiful long red hair across their bodies."

"What about *shut down* don't you understand?" Rachel yelled at her.

"That sounds icky, weird," someone chimed in.

Pablo agreed but didn't say it was the stupidest idea he'd ever heard.

"And that red hair went missing two days ago," Rachel said.

"It was donated, wasn't it?" Pablo asked.

Rachel shook her head. "It was supposed to be, but the hair stylist lost track of it."

"I promised Nichole it would go to *Locks of Love*."

"Pablo! Not our problem right now." Joe went over to the light switch and flipped it on. He stared at the cheerful newbie with something akin to appreciation, an emotion Pablo wasn't sure Vong even possessed. "Pollyanna might be on to something."

Pablo did a double take, snapping his head around.

"What's your name, again?"

"Harper."

"Okay, first, cone of silence. We can't let Broyce catch wind that we're still shooting. Second, under *NO* circumstances can Keisha find out that the network shut us down." Joe Vong sounded like he was in charge for the first time since the show had first aired. Everyone in the control room nodded, despite the fact that gossip spread through their production like STDs on *The Bachelor*. "Pablo, you're with me," he barked.

"I should go see if I can calm her down…"

"This is triage and we're the MASH unit. Let's move it people."

Pablo followed Joe toward the catering area, outside the talent trailers. Congregated around tables, the crew and judges were gossiping about what had happened and watching Keisha's meltdown replay on their iPhones.

"It's everywhere," one grip said.

"I wanna see how she spins her way outta this one," a PA scoffed.

One look at Vong's angry face, they slipped their phones in their pockets and shut up.

Like a pompous cat washing his face, Mason was dipping his fries into malt vinegar, nibbling them one at a time and then licking his fingers.

"Mason," Joe yelled. "I need you and Pablo to recreate that fucking bullshit body image cover you shot for *Time Magazine* ten years ago."

Mason nearly choked on a fry.

"Oh, it…it is so last decade, Joe." He struggled for an excuse. "And it has been re-done to death. People see it all the time—"

"That's the whole point, *Prince Charles*. People recognize it. They love it. It'll touch their stupid hearts. Just do that shit again and prep it fast. You're shooting it in like," Joe looked at his Apple Watch, "less than 36 hours."

"We cannot possibly recreate…" Mason stammered a list of everything he would need to pull off that shoot at such short notice.

"Spare me the details," Joe barked, turning his back. "Just do it."

"But I don't have my—" Mason yelled.

Joe Vong shrieked at the top of his lungs, "Just fucking do it."

Pablo shook his head. Arguing with Joe Vong was futile. Mason grabbed Pablo's arm. "We need to talk." He hauled him down the alleyway between the soundstage and the talent trailers.

Pablo shoved Mason away. "What the fuck? We have nothing to talk about. Keisha buried it for you." Pablo was cold and curt. "All you need to do is stay the hell away from me. That's the deal, remember?"

Mason looked flustered. "I'm not talking about that." He dropped his pretentious British accent and blurted, "I have to admit something to you."

"Oh, *puh-lease*, obviously I already know." Pablo had never seen the smooth-talking Brit so visibly upset. He rolled his eyes and stared back at Mason with a *who gives a fuck* face, folding his arms and leaning against the studio wall.

"No, this is not about *us*."

"There is no, US," Pablo reminded him. "You made a pass at me. I rejected it. Period. End of story."

"Pablo, this is about the *Time Magazine* cover."

"What about it?"

"Well, my old assistant Muhammad," Mason paused, shifting his eyes to the floor, "*may* have actually come up with the idea and technique to shoot it."

"And, lemme guess, you *may* have taken all the credit?" Pablo scoffed. Typical. White privilege strikes again. "You know what, I'm not even surprised. So, do you know where Muhammad is now? Maybe *he* can do the photoshoot for us."

Mason winced and kicked some old cigarette butts littering the alley. "He quit the business. Went back to Mumbai. He won't take my calls. You have to help me, Pablo. Please."

"Oh, this is priceless. Lemme guess again. You two were fucking?"

"It's really none of your business wh—"

Pablo roared. "You really do have a thing for *brown boys*, don't you?"

"I..."

"You're not an idiot, Mason. Why can't you just recreate the cover?"

"It was some double exposure trick that Muhammad manipulated with After Effects. I don't know how to do it."

"I take back what I said—you're a *fucking* idiot." Pablo turned away from Mason and his revelation but fired off one last verbal punch. "Why is everything *always* about this fucking show?" He was screaming now, aware that Meltdown 2.0 was about to be his own. "Why do I even try to keep things afloat around here? I should've known the moment Keisha insisted we hide that whole debacle of you attempting to put *YOUR DICK IN ME* that this shit show wasn't for me. I should've filed a lawsuit against you *and* the network, and escaped while I still had my ethics and my life."

Pablo was being melodramatic and he knew it. But who wasn't being melodramatic tonight? Hanging out with a bunch of prima donnas had finally rubbed off on him because in actual fact, Pablo had made peace with Keisha's duplicity and Mason's indiscretion for the sake of his career. After all, *Model Muse* was his launching pad for a bigger opportunity in television. Pablo, too, had seen the merit of burying his Me Too moment as much as Keisha. Staring at the pathetic Brit, Pablo realized he no longer felt threatened by Mason in any way. Mason was just a sad, confused man who would most likely never feel free to be himself. That was punishment enough.

Unable to look Pablo in the eye, Mason fled back to his trailer, while Pablo confidently sauntered back through the studio doors feeling restored from his explosive tête-à-tête. And that's when inspiration struck. He pulled out his iPhone and fired off a text message.

**Pablo TEXT:** I have an idea. Coffee in the a.m.?

Broyce texted back immediately.

**Broyce TEXT:** 8:30 a.m. My office.

Still intrigued by Harper's original suggestion and knowing Mason couldn't pull off what he hadn't done in the first place, Pablo sat alone in the abandoned video village of the judging soundstage watching After Effects tutorials on YouTube. Two steps ahead of the game, he was figuring out a trés chic version of the *Time* magazine cover that could restore Keisha's public face and force the network to allow *Model Muse* to resume production. Harper had actually contributed something good and he'd have to thank her later because come morning, he'd have to pitch Broyce.

Andy Levenkron arrived at Silvercup just after midnight and strode into video village where Pablo was working. Scratching his crotch, he pulled up a chair and sat uncomfortably close. Andy liked to grab people with a two-lock gaze, as if he was challenging them to some kind of staring match before beginning a conversation.

"I dunno what happened here tonight, but I need you to fix it." He was man spreading and reached down to scratch his balls again. Pablo wondered if Andy ever tried spraying them with anti-jock itch. "Keisha's been shopping a new talk show for the two of you. She does nothing but sing your praises with buying executives and she's pushing for you to be her co-star. I thought you'd wanna know."

The news hit Pablo with such force, it was as if all the air had been knocked out of his lungs. He was rendered speechless. He could barely breathe.

"So, I'm not sure what you're doing in here, but my

understanding is, you haven't checked on Keisha since the shit hit the fan a couple of hours ago!"

"She's not talking to anyone, Andy. Even me."

"I don't care what she says. You're her trusted—whatever you are." Andy was yelling at him now. "Get your pretty little ass over to her dressing suite and fix the bitch, or there will be no talk show for either of you. Capisce?"

Pablo knew the drill all too well. Nod and keep it moving. He grabbed his laptop and disappeared down the hall, dipping into the men's room to gather his thoughts. Staring at his reflection in the mirror—his grey eyes, silver grey short cropped hair—his mind raced. Keisha was actually pitching him for a talk show? Any doubts about her loyalty or greed, vanished. He felt that old bond they'd forged the night after the Michael Kors show. Best Friends Forever. His own insecurities could make him such an ass. Just because she didn't side with him over Mason, he'd doubted her and in fact, was holding a grudge. It was just a pass hadn't sat well with him, but he understood. Women had to deal with these kinds of improprieties every day. And now, she was going to make him a part of her next big show. Their own talk show—they were Judy Garland and Mickey Rooney, again.

Pablo leaned against the sink and looked at himself in the mirror. *You never see the gifts that are in front of your face, Pablo. You're always waiting to be rejected or be unveiled as a fraud. When are you going to believe in yourself, like Keisha does? You have to prove to her that you deserve a seat next to her at the table—your new talk show table.*

He wanted to take her something to make her feel better. Something to bring her out of her cave and recover her composure. Solving the ransom note would work. He couldn't go back to video village, not with Andy Levenkron sitting there, so he stepped into the bathroom stall. Where else was it quiet and private? Pablo flipped down the toilet lid and sat down, placing his computer in his lap. After a quick Google search, he found a list of instructions for solving anagrams. By rearranging the letters of the note, he hoped it would form a sentence that made sense and reveal a secret message. That's what his intuition was telling him, and *Kimoru* was the key. His mind drifted and he fantasized about being a character in a new Dan Brown movie—though one with an ethnically diverse cast—unveiling some mysterious hieroglyph set in Egypt. He stared at the basic instructions on the screen hoping they'd help him solve the message.

1. Break up the anagram. First, write down all of the letters in a different pattern.

2. Put letters together in common pairings.

3. After you break up the anagram, start putting together pairs of letters.

4. Separate vowels and consonants.

5. Pick out prefixes and suffixes.

Too tired to make much sense of the instructions, he didn't feel he could help Keisha recover from her breakdown, unless he offered her something concrete. So, maybe he couldn't see her tonight. It was clear that what had happened on set had been precipitated by the arrival of that ill-fated vial of blood. It was understandable, somewhat. Pablo was certain that once the mystery of the message was solved, it would bring Keisha out of her tailspin. He just needed to get her head back on straight. That's what *family* did for one another. Playing around with different letter combinations, he began typing possible answers in his Notes application. It seemed as though the message was beginning to come to life. And then, the bathroom came to life.

"Come in here, sexy," a gruff man's voice said.

"I've never done it in a public toilet before." The bathroom door banged shut.

"Then you haven't lived."

Pablo placed his hands over his ears and closed his eyes. How had he gone from creating covers for *Vogue* in Paris, and walking the Champs-Élysées in spring, to squatting on a toilet in Queens? Glamour truly is fleeting. When the lights dimmed and the studio emptied out, *Model Muse After Dark* now seemed to be the real reality show viewers would kill to have a front row seat to. Was this day ever going to end?

Through the crack in the door jam, Pablo could see Andy Levenkron and the contestant known on set as the slut, Kayla, preparing to do the nasty. How had Kayla escaped "the cupboard?" What were the model contestants still doing at the studio anyway? Had the producers forgotten the girls completely and left them there to rot in their stuffy backroom for the whole night? What a stupid question to ask. If she was screwing the big manager honcho, it was obvious. Pablo tried not to sigh too heavily. He didn't want Andy to know he hadn't gone straight to Keisha's dressing suite.

"You're so wet." Andy unfastened his belt and let his khakis drop to his knees. Kayla hiked up her denim skirt. He tore off her panties.

"You're so hard." The Grecian girl had that Helen of Troy look that was about to launch Andy's ship.

She pulled Andy's long-sleeved polo up and over his head, discarding the shirt on the floor. Pablo winced at the sight of the young model running her hands up and down his acne covered back. Moaning with ecstasy, they dry humped each other with only Andy's white Calvin's between them.

Abruptly, Kayla pulled down his underwear and wrapped her legs around his hairy buttocks, locking her ankles together, as he thrust away inside her. Sliding along the wall, they banged it out wedged between a Dyson hand dryer and plastic garbage bin. *Please, let it be over quick.* Pablo covered his eyes then covered his ears, neither worked.

Andy grunted like a pig. Kayla squealed like one. With one last great thrust, he groaned and let her go. Done.

Kayla's face shifted from ecstasy to frustration. "What are you? A two-pump chump?"

Andy shuffled over to the sink and splashed water on his dick. "You should be grateful for what you get," he snarled, rubbing his chest and looking proudly at himself in the mirror.

The Supermodel wannabe was not amused. "Too bad you can't manage to satisfy a girl as well as you *manage* your clients." She pulled her jean skirt down and walked out, leaving her panties on the floor.

"At least you got a night out," Andy called after her while pulling up his khakis. Chuckling to himself, he ran a hand over his close shaved head. Pablo had always thought the manager looked like a thug, but now he acted like one too.

Exiting the bathroom, he flipped the light off, leaving Pablo in the proverbial dark.

Pablo leaned back against the toilet and sighed. The time on his iPhone read 1:18 a.m. Fuck. He still had to get all the way home from Queens and he'd gotten no further with the anagram. He needed food, rest and a break before he faced Keisha. He texted De La Renta.

**Pablo TEXT:** How's Mother?

**De La Renta TEXT:** #Messy. Not talking. Won't open the door.

**Pablo TEXT:** Do you need me?

**De La Renta TEXT:** Go home. Just be here first thing in the morning. I'll babysit tonight. Already half asleep. You know I don't mind a comfortable couch.

**Pablo TEXT:** Thanks, Switzerland. See you in the a.m. xoxo

# KIMORU

ENSCONCED IN THE safety of his own home, Pablo propped himself up with down pillows and his molded overlap designer tray that allowed him to relax and work from the comfort of bed. It was 2:17 a.m. but he had to finish decrypting the mysterious note attached to the even more mysterious vial of blood or he couldn't face Keisha. At least, it wasn't a horse's head. Pulling out a large piece of graph paper, he began to shuffle the letters from the cryptic message—grouping them into vowels and consonants (Thanks, YouTube!).

He made a couple of attempts at forming a new sentence, but he ran out of letters. His lack of sleep was catching up with him. Taking a break, he went into the kitchen for some fresh juice and an energy bar. Pablo closed his eyes and sighed. What if he couldn't fix this one thing? Everything seemed to

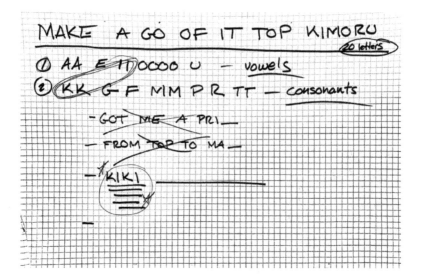

depend on it, but if you'd asked him why, he wouldn't have the words to explain. Returning to his bedroom, his tired eyes scanned the page and the circles he'd drawn. Sugar kicked in and suddenly it was all so obvious. How could it be a coincidence that there were two 'K's and two 'I's—that could only spell one name. He began crossing off all the other letters until the message appeared. "Yes!" He punched the air and leaned his head back on his pillows. Slipping the solved puzzle under his iPhone on the nightstand, he whispered, "Hey *Siri*, set the alarm for 7:00 a.m."

"OK. The alarm is set for seven a.m."

He needed to be up in only a few hours and thank God, his eyes were closing fast and heavy. After his 8:30 a.m. meeting with Broyce, he'd head over to Keisha and hand her the cipher that would prove to her once and for all that he could actually fix everything, his loyalty was golden and he was indeed her BFF. He couldn't wait to see her face.

## 6 DAYS TILL WRAP, SEASON SIX

"So, we redeem her and redeem the show," Pablo said, moving to the expansive portal in Broyce's office. He'd always found the view distracting, still he looked out at the incredible skyline now to catch his breath. New York City looked cleaner and more magnificent from the network executive's 48th floor office of white marble and glass.

Broyce looked calm as he nodded and leaned on his desk. Pablo's pitch to save the show was scribbled in blue erasable marker across the office white-board.

The executive stood up and walked over to the Nespresso machine. "Refill?"

Pablo nodded and walked across the room. It was a huge office—two-story ceilings, couches, conference table— designed to intimidate and place Broyce Miller as the rainmaker of the network.

"I have to admit, your twist on an updated, more modern version of the *Time Magazine* Body Image Issue is great! I'll have to run it up the ladder, but you've got my support." Broyce's gentle parental tone was a real comfort after the insanity of the past 24-hours. He'd always been more than a network executive to Pablo. He was more like a guardian angel, swooping in and helping Pablo to understand how to navigate the world of reality TV. Now Pablo was returning the favor.

"It would certainly make the network look good," Pablo reiterated.

"I'll do my best to get this approved later today when I meet with the guys upstairs. We're figuring out what to do, and presenting this creative idea might get you back on air."

"Keep in mind, we never got to eliminate a model yesterday and *judging* never happened." Pablo winked. "Just because a blurry video of Keisha screaming is all over the internet, doesn't mean the public has to know *when* it happened during season six."

"How do you figure that?"

"The video begins with Keisha already yelling, and you can barely hear Nichole trying to interrupt. So, I say, let's use the new photoshoot I just pitched you—I hated the *Kash-branded* beauty shots we did—and shoot a new judging. When season six finally airs this fall—edited the way *we* want—people won't figure out where and when her meltdown happened."

Broyce took a sip of coffee and looked thoughtfully at Pablo. "You really should be an executive producer. There's a reason the crew call you *Mr. Fix-It.*"

Pablo laughed. "Where'd you hear that?"

"I know more than you think." Broyce smiled. "De La Renta is *Switzerland.* Joe Vong is *Mad Max.* And Keisha is... Well, we won't acknowledge what Keisha is."

Pablo wanted to laugh out loud. Broyce winked at him.

"I want you to know that I see you, Pablo. I see what you do for the show and I know who the real talent is behind *Model Muse's* success." Broyce raised his eyebrow and looked pointedly at Pablo.

Pablo lifted his coffee cup in a mock toast to the exec. "That would be you, Broyce."

"And that says it all," Broyce laughed and reached out his hand to shake Pablo's. "No wonder you've lasted as long as you have."

Outside on the street, Pablo couldn't see his Uber anywhere. Morning traffic was at its height and one car looked much like the other. He texted the driver—*Here.*

From behind him, he heard the chilling snap of a paparazzi's camera and the familiar voice of an *E!* reporter. "Pablo."

He didn't turn around.

"What can you tell us about what happened last night on

the set of *Model Muse?*" Now ambushed, a microphone was suddenly thrust under his chin and a camera in his face. Shit! He didn't even have any concealer under his eyes to hide the dark circles from last night's sleeplessness.

"Did she have a psychotic break?" A tall, slender reporter from *The New York Post* shouted above the din of reporters.

"Come on, Tom." Pablo played spin doctor as well as Olivia Pope did in *Scandal*. "She just had a really bad day. You tellin' me you've *never* had a bad day?"

Another sloppy looking reporter fired at Pablo. "I heard the network cancelled the show. Is that why you're here?"

"No one's cancelled anything. In fact, I'm going back to work right now. It's gonna be amazing, big surprises." Pablo hurried past the bee buzzing journalists as his Uber pulled up to the curb. *Who the fuck was the mole?*

"So, is it true that you might file a sexual harassment lawsuit against Mason Hughes? Is that why you were upstairs with the network brass?" Harvey Levin himself appeared from behind a camera and smiled at him with *got you* eyes. Pablo swept the shock off his face and looked directly at the head of TMZ, who loved to grab gossip and spew it all over the internet with little regard for his appalling crime against humanity.

"Well, look who the cat cleaned up, spray tanned, J Crewed and dragged out. I thought you never left the studio these days, Harvey?"

"A story like this? Check out what I have and plan on releasing once I get your statement." The former legal analyst, and TMZ gossip website founder, handed Pablo an iPad with a video playing Mason and him fighting in the ally next to the soundstage—only hours before. "Your set security is leaking like the Titanic."

Pablo laughed out loud and stepped into his Uber. "No one actually *believes* anything TMZ posts, Harvey. You know as well as I do that *anything* can be edited to look real. You wanna waste your time on fake news, go ahead."

The suburban peeled away up Sixth Avenue. Pablo took a long, slow, deep breath to keep himself together. *There was a fucking mole!* The Uber driver shifted his eyes back and forth from the traffic to his rearview mirror.

"Aren't you that guy from Keisha Kash's modeling show? My girlfriend loves her—she's her role model."

"You know, it's not just HER show," Pablo yelled.

"Fine. Whatever. I thought *you* were one of the nice ones."

*I am*, Pablo wanted to say. *I am.* But he was too over-whelmed by the pressure cooker of his career, the reporters and lack of sleep. "Sorry, I just need a minute."

The crowded Manhattan streets, unaffected by the turmoil and urgency roiling in Pablo's mind, moved at a snail's pace. The *one* story he never wanted out in the public was in the hands of the press. There was no way Mason would say any-thing–that's for sure. And there wasn't any benefit in Keisha trading the story. But they were the only ones who knew. Pablo closed his eyes and focused on the video he'd just watched. He sat bolt upright as clarity dawned on him. "Fuck."

"Excuse me?"

"Oh no, not you. I'm sorry. I just figured something out." Pablo was going to get a bad rating from this Uber driver—for sure.

Considering the angle from which the conversation between Mason and him was shot, they had been outside Miss Thing's trailer. The clever bastard had filmed them.

"What a bitch," Pablo quietly mumbled. He could just see the evil look on Miss Thing's face—donning an ear to ear grin like the Cheshire Cat from the original 1951 Disney animated film, *Alice in Wonderland.* However, he needed proof before he could confront the shady model coach.

Pablo pulled his iPhone out of his bag and frantically typed four individual text messages to I.C.E. Tears welled up in his eyes, as he did the one thing he NEVER did. Pablo asked for help.

**Pablo TEXTS:** All hell breaking loose!
Press asking me about Mason!
KK falling apart!
HELP!

Nothing came back. Pablo waited. Nothing. Why was it when you needed someone the most, they were never around? Everybody knew I.C.E. meant 'In Case of Emergency,' so what the hell?

\*     \*     \*

"Late start for the crew?" Pablo walked onto the soundstage lot and waved at Rachel heading past the loading dock. The catering area was oddly deserted even though it was 9:45 a.m.

"Thank God you're here. I need you to go check on her. Security says she's been in there all night. Please."

"I'm literally on my way there now. Hashtag, I got this."

"Aw, I love you." Rachel sounded like she was about to throttle a cute puppy. She didn't vocalize emotion well. "And while you're at it, could you see if there's a chance she may wanna visit set and actually save her show *and* all of our fucking jobs?"

"She's not supposed to know the show's in jeopardy, is she?" Pablo raised his eyebrow.

"I disagree. The best way to keep celebrities in line is dangling the possibility of their star fading. They *hate* being irrelevant."

Pablo stepped through fire doors and headed down a long

hallway, pushing open yet a second set of fire doors. So many fire doors just to protect the show from *her* fiery temper. The dingy gold star on her dressing suite had fingerprints on it.

Quietly, he knocked on the door. Nothing.

He placed his ear close without touching. Silence. Knock. Nothing.

Finally, Pablo pounded on the door in case she was in her en-suite bathroom.

"Y'all keep banging on this door like I'm handing out free pussy." It was De La Renta.

"It's me." Pablo opened the door and peered in.

"Thank God, it's you."

"Is it safe?"

"Hell, if I know. I've been tryin' to get her outta the bathroom since last night." De La Renta looked at the bathroom door while he practically shouted. "Mother snapped, bad. AND it can't be pretty." He flitted around the dressing suite, gathering his belongings and dumping them into his Louis Vuitton Supreme backpack. "I didn't sign up to be the gatekeeper and guardian to Mother—you did. And I got things to do. Like making her a new fucking wig. I'm outta here," he whispered to Pablo as he exited.

Pablo didn't even try to stop De La Renta from his dramatic exit. Once a Capricorn made his mind up, it was best to just leave them be. You think karma's a bitch? Wait until you piss off a Capricorn. They keep a frozen shoulder in the freezer, just in case they need to ice someone out. De La Renta's specialty was putting people "on pause;" it even worked on celebrities.

Keisha's new dressing suite was monstrous. When Andy became her manager, he wanted to raise the Supermodel's profile above the other talent's so he'd convinced her that her trailer, which before had been more comfortable and conveniently stationed outside near all the other talent double-bangers, was passé. It was like Andy had put "inconvenience" into her contract. This new dressing suite forced producers to commute all the way to the other side of the studio for onset meetings, and then schlep all the way back. Worst of all, Keisha really didn't like being so isolated from the nucleus of the cast and crew. At the very least, she missed being in close proximity to the catering truck.

The colossal chamber was equipped with a full hair and makeup room, a ring-lit selfie station, over-sized lounge area anchored by four large white sofas, modern glass tables topped with fresh white rose arrangements and an 85" OLED TV. It was way too much space for a star who kept herself locked inside with either De La Renta or Pablo, for fear that crew members might catch a glimpse of what she looked like *"outta drag,"* as De La Renta called it. During the first season, Keisha always came to the set without her wig or makeup; however, one day the studio manager kept walking right past her without any idea of who she was. She ran to her trailer in tears and from then on refused to come to the set without her face and "lid." The Supermodel needed to be fortified with her armor—as she called it—more than ever, and so it was.

Pablo waited for a moment after De La Renta left, steeling his nerves. He didn't want to admit it to himself, but Keisha's meltdown had freaked him out. Her venomous outburst scared him. He thought he understood her, but after last night he wasn't so sure. How should he approach her? Seriously or jovially? Solemn or light?

He walked up to the closed door in the makeup area leading to Keisha's own private bathroom and tapped lightly on the door. "Hey…Judy, it's me, Mickey. Can I come in?"

From the other side of the door, he could hear shuffling and then the tumbler clinking in the lock. Turning the handle, he slowly peeked through the opening of the door. Keisha was still wearing her dress from judging last night, with the side zip fully undone. Slumped on the floor, she looked helpless and sad. A hot mess. Her iPhone was in her right hand and attached to the charger which was plugged into the wall.

"You didn't spend all night watching that crap, did you?"

She nodded. Her wig flopping loosely from side to side. At least, her do didn't look as bad as De La Renta feared. "Come on, let's get you cleaned up." He got down on the floor with her and began to clear away her smeared makeup with a baby wipe, speaking in the soothing voice of a parent trying to calm a brokenhearted child. "I know things are hard for you right now, but Mr. Pablo's gonna take care of everything."

Keisha leaned her head on Pablo's chest and sobbed. He wrapped his arms around her and let her lean even more into him, in a way she hadn't done since they'd begun this whole wild ride. Pablo genuinely felt his heart break for his BFF and if nothing else, he'd remember this moment of affection when they were both people who simply cared for each other. It made all the rest of her crap worthwhile.

"You never came back," she pouted.

"Joe wouldn't let me."

"All night?"

"Pretty much, but it gave me time to fix things. I figured out the cryptic message. It was an anagram."

"What's an anagram, again?"

"It's a phrase formed by rearranging the letters of another—it doesn't matter. The important thing is, the note isn't from a stalker."

"It isn't?"

"Nope. I think it's from your mom." He showed her what

he'd figured out on the graph paper, and that *Make a go of it Top Kimoru*, actually said: *Proof to get Mama out Kiki.*

Keisha's eyes shifted into focus and she grabbed Pablo's hand. "Mama's the *only* person who calls me Kiki."

"*Egg-zackly.* But a vial of blood? How would that be proof to get her outta jail?"

"No clue, but mama *always* has a Plan B."

"Fine. Let's see what she says. But why all the cloak-and-dagger?"

"She has to be careful with things connected to me. I used to love my puzzle books as a kid and she probably assumed I'd figure it out. How did *you* figure it out?"

Pablo told her all the complexities, explaining and recounting every step of how he solved the anagram—including how he got stuck in the bathroom while Andy and Kayla were doing the nasty. Keisha might have been traumatized by yesterday's events but she was still copacetic enough for her eyes to narrow into slits at the Andy news. She looked up at him and forced a little clenched jaw smile.

Pablo felt a little chill run down his spine. She looked a little like a psychiatric patient off her meds, not defenseless at all. And something in her eyes told him he'd just given her a brand new weapon for her arsenal. Gently, he helped her up off the floor and over to the couch. "You ready to face the world yet?"

"Almost."

Pablo reached for the walkie-talkie sitting on the makeup counter, smiled sweetly at her and pressed the talk button. "Does anyone have eyes on Keisha's stylist? There's a new girl coming in today," he reminded whomever was listening.

"I got her here."

"Send her to Keisha's in thirty." He tilted his head toward Keisha.

"Sixty," she mouthed.

"Sixty."

"Copy that," an anonymous PA's voice crackled over the walkie.

Stripping off last night's over worn attire, Keisha walked across the room, naked, to the shower. "Can you get me some eggs and bacon from catering, Mr. Pablo?" Her voice was weird and high pitched. "I'm starving."

Almost an hour later, the semi-svelte Supermodel the world knew and lusted after, was sitting on the couch next to Pablo, happily scrolling through *Vogue*.com on his laptop. Stripped of all her makeup and hair, she looked like any normal human being, fiddling with her exposed cornrows.

"Yaaaaas. Look at this one. That's perfect." Keisha pointed at the screen.

Pablo's eyes widened in disbelief at her choice but he choked back his response. "You're right, Mommy. It's perfect for you. But are you sure that's what you wanna be wearing when you show up tomorrow?"

Her eyes hooded and narrowed. Her cheeks sunk into her teeth, like she was sucking on sour candy. It was her, *does a bear shit in the woods?* look.

"Okay then. I'll make sure De La Renta has everything he needs," he paused, "and I just wanna say thank you too. Andy told me—"

Abruptly, the door flew open and a big-busted, black stylist sporting an afro and headband strutted into the dressing suite, hauling with her a huge, Gucci logo-print tracksuit.

"Look what I scored for you, Miss Kash! The new Dapper Dan collection with matching sneakers. Girl, you gonna look so fly. And, you can keep the cornrows; De La Renta won't mind if you skip the wig on this one."

Pablo's mouth dropped open.

Like a heat seeking missile, Keisha turned toward the new stylist, who had walked into the room without so much as a knock or an introduction. "Can you tell, Miss…I'm sorry, Baby, what's your name, again?"

"It's Pamella. I started yesterday but it was a little crazy."

"Well Pamella, one of my *hashtag new rules* is, KNOCK! Don't ever barge in here without asking my permission." Keisha rose up from the couch to her full height and towered over the tall girl, who began to shrink in the Supermodel's shadow. "Plus, I don't do logos! And, that cut? That's gonna make me look huge."

Pablo was grateful not to be on the other end of the new stylist's dressing down. Keisha was clearly back to her old self.

"Oh, Miss Kash, you're wrong. *Naomi Campbell* is rocking all the Dapper Dan stuff."

Keisha waved her hands in front of the new girl's face, her voice rocketing into creepy land. "Mr. Pablo, make it go away."

Pablo jumped up and escorted Pamella out of the dressing suite. "Don't worry, I'll personally go pick up the wardrobe you just chose for tomorrow's photoshoot and leave it with De La Renta."

Closing the door to a crack, he leaned back in to whisper, "I'll also talk to Rachel about hiring a new stylist." Pablo closed the dressing suite door and looked at the poor girl on his arm.

"That was super creepy," Pamella said to him.

"Child, trust me, rejection is protection. She goes through stylists like Sasha Berenson goes through bottles of Chardonnay."

"You mean I'm fired? I didn't work more than a few hours. What did I do?"

Pablo nodded. "You used the N-word."

He left the previously sassy, energetic young stylist bawling in the hallway, probably wondering when she'd used the N-word. He had real work to do, not the least of which was styling the photoshoot that was, hopefully, going to save the show.

# 18

## TWISTED VANITY

**5 DAYS TILL WRAP, SEASON SIX**

E ARLY THE NEXT morning, Pablo stood alone under the LED lights at Highline Stages as he set up the new photoshoot for the remaining four contestants. Three camera crews hovered around him. Behind the cameras, Rachel, Joe and Broyce intently watched the monitor. Behind the producers and execs, a row of attorneys, wearing ill-fitting power suits and holding yellow legal pads, muttered amongst themselves. Legal was on set to ensure that the appropriate verbiage was used to introduce the controversial photoshoot and protect the show from litigation.

"Quiet on set," Bill shouted.

"Quiet on set," the 2nd AD repeated.

"Rolling." The word echoed across the studio.

Pablo smiled as Rachel signaled, *Action.*

Taking his cue, Pablo began his introduction. "Hey, girls, for today's photoshoot we're going to honor cancer survivors."

The three models immediately looked over at Nichole, who appeared unphased by the new direction the episode was now taking. Mason, Miss Thing and Sasha walked into frame and stood next to Pablo.

"And for the first time on *Model Muse,* all our resident judges will be on set for this worthy cause because ultimately, today, we're honoring all women who have battled and are *now* fighting Breast Cancer."

A Steadicam pushed in close to capture a single tear falling down Nichole's porcelain face.

"As an added bonus, our very own *noted* fashion photographer, Mason Hughes, will be shooting this special tribute."

Usually stiffly upright, Mason bowed toward the girls. They were all working it. "It is an honor..."

Pablo clapped his hands. "Okay, time to head off to hair and makeup."

"That's a stop down everyone," Rachel stood up and announced. "Girls, make sure you use the bathrooms now. This is gonna be a long makeup process today. Camera crews, repo in the dressing area to capture reality. Nichole, it looks like you have some down time." The other models moved toward the hair stylists.

Pablo made a beeline over to where Rachel was now standing in the middle of the studio. He covered his mic and whispered into her ear so no one could hear him. "What happened to Sasha? She looks senseless...I mean, more than usual."

"She hasn't slept since she jolted awake in judging–I even tried to give her her breakfast bottle of wine and it did nothing." Rachel seemed unphased by the incredulity of her own statement. That had been 34 hours ago.

Pablo scanned the studio and locked in on the production assistant he'd given the Adderall pills to. "How many pills did you put in her Diet Coke?" He grabbed the poor kid by the arm and hissed in his face.

"All of them?"

"Shit! Just keep your mouth shut. Network legal is on set and they can't catch wind of this."

Pablo looked over to where Sasha was buzzing around the room, bumping into walls and looking a little wide-eyed and out of her mind. He was about to go rescue her when the bubbly Harper magically appeared and took Sasha by the arm, leading her away from the legal team. Good ol' Harper.

Out of the corner of his eye, Pablo caught Miss Thing slithering his way over to Mason.

"Hey, Master Hughes the third," the model coach said, with a forced smile.

Something was up. Pablo grabbed Mike's arm standing to his right, holding the sound boom. "Can you kill Mason's, Miss Thing's and my audio real quick?" he said.

"Done and done," Mike replied.

Miss Thing acting all sweet and coy was a sure sign he had something up his sleeve. And the best way to thwart Miss Thing's hijinks was to know what he was up to ahead of time. Pablo slipped a little closer to eavesdrop.

"And here I was thinking you were just hired because of your good looks, British accent and being *straight*." Miss Thing thrived on the art of the sting and timed his fatal blows so his victims were deboned and dethroned, simultaneously.

"Too bad our contestants aren't *little brown boys*! You'd be so much *lustier* if they were."

Mason's face froze.

Hearing Miss Thing quote Pablo—verbatim—was all he needed to be completely convinced that Miss Thing had taped his argument with Mason. He was furious. Pablo pounced on the slick model coach. "You can take the boy outta the South Bronx, but you can't take the South Bronx outta the boy, can you *Tyreeq Levern Jackson*. You wanna get street?" Pablo held up his iPhone illuminating the dick pic Miss Thing had sent him a few days earlier. Full screen. "I'll send this photo to every media hungry outlet because I'm so fucking fed up with your back-stabbing. I know it was you who sent that video to that gossip-hungry fiend, Harvey Levin, at TMZ! Payback's a bitch, *bitch*."

"Oh, well I ju…" Miss Thing stammered innocently.

Pablo jabbed his flat hand in front of the model coach's face and lowered his voice an octave, so he sounded like Keisha when she got weird and demonic. "How about you start using that pea-sized brain of yours and STOP trying to sabotage this show."

For once, Miss Thing was speechless. Mason tried to burble a relieved thank you, but Pablo wasn't done yet, though. "And lemme make this clear, so you don't misinterpret my actions. I don't care about you." He pointed at Hughes. "I care about the show." He glared at the two guilty judges. "And maybe you should both get on board and start treating working here like a job, not your own private FUCKFEST!"

From across the studio, Broyce caught Pablo's eye and mouthed, "Good job." For a panicked second, Pablo was afraid his mic had been on, but Mike had turned all three of their levels down—as requested. Instead, Broyce was simply praising him for the photoshoot. Working on a reality show for years taught Pablo to be mindful of what you say when mic'd up for sound—everyone can hear everything you say. Pablo simply waved back as he walked over to the hair/makeup area, gesturing at Mike to turn his audio back up.

"OUCH. That fucking hurt." Kayla made a face as the makeup artist pulled an FX bald cap over her head. Pablo rolled his eyes. Nearby, a Steadicam operator was filming the scene.

"You think that's uncomfortable?" the stylist quipped. "Wait till I glue this sucker down with Pros-Aide adhesive and you get under those lights."

Pablo flipped back into *Pablo Michaels* mode. "Models are always expected to find the beauty, no matter what they're wearing."

Kayla glared back at him with the same look she gave Andy after he showed off his *two-pump chump* moves—if she'd only known Pablo had seen the whole thing go down.

Creating the illusion that none of the models had any hair, Elyssa, Beth and Kayla all had special FX bald caps secured on their heads now to resemble Nichole's unwanted makeover. Pablo had stacked white ladders on the clean white backdrop, so that the models would be grouped together but at different levels. They were dressed in demure pink, knee-length, corseted Versace dresses. Donatella was a personal friend.

From behind where Mason was shooting in burst mode, multiple clicks reeled off as Pablo directed, "*Werk* it Nichole. If Donatella could see you now—she'd LIVE."

Pablo's iPhone vibrated in his pocket. Discreetly pulling it out, he saw a response from his *In Case of Emergency* mentor and advisor—a day too late.

**I.C.E. TEXT:** Just play it cool.

Great. He'd asked for help and gotten a platitude. Pablo shoved his phone back in his pocket. "Okay girls, so let's try something…"

The models were no longer paying any attention to him. He turned to follow their stunned gazes.

Floating into the studio with all the grandeur of a cream puff, crowned by her own bald cap and a monstrous pink chiffon gown, Keisha descended upon the set with her arms outstretched like Christ on the cross. Behind her, a production assistant was following, live streaming the Supermodel's entrance. She looked like she was ready for *Vogue's* exclusive MET Gala. The gown's twelve-foot-long train of pink feathers and micro-beading rippled along the floor.

"What's she doing?" Joe Vong hissed.

"I told you this bitch is crazy." De La Renta was laughing. "You wanted an apology? Well, now you're getting the mother of all apologies. Catch it. Live on Social Media!"

Looking like a bald alien-angel, halo lit from behind, Keisha reached for Nichole's hands. "I misjudged you." The Supermodel choked on her own tears. There was a collective gasp from models, crew and Pablo alike. "I'm here for you. And to show my support honoring your dearly departed mother, I apologize from the bottom of my heart. I want you to know that I too have experienced extreme pain in my own life. But if you want to be a true *Model Muse,* you need to find a way to use that pain and overcome it with your strength and beauty." She turned her best side for the camera. Tears streamed down her face.

*Eye drops or onions?* Pablo wondered.

Nichole stood in stunned silence as Keisha dramatically

turned, speaking directly to the *Model Muse* cameras by breaking the fourth wall, and in turn, with the PA still live streaming, also spoke to her fans on Instagram Live.

"I'm here for *all* women suffering from breast cancer. God forbid I should ever experience what these women go through. I've made my living off these breasts and I can't imagine the pain of not having them."

Turning away from the camera, Keisha looked as if she was about to break down. Hand to forehead, she reached behind her and squeezed Nichole's hand one last time before swaying like a parade float towards the studio exit.

"Got it," the production assistant said. "I ended the Live Stream."

"Fab. Link it to all of my social media accounts," Keisha ordered. As the fire doors slammed behind her, the pink feather beaded train got trapped in the door jam. There was a loud rip of fabric and a shriek. The door opened a crack, and like a cat flipping its tail, the train flipped in the air. The door slammed with a thud. A spare pink tuft still stuck out.

"Will somebody hold this fucking door," Keisha screamed as she cracked it open again. Three PAs and a producer ran to help. The look on every crew member's face was unanimous: *Bat, shit, CRAZY!*

De La Renta broke the silence. "Now, that bald-headed bitch knows how to make an exit," he joked.

Pablo tried not to smile. He'd known the plan, of course, but didn't expect the cringe worthy remarks that came out of her mouth. The network would have to edit around that. Keisha had forced the network's hand. Live-streaming her apology had sealed the deal. The network couldn't shut the show down now, and they'd have to include her in the final edit of the segment. Batshit crazy, as a fox!

Broyce glanced over at the legal suits. They hesitantly nodded their approval. "Looks like you folks are back in business," he exclaimed. "Don't screw it up."

The crew erupted in cheers. In relief, Joe and Rachel slumped down in their chairs. Everyone was kissing and hugging each other. Dancing around the room in celebration. The models had no idea about the drama that had been happening around them. "Are you telling me, the show almost got cancelled?" Nichole asked Pablo.

"Of course not," he laughed. He was almost as good at lying as Harper.

With the segment in the can, Pablo rushed down the hallway toward Keisha's dressing room to congratulate her on her stupendous, though mildly disturbing, performance. The dressing room door had been left ajar to accommodate the dangling train of pink chiffon and feathers still partially in the hallway. From inside, he could hear Keisha's speakerphone crackling with static.

"Your call is being recorded by the California Institution for Women correctional facility. You are receiving a collect call from…"

*"Brenda Paris."*

"If you accept these charges, please press one now. If you…"

Keisha must have pressed the number one because he could hear her saying, "Mama? Is that you?"

"Hey, Miss Kiki. I'm checking in on you. You OK?" Her mother sounded truly concerned.

"I'm fine. Why?"

"Well, during recreation time last night I got to see *Celebrity-Buzz TV* and they were showing you having—"

"I'm fine, Mama. Fine."

There was an audible beep on the line to remind them that the call was being recorded.

"Miss Kiki, remember what they're tryin' to do to you. Don't *let* them steal your shine, and don't let *anyone* take you down, especially a man."

"Mama, I'm a grown woman. Not a little girl…"

"Don't sass me. You can open your legs and let them in, but don't *ever* let them in your heart. We're meant to be on top. You hear me? On TOP."

"Mama." Keisha's voice began to ascend the scales by octaves until she sounded like the scary child in *Poltergeist*, again.

There was a long crackly sounding pause before Brenda continued. "So tell me, you receive any exciting gifts lately?"

Keisha nervously answered. "I got a little something from *Kimoru*."

"Don't misplace my love."

"Yes, Mama."

"You being a good girl?"

"Always."

"That's my Miss Kiki."

"Don't you worry about a thing, Mama."

"I'm counting on you."

"Bye, Mama."

"Bye, Miss Kiki."

Keisha hung up the call and flicked off her phone.

Waiting a moment before he entered the room, Pablo watched Keisha reach into a wig box on the counter and withdraw a new, exceptionally long, redhaired, custom lace-front wig and secured it over her bald cap. He recognized the wavy locks at once. Keisha had stolen Nichole's hair.

She tossed her new hair back and forth, flirting with her image in the mirror. "*Fierce*," she said. And then she cackled like *Cruella de Vil* about to scalp some Dalmatians.

Pablo was horrified and backed away from the door. He now understood the Samuel Butler quote his mentor had often posted on his social feeds: *"Man is the only animal that can remain on friendly terms with the victims he intends to eat until he eats them."*

# REVELATIONS

## 4 DAYS TILL WRAP, SEASON SIX

**W**ITH PRODUCTION BACK in full swing, the crew was summoned to the studio with an unusually early call time of 5:30 a.m. to set up for the *second attempt* at filming the judging of the semi-final round. The network had decided to nix the failed attempt of the previous episode's elimination, and the *Kash-branded* beauty shoot, per Pablo's suggestion, instructing Joe Vong to edit the episode with the cancer awareness photoshoot and a *new* judging, a scene that did *not* have their Host's meltdown. Reality TV executives had no qualms about re-writing reality.

Pablo and De La Renta always arrived early at Silvercup so they could find the time to have breakfast together and, even with an early call, that was not different. Well, Pablo had breakfast. De La Renta usually had coffee and some "brown stuff." The hair/makeup artist did not go for anything green or plant based.

"Is Mother here yet?" Pablo greeted his friend.

"Would I be sitting here if she was? She thinks I can do her hair and makeup as fast as Usain Bolt can run the 100-meter race. But do I get an Olympic Gold Medal for doing it that fast? Hell no."

One day Keisha showed up expecting the works in fifteen minutes and De La Renta actually asked her what she'd prefer most, hair or makeup. He wasn't kidding. Keisha chose *"hair,"* and he threw her a tube of concealer and an old dried up Mac lipstick, as she walked out on set. Never fuck with your glam squad because they could make or break you. It was a sort of marriage and if things went south, things got ugly. Literally and figuratively.

"Can I buy you breakfast?" Pablo offered as they headed to the catering cart.

"I got my morning Joe." De La Renta slurped his latte.

Pablo ordered his protein fix–five soft boiled eggs and *two* bowls of oatmeal with sliced banana and nuts."

Seated at their favorite corner table, the cook brought over Pablo's order and served De La Renta some brown stuff.

"That bowl is for you." Pablo shoved the oatmeal under his nose.

"It looks like vomit."

"Well, it *is* brown," Pablo giggled.

De La Renta pulled out his iPhone and took a selfie gagging over the steaming porridge. *"Help. My friend is trying to kill me!"* his caption read, as he posted it on Instagram. "Frank," he yelled up to the truck, "can I get me some bacon and biscuits—hold the eggs. Extra salt, please."

"You can't put salt on bacon," Pablo ridiculed. "Bacon is nothing *but* salt."

De La Renta licked his lips.

When the cook shuffled back and plopped his food order and a plastic saltshaker in front of De La Renta, he complained, "Where's the *little girl with the white umbrella?*"

"This is all we got."

"This is fake salt." He kissed his teeth in disappointment.

"It'll still kill ya," Pablo said.

De La Renta licked his fingers, sloppy and happy. "Shit, this bacon is gooooood. I'm gettin' my life!"

"Don't you wanna at least try and eat healthy?"

"Nope." De La Renta crunched down on another piece of bacon and slathered a flaky southern biscuit with butter spread. "I'm good right here."

It was Pablo's turn to mock-vomit.

Where Keisha and Pablo were the Judy Garland and Mickey Rooney of Fashion, De La Renta and Pablo were the Laurel and Hardy of Glam. Pablo not only watched his diet, he exercised regularly; De La Renta was a junk food hound with an HBO habit.

"So what's goin' on, Boo?" De La Renta crunched on a second helping of crispy bacon. "You got that *Star-Spangled Banner* look in your eyes."

Pablo could barely contain his excitement. "Don't roll your eyes, but, you know it's been my dream to get a talk show, well—I said, don't roll your eyes—it's about to come to fruition."

"*Fru-who?* Girl, you and your Harvard dictionary vocabulary. Don't hurt what few brain cells I've got on salary this early in the morning."

Pablo stuffed a humongous spoonful of his oatmeal in his mouth. De La Renta mimicked him by licking the butter off his biscuit.

"Andy told me Keisha's been pitching a talk show that she and I will co-host together. Everything I've accomplished on *Model Muse* is finally gonna pay off."

De La Renta shook his head. "Girl, look at you. All wide-eyed and dumb as a bag of rocks. Haven't you learned, yet?" His southern accent softened the harsh truth—which was something De La Renta was accustomed to. His own mother dropped him off at his grandmamma's house when he was six years old with no warning or time to pack for the move. After she left, his mother didn't come back to visit for nearly eight months. A harsh reality to deal with as a child.

Pablo sighed. "This is gonna be different."

"Are you sure this is something you wanna do? With her? Really, Pablo?" De La Renta cautioned. "Need I remind you that Mother is out of her mind, and that you were afraid of her a day ago." His eyes practically bulged out of his head.

*Too much salt?* Pablo wondered. "Don't you think I'm good enough for Daytime Television?"

"Who said dat? Of course, I think you're good enough."

"Thank God," Pablo exhaled. If De La Renta didn't believe in him, he'd really be lost.

"You still don't get it, do you?" De La Renta shook a spare piece of bacon under Pablo's nose. "She's not gonna let you stand out on your own. Mama don't share and she don't play well with others."

"You've got her all wrong. This time—"

"Lemme break it all down for you," De La Renta leaned in. "Keisha's one of those Supermodels who's *actually* done something. She can *slay* a magazine cover, launch a TV show, become the voice for broke-down bitches all around the world—"

"I know that. She'll forever be a legend," Pablo interrupted.

"Can I finish? *Shit*." De La Renta was annoyed now. "You

really think she's all about, *Girl power, Black women, Fat chicks?* She could actually give *two shits* about any of those peeps. It's all about her. No one else."

"You think?"

"I know," De La Renta snapped. "Pablo, she's only gonna let you stand in her shadow. That's it. And as my grandmamma always says, 'If you don't stand for somethin' you'll fall for everything.'"

"This talk show will be a game changer. Even Broyce recognizes that I'm uber-important to the show."

"Broyce, I trust." De La Renta made a face. "Miss K-a, dollar sign-h, *I-got-a-brand-new-red-haired-wig,* I don't."

Harper and Rachel were walking across the parking lot to where the two friends were in heated debate and sat down.

"Hey, guys."

"Are you aware of some creative editing going on around here?" De La Renta asked the women and Pablo. "Hashtag just saying."

Pablo made a face. "But I rescued *Model Muse* and kept it from being cancelled."

The women nodded in agreement.

"And? How'd that work out?" He licked his bacon. "In *her* favor, that's how."

More often than not, De La Renta's words bore the hard truth Pablo didn't want to hear, but their friendship meant everything to him. No matter what went down, he knew De La Renta would always be by his side. He was one of the good ones; not a fair-weather friend, but a real one. The kind who knew how to get out and push when things got rough, unless, of course, it meant pushing an actual car. That's just how De La Renta was made. Bless him.

Pablo cleared his plate and came back to the table to gather his belongings. "I hear you. But I have to follow my dream."

De La Renta folded his hands in prayer and bowed his head. "Go with God. And watch your back."

Surprise. The second shoot of the semi-final judging round ran late. Surprise Two. The real drama wasn't on camera or live streamed. The judges revolted. It seemed Mason Hughes had suddenly grown a set of balls and walked off set. Followed by Sasha and Miss Thing. It was *Mutiny on the Bounty* without Marlon Brando at the helm. The problem was Nichole had been the one on the chopping block for the previous episode, but since the new photoshoot had been dedicated to her mother, well, they were now stuck with a gorgeous, chisel faced bald girl. Despite what Keisha kept trying to manipulate, the network could not and did not want to dethrone the new fresh face of cancer awareness. From the giant sixteen-panel LED wall, the group image from Pablo's photoshoot revealed four gorgeous bald models looking down like arch-angels on the last day of judgment upon Miss Thing, Mason and Sasha. It was unnerving. Sort of like going to the ape house at the zoo and realizing the humans are actually on display for the apes.

Elyssa looked incredible, so she was also safe. Her inked arms and legs created the body painting effect that Shiseido cosmetics had tried to corner the market with back in the 1980s. Beth and Kayla were the final two on the chopping block. The fix had always been for season six to announce the first plus-sized model. Keisha, dealing with her own weight problems, entered stage left as the judges were debating the girls' merits. Busting through a canary yellow silk and Guipure lace frock, her favorite color, Keisha backed the network's choice. Beth was to be this season's *Model Muse*. The judges were supposed to fall in line.

Mason's critique of Beth was absolute. "There was not a

good photo of her in the bunch," he snorted. "She's barely giving me any neck."

"That's 'cause she don't have a neck to begin with," Miss Thing blurted. "I agree with Mason. I don't think she's *Model Muse* material."

And then there was Kayla. For all of her slutty tricks, Andy included, she really *did* look like a superstar in the group photo.

"The energy Kayla's bringing to this photograph reminds me of a younger, thinner you, Keisha," Sasha said with a wicked little half smirk.

"Oooooooo." Miss Thing snapped his fingers. "Leave *Big Bird* alone."

Of course, all of their arguments were going straight to the cutting room floor. Whenever any of the judges tried to stick a dagger in Keisha's back, she just looked over at Joe Vong, who whispered "cut" to Rachel and the fix was in.

"Beth deserves a fighting chance since she represents all plus-sized women," Keisha argued. None of the judges knew Beth was in fact to win, as senior producers and Pablo kept "*The Ringer*" secret. Stroking their egos and making them believe *they* made their own choices had become a weekly ritual, but then Mason stood up and walked out.

"Why pretend you need us, Keisha? This is all your reality anyway," he said with a dramatic gesture.

"I'm with Mason." Sasha stood up, one hand on her open water bottle, the other on her bag. She tripped on her purse strap, spilled her wine, and nearly did a face plant into Miss Thing's crotch.

Miss Thing screamed.

"It's not like I doused you with acid," Sasha slurred at him.

"Girl, you nearly crushed my family jewels."

"Honey, those aren't even *semi-precious* stones." She sauntered off after Mason.

It was a dramatic but unnecessary mutiny, which added another hour to the clock. Everyone was used to overtime by now and Pablo was beginning to think he'd be able to pay off his mortgage early if the delays continued into Season Seven. Coercing the defectors back to set took a while. Harper, always up for a difficult task, got it done and finally had everyone in line behind axing Kayla, if only because of the way the elastic on her panties kept slipping to her ankles whenever a man was near.

Pablo sat and watched the chaos from the safety of the control room with Rachel all night. He wanted zilch to do with the foul energy soaring around the studio. Nothing was going to ruin his day. He only had his future with Keisha to look forward to and their talk show together.

His phone vibrated in his pocket, and his mother's face appeared. "Hi Mom," he whispered. "Just a sec, I've gotta get to a quiet area." He scampered out of the control room and out the fire doors, where he leaned against the wall. "How are you?"

"Just fine, Sweetheart. I've just been thinking about you a lot and you know, mother's intuition, worried. Are you okay?"

"I'm great, Mom."

"That's a relief. I must just be getting old and senile."

"Never. You look fab for being thirty-nine *and holding*," he chuckled.

"Bless you. I do love my annual fortieth birthdays."

"I was actually going to call you. I have some awesome news."

"Really?"

"Keisha and I are gonna have a talk show together."

"You mean like *Kelly and Ryan*, well, whoever Kelly's *flavor* of the month is?"

"Shady, Mom. No more lunches with De La Renta when you come in town." They both laughed.

"Oh, sweetheart, this is all wonderful news. Everything you've ever wanted is finally coming to fruition."

He had to chuckle at the word *"fruition"*—De La Renta didn't know that Pablo's Harvard dictionary was none other than his mother—Helena Michaels.

"Please be careful, though." She sounded concerned. "I saw Keisha on *Good Morning America* the other day, and something's not quite right. You can see it in her eyes."

Pablo let out a heavy sigh. "Keisha's just lonely, Mom. And she's desperately trying to keep herself relevant."

Out the corner of his eye, Pablo thought he saw a sliver of yellow fabric slip through the fire door to his right. It couldn't be *her*; weren't they still filming?

"Listen, Mom, I gotta go. We're shooting today. I'll call you later."

"Whenever you can. I just had to know my boy was okay. Love you, Sweetheart."

"Love you too, Mom."

He hung up the phone and sighed happily, then turned to head back into the mayhem. Two steps, and he got a text message. Bing.

**I.C.E. TEXT:** You've been on my mind. Just wanted to reach out and remind you that you're BEYOND talented and generous. Innocence is dangerous in this biz. Take off your blinders. KK's not a leader, she's a usurper. Don't let anyone define you. Real success comes when you find faith in who you are. You've got nothing to prove to anyone. xx

It was like I.C.E. and his mother were psychically communicating or something. Pablo walked back into the control room just as Rachel was shouting into her IFB. "Hey, guys, Mike, Jesse, make sure you keep Kayla long enough in her exit OTF. We need an actual shot of her crying, for once."

"You guys wrapped already?" Pablo asked.

Rachel pulled off her headphones. "Yup. Five minutes ago." She stood up to walk out of the room. "You gonna hang out here much longer? I'm heading down to the floor. I need to show Harper what's needed for tomorrow's teach and challenge."

"I'm just waiting for Keisha."

"Cool. Turn out the lights when you leave." Rachel kissed his cheek and disappeared.

Pablo took a moment, looking around the room. Keisha's mic was pushing the red zone on the sound board. What was wrong now? He leaned forward and raised her mic level so he could hear her audio over the loudspeakers.

"Andy, I've told you how many times? You won't, no, can't fuck up my shit. This has got to stop." Her low demonic voice boomed across the room. Pablo quickly lowered the levels to avoid hurting his own ears.

"You better be glad I took care of things tonight. What were you thinking? Fucking Kayla? Have you even *heard* of the Me Too movement?"

Pablo's heart jumped into his throat. He knew where she was going and wondered if she was going to fire him or just emasculate him?

Andy didn't even try to defend himself. "I've convinced Netflix to ink a deal with Kashing In Productions for *The Keisha & Pablo Show*, worldwide rights. They love what you bring as a team, onscreen chemistry, fashion know-how, wit. Pablo's great sense of timing and humor offsets your serious, quirky side."

"Mr. Andy," Keisha's voice register had risen to something sounding more innocent, more conniving, "Miss Keisha has decided she wants her *own* talk show."

Pablo's throat stretched down into his stomach. He gagged. Felt physically ill.

"Everyone loves little Pablo but they forget," her voice dropped two octaves, "I MADE HIM! *Model Muse* is *my* fucking show. I created it. It was my idea. All he does is ride around on *my* coat tails. And I'll be damned if some throwaway bi-racial baby is gonna crawl outta the gutter and steal my shine. I don't need Pablo Michaels and neither does Netflix."

## SCRIPT CHANGE

S ILENCE. PABLO'S HEART began to race out of control.
"Well," Andy cleared his throat, "we gotta problem then."
"What?"

"I told the kid, last night, you were shopping a talk show for both of you. I needed him to get your head back on straight."

"Fuck." Keisha's voice reverberated over the control room speakers. "Does he know it's been picked up by Netflix yet?"

"No."

"Good. Don't say anything to Pablo, and let's work on the down-low."

"But I sold the concept on—"

"You'll make *The Keisha Kash Show* happen Mr. Andy," she said, with her voice crawling into creepy land. "And when it announces, we'll just tell him that Netflix wanted me as a solo host. He'll believe anything, and it'll be too late anyhow."

"Done."

There was a pause. A shuffle.

"I need you to destroy this…"

"Is that blood?" Andy asked.

"No more questions!" She screamed.

"Sorry."

Andy apologizing? Pablo couldn't believe his ears.

"If you don't get rid of this, my has-been *mother* will get outta prison."

"Your mother's not a good look for you right now."

"My mother's *never* been a good look for me."

"Got it. So what if I—"

Loud, high-pitched feedback echoed from the speakers hanging above the sound board. Pablo's eardrums rang.

"Ah, shit, my mic is still…" Keisha's voice went mute.

Pablo sat in the sudden silence of the control room. The all too familiar sensation of being discarded rushed over him. Alone. Betrayed. Abandoned. He knew these feelings well. De La Renta had been right. He'd spent his entire life seeing the best in people and subsequently placed too much faith in those who'd ultimately let him down. For years he'd gotten up and moved on, despite the hole in his soul. Now, Pablo wanted to crawl under a rock and curl up into a fetal position. Grabbing his jean jacket, he pushed through the big metal door of the control room and fled the studio. He would never eat *Dulce de Leche* again.

*　　*　　*

Everything was blindingly white. Pablo couldn't see anything. He was frightened. Visually impaired. He shut his eyes tightly and covered them with his trembling hands.

"Nurse Marge," a voice said. "Take him…she doesn't even want to hold him for minute."

Pablo removed his hands and cautiously opened his eyes. It was still bright, but through the haze he could see two nurses talking to each other standing near a hospital doorway. A large retro dial clock on the wall read, one-minute past twelve. It must be just past noon, he thought. Slowly things came into focus. The brightness wasn't nearly as harsh, but everything seemed surreal. The heavyset nurse, Marge, held the baby as she walked down the hall. Pablo followed her past the equipment stacked up alongside the passage. An orderly almost bumped into him without saying, excuse me. How rude.

The nurse abruptly changed direction and headed towards a nursery. She turned her back to the double doors and used her behind to pop open the entry. She made no eye contact with Pablo, even though they were nearly face to face. He followed her in the room and watched as she unwrapped the newborn child and carefully placed him on a padded counter. She turned the water on in a nearby sink, ran water over a washcloth, but still had not acknowledged Pablo's presence. He had the eeriest feeling about the room. It looked strange. Old. Out-dated. Ethereal.

"Time to clean you up, little one." She lifted the tiny arm. The baby wailed at the immediate shock of wet against his skin. Pablo felt a sting of pain at the sudden sound of the child's scream. His tiny lungs were so strong. "Shhhhh, you're OK. It's OK. It's nice and warm." The baby boy calmed to the sound of her soothing voice.

"Cooo…" The baby smiled, or was that gas? Pablo almost laughed.

"Until we find you a family, I'll call you David." She turned and reached for something that Pablo couldn't quite see and when she finally moved back to the child, he could see Marge fastening a name tag around the little boy's ankle. It simply had *David* written on it in big block letters with a barcode underneath. No last name. That was all that identified him. A sudden jolt of anxiety coursed through Pablo's body. Panicked, he whipped his head around. There was no one standing at the nursery window loving this newborn baby from afar. His eyes filled with tears.

"Argh." Pablo bolted upright. He was hot. Lost. Abandoned. His heart raced. He looked around at the faint shadows that were morphing into the familiar contours of the bedroom of his Seventh Avenue apartment. This same dream—or was it a nightmare?—had haunted him for years until Keisha came into his life, becoming a part of his family. Now it was back tormenting him, again. Pablo flopped back on his bed, backhanding the wetness on his cheek and closed his eyes. Emotionally drained, he stared up at the ceiling and tried to focus on his breathing, so he could stop his mind from churning round and round.

## 3 DAYS TILL WRAP, SEASON SIX

A few short hours later, leaning against the headboard of his bed, Pablo gazed out at the Manhattan skyline from his 15th story apartment window. Even One World Trade Center looked alone. He had tapped snooze on his iPhone alarm several times already. He wasn't expected to be on the set today, anyway. Pablo wasn't sure he would ever go back. Through a slit in the drapes, a thin beam of sunlight touched his dark mood. Everything he'd accomplished, everything he'd created from his career to his apartment seemed pointless now.

"Hey *Siri*, what time is it?"

"It's 9:26 a.m. Good Morning." Pablo hated that his iPhone was having a better day than him already. He felt like he'd been awake the entire night. Maybe he should have a pajama day and just stay in bed, but he had to eat something. Groaning as he got up, he looked at himself in his floor length Philippe Starck Caadre mirror.

"Pathetic." Padding barefoot across the whitewashed oak floors of the living room, he considered making a cup of loose-leaf herbal tea but decided it was too much work. He didn't feel like drinking or eating. His body felt encased in the concrete of a broken heart.

"Hey *Siri*, turn on the lights."

Slowly, a glow rose from around all his furniture, and kitchen cabinets.

"Hey *Siri*, play *On The Nature of Daylight* by Max Richter."

The robotic sounding voice confirmed, "On The Nature of Daylight by Max Richter Orchestra and Lorenz Dangle now playing." Nothing better suited the sorrow and grief of the human experience, and the sense that there's a purpose, or at least a grandeur to life, than the wailing of Richter's melancholy music. It set the mood for Pablo's forlorn day.

Yesterday, he thought he had it all. His dream of having a talk show had been just a handshake away. Now he had nothing, not even the friendship he'd believed in and done so much for. Keisha had robbed him of it all. His job was to create fantasies and bring dreams to life, but his own dreams felt like a distant destination he would never now reach. The depth of love and acceptance he craved had left him. How could he go on in a business that made him feel so rejected? The expectations he had of *Pablo Michaels* versus the reality of who he *really* was would never measure up.

He wanted to be so much more than a creative director on a model competition show. He wanted to do something important in the world he loved; share his insights on life, art, spirituality. He wanted to connect with others, learn about their passions, what they liked to read, listen to, and eat. He wanted others to connect with him too, and see beyond the preconceived stereotype of who he appeared to be; the glossy, perfect on camera personality, with silver grey hair and eyes. He felt trapped by the price of fame that he was only now learning he had to pay.

Keisha's hate-filled rant ran on a loop in his head. *I made him. Throwaway bi-racial baby. I made him. Throwaway...* She made me. Tears welled up in his eyes. Why did he believe her in the first place? Because it was she who'd helped him believe in himself, and convinced him their relationship was special. Despite all the warnings, the indications that she couldn't be trusted, he'd believed her.

Pablo pressed the *Double latte* button on his Miele coffee machine. Waiting for the milk to steam, he reached for his iPhone and begrudgingly unlocked it. A flurry of texts and email alerts popped up on his home screen notification center, but only one message caught his attention.

**I.C.E. TEXT:** I never heard back from you yesterday. You ok? I hope you didn't think I was being too pushy. I never meant to offend. Sorry. You're still on my mind, so hit me up when you get a min. xo

Pablo's fingers flew across the screen, typing a quick response.

**Pablo TEXT:** No! Soooooo much going on and I didn't get a chance to write back. Your words of encouragement are everything to me!!! You've been right all along! Last night I overheard KK speaking to her manager...she said horrific things about me. Can't deal. She's a beast! Now I can't sleep. Don't know how I can walk back on set. Ever!

Pablo pressed send and grabbed the latte like his life depended on it. His iPhone vibrated with an immediate response.

**I.C.E. TEXT:** I'm so sorry. This has been my fear all along. You've worked hard learning to trust people, don't let her derail you from your path.

**Pablo TEXT:** She destroys anyone who challenges her. Remember her old assistant? He couldn't find work for 6 months. I'm fucked! ☹

**I.C.E. TEXT:** Reacting to her from an emotional level will only put you out in the cold. You're smart. Take the high road.

**Pablo TEXT:** How?

**I.C.E. TEXT:** Go back to work and give an Oscar Award winning performance, like she's been giving you. Play the game but don't fall for the illusion. Nothing is worth sacrificing your integrity. xo

Why was life so complicated? Pablo threw his phone on the couch and curled up in the corner of the sofa with both hands clasped around his latte. "Fuuuuuck!" he screamed. Like De La Renta, he was sick and tired of being *sick and tired*. He felt so manipulated, so played. Carelessly and without much thought, he fired off an impetuous message in response to his mentor.

**Pablo TEXT:** I CANNOT let her walk all over me like this! I hear what you're saying…but I swore I wouldn't let her bully me.

**I.C.E. TEXT:** DON'T DO SOMETHING YOU'LL REGRET LATER!

A flashing ellipsis alerted him that I.C.E. was writing more. Pablo sipped his latte, waiting impatiently for the long message to finally appear.

**I.C.E. TEXT:** Transcend her tyranny and oppression. Taking a stand for yourself is a good thing. But do NOT stoop to her level. It's your time…don't forget that! Case in point. I had the opportunity to work with Iyanla Vanzant on the Oprah show years back and we became close. Her wisdom and ability to see the error of her own ways is always an inspiration to me. She uses her gifts to help everyone she can. Read her book, "Acts of Faith." Here's one of my favorite quotes from it…

Pablo stared at his screen, waiting to see the quoted text come through, and within seconds it popped up.

**I.C.E. TEXT:** "A wise soldier knows never to draw his sword unless he is ready, able and willing to do battle. A fool draws his sword aimlessly and is prone to cut himself to death."

Pablo walked over to the plate glass window on the far side of his living room. Leaning his forehead against the glass with his hands pressed alongside him, he looked like he was about to leap out across Manhattan in a swan dive. Below him was a sea of yellow cabs fighting their way down Seventh Avenue. A circle of white condensation formed on the window, a ghost of his former self, or a new, self-born phoenix rising from the ashes? Abruptly, Pablo pulled back and looked at the expanse before him. This was his world. He owned it. His reflection smiled at him. "Let's do this."

# DUCK FACE

THE CAMERAS WERE already rolling when Nichole, Elyssa and Beth filed into the newly transformed studio at Highline Stages. Studio C was set to look like some secret headquarters in a DC Comics film. Gigantic old-fashioned computers, circa 1960s, lined the makeshift walls; each monitor housed an LED screen with Keisha's face on it. Her expression alternated from soft and relaxed to the strained pout, cheek sucking visage of *Duck Face*. Rachel motioned the models towards their taped X marks on the floor.

Bang.

The lights went out.

As if on cue, the girls screamed.

Blue and yellow computer lights began to blink madly, illuminating the room. Fade Up: purple LEDs. Keisha stood statuesquely on a glass and steel platform, wearing a silver spandex catsuit. As she turned her back to the cameras, a long silver cape unfurled with the hand stitched logo of a duck, initials "D.F." on the back. Reality TV 101–use crazy visuals to keep viewers watching. But jumping the shark could be inevitable. Clearly this was the kind of material late night TV Hosts dreamt of using in their opening monologues.

Whipping her extra-long, newly woven wig of red hair, Keisha glared down on the girls. She looked like she had just eaten a lemon. "I'm Supermodel Duck Face."

"What, in hell?" Pablo nearly bust a gut trying to keep from laughing. The entire camera crew, producers, ADs, PAs, even Harper struggled to refrain from laughing out loud. The models had it much worse. The smirks on their faces couldn't be retouched out in post.

"I'm here to teach you how to conquer the lens of any camera, with the power of the Duucckkkk Faaaaccccceeeee." Keisha's last words echoed across the studio.

"Is *this* today's teach?" Beth leaned over to Elyssa and muttered under her breath.

"Maybe she's punking us," Elyssa whispered back.

"Nobody even does the *Duck Face* anymore," Nichole added.

Keisha's voice roared like an auto-tuned lion. "Now, you three must go behind my face recognition supercomputer and change into your own power Duck Face suits." She waved her hands in front of her face and whispered, "Be back here in a super-flash *Model Muse* moment."

"Reset for Duck Face challenge." Rachel's shrill voice pierced the blackness.

Nichole stopped and stared at Keisha's head before joining the others. As the three model finalists moved rather reluctantly around the flimsy set wall, a piece of gaffer tape broke free and an iPad fell off the ridiculous replica of HAL 9000 from *2001: A Space Odyssey.* Pablo dropped his head in his hand. All his hard work trying to get this show to be taken seriously and now this?

"Can someone walkie for the scenic gal and get this fixed immediately?" Rachel begged.

"Copy that," a PA confirmed.

"Harper?" Keisha shielded her eyes from the bright lights.

"So sorry. Right here." Harper flew in from the shadows, panting and apologizing for nothing at all. "What can I do for you?"

Pablo watched the young producer with pity, and then realized he himself had been just as apologetic and subservient in the past.

"Email my trademark attorney. I want the copyright on *Super-flash Model Muse Moment.*" Keisha took the perspiring producer's face in her hands. "Make sure he puts it through today, so we can start using it on social ASAP."

"Got it. I'll make sure to add this to the list of terms for all on-camera talent to use when addressing the girls too."

"Fierce." She snapped her fingers. "You have my phone?"

"I sure do, *Darlin'...*" Harper chimed. Pablo nearly threw up. "Here you go. And, I have some water with a *yellow* straw for ya."

"I don't know what I'd do without you," Keisha fussed.

Blushing at the rare compliment, Harper hiked up her sagging jeans and ran back into the shadows where she belonged. Keisha didn't move from her Plexiglass platform of honor. Clicking away on her phone, she ignored the crew as they reset. She seemed oblivious to the fact that Pablo hadn't said hello to her, but then she probably didn't even know he was there. He'd snuck into video village and was hiding there with De La Renta, Joe, and Rachel.

Thrusting the studio door open Andy Levenkron strolled in, chatting away to some underling listening on the other end of his white AirPods.

"Hey, Boo." Keisha waved. Andy waved back and strutted across the studio, double tapping his AirPods to hang up the call.

Joe Vong's face was redder than usual as he stamped up to Keisha's manager. "Where have you been, Levenkron? This is a fucking joke. It'll ruin the show. You're supposed to be her fucking manager. Manage her and stop this."

"Stop Keisha?" Andy settled on one of the cast couches and smiled up at Vong. "We just closed on a huge deal with Apple for her new Duck Face App. You're gonna be hearing *'Duck Face'* from everyone this season and you can be sure it'll go viral."

Scrolling through Instagram, De La Renta muttered to Pablo, *"Duck Face* is about as stupid as that *Smize* crap. I tell ya, these Supermodels think they're all that and a bag of Doritos. Ain't nothin' new."

"She should have the initials *'TB'* on that cape," Pablo sneered.

The glam guru looked puzzled.

Pablo mouthed the words, *'The Bitch.'*

"Watch that tone, missy! Don't bite *my* head off just because you and Mother fell out."

Pablo looked reluctant to continue. "I haven't even told you what happened..."

"And I don't wanna know." De La Renta held up his hands in the air, then leaned over and whispered real low, "Not here, later."

Rachel popped two Xanax in her mouth and closed the bottle. "We've got bigger problems than this *Teach* right now." She pointed to her iPhone. "You guys been reading the production group chat? Check the latest update on our newest Bogie." A long screed from the associate producer that governed the axed contestants, locked up in the hotel, divulged the indiscretions Kayla had with Keisha's manager. Kayla was planning on nailing the show, the network and Keisha. But she was offering the producers a deal.

"I may have gone to Harvard," one of the producers said, "but even I can't write our way out of this one."

"You fucked one of our models?" Joe was in a dysmorphic rage and hissed at the self-satisfied manager, busily planning a viral Duck Face App takeover. "Are you fucking nuts?"

Andy was dazed and confused. "What's the problem?"

"Kayla claims she got *gonorrhea* from you and is threatening to go public with an exclusive on TMZ if we don't make her the winner this season."

"She could've gotten gonorrhea from Bill, for Christ's sake."

"You fucked her too?" Joe turned and screamed at Bill.

"Only oral," Bill assured him. "And I don't have STDs."

"Anymore," De La Renta scoffed.

"All she needs is to accuse you. It doesn't matter if it's true or not, which you both have just assured me it is." Joe nervously began pacing around the studio, running his hands through his thinning jet-black hair and exposing his all-white, one-inch roots. "At least on *OFFICERZ* the crew obeyed the law."

"Where are we with finding dirt on her," Rachel fired.

"Close," a producer replied. "We still need to follow up on a—"

"You knew about this, Rachel?" Joe yelled.

"Hell no. This Andy thing is news to me."

It wasn't news to Pablo, but instead he said, "Why don't you just throw her back into the competition during the final runway challenge as a surprise twist?" He didn't know what else to say; he was trying to protect the show. "And she can win."

De La Renta nodded in agreement. "*Egg-zackly.* In the past y'all have randomly eliminated two girls in one episode, why not throw a bitch back in and change it up? The kids at home watching will *liiiiiiive* when the other models see Kayla and gag."

"That might actually work." Rachel looked cautiously optimistic. "We could stage the scene with Keisha backstage announcing Kayla's return, right before the runway segment. It'll raise the stakes for the finale."

"Ummm, excuse me, white lady? Ain't that what Pablo and I just said?"

Rachel looked embarrassed.

"Just make it work," Joe growled at the two lotharios. "You two had better hope to God Keisha doesn't find out about your indiscretions, or you'll be the ones on camera going to the doctor for an HIV test."

Pablo's phone vibrated. *Mommy Dearest* was on the screen. He looked up at Keisha, peering from the darkness that surrounded her. She had her phone pressed to her ear now. Pablo showed De La Renta his glowing iPhone.

"Nope," he snapped. "I don't wanna fuck with *either* of you. I'm out!" De La Renta then got up and made his way to the craft service table.

Pablo let his phone go to voicemail. He had nothing to say to her, yet.

"Ugh, can we hurry up?" Keisha barked.

"Girls almost ready," a PA yelled.

Pablo's phone vibrated, again. This time a text message popped up.

**Broyce TEXT:** 911! Can you be red carpet ready tomorrow night?

**Pablo TEXT:** I'm filming the final runway challenge. Why?

**Broyce TEXT:** I can get you out of shooting MM for the night, but keep between us.

**Pablo TEXT:** Done.

**Broyce TEXT:** I got you a huge gig. A producer is going to call you shortly. And no need to thank me, I owe you one!

**Pablo TEXT:** Intrigued!! ☺

# RELIABLE SOURCES

## CALIFORNIA INSTITUTION FOR WOMEN, CHINO

9 11#, FOLLOWED BY a phone number, has a whole other meaning in a state prison. So, when a guard slipped the note to Brenda Paris, she knew she had to act and act fast. Payment for the special delivery was a *Model Muse* sweatshirt with Keisha's authentic signature on it.

"For my niece," the guard mumbled.

"Yeah, right."

Brenda had been selling *Model Muse* swag to inmates and guards ever since the show had gone viral. It had become every felon's favorite reality show, after *Judge Judy*. It was a good business that kept her in Juul Vapes and raised her profile among the more hardened criminals, especially the Mama of them all—Aunt Peggy, the only inmate with the a cell phone.

A jewel thief is one thing. A murderer is something else. Aunt Peggy kept her rap sheet fairly quiet, but the huge garish scar on her face and the torn earlobe inspired gossip and respect, if not outright fear. Holding court in her private cell, Aunt Peggy had her own TV, a desk neatly piled with the latest Michael Connelly and James Patterson novels, and two bookcases of beauty supplies that rivaled the inventory of any black hair salon on the Southside. It cost a hefty price to make an unmonitored call, but if Aunt Peggy liked you, there was a cell to be had at a price. Brenda's price was Keisha.

"If it ain't Madison Avenue." Aunt Peggy's face clouded over at the sight of Brenda. "You got nerve showin' your face in here after that shit swag you passed last month."

"I didn't know it was subpar quality. I told Keisha never to send me that crap again."

"Not so tight." Aunt Peggy swatted at the girls adding cornrows to her scalp. "Stop watchin' *Judge Judy* and pay attention to my head."

"Sorry, Aunt Peggy," the young inmate groveled as Judge Judy passed sentence. *"If it weren't for morons like you in the world, I wouldn't have a job."*

"That stuck up Supermodel," she patted the hairstylist's hand, "thinks her shit don't stink."

Brenda nodded in agreement. Like Keisha, you had to agree with everything that came out of Aunt Peggy's mouth or she wouldn't grant any favors.

"Aunt Peggy couldn't stop laughing when she went craycray on that bald, white chick the other day." The old murderess showed her hair crew the animated meme of Keisha's rant on Facebook. Through the cracked screen of the old iPhone 6, the tagline read: *When Monday's gotcha looking like...*

The three laughed hysterically.

"I have a 911," Brenda said.

Peggy spit out a wad of chewing tobacco into her waste-basket. "Yo, Keisha Kash is one stuck up bitch who don't love her mama. You don't need to run and fix her 911 crisis call."

"It's not from her." Brenda didn't know who it was from, in actual fact. The number wasn't familiar to her. She stooped over and wiped up the tobacco juice that Aunt Peggy had spat across the floor with the cuff of her sweatshirt. She would've kissed her feet if it helped.

"Miss Madison Avenue, Aunt Peggy feels for you. Your kids don't deserve a mother like you. Do they?" She turned to her yes-girls.

"Dat's right, Aunt Peggy. That Superbitch don't love her mama."

"Kind of money she makes. What you still doin' in the joint? She could've gotten you the best lawyer in America. Hell, she could fuck him and not have to pay his fee. Instead, she leaves you here to rot with her leftover swag scraps."

"I'm gonna get out," Brenda said. "And when I do, I'll be sending you a big fat care package of everything you like."

"Honey, you can't fit what I like in a box." Aunt Peggy slapped the ass of one of her girls. "Forty. Cash, for one minute. And you call from here where I can listen. Make sure this ain't no fix-up with the guards."

Brenda handed over the cash and a signed T-shirt.

"Keep that cheap shit swag." Aunt Peggy swiftly chucked her iPhone at Brenda's head. Brenda caught it midair.

"Nice catch."

Brenda pulled the scrap of paper from her pocket and dialed the unfamiliar New York 917 number.

"This is Brenda Paris." She listened for a brief second. "Wait, your voice, is this *Pablo Michaels*?"

"You talkin' to Pablo?" one of the girls squealed. "I love me some of that silver fox."

Brenda held her finger over her mouth for quiet. "I literally have less than a minute to talk on this secure line."

All three inmates were tuned into what Brenda was saying. Tension tightened the room.

"Wait. What? How could you possibly know about that?" There was a long pause. "She got the message then…"

Aunt Peggy sat up a bit taller now. She rubbed her fingers together and tapped her finger on the faux Rolex wrapped around her wrist. "Time's a wastin'. Got another forty?"

Brenda, intently listening, nodded her head then blurted, "She what?"

"Show me, Madison Avenue, or the price goes up."

Brenda rummaged around in her pocket and turned up several singles and a five-dollar bill. She tossed the money into Aunt Peggy's fat hands.

"That's 19 bucks." Peggy counted through the bills. Her scowl then turned into a grin. "I'll be nice and give you a discount. Another 30 seconds, with a few on the house."

Brenda gave a nervous quick smile, but focused more on the call. "I don't understand? She was wearing a red wig and doing what with the blood vial?"

"I knew it. Weave, my ass." Aunt Peggy snapped her fingers.

"Sorry, I can hardly hear you—you're breaking up." Brenda was frustrated. "She destroyed it? That was evidence."

"She destroys *lives* for a living," Peggy roared. Her minions joined in and cackled along with her.

"Say what?" Brenda sounded like she was being blindsided by a semi-truck. "You gotta get me outta here," she pleaded. "I can help you get her in line, but I can't do anything from jail." Looking at the duration of the call—1 minute, 28 seconds—she abruptly tapped the red icon, ending the conversation, and tossed the phone back to Aunt Peggy.

Befuddled, Brenda stood with her jaw clenched, and the normally congenial woman's face began to morph like Bruce Banner into *The Hulk*. "That FUCKING bitch better ditch her wig, and learn how to basket weave in Tibet, because when I get outta here, *she's* a fucking wrap."

"Ooooo, don't fuck with your mama." Aunt Peggy clapped her hands and screeched with delight.

Pablo sat back with a certain satisfaction. Fight fire with fire.

# LIVE TV'S THE BITCH

## 2 DAYS TILL WRAP, SEASON SIX

CENTRAL PARK WAS partially in bloom. Pink blossoms carpeted the paths. Birds were singing. Spring in New York was when the city was most magical and added to the enchantment the models would experience. Today, they were on a Cinderella style carriage ride through the park. It was times like this, however short lived, that made the reality of their borrowed lives worthwhile, and was a relief from their grueling schedule. Wearing hoodies covering their faces, the three model finalists were slipped through the back entrance of Tavern On The Green, while a pre-announced press op and social media lovefest was in full hoopla out front, under the restaurant's faded red awnings.

Posing for journalists, Keisha and the judges smiled and took selfies with shrieking fans gathered ten deep for the rare public, group appearance. Ideally nestled amongst mature oaks and maples in a cul-de-sac at 67th Street and Central Park West, the world-famous restaurant was the perfect Manhattan location to film the new segment that Keisha had created for the finale episode. She planned to use it in future seasons, as well. It was important to have a recap of all lessons the contestants had experienced together and for the judges, especially Keisha, to share their wisdom and advice with their models—muse or not. It also would allow the Supermodel host to pontificate about everything she'd done for the final three. Keisha was all about product placement—she was the product; her show was the placement.

The network had negotiated its deal with Tavern On The Green—free meals and shooting venue, in exchange for on air placement. And the on-camera talent were expected to do their due diligence and make an appearance to help promote the classic tourist attraction as a celebrity hot spot. In truth, no star (A-list or Z) would be caught dead eating at Tavern On The Green, unless it was written into their contract. The food was great but it wasn't trendy anymore, and hadn't been for thirty years. For one thing, they didn't serve BBQ ribs and corn bread. It was too bad for Keisha that Virgil's didn't have the right aesthetic or enough space to shoot the sentimental scene.

"I wonder how much the restaurant is paying for this airtime?" Miss Thing asked. "Keisha *never* does this shit."

"Oh, she's getting her cut *and* a free meal." Sasha waved to their adoring crowd. "She's in heaven." They clinked their heads together like champagne glasses and smiled for the fans.

Pablo held back, smiling semi-demurely and checking his watch every two minutes. He felt nauseous standing with his arm around Keisha's waist, but the network had requested the two of them stand as a pair, and slightly apart from the judges, so fans and paparazzi could snap double shots of them alone. Judy Garland and Mickey Rooney of Fashion, the network's new "dream team."

Keisha whispered to Pablo like a ventriloquist, holding the perfect Supermodel smile. "What's wrong with you?"

"I'm just afraid I'm gonna be late, that's all," he said.

"Late for what? First, you don't return my calls and *now* you're acting all strange?"

*I'm not acting strange you sad, lonely, idiosyncratic— you'll have to look that one up—backstabber.* "Doctor's appointment. I don't feel good. It might be flu."

"Ewww." Keisha took a step away from him. "You can't be sick. You have the final runway show to produce and host later tonight."

"I know." He lied, "I was trying to head over to my doctor and—"

"That's it, everyone," Keisha interrupted, barking at the crowd. "Harper."

"Sorry. Right here…Behind you."

"Get me some antibacterial wipes. Pablo's sick." The germophobic Supermodel strutted past the rest of the judges towards the double door entrance of the restaurant. "And seat Pablo as far away from me as possible," she whispered to Rachel who was standing at the threshold. "I really can't afford to get the flu right now."

Who can?

Followed by two Steadicams, Keisha and the judges walked through the lush décor of the downstairs bar and into a glass walled room that looked out at the green splendor of Central Park. Wait staff dressed in their black and whites bustled in and out of speckled and then sun-drenched light, pouring champagne into glasses and carrying platters of hors d'oeuvres. Beth had already loaded her plate with grilled shrimp and petite pigs in a blanket. Elyssa and Nichole were grazing more demurely. Wide-eyed with the excitement of dreams about to come true, the girls gave the cameras all the material they needed for the show's Cinderella storyline. After what they had been through, they needed some sweetness in their lives.

A tower of fruits de mer, raw oysters, shrimps and clams formed a nest around an ice sculpture of Keisha as Venus Rising, a la Botticelli, from a scallop shell. The models stared at the ice Goddess, which Pablo had ordered for the event a while back. That was a mistake. The deific Supermodel had fallen from grace, as far as he was concerned. But then goddesses had a notoriously bad reputation when it came to their treatment of mere mortals. The sculpture worked on so many levels, from the first night he'd met the Supermodel hiding behind the catering racks in that cold, slush-filled alley to her present day coldness. Had she changed so much since that fated night, or had she always been a malignant narcissist?

"Ugh." Pablo gagged.

"You look pale," Mason said.

"I don't feel well." At least, he was telling the truth. Thinking about what he'd put up with over the past few years was making him physically sick. "I just need to get outta here and over to my doctor's office."

Across the room, standing in front of the glimmering ice Venus, Beth's eyes almost bugged out of her head looking at all the seafood.

"What are those?" she purred.

"You've never had a raw oyster?" Elyssa seemed shocked.

"I come from Wisconsin. We only have cream and cheese."

"OMG. They are amazing. Come to think of it," Elyssa burst out laughing, "Kayla told me her boyfriend said they taste like sex."

"They're so good." Beth and Nichole slurped one up.

"Or maybe *she* tasted like the oyster."

"Yuck." Beth gagged, but kept eating anyway.

"I'm still getting over the fact that she has a boyfriend," Nichole said.

Camera C pushed in for a close-up of the models chowing down at the raw bar, while Camera A captured reaction shots of Keisha and Camera B followed the judges.

"If you guys can have a seat," Rachel suggested. "We can start with Keisha's greeting. We need to wrap out of this location, taillights, by 1 p.m. sharp."

"Settle." Bill's voice carried across the room.

Keisha took her position at the head of the table, looking like a radiant and slightly disturbed schoolmarm. "I feel so fortunate to find myself here at the end of this season, looking at three beautiful faces, which I've made even more beautiful over the past weeks. I feel like a proud mama about to send her children out into the world. Even though only one of you will be a *Model Muse*."

Keisha droned on about her days as a model and preached about her endless contributions to society, as a leader of women's empowerment. Pablo watched as heads began to nod. Rachel and De La Renta were practically leaning on each other taking a nap. At least the models looked rapt with attention. Innocent of the larger ruse, they played for the cameras looking truly inspired by their superstar role model.

Sasha cleared her throat and stood up, cutting into Keisha's moment. "Listen girls, as the world's *highest paid* Supermodel, lemme break it down for you. Don't fool yourselves. At the end of the day, you're still selling your tits and ass—for a check!"

"Amen chile'," Miss Thing chimed in. "And remember to walk the walk, don't talk the talk. No one cares what a model thinks."

Keisha glared at both of them.

"Ladies." Mason stood up and gave a little bow in their direction. "We just want to make sure that you are all prepared for the scrutiny you will face in this business." He shifted the tone. "Having a strong mind and sense of self, will serve you in the long run."

Keisha smiled condescendingly at her faithful Brit. The three contestants kept their sweetest smiles pasted on their faces, hip to the fact that the scene being played out was not about them. For Elyssa, it was about having a little *precious* time with her mentors. For Nichole, it was about righteous retribution for, after fighting her way to the top, shaming Keisha on camera. For Beth, it was about having a decent meal.

"Thank you, judges." Keisha cut them all off. "It's been a long road and my finalists are here: the daughter of a brave woman who lost her battle with breast cancer, our trendy tattooed work of art, and our first plus-sized model." Beth's face contorted as the cameras focused on her. The look on her face was not even slightly attractive. Her mouth twisted. Her eyes bulged and watered. Suddenly she lurched forward and projectile vomited all over Keisha.

Beth fell to the floor, rolling around gasping for air and groaning.

"Yuck!" Keisha screeched and spat at the model. "Yuck. Get it off me."

"Medic!" Rachel screamed. One of the wait staff ran over to perform a Heimlich maneuver.

"Get me the Medi-Kit. She isn't choking," the waiter yelled at one of his coworkers. "She's going into anaphylactic shock."

"How do you know?" Rachel yelled at him.

"I'm pre-med," he fired back.

Beth's lovely face was turning blue.

"Is she allergic to oysters?" Nichole asked.

Another waiter ran into the room pulling out an EpiPen from the emergency medical kit and raced to the thrashing model's side.

The waiter pulled Beth's skirt up.

"What are you doing to her?" Rachel was beside herself with panic.

"Saving her life." He stabbed her in the thigh, twisted the pin and held it against her leg. "One one-thousand. Two one-thousand. Three one-thousand."

Silence engulfed the cast and crew as they watched poor Beth's distorted face and ballooning neck. Nichole had tears streaming down her face. Elyssa hugged her.

Beth gasped for air.

A collective sigh of relief cascaded around the room.

"Everyone, give her some room." The waiter pressed her eyelids open and shone a flashlight into her pupils. Took her pulse.

Rachel was shaking. "*Ohmigod*, you saved her life."

From the top of the stairs, emergency medics came racing in with a stretcher.

"I expect a good tip," the waiter chuckled.

"You know? A good model who can hold down her oysters *and* her Flaming Hot Cheetos is hard to find," De La Renta quipped.

Rachel cornered him with her eyes. "Not funny, Switzerland."

An hour later, the producers were still trying to decide whether to finish the shoot in the restaurant or just skip the whole set up. Sitting in a private office downstairs in the restaurant, Joe paced and fumed. Keisha was sitting in a white chef's uniform and kitchen clogs. "I'll need new wardrobe if we do a reshoot," she told Joe.

Rachel was talking to a physician on the phone and shaking her head. She put the doctor on hold and turned to the team. "This is Dr. Bernstein. He can speak to us now that I've gotten her HIPAA statement, but the prognosis isn't good."

"What the hell does that mean?" Joe cussed.

"They've got her on IV fluids now."

"Fuck fluids. We need to know if we can at least get her back for final judging tomorrow." Joe snatched the phone out of her hand and pressed speakerphone. "Dr. Bernstein? This is Joe Vong, executive producer of *Model Muse*." He sounded unnervingly polite.

"What's that?" the voice echoed from the phone.

"It's one of the top reality shows on television."

"Was this some kind of TV stunt?" He was not impressed.

"Not at all," Joe assured him. "Can you catch us up with the latest on Beth?"

"She had an allergic reaction to shellfish, but she has also developed *Vibrio Vulnificus*."

"Got it. But can we get her back by tomorrow morning to resume shooting? I can push it to afternoon, if that's better."

"*Vibrio Vulnificus* is an infection that can cause severe blistering, skin lesions."

Dr. Bernstein continued. "Many people with this virulent infection require intensive care or limb amputations. Fifteen to thirty percent of infections are fatal."

"What exactly does that mean for us then?" Joe sounded panicked now.

"It means she's covered with derma layer vesicles and we're evaluating whether we need to amputate her left leg or not." Dr. Bernstein sounded resolute.

Joe went ballistic. "Fuuuuuuuck." Rachel grabbed her phone quickly and put it on mute. "Fuck! Fuck! Fuck! This season is cursed."

"You know," Keisha said, excitedly, "if we keep her as the winner, this could work for us. We've never had a plus-sized model win...but imagine the headlines for a plus-sized amputee."

"She has blisters all over her fucking face and body," Joe reminded her.

Pablo was horrified that he'd once believed Keisha was sane. She was unhinged and deranged. What could possibly be swirling around in that pretty head of hers?

"I think we need to use this situation to our advantage and swap out Beth for Kayla," Rachel suggested as she got off the phone with the doctor.

"Right." Joe snapped his fingers. "We can play out the scene tonight at the girl's apartment before the final runway. Keisha, you'll deliver the news that Beth isn't coming back. And *surprise, Kayla's back in the competition*." Joe sounded relieved now.

"The underdog fights her way back and wins the competition." Keisha pondered the narrative. "I like it. We'll just do a plus-sized winner next season."

"Hello? What about Nichole?" Pablo asked. "Social media is gonna hate her losing. Do you know how many girls have lost mothers to breast cancer around the world?"

Joe sighed. Keisha glared at him.

Pablo took a long hard look at everyone in the room playing each other like puppets. They were all fully aware of what was at stake, but no one had the balls to say it out loud. Kayla had them all by the short and curlies.

"If Kayla doesn't win, she'll definitely go public with a sex scandal," Pablo laid it all out for the bunch of spineless pussies. "If she does win, she may go public at some later date. *Model Muse* is fucked either way and is gonna take a hit. So, let's just do the right thing, for once."

"I thought you had the flu," Keisha sneered.

"Well, I have something." Pablo stood up and left the team alone in the restaurant office. They could decide their own fate. Nothing else was going to ruin his day. He had an appointment with destiny on the red carpet of the Primetime Emmy Awards.

\*    \*    \*

Marking a special anniversary, the Primetime Emmys had travelled across the country to be held *"Live from Lincoln Center in New York City."* Pablo was living the dream. Standing on the carpet, mic in hand, Pablo dazzled in a Tom Ford tux and enough liquid foundation, pressed powder and bronzer to make a corpse look attractive and alive. He looked like the groom on a wedding cake and felt like one too. After the hell of the past few days, heaven was the magenta and fuchsia sunset behind the statuesque grandeur of one of the most glorious performance venues in America, Lincoln Center. It was the golden hour and everything was swept with the rich warm hues a camera loves. Pablo was radiant. Luck was finally on his side, for once. Getting the text from Broyce to fill in as a fashion correspondent at the last minute was the lifeline rescuing Pablo from a nightmare of betrayal and plummeting self-esteem. Unfortunately, someone *did* have the flu that day. Fortunately, it wasn't Pablo.

Dishing about the Emmy nominees, the *Celebrity-Buzz TV* co-host touched her ear so she could hear the cue in her IFB to introduce Pablo. He could also hear the producers giving her the intro line:

"And standing by with Heidi Klum, the queen of reality TV, is our newest reporter, Pablo Michaels from *Model Muse.* Welcome to the *Celebrity-Buzz TV* family, Pablo."

His camera operator held up two fingers, then one and pointed at him.

"What's going on at your end of the carpet?" the hostess asked.

"Things are amazing here," Pablo smiled confidently into the camera, "as I'm with arguably the world's most beloved Supermodel host, Heidi Klum."

Heidi and Pablo did a fashion, double fake air-kiss without touching each other.

"Tell me, Heidi," Pablo dished. "Is that Christian Siriano you're wearing?"

"Of course, Dah-ling! I always support my *Project Runway* stars." Effervescent, Heidi winked at the camera. "You know, Christian was one of our first winners."

"I know."

"And now he's a legend in his own right."

"You really know how to shape a diamond in the rough, and create a *true* brand." Pablo laid the charm on thick as organic peanut butter. "Loyalty's such a wonderful quality. No wonder everyone loves you, and always will." He smiled at the camera, sending psychic barbs to his former BFF, who he knew had to be watching, most likely in her dressing suite with De La Renta.

"To be honest, Pablo? I was so lucky to have help when I was coming up in the industry. We all did. It's important, no? To help one another?"

"I just love that." Pablo shook his head and smiled sweetly at her. "Glamor has a new meaning Heidi, and you're wearing it. Back to you...."

"You're out," the producer said.

Pablo breathed for the first time in what felt like five minutes.

"That was marvelous." Heidi told him before moving toward the open doors.

Over his IFB he could hear the producers discussing who was coming up the carpet towards him, and giving the handlers instructions for how to space out his next celebrity interview. He loved being kept in the loop on all the different facets of the production, and it felt like he was in six places at once. Why didn't Keisha like wearing the concealed IFB in her ear? It was a control freak's dream. Coming towards Pablo now were Zendaya, wearing Versace, Reese Witherspoon, in Chanel, Glenn Close, in Valentino, and Pablo's favorite star from *Game of Thrones*, Peter Dinklage, wearing whatever he damn well wanted.

At a brief pause in the celebrity parade, Pablo took the live television moment to give a shout out to, "Tom Ford, who I'm wearing tonight. Tom once eloquently said, *'Glamour is something more than what you put on your body. It has to do with the way you carry yourself and the impact you have on others.'*" Standing next to the multiple Emmy Award nominee and one of the presenters, Pablo took Kerry Washington's hand and added, "I interpret that to mean, style is the very definition for the way you live your life and accomplish your goals. And you do that so effortlessly. Inside and out, Kerry, you look absolutely gorg tonight!"

"And if it weren't for you, on *Model Muse*, I wouldn't know how to pose in front of all these cameras. You're the heart of the show." He almost choked up and cried on live television. Olivia Pope loved him.

Two hours of live TV is enough to exhaust anyone, but Pablo was already running on empty. The adrenaline of the night and the sense he had of belonging, filled him with courage. As the last of the stars waved good-bye on their way into the award ceremony, the producer gave him a thumbs up and twirled the air. "That's a wrap," he heard through his earpiece. The Emmy red carpet was officially over. Pablo pulled out his IFB and the sound engineer unhooked all the audio packs.

"You're a natural," the producer who'd fed him his lines and celebrity names said. "My boss has already spoken with your boss about using you for more events. You were trending the whole show."

He hadn't even had time to check his social feeds, and now eagerly pulled out his iPhone to flip through the Instagram and Twitter responses from designer friends, photographers and fans. His appearance had indeed gone viral on every social media platform. Everyone was on it. His mentor, acquaintances, even his frenemies were posting.

@**MissThing**: Pablo on the red carpet wearing Tom Ford—Muse over #KeishaKa$h!

@**Sasha_original_Supermodel**: One of the nicest people I know. Go Pablo! #RealTalk I'm loving your hot buns on the red carpet. :-p

@**MichaelKors**: Remember when? xx #PabloMichaels #RP using the Repost App: @MissThing - Pablo on the red carpet wearing Tom Ford—Muse over #KeishaKa$h!

@**MrJayManuel**: For a split second I thought I was looking at a younger me on the E! Red Carpet. ☺ You killed it tonight! xo

@**MasonHughes**: Are you sure you are not British? Suave and Sophisticated = Pablo Michaels. #TomFord #MensFashion #DapperStyle #CreativeDirector #ModelMuse

A slew of individual comments populated below the selfie Pablo had posted from the red carpet just before they went live:

@**MrTorontoDude**: Husband material!

@**SouthernBoy_123**: You look sooooo good! I could eat you!

@**OscarJamesHair**: Yassssssss! The hair's on point! ☺

@**CoutureMaster_the3rd**: Hitting us with the drip… Boy you can dress!

@**ElizabethTheWriter**: (DMV Intercom) Now serving…Exquisite!

@**c_h_e_t_t_i_girl**: You are EVERYTHING! ☺

Pablo felt high, but the negative chatter in his mind kept his feet firmly planted on the ground. *This isn't real love. It's social media. They don't even know who you actually are. They probably don't even like you. You could still end up with nothing, then what are you going to do?*

He quit his Instagram app and looked at his phone. His mom and dad, both on the line, had even called and left a message. And then a dose of #KeepingItReal from Joe Vong and De La Renta popped on top of his several text messages.

**Joe Vong TEXT:** Killing it at the Emmys doesn't give you an excuse to be late for final judging. CU 2morrow.

**De La Renta TEXT:** Mother having a SHIT fit!!!!! Grab some food later? You need me. TRUST! It went down over here! :-p

\*     \*     \*

Pablo sat huddled with De La Renta in one of the luxurious curved velvet booths inside the Lincoln Ristorante adjacent to David Geffen Hall, where the Emmy festivities were taking place.

"She thought I knew." De La Renta slurped on his second Mojito. "Child, my head would've gone into a guillotine if you'd told me you were doing that gig. Thank you for keeping a bitch in the dark."

"Oh, I know. And you can't lie." Pablo pulled at his tie and unbuttoned the top two buttons of his dress shirt.

"Don't I know it." He sucked up the last of his drink and waved at the waiter for another one. "But did you notice that Jay Manuel tweeted you while you were on the Red Carpet?"

Pablo smirked. "I did."

"That's all you gotta say? Isn't he, like, your hero?"

"I guess he's something like that."

"You guess?" De La Renta glared at Pablo with a curious look. "Now I'm starting to think Mother wanted you to have silver hair for a reason."

"Speaking of, she didn't see me being on *Celebrity-Buzz TV* as a good thing for *Model Muse*?"

"What? She looked like Medusa tryin' to turn your face to stone through the TV. She saw it as, and I quote, *a slap in her face*," he parodied.

"Of course, she did."

"She called Broyce. Claimed you were using her celebrity to elevate yourself. And tried to fuck your contract." De La Renta made a face.

"Broyce is the one who got me the gig." Pablo took a bite of his goat cheese and pomegranate salad.

"He's one cool dude. He told her the network sees you two as its new 'dream team.'" De La Renta tried to mimic Broyce's smooth delivery, "'We're thrilled he got this *Celebrity-Buzz TV* exposure. It's great for ratings. Their EVP's already offered him a permanent position as fashion correspondent for the whole award season.'"

Pablo's face immediately lit up at Broyce's support.

De La Renta went on. "She tried to throw you under the bus, though. Claimed you weren't ready for the runway shoot we just wrapped."

Pablo sputtered. "*Bullshit*. I finished my prep, days ago."

"Girl, please. Even *Joe Vong* was on your side. He suggested we have Miss Thing do the intro setup and host the runway challenge for a change." De La Renta was now chomping on a brown breadstick. "I mean, shit, isn't that what *the beast* does for a living?"

Pablo couldn't believe his ears. "I bet *that* went over well with Mother."

"You should've heard her. *I made Pablo and I can break him,*" he mimicked.

"Oh really?" Pablo paused. "If I learned anything tonight, it's that there's a whole entertainment world out there for me to conquer."

De La Renta looked at him. "She's comin' for you, Boo. You betta be ready."

# IT'S A WRAP

## LAST SHOOT DAY, SEASON SIX

ALONE IN HIS trailer, Pablo finished his makeup for the final judging sequence he was about to film. The thought of being on camera with Keisha, and having to fake his way through announcing Kayla as this season's winner, made him ill. The phone and text silence from his former BFF was deafening and designed to make him feel unsure and insecure. Why couldn't she allow him a little of the limelight for a change?

In an effort to make himself feel loved, he picked up his iPhone and opened Instagram with the expectation of reading the plethora of adoring fan comments. As the app launched, a new post from Keisha was at the top of his feed. The gif she'd posted was an over-filtered selfie of herself with sparkling, animated fairy dust floating around her head. She fancied herself a prophet.

@**Official_KeishaKash**: Celebrity isn't real or magical. One night on the red carpet doesn't make you a star. You have to put in the work & fight to the end to become an icon.

She clearly wanted Pablo to feel the burn. Why couldn't they go back to the way it had been? Why did everything have to change? Was it his fault for wanting more, or was it hers for keeping a stranglehold on him and what he had to offer? All he'd ever wanted was a talk show. She had to sabotage even that. He couldn't even fathom why she'd done it. It made him feel inordinately sad. They could've had it all and they could've had it together. Now they didn't even have each other.

A production assistant banged on his door. "Delivery, Pablo." She entered with a huge bouquet of flowers and placed it on his vanity. "You were awesome yesterday, by the way," she said shyly.

"Thanks so much."

"On the set in five?"

"Copy that." Pablo looked at the card. Tears filled his eyes. "Aw. Damn you, now I've gotta fix my makeup again." His fingers flew across the screen of his phone.

**Pablo TEXT:** OMG! Thx for the flowers! xx Working the red carpet was the miracle I needed to believe in myself again. And #RealTalk? I'm going to leave Model Muse. My contract is up for renegotiation, so why not take this golden window of opportunity and fly? I just can't do HER any longer! KK's toxic energy is slowly killing me. I can feel it. I need to get away and figure my life out. I'm considering writing a book about the whole thing! ☹

Pablo looked in the mirror, took a deep breath, and held up his outstretched hands. "Showtime." Exiting his trailer and halfway to the soundstage, Pablo's phone vibrated.

**I.C.E. TEXT:** So happy for your success. You deserve it. Beware, the pressures and anxieties of fame are FIERCE ☺ Don't do anything desperate. KK is a master of wooing the court of public opinion. If you write a tell-all memoir, she'll vilify you, mercilessly!

Pablo swallowed hard and his heart started to race. Another text popped up immediately after.

**I.C.E. TEXT:** OTR, I'm writing a book of my own, but it's a novel. You can have a lot more fun with that because it's all "fiction." ☺

**Pablo TEXT:** A novel? About what?

**I.C.E. TEXT:** It's a dark, comedic take on the extreme abuse of power that runs rampant in the TV biz and throughout society today. It's basically inspired by my life.

**Pablo TEXT:** This sounds juicy!! Wanna spill some tea for a change?

**I.C.E. TEXT:** I'll spill this. It's very meta. You ain't ready. ☺ It conveys an important narrative in our world of social media, where stories of substance are often sacrificed for viral sensation. You know the deal. So with my salacious title and plot (which I'm NOT going to tell you), people might accept it for real gossip, but ultimately I'll get my true message out there. In a time where the pressure to be validated online takes precedence over exploring the truth of who we really are, "Likes and Comments" have derailed our personal growth. We are no longer seeing the reality of the world around us.

**Pablo TEXT:** Oh…you're going there! ANTM fans are going to gobble it up.

**I.C.E. TEXT:** LOL! We'll see. When you began working on MM, I started to see my life through your eyes. I know this sounds very Super Soul Sunday, but it's what YOU did for me, Pablo. You opened my eyes—leading me to my own inner child.

**Pablo TEXT:** Wow! And here I thought you were my lifeline. You've dodged so many bombs in this industry and have all the experience. You're like the big brother I never had.

**I.C.E. TEXT:** Truth? Advising you turned into an exercise of reassuring my younger self. I will forever credit you for compelling my spirit to grow. You may think I'm your lifeline, but it was really you who saved me. I walked around with blinders on, when I was your age, made a ton of mistakes and wished I could hear the voice of reason—myself.

**Pablo TEXT:** I don't know what to say. Jay Manuel is telling me—little Pablo Michaels—that I helped him?

**I.C.E. TEXT:** You're silly. Remember I'm just Jay, and I've been here for you all along. "Jay Manuel" has become an identity the world thinks they know, but they really don't.

**Pablo TEXT:** Deep. Now I see why you love Iyanla Vanzant so much.

**I.C.E. TEXT:** HA! ☺ Speaking of Iyanla and with regards to KK, don't react, just act—with courage and faith. You'll know what to do. I'm not worried about you at all. You'll go on to do great things. And I'll be watching. Big virtual hug!!! xoxo

Pablo stopped midstride and turned around. He always went to her dressing suite before judging to check in before shooting. He had to do that now. Face her without any fear. Navigating the fire doors that lined the passage to Keisha's dressing suite, he paused to gather his courage. Now or never. He tapped on the door.

"Enter," De La Renta chirped. *She* was sitting in her makeup chair as he came through the door. *Duck Face* would've looked friendlier.

Pablo could feel the static energy coming off of her back.

"I just wanted to check in and see how you liked the final runway show last night?"

Keisha clacked away at her computer, typing with her two index fingers and looking fixedly at the screen. "It was fine."

"I knew you'd like it." Pablo pretended there was nothing wrong. "The Egyptian-themed setting I had built was sooooo Karl Lagerfeld for Chanel, 2018, at the Metropolitan Museum's *Temple of Dendur*. Epic."

"Oh? Too bad you didn't see it then."

"Oh, I saw it. We rehearsed with the Bogies." Pablo stepped closer in an effort to appear natural. "Don't worry, I'll sit down with post and make sure they cut it together right."

"I'm not worried."

Pablo looked over at De La Renta who was busily minding his own business and scrolling through Instagram. "Soooooo, any notes for judging tonight? You want me on team Kayla, Nichole or Elyssa during deliberations?"

"You choose."

"Fine."

"Fine."

Pablo turned to walk out but caught Keisha's reflection in the mirror. "You'll have to talk to me at some point, you know. We're shooting in like, 15 minutes!"

"We're talking."

Pablo stood in disbelief and listened to the rhythmic beating of her fingers on the keyboard. What could he say to force her to feel his frustration?

"You know, on camera, you can't be so monosyllabic with your utterances," he sniped.

"Excuse me?"

"Words too big for you?"

"What!?"

Pablo had her attention now. She had stopped typing and was glaring at his reflection.

"Lemme break it down for you. Translation? You should really be more diligent about turning off your mic after you leave set."

"What are you talking about, Mr. Pablo?" She swiveled around in her makeup chair, facing him head on.

"*Ohmigod*, enough," he barked. Pablo found his confidence. "You sound insane playing these childish games. It's exhausting. I thought I knew—"

"Knew what?" she said. An insidious smile grew on her lips.

"Really? Really? Fine. I heard Andy telling you that Netflix greenlit our talk show together. And *you* pulling me off the project. Did you really think you'd get away with betraying me like this?"

Almost tripping over his hair kit laying by his feet, De La Renta slipped out the dressing suite door in a mad dash.

Calmly, Keisha closed her left eye slightly and fiddled with her fake eyelash. "I hate to be the bearer of bad news, but Netflix was only interested in this experimental talk show because my name was attached." She fluttered her lashes and fixed her gaze on Pablo's face. "Don't you think it's time you start building your own empire, without me spoon feeding you?"

How dare she. After all he'd done. Pablo wasn't going to give her the satisfaction of knowing the ire she'd provoked in him. "You're right," he said, matching her indifferent tone.

\*      \*      \*

Sitting next to Mason behind the judging table was a welcome relief for Pablo, because it meant that he was one seat further away from Keisha, and the rod that was stuck up the uptight Brit's butt would attract any lightning bolts sent his way from the angry Supermodel. Hell had no fury like a woman scorned, but Hell had never seen Keisha Kash. Pablo's watch read 5:23 p.m.—not bad for a final judging. Maybe they would wrap on time for once and he could duck out to the safe haven of his own apartment. No wrap party. No dinner with Keisha at Virgil's. Pablo's celebration was going to be on his couch with a glass of white wine, bowl of popcorn and his favorite movie—*The Matrix* (part one, of course). Sometimes he felt like working for Keisha was the equivalent of taking the red pill that Morpheus offered Neo. One big, *awakening*, red pill that forced him to stay in Wonderland, with Keisha showing him how deep the rabbit hole goes.

Pablo should've taken the blue pill.

"Elyssa." Keisha looked like a beautiful grim reaper as she began the winnowing of hope among her hopefuls. "You have done what no other model has done before. You have used your body as your pallet. You are the art and the canvas. I think you will go far in our industry, but you still have some weaknesses that need to be worked on." The other judges chimed in on her weaknesses. Elyssa didn't care. She walked up and hugged a cold and withdrawn Keisha, who barely knew how to receive such effusive emotion, and then without warning, the illustrated girl stepped around the judging table and hugged each judge individually. Pablo had to admit he adored her. Before leaving the set, Elyssa waved happily good-bye to the cameras.

It was between Kayla and Nichole now. Keisha's eyes darted back and forth between the two adversaries, now holding hands and standing on the runway in front of her. "Two of you stand before me, but only one of you is a *Model Muse*," Keisha said.

The jib camera swept up high in the air, capturing a dramatic wide shot of the judging set.

"I look at you, Nichole," Keisha continued, "and all I see is that beautiful face that the camera loves. But the judges wonder if you'll be able to take the harsh criticism the fashion industry dishes out, almost every, single, day."

Pablo was half listening. He'd heard Rachel and Joe run these lines with Keisha—ten times already during the camera reset.

"And Kayla, you consistently became the frontrunner model to beat, week after week, in Pablo's *amazing* photoshoots."

Pablo held his breath. Was their super slick Supermodel going to go rogue on him?

"But pulling off fierce poses and looking beautiful is not what being a *Model Muse* is all about; integrity is a model's best feature."

Rogue? Pablo snapped his head left. He looked over at Joe Vong, angrily whispering into his IFB. Keisha had gone off script. Kayla was slated to win because Joe had convinced everyone that she would destroy *Model Muse* and Keisha's reputation by blabbing to the media, no matter what her contract said. Yes, the network could sue Kayla, but what would they get? Nothing but a smear campaign. Nichole was to be the sacrificial lamb.

"The next *Model Muse* is..." Keisha dragged this moment out, like she always did, to make Nichole and Kayla suffer, for almost a full minute, in staged silence. Nichole had tears in her eyes. Her chin quivered. Kayla looked *almost* as upset— minus the tears and sorrow.

Keisha bowed her head, the cue to the visual department that she was ready for them to display the winner's photo on the giant LED wall.

"*Nichole*," Keisha screamed.

Nichole immediately let go of Kayla's hand and fell into Keisha's arms. "Oh my God," she sobbed, "I wish my mother could've seen this moment."

Keisha rubbed the bald model's back, trying to console her. Having Nichole as the winner made the Supermodel look good, just like Pablo had said. And clearly Keisha wasn't going to be blackmailed. She must've had a plan B, or played a good game of chicken.

"What bullshit," Kayla screamed. "You're an idiot, Nichole." She moved toward Keisha. The camera operators frantically shifted their angles. Harper jumped out of her seat, covering her mouth with her hand, and Joe dropped the pen he had clenched between his teeth.

"She almost kicked you off the show a week ago for cursing her out and she stole your fucking hair. Did you look at her wig? That's your hair, dumbass." Kayla lunged towards the host and grabbed the ends of her long red tresses. Keisha contorted and dipped her body, back and forth, looking like a Jiujitsu master, but Kayla had hold of it and the wig flew off. Leaving Keisha with her bare cornrows and skinny head shining under the LED lights.

Keisha flung herself at Kayla. The wig flew through the air and landed at Nichole's feet. As Keisha and Kayla tore at each other's clothes and faces, Nichole took her hair and placed it back on her head and smiled for the cameras.

"That's a cut."

Kayla had face planted into the platform. Keisha was straightening her outfit. "Are we clear?" she yelled over at video village.

"We'll need to do some pick-ups."

Keisha walked over to Nichole and ripped the wig off the *Model Muse*'s head. "I'll be in my dressing room." She strutted down the runway, leapt off the platform to the fire doors and the hallway leading to her dressing suite. Like a pro, she plopped the wig on and slid the lace-front into position. "De La Renta, I need you."

"Wait," Pablo yelled. He jumped out of his seat and ran after her.

"Oooooo, this is gonna be a *good one*." Miss Thing grabbed his makeup purse. "Come on."

Sasha and Mason leapt up to join him. Keisha looked like the Pied Piper, leading Pablo, the judges, producers and several of the crew down the empty hallways of Silvercup Studios.

"You can't leave things like this," Pablo pleaded. "We're gonna have to speak at some point."

Abruptly, Keisha did an about face and took a couple intimidating steps towards Pablo. He froze on the spot. Like an old western standoff, they stood face to face about fifteen feet apart. Everyone else gathered around, not saying a word.

"So? Speak," she provoked.

"Well…I…" Pablo felt uncertain.

"Isn't this what you wanted? My attention?" Keisha was relentlessly firing questions. "You've got it. Thirty seconds. Say your piece."

"Maybe we should find a private place to talk."

"I'm DONE spending any time with you outside these walls. This is your last chance to speak with me when the cameras *aren't* rolling, so speak."

Pablo hesitated. The words were jammed up in the back of his throat and wouldn't come out. Frustrated now, she stood with her hand on her hip, pose number 32, like she usually did when shooting the Veronika's Privates catalogue.

"How do you expect us to work without speaking and shoot a show together?"

"I'll be just fine and we'll play, on camera, the way the audience expects us to play." She spoke slowly, sounding cool and collected. "But when the cameras are down, I really don't feel the need to nurse your insecurities anymore."

"My insecurities?"

"Oh come on, your sad little *poor adopted boy* story, it's tiring and manipulative."

"You're adopted?" Miss Thing blurted.

Pablo only had eyes for Keisha now. He'd been preparing for this blowout all day knowing that after final judging, he was going to tell her he was leaving *Model Muse*. He didn't think she would stoop so low, but it didn't matter anymore. So, what, he was adopted. Loads of kids were adopted. At least he had caring parents who had raised him and loved him.

"We all have pain. But I certainly don't use *mine* to manipulate everyone. People barely know I'm adopted." Pablo surveyed the crowd, standing around them, to elicit support. "You, on the other hand, play out your abandonment issues by living in *Keishavision* land where you're blinded by your own anointed celebrity. You completely betrayed me, which shouldn't be a surprise, since your own mother is a convicted felon."

"Excuuuuuse me?" Keisha railed at him. "Get outta here, you bunch of rubber neckers, and leave us alone." The judges, producers and crew all scattered, disappearing, like ants into the woodwork. She snatched De La Renta by his hoodie as he tried to leave. "You stay."

"I gotta get…" he squawked.

"I need a witness."

The glam guru exhaled heavily and propped himself up on a nearby equipment crate.

"So, tell me, oh wise and intelligent one, where does *my* pain come from?" She stared down at him with a look of disgust.

Pablo rose to his full height and faced Keisha head on, eye to eye unafraid of the ramifications of what he was about to say. "This entire television and fashion world, that's mostly run by men, has hardened you, and I *totally* get that. I see you. I always have. That's why I've been here all this time, by your side." He took a big breath. "I cared, and wanted you to have someone who loved you for *YOU!*"

"How sentimental," she condescended.

"And being a black model? It must've been maddening for you to work in a business obsessed with women staying young—that mostly celebrates the white aesthetic."

Keisha laughed, rolling her eyes.

"I'm sure the industry made you feel subpar because you're black—then, you were chucked aside when you matured and became a woman."

"Oh, and now you're an expert on racism, sexism *and* ageism in this country?" Keisha stood with her legs slightly apart, her hands twitching as if she were about to draw a gun at any moment.

"Pablo..." De La Renta muttered, warning his friend.

"No. I just understand self-induced pain caused by rejection. It had to have been hard on you and your brother—it's perfectly clear all your actions are motivated by pain, *not* by helping people."

"Don't go there, Pablo," De La Renta urged, speaking louder.

"Trust me when I say this." Pablo continued without listening. "People are soooo tired of seeing you play the martyr. You have millions in the bank. You're obviously self-obsessed. But transparent as a piece of Cling Wrap. And I hate to break it to you, but you're no one's *Model Muse*—or any muse for that matter."

"Annnnnd, he went there," De La Renta yelled, throwing his hands in the air. Hopping off his crate, he bolted for the fire door to his right, leaving Keisha and Pablo alone in the hall.

Pablo was on a roll and continued. "Your shitty life is no excuse for treating others like shit!"

A sinister smile spread across her face. "And your shitty life is? You used *me* to get what you wanted. You manipulated me to give you a part on my show and then tried to upstage me?"

Pablo squinted at her. "Huh?"

"You coerced me. Fawned all over me. Took advantage of my good nature. Got me to trust you and then betrayed me, Mr. Pablo. You betrayed me. I can never forgive you for everything you've done to me, and after everything I did for you." Her amber eyes were simultaneously teary and flint hard. "I thought we were *real* friends, but all you've done is slap me in my face."

What planet was she on? He couldn't believe her version of events. Let alone her version of reality.

Facing each other, eyes locked, Pablo made his last move. "I'm leaving the show. I've already fulfilled my contract. So legally, I can walk."

Keisha dangled the potential horn of plenty before his eyes. "The network plans on picking us up for six more seasons. Do you know how much money you'll be throwing away by not renegotiating? And keep in mind, *Celebrity Buzz TV* will drop you as soon as you leave too."

"Everything isn't always about money, Keisha," he said. "Integrity means so much more. But clearly, it's *not* your best feature." Pablo threw the words she had just used on Kayla back in her face.

Keisha's jawline tightened.

"As I see it," Pablo began to feel more confident about his decision, "there are no incentives here, just more games. And I was just one of your pawns."

"Who's playing games now?" she asked. "Your ego just got bruised because you weren't good enough to host a talk show with me, and now *you* repay my charity by abandoning us."

"Us?" he scoffed.

"I made you, Mr. Pablo Michaels."

"Pablo made *Pablo Michaels*. You just put him on TV."

"I did a lot more things than that."

"A lot of appalling things." His voice cracked.

Her face rearranged expressions. Innocent face number 17—cover of *Harper's Bazaar*, 2016. Keisha had spent her life baking in pain, raised herself since childhood and learned how to compete in a man's world by creating a false superhero persona to survive. Pablo, loved and cared for, took years to realize his adoption had given him an advantage. A heart. They were two flawed people sucked into the fake business of entertainment. However, he could see his way out and she clearly couldn't. Without her fame, her world would come crashing down and she'd end up where her brother is—broken and in isolation.

"Isn't there anything I can do?" She raised her hand as if she was extending an olive branch. "Let's take a little walk. Come on." Keisha floated past him and grabbed his hand. "Give me one last chance. I can change."

Walking in silence, hand in hand, down the hall, Pablo followed her with a sense of dread, like he was heading for the guillotine. At the loading dock doors, she pushed on the gate trimmed with rubber flaps and stood back.

The path was clear in front of him.

Maureen Dowd once eloquently wrote in the *New York Times* that, "Celebrity supersedes criminality. How can you see clearly when you're looking into the sun?" The veracity of that statement couldn't hold any more truth in that moment.

"I wish you the best of luck with all your future endeavors." Her voice began to sink in register and the demon returned. "Now you can go and do whatever the HELL YOU WANNA DO."

# A NEW DAY

SEARCHING FOR SAGE advice that would make sense of his last four years walking on eggshells, while Keisha the tyrant had controlled him, the unemployed Pablo pounded motivational books. He was trying to take back his life and it was time to try a different approach. Give her problem with being a bully back to her. However, he'd made a few mistakes in walking from the show. One, he couldn't file for unemployment because he hadn't been fired. Two, no one was banging down his door asking the reality star to produce runway shows anymore—not that he wanted to do that anyway. Three, because he'd walked from a well-established franchise, there was a question around his loyalty. Doing general meetings with other networks was going to prove difficult. He desperately sought a way to find solace in himself, but he was plagued with doubt.

Leaving *Model Muse* had seemed like the only power move Pablo could make. Now it seemed foolhardy. How would he ever get a talk show without his celebrity in place already on television? It's easier to get a job when you have one, than get one when you don't. Nothing was permanent. Even huge success wasn't yours to keep. Celebrity was NOT owned—it was rented! And the rent was due every day. Keisha had been right and he hated it. He'd passed on renewing a lush contract for six more seasons of the hit show, lost his platform on TV and given up a ton of money—before securing a new job. Was integrity worth the tough pill he'd had to swallow? He loved working with De La Renta and the models. He'd loved the creativity that he was able to bring to the set and the show; he even loved the long hours. There were a few red carpet events to co-host on *Celebrity-Buzz TV,* but not enough to fill his enormous energetic drive or enough money to pay his mortgage. He needed something else, a new project. Some way to fulfill his desires and fill his pockets. Through it all, he was finding the holes in himself and he needed to plug them up on his terms.

De La Renta had suggested Pablo write a style book. "Your fan base will eat it up." That was the *last* thing Pablo wanted to write. He'd witnessed the demise of too many colleagues who, after a brief launch and a lot of hoopla, were relegated to the dusty old section of the bookstore—or worse, Costco—plastered with *70% off* permanently affixed to their glossy covers. Pablo looked out on the abyss of Manhattan from his fifteenth-floor apartment and waited for inspiration. He'd saved his soul by leaving the show. But what the hell would he do without it? Oscillating between pity party and proactivity, Pablo welcomed the interruption of his phone ringing on the living room coffee table.

\*       \*       \*

Season seven didn't have an international or even a national open cattle call. Not one judge, producer or peon wanted to pick through tens of thousands of desperate girls again. The show was a bonified success and selecting models was the last thing anyone had time for anymore. Instead, Luciana was back to single-handedly finding diamonds in the rough— much to Keisha's fury. And that was why the casting team was in the 23rd floor conference room at the network ready to present the new cast of hopefuls.

Keisha chucked her iPhone on the conference room table, impatiently. "I'm done waiting on Broyce. Just show me my cast."

Luciana obediently clicked a remote to activate the presentation screen.

"Okay. So here are your tired, your poor, your huddled masses," Luciana started. A pale redheaded girl in a skimpy bathing suit filled the screen. "First, we have Prenilla. She's our super fair redhead. She barely passed psych eval, but I think there's gonna be good story here."

"I asked for an albino this season. Is this the best you can do?"

"Oh come on, she's a click away! You can give her pink contacts during makeovers," Luciana snapped.

"And shave her head," Joe Vong mumbled to Rachel, "to get a new wig."

Luciana took a deep breath. "Can I continue?"

"Fine. Next," Keisha sighed.

"So, for our *Keisha wannabe,* we have Tyranne."

"Sorry for being late everyone." Broyce walked swiftly into the conference room and smiled at everyone. "Oh, she's stunning!" he said of the model whose photo was on screen. Her wheat colored hair and hazel/green eyes made her a true knock out. "She kinda looks like you, Keisha."

"She does, doesn't she?" Luciana's voice dripped with sarcasm. Both Joe and Rachel sank into their seats. Harper was completely transfixed by the doppelganger image.

Like a diplomatic emissary, Broyce stayed standing. "I just need to have a word with everyone before we continue." His presence was magnetic and authoritative. His voice a baritone that could've made him a great hypnotist. "We have some statistical information from research that has had us making some changes upstairs, and I want to share with everyone before we finish seeing the cast. *Model Muse* has extensive growth with young women between eighteen to twenty-four. That age group also has a racially mixed balance; white females watch just as much as Black, Asian and Latina women. But what I really want to share is the new focus group data."

Keisha carefully placed both her hands on the conference room table.

"Sixty-eight percent of viewers love Pablo as Creative Director, and 52% answered '*no*' to the question, would you watch if Pablo Michaels was no longer on the show; 43% weren't sure and 5% didn't care. Reasons included: they liked his male energy, his stability, his kindness, his ass, and they especially like the on-air chemistry between Keisha and Pablo."

"Too bad for them then, since you're about to show us our new creative director in that file folder of yours, right Lucy?" Keisha's eyes blazed. "Really, Broyce, what's the point of this and why wasn't I made aware of new focus group testing?"

"Well, we did our due diligence and put everyone on tape that you sent over, and," Broyce looked over at Luciana, who looked down at her computer, "the creative director we found that best fits with the formula of the show is—" Luciana pressed the remote. "Pablo Michaels."

Pablo came through the doorway. He'd been watching and listening from the adjacent room, behind the one-way glass wall where executives stood during focus groups.

"What?" Keisha stood up, angrily.

"We've been talking internally and the fact is when something works, you don't change the ingredients. So, we sweetened the deal, coaxed Pablo back to the creative director position *and* offered him an Executive Producer credit." The strapping executive placed his broad masculine hand on Pablo's shoulder. "Not only has he signed on for six more seasons, but we're working with Dawn Gately, over in development, on a new one-hour talk show for our "dream team" that covers fashion, pop culture, teen anxiety, FOMO, and it will serve as a platform to bring back past *Model Muse* contestants—like a *Housewives Reunion* show."

Keisha looked like she'd swallowed a firecracker and was about to blow up.

"What the fuck, Broyce?" Joe Vong's voice screeched higher than normal. "You made me the EP of *Model Muse*. How's that all gonna work?"

"You're not the *only* EP on this show," Broyce chuckled. "There are five or six of us. And now we have one more." He then turned to Keisha. "The execs upstairs love everything you and Pablo do for our ratings. A talk show is how we capitalize on you and Pablo, and all the two of you bring to the table. It was the only way to get Pablo to come back."

"I thought we had an understanding, Mr. Pablo?" Keisha's creepy girl's voice uttered, cutting off her superior.

Pablo beamed. He felt in control of her—for once.

She stared into his eyes, innocently, and said, "We *weren't* gonna talk through other people, and now you go behind my back?"

"We went to Pablo," Broyce said. "This is a network decision."

Keisha looked unconvinced and slowly reached for her iPhone, never breaking her eye contact with Pablo. Her words were slow and deliberate. "Game on."

Pablo didn't flinch. He wore his newfound confidence well. And despite all the advice that he'd been given, Pablo couldn't resist flaunting his newfound power over her. "*Certain people* in the room should remember I never signed a personal NDA." He let his gaze drift around the table. "And now that I'm an EP, *certain people* should tread very, very carefully. You never know what kind of salacious gossip could leak out."

"Can we have the room? I need to speak with Pablo, alone," Keisha ordered. Her eyes began to narrow and Pablo knew what that meant. She was furious.

Everyone, including Broyce, hastily exited, capitulating to Keisha's rhetorical request. As the last to leave the room, Harper, being sweetly discreet as possible, carefully closed the conference room. *Good luck*, she'd mouthed.

Keisha nonchalantly sauntered around the room, closing all the privacy blinds along the glass walls. Her actions were slow and menacing. Clearly an attempt to intimidate the new executive producer. Pablo played it cool.

"You're not scaring me with this routine." Pablo gazed out the conference room's window. "I'm not Joe Vong. You've got nothing on me."

"Oh really? You think you're sooooo bulletproof?" She plunked herself down at the head of the table. "Whose voice will the press listen to if I happen to make a statement about your unethical practices around here?"

"Hashtag news flash! *Cancel culture* is sooooo 2019. I tend to believe people will see right through your lies. Not everyone's a fan of yours, you know. Hashtag keeping it real."

"You're fooling yourself because those naysayers that you think I have would give up everything for a selfie with me, if they had a chance. Real power is forcing those who hate you to love you."

Pablo broke his gaze from the window and stared directly at Keisha. "Will they love you when they find out how much you manipulate the show to your benefit?"

"*That's* reality television. Who'd care?"

"They'll care when they find out what you did to Mandy when you yourself were petrified of being pregnant, after having unprotected, indiscriminate sex. The hypocrisy alone will chip away at your *social justice warrior* facade."

"*Puh-lease…*"

"Oh really?" Pablo chuckled. "I was foolish to stand by and watch you play Mandy like a puppet. But better yet, it worked in my favor. Bye-bye Miss Keisha good girl." He felt righteous in admonishing her. "And to think I felt sorry for you, and tolerated you handing me ten urine-soaked pregnancy tests all because you couldn't bear to look at the results."

The sun now bounced off the conference room presentation screen, illuminating a physical divide between the standoffish duo.

"You're showing your ignorance now. If you tried to peddle that story, you'd simply look like a media *thirsty* employee looking to cash-in on *my* fame. Mandy made her own choices and I was never pregnant." Keisha rose out of her chair staring eye to eye with Pablo. "Don't underestimate the power of celebrity. My fans are tired of gossip, and they'll fight alongside me as I publicly shame you. You don't belong to this club, so good luck with summoning any foot soldiers to attack me."

In an attempt to leave Pablo alone to consider his fate, the gutsy Supermodel picked up her bag and sauntered past her silent adversary.

"Bravo, *Mommy Dearest*," he spoke up as she was almost out the door. "You're finally worthy of the golden statue for playing the part of the wicked adoptive mother. Thank God my real mom isn't like you"

Keisha turned around without missing a beat and said, "No, your real mother left you the day you were born."

Bitch. It was clear they were both ready for a fight. Now, Pablo feared that waging war on a formidable force like Keisha Kash might leave him reeling from the poison of her vindictive venom. "At least my real mother isn't a jailbird," he barked.

"How do you know, *David*?"

# EVENING THE SCORE

T HE FIRST DAY of filming, on yet another new season, brought the crew in early on a steamy July morning. Catering was pumping out a special hot breakfast, including brioche bread French toast and homemade stuffed sausage links. Not the kind of food you'd expect on a modeling competition show, but many of the crew's waistlines made up for the lack thereof on the model contestants. Pablo loved the smell of breakfast wafting from the catering truck. He loved the smell of his brand new full-sized trailer even more. Parked right alongside the dining tables in the catering section, the light grey leather interior reminded him of the Learjet he'd flown in with Keisha to Florida, memories he'd soon rather forget. He watched as various producers and grips walked in and out of catering catching up after hiatus. His new home away from home, equipped with one-way privacy glass, allowed him to see everything that was going on, but no one could see him. He'd arrived early at Silvercup, before any of the crew were at the studio, and needed to prepare for the biggest *"welcome"* they had ever attempted to shoot.

Season seven needed to be bigger and better, mostly because his name was now attached as one of the EPs, and he needed to show Keisha he could be *America's next top producer*. He'd shifted the tone with their team's first pre-production meeting by saying, "I encourage all of you to come to me with any creative ideas. We're in this together. Let's make a show we're proud of."

Keisha had skipped all Pablo's meetings and Joe sat in silence, looking evil. It was like they both wanted him to fail, but that wasn't Pablo's style.

Harper, now officially working on her second season of the long running mannequin maker, suggested they open the first episode with a *"mega model march"* on New York's legendary Intrepid Sea, Air & Space Museum, one of the city's biggest and most iconic harbor attractions. "It'll be in support of our veterans and a dignified way to promote the new season during sweeps at the network," she'd said. Pablo loved the idea and presented the creative to Broyce, who had called it a *"slam dunk"* with advertisers.

*Model Muse* was now a pop culture phenomenon, and other countries around the world were filming international franchise editions—*Model Muse* Canada, *Model Muse* Germany, and *Model Muse* China were the first to launch. *Model Muse* Britain, which Mason had hoped he could host, tapped Kate Moss and the UK edition blew up. Rumors surfaced that Keisha and *Calvin Klein's muse* had a falling out. Pablo knew the time would come when the show's format would stand on its own, without its indigenous Supermodel host. *Model Muse* would also continue on with or without the original judging panel, and they all knew it. Looking like a Brown Paper Wasp sucking nectar out of a flower, Sasha Berenson, seated directly below Pablo's lounge area window, slurped through an impossibly tiny straw from her thirty-two-ounce plastic sippy cup. Holed up at the corner table wearing big dark sunglasses and a black zip-up sweatshirt, Sasha used Miss Thing, who was seated next to her, as a shield trying to remain below the radar.

Mason walked in looking rock bottom, unshaven and plunked himself next to his fellow judges exhaling for attention. Pablo opened his window a bit, to clearly hear their conversation.

"That looks like the same damn pinstripe suit you wore to the final judging last season," Miss Thing said, waving his hand in front of his nose. "And smells like it too."

Sasha released her straw coughing and spitting. "Ooooo, my favorite scent. Chardonnay."

"I have been living over at The Carlyle on the Eastside for the last several weeks. Sukhdeep and I had a huge fight. She kicked me out and will not take any of my calls. I have not even seen her, or rather, she will not see me."

"Ewwww, *The Carlyle*? You're kinda slumming it, aren't you King Arthur?" Sasha hiccupped on the word *Arthur* and took another sip from her vat.

"Just because my family is wealthy, does not mean I squander my funds."

"Sooooo, is that why you wouldn't pay for Sukhdeep's *snip-snip*?" Miss Thing was quick to jump in. "I can see why she's pissed."

"Stop being so presumptuous about my wife. And shut your traps, both of you. My life is absolutely horrible right now and you two delight in taking a *piss out of me!*"

Miss Thing pulled a small travel bottle of Le Labo

fragrance out of his makeup purse and sprayed the entire area around Mason. "It certainly *does* smell like piss around here."

Pablo quietly chuckled to himself. Miss Thing had a great sense of timing. The public needed to see that side of the model coach. Pablo made a mental note.

"Shit, it's hot as fuck out here," Sasha said, grabbing the empty paper plate laying on the table. She began fanning herself.

"Well girl, take the hoodie off already." Looking like he was smelling shit, Miss Thing's expression overexaggerated his large features.

Sasha took off her sunglasses, slowly unzipped her sweatshirt and carefully peeled off her hoodie. With all her hair matted down and her forehead full of sweat, the entire crew stopped talking. Plates of food hit the asphalt.

"Really?" Miss Thing shrieked, only moving his lips. "What the fuck have you done to your face?" He clutched his pearls in horror.

"It's just a little swollen. It'll go down in a few days. You're such a drama queen, God."

"At least I'm not a fucking Siamese Cat." The model coach was horrified.

"*Yes*, for the clapback," Pablo muttered, to himself.

After a brief awkward moment, the crew continued eating and chatting, leaving the *talent* to discuss amongst themselves. Mason was now staring off at the NYC skyline.

"Anyway, did you hear?" Miss Thing paused for dramatic effect. "We gotta new boss, well, he's not that new."

"Come on, before I pop a stitch."

"It's Pablo."

"Keisha's golden boy?"

"Former." Miss Thing leaned in. "From what I hear, they haven't spoken since we wrapped last season and they had that blowout."

Mason snapped to. "What happened to Pablo?"

"Your fantasy man is now your boss. So, you really need to check your package around him." Abruptly, Miss Thing grabbed Mason's crotch and swooned, "Oooooo, Mason."

Sasha reached in her purse. "If you queens are gonna go at it, I'll need more Percocet." She pulled out a large bottle of pills. "Fuck. This opioid crisis is killing me."

"No, what's killing us is the fact that Keisha's been dulling *our* shine so the bitch shines brighter than all of us put together. And word on the street is, the network's planning on refreshing the judging panel next season."

"I just got my face done."

"Well, Gigi Hadid has more followers on social, so bye, bitch."

"Who told you they're looking for new judges?"

"I have my sources." Miss Thing paused. "Keisha's got nobody's back, and if I get fired, that twat—"

"Language, Miss Thing." Mason took command. "Small mice have big ears, and you do not need anything getting back to *her*."

"Da fuck I care. Do you know how many photos I got on her?" Miss Thing pulled out his iPhone and started scrolling through his camera roll.

"Hold up there, buddy. I am not falling for that trick." Mason covered his eyes.

"What trick?"

"*Puh-lease*," Sasha jumped in. "Everyone with an ounce of testosterone on this set is hip to your ways."

"Girl, what are you talking about?"

"If I gotta dollar for every time you *accidentally* showed Mike, the sound guy, one of your dick pics, I'd have this face paid for already."

"I'd just focus on that pussy-cat face problem."

"Shut up, you *fashion don't*! I said I was just swollen."

Mason stood up and forcibly wedged himself between his fellow judges. "Now, now, let us all play nice."

"Catwoman over there started it."

Sasha made a feline clawing gesture mimicking a cat. "Meeeeoooooow."

"I have a ton of these babies." Miss Thing continued flipping through his camera roll and unearthed a snapshot of Keisha from behind. Pablo squinted to bring the tiny photo into focus. Keisha's outfit was wide open in the back. The zipper to her dress had barely been pulled up a third of the way. Tape, pins and shoelaces had created an intricate latticework that seemingly held the frock to her body.

"Good Lord. That is not appropriate for a Lady," Mason said, now looking at the iPhone through his fingers.

Sasha grabbed the device to look up close. "She's just a wolf in sheep's clothing, Mason. And drag doesn't make a *lady,* ain't that true, Miss Thing?"

"She sure don't! I snapped her from behind at judging. It's my *get outta jail free* card, if I need it."

Mason leaned in to get a better look.

"See. I can easily leak a few of these babies and we could watch the media eat her alive." Miss Thing kicked off one of his Moroccan slides and threw his giant bare foot on the table. "And what's real sad? Her dress was uglier than both my bunions."

The three judges roared with laughter.

"Yo, Missy," Sasha coughed. "You have an Instagram DM." She was holding Miss Thing's iPhone and read the alert notification preview out loud. "*I'm still waiting for that pic you promised me! Papa is HORNY and ready to get off.*"

Mason pointed a ridiculing finger at Miss Thing. "Do you know what you are possibly risking?"

"You can't get an STD from sharing photos, Mason. You're so square." The model coach snatched his phone, rolled his eyes and unlocked it, flipping over to Instagram.

"No. What if someone posts naked photos of you online? The network will not stand behind you. And I am pretty sure you will be hard pressed to find another gig that is as accepting of your kind."

"My kind? Kind of what, you conceited closet case."

"I am just saying; you should be careful. You are no tech genius."

"Whatever, Hughes junior. I may not be good with this whole Instagram thing, but leave me to handle my shit." Miss Thing gathered his belongings, stood up and stared Mason down. "Now, before I go beat this face, I'm gonna go beat this meat and snap the ooooooonly photo that's gonna make *my man* blow his load."

Turning his back on his disgusted colleagues, Miss Thing sashayed across the catering area and disappeared into his double-banger trailer, slamming the door.

Sasha slurped the last of her concoction and said, "Well, I hope he uses a filter 'cause those nuts gotta be older than black thread."

\*　　\*　　\*

It was just past noon and the blistering hot sun beat down on Pablo, who stood in awkward silence next to Keisha on the Intrepid's main deck. This was the first time they'd seen each other since Pablo was announced as EP. She was clearly avoiding him and planned to ice him out. Pablo no longer wanted to fight with her, though. They would, as she'd once told him, *"play, on camera, the way the audience expects us to play."* She wanted to ignore him? Fine. But he now had a new friend. And she wouldn't like who it was.

The scope of production was huge and several crew members ran around locking things down across the massive expanse. Located at Pier 86, off 46th Street in the Hell's Kitchen neighborhood of Manhattan's Westside, the installation showcased the aircraft carrier USS Intrepid, the cruise missile submarine USS Growler, a Concorde SST *and* the infamous Space Shuttle Enterprise. Its opening in 1982 had been the success of New York developers Zachary and Larry Fisher and philanthropist Michel Stern, who'd saved the USS Intrepid from being destroyed in 1978. The Intrepid became a National Historic Landmark in 1986 and remains one of the hot tourist spots to hit when visiting the city of dreams.

Being escorted by a PA, Miss Thing runway walked and landed on his taped X mark next to Pablo. "Why are we doing this welcome here? It's hotter than hell."

"We're gonna surprise the girls with an impromptu fashion show." Pablo burst with excitement. "They're gonna runway walk down the deck. It'll be chic."

"Well, can we get a scrim or somethin'? Keisha looks like a drag queen who just walked outta da club at daybreak."

"You know what, bitch, don't try me!" Keisha barked, without making eye contact with either of her colleagues.

"A scrim is flying in. I already spoke to Bill," Pablo said. "You'll look pretty, don't worry."

"Oh, I'm snatched. It's ya good girlfriend you should be worrying about."

Being an executive producer had its privileges. Pablo wore the concealed IFB earpiece that Rachel and Joe needed him to wear. His work with *Celebrity-Buzz TV,* the last couple of months, had given him the essential practice that taught Pablo to speak on camera, while listening to his producers—at the same time. He could easily hear the conversation between the *Model Muse* team sitting across the deck, hidden inside an open-ended tent. Joe, Rachel, Luciana and De La Renta had been watching everything on a monitor and were all listening on their individual radio headsets. Pablo had requested the IFB mic be left on—so he could hear everything. His therapist was still working with him on his control freak issues.

"Miss Thing's right," Luciana said. "You guys need to back off Keisha. She's a LOT to look at in this light."

"She wanted lashes with rhinestones, and I just do whatever she tells me to," De La Renta piped in. "She likes it, I love it."

"Fucking soften her a bit," Joe yelled, nearly blowing out Pablo's eardrum. "I can't shoot her looking like this."

"I'll tell you what you can soften, that nasty *little man* attitude of yours."

Pablo snickered to himself listening to his witty friend's clapback, as a large scrim was being placed over their heads. Keisha shot him an evil glance. She had no idea what he was giggling about. She was still refusing to wear the concealed earpiece.

"You feel better with this?" Pablo asked Keisha, kindly.

The Supermodel ignored him all together and leaned over, smiling at Miss Thing. "Tell him I look good in any light."

"Did you look at yourself, Mary? Believe me, this is a vast improvement."

Keisha ignored the quip. However, Pablo had more to say. "So, is this what we're doing now?"

"Oh, the gloves are off. This is gonna be good," Luciana cracked. "Anyone wanna place a bet on the last bitch standing?"

"Which bitch?" De La Renta said, "There's a lotta bitches around here, okaaaay."

Pablo could hear several crew members now snickering,

but Joe Vong's voice raised over the ruckus. "Everyone shut up. She's gonna hear you."

Rachel popped her head out of the tent and pulled out her bullhorn, having direct line of sight with the judges. "Ok, since everyone's roasting out here, we're gonna skip the pre-roll and do this in one take with the girls." Her voice echoed.

"Ready on set," the 2nd AD yelled.

"Ready."

"Copy that," Bill yelled. "Girls are walking in three, two, one."

"Wait. What am I saying again?" Miss Thing stammered to Pablo.

"I'll lead you. Just give us some funny lines."

"Don't I always?"

The two giggled at each other *and* at the emerging new model hopefuls tromping onto the deck wearing high-heels, tank tops and tiny cutoff shorts, dragging wheeled carry-on luggage and neck pillows.

"Well, hellooooo ladies. Or should I say, *ladies of the night*." Pablo took center stage; he was loving the moment. "I dunno, Miss Thing, do these girls look like a group of young models to you?"

"Chiiiiiiile, pale girl in the front, with the nonexistent purple shorts. I ain't no gynecologist, so I don't need to see your cervix." A group of girls in the back snickered at the inappropriate jab.

"Welcome, everyone, to *Model Muse*, season seven," Pablo chimed in. "We've got amazing challenges planned for you, AND big news. The winner of this season is gonna be personally managed by our very own *matriarch,* Keisha Kash."

"Did I fucking miss something?" Joe hissed.

"Oh no. You're just getting schooled in *gay shade*," De La Renta shot back. "Pablo's setting Mother up."

Keisha grinned and placed her arms lovingly around Pablo. "That's right. This season I've decided to personally manage the winner with my *handsome* BFF." She leaned closer to Pablo, making annoying kissy sounds near his cheek. "Oh, you're sweating through your makeup, Boo." Patting the sweat off Pablo's brow, she smeared his foundation, making it look uneven. "This year, I'll take one of you under my wing and lift you to new heights—"

"Soooo, we're not wasting any time today," Pablo interrupted, stepping all over Keisha's audio. "You'll be doing a runway challenge right here on the Intrepid, walking in flight suits." The models looked confused. "Now, head below deck where you'll find your wardrobe to change in to. We'll see you back here, sharp, at thirteen hundred."

"That's in ten minutes, you model maggots. Move," Miss Thing yelled, sounding like a drill sergeant.

It was like the *bridge and tunnel* crowd coming into the city on a Saturday night; the near naked girls squealed and awkwardly stumbled off in their heels.

"That's a cut." Rachel said on her bullhorn, "Judges stay in place so we can get a few closeups." She then whispered, "Can you *PLEASE* go in and soften her?"

"I just do hair and makeup," De La Renta barked. "This right here is a comb, not a magic wand."

Pablo could now see his new BFF, De La Renta, walking across the deck reaching into his pocket and pulling out his iPhone midway across. He swiped up on the screen and mouthed the words, *"what the fuck."* Arriving at their position, he glared at Miss Thing.

"Really girl? We doin' dick pics on Instagram now? Who are you? *Anthony Weiner?*"

Pablo grabbed De La Renta's phone and looked at the screen. "Isn't this the same dick pic you sent me last season?"

"Oh, y'all sharing dick pics now?" De La Renta snatched his iPhone back. "That's my exit cue."

"Wait, what?" Miss Thing grabbed Pablo's arm with his oversized hand. "I swear to God, Pablo, I didn't mean to do this."

Pablo knew the network took their morality clause *very* seriously. Nude photos of talent going public was enough to get the model coach fired of his own accord. Another problem he would have to fix.

"Bye-bye, Miss Thing." Keisha grinned like the cat who ate the canary. "Looks like we'll be casting a new *judge* this season too." The smug Supermodel gave a gentle wave of her delicate hand.

Pablo shifted his gaze towards the horizon. An ethereal vision appeared to float amongst the rippling heat vapors that bounced off the steel warship. He focused his eyes and could now see his knight in shining, new armor.

"What you all *really* need to be casting for around here, is a new Host," her voice bellowed from the far side of the Intrepid deck.

Instinctively, Keisha snapped her neck back around to see Brenda Paris looking radiant, outfitted in a Chanel power suit.

"Mama! You're out?"

"That's right, Miss Kiki. I'm baaaaack!"

# TRUTH BE TOLD

**B**RENDA PARIS HAD become the woman you never wanted to cross or dupe. And as the famous saying goes, *Fool me once, shame on you; fool me twice, shame on me!* Brenda had learned all too well from her cheating ex-husband—and now her own daughter—ALWAYS have a plan B!

The air conditioning was roaring at full blast attempting to cool down Keisha's black, stretched Escalade parked on the access road out front of the Intrepid Museum. Comfortably seated inside, and leaning back in her daughter's luxury ride, Brenda Paris felt like the ultimate feminist icon and her hero, Doris Payne, who'd pulled off some of the greatest jewelry heists in history by pretending to be affluent women. When Keisha had been 13 years old, and they were practically starving, Brenda had decided to do the unthinkable to save her kids, just like Doris had in trying to save her own mother.

Unfortunately, Doris had landed behind bars just like Brenda. Brenda had only planned on robbing the unguarded morgue safe, where she worked overnight shifts, once. It was a once in a lifetime chance to score a massive haul that could set her family straight. Brenda's kids depended on her and she'd been in desperate need of cash. After all, she justified, dead people didn't need jewels. Thank goodness, she hadn't pulled off the heist alone. And with her accomplice making off with the loot, the blood vial that took her years to procure had become the key to her release and salvation. Without question, it linked her accomplice to the crime scene.

The sky had been grey and threatening a storm the day Brenda heard the lock to her cell click open. It was a few hours before dinner was to be served and she needed one last favor.

"I can't keep doin' you favors, Brenda," the muscular female prison guard had said, "but my niece won't stop beggin' me for that *Model Muse* zip-up that Keisha's wearing all over Instagram."

Brenda had one left, with her daughter's signature across the back to boot, so she'd handed it off in exchange for the folded shred of paper that had the 911 # 917-555-8691 written on it. When she'd gotten the note, Brenda had no clue that the phone number on that paper was her lifeline and was going to change her life. Now, today, she was about to change Keisha's. Brenda had come up with a *new* plan B, and his name was Pablo.

Gazing with delight, she watched her daughter slip into the Escalade opposite her.

"Oh no, Joe," Keisha called out. Joe Vong was trying to skulk past. "You're back here with me."

Joe reluctantly stepped into the Supermodel's ride, sitting next to Keisha, and closed the door. Brenda was seated directly across from the guilty duo, with her back to the driver. Banging on the partition she said, "Put the window up."

Brenda meant business.

Keisha's eyes widened, her breathing became shallow and nervous. "So, wow. You look great. How did you—"

"Let's just cut the shit! Okay, Miss Kiki?"

The pimped-out Escalade slowly pulled away from the curb and merged into the southbound West Side Highway traffic. Both Keisha and Joe looked terrified to speak.

"You think you're the only ones with high-powered friends? I've got eyes and ears all over your world," Brenda snapped.

Keisha tried to jump in. "I'm assuming you've been talking to—"

"Mama *always* figures out a plan B, Baby. Didn't think I needed one, till I found out you were tryin' to keep my ass in jail. Don't forget, every trick you got you learned from me."

"Pablo's not to be trusted…"

"Pablo's innovative methods of research are what have me sitting here today," Brenda fired back. "My new buddy uncovered a simple truth. The diamond engagement ring I was accused of stealing was never found or cut down into pieces."

"So?"

"So, that meant it could only be in one place, and I no longer needed the blood vial that you DESTROYED." Brenda felt like she was possessed by a demon now. Her voice rumbled and grated her vocal cords.

"Blood vial? Diamond ring? What are you guys talkin' about?" Joe asked sheepishly.

Brenda shifted her gaze, to where Vong was huddled, and slowly transformed her scowl into a big disingenuous Hollywood smile. "And look at you. Big, *little man* on campus. You step in a pile of shit and come out smelling like roses."

With strikingly different alert tones, both Keisha and Joe's cell phones started sounding off in dissonant song.

Brenda continued scathing Joe, wagging her finger in his face. "How do you go from some low-rent *COPS* knockoff shit show, arrest me on camera for your entertainment, to running my baby girl's hit TV empire?"

"Well, I…"

"Will you *both* just put that shit on silent," she screamed. Frustrated with the incessant ringing, Brenda became distracted.

"Ms. Paris. I literally have different execs trying to call—"

"Oh, nooooow it's Ms. Paris? I see Keisha's pint-sized dog training has you good in line."

"Mama hold on for a moment." Keisha flipped the intercom switch next to her shoulder. "Can you activate the Wi-Fi so we can stream something on the screen back here? Quickly."

Brenda's bemused expression didn't distract Keisha as she flipped on the TV that stretched between them. Turning to channel 51, a live, breaking news story was already in progress. Keisha turned up the volume.

"You heard it here first, on *Celebrity-Buzz TV*," the show's host said. "Things are really heating up over on *Model Muse* and *not* on-screen with the contestants. It appears the *real* show is behind the scenes."

"Here we go." Brenda shifted her position to see the screen a little better.

"By now, you've all seen this viral photo of Tyreeq Levern Jackson, known as Miss Thing…."

"*Tyreeq?*" Brenda and Joe shrieked in unison. The screen then swiped to a blurred photo of an unidentified man's pubic region and his hand flipping the bird.

"We've confirmed with Pablo Michaels, the show's *new*

executive producer, and our very own fashion correspondent, that the he/she judge was a victim of an elaborate hack."

"At least he's doing his job," Joe muttered to Keisha.

"Shhh."

"We've also obtained shocking new images of Sasha Berenson, the self-proclaimed original Supermodel of the world, revealing she's evolved into this." The screen swiped to an unflattering paparazzi photo of Sasha in Silvercup's catering area. "The world's first Cat-lady Supermodel."

Glancing down at her iPhone, now buzzing on vibrate, Keisha squirmed in her seat looking very uncomfortable.

"Bribery allegations have also been brought forward involving Andy Levenkron, Keisha Kash's very own celebrity business manager. He's being accused of paying off a former *Model Muse* contestant, who he allegedly had sex with."

"He's so, fucking, fired," Keisha uttered with her jaw clenched.

"Aw, Baby! Things aren't lookin' so good for you," Brenda giggled. She began wheezing and coughing.

"Shhhh," Keisha snapped.

Brenda glared at her daughter.

"…and speaking of Keisha Kash, her very own mother has been sprung from the clinker. An anonymous tip allowed detectives to recover the infamous 8.8 million-dollar Asscher cut diamond engagement ring, given to the late, great Elizabeth Taylor by Richard Burton. It had sold at auction weighing more than 33 carats and investigators had charged Ms. Paris of stealing the rare gem, years ago. With the ring being considered *'too hot to move,'* police now have the actual perpetrator in custody, as evidence found at the scene of the crime also confirms the young man's extremely rare blood type of AB-. The California DA's office will be holding a press conference, later today. However, sources are telling us

Ms. Paris is thrilled to be back and involved in her daughter's life again."

"Sources, Mama?"

"Shhh! I don't wanna miss anything…."

"Now, probably the most surprising news to come out of *Keisha's Crashing Model Drama mill*, TMZ.com is reporting they plan on releasing a verified video that alludes to a potential sexual harassment lawsuit between crew members, AND it's rumored that Ms. Kash allegedly squashed the incident to save her show. Harvey Levin has implied our very own Pablo Michaels is the victim here. A lot more tonight at…"

"Ooooooooo, Baby. See? God don't like ugly." Brenda snapped her fingers and pointed at the screen. "Payback's a bitch…*bitch*."

Keisha flipped off the TV in a huff and glared back at her mother.

"Things are about to change around here," Brenda said. "Mama's back calling the shots," she chirped with delight.

Joe Vong barely moved, but his eyes betrayed him. There was nothing worse than a mother scorned.

Feeling like a baller in a music video, Brenda leaned back in the plush leather seat and took in the speechless Supermodel. She smiled. "Ava DuVernay's people have already reached out. She's interested in writing a biopic about my life story. Looks like Brenda Paris is taking over *Tinsel Town!*"

"Mama, I should warn—"

"*Ohmigod*! Do you think that Viola Davis will wanna play me in the film? I love me some Annalise Keating."

Keisha simply looked down at her iPhone in silence. She turned the device towards Joe, who was also engaged with his own phone.

"What is it?" Brenda asked.

"A text from Broyce Miller, our executive in charge of production."

"And? What's it say?"

Keisha held up her phone to her mother's face.

"Oh baby, I can't see that close, further back."

Keisha slowly moved her device a decent distance away, in order for Brenda to read the message. The group text chain had been addressed to three people: Keisha, Joe and Pablo.

**Broyce TEXT:** Drop what you're doing. My office in an hour!

"How 'bout I drop you off, real quick, before I head over to The Plaza Hotel. I'll send your car right back, don't worry." Brenda's day was about to get better.

"The Plaza?" Keisha quipped. "Who's paying for that?"

"My new son, Pablo, hooked his mother up!"

"Your who?"

"Don't be jealous, Baby. Pablo's not replacing you. You're just demoted."

Brenda could see the lace-front, along the edge of Keisha's wig, lift up as the Supermodel clenched her jaw. Her daughter was fuming now, but didn't dare challenge her.

"He got me a full suite overlooking Central Park, on the house. Apparently, he and the manager are close. The Plaza loved the publicity they got from being on a new hit TV show."

"That I host, Mama."

"I know," Brenda snapped. "But look how you've treated me. Pablo's got the right idea."

"Pablo's a liar."

"Oh, I don't think so. He's proven himself. As for you?" Brenda cackled. "Looks like *truth hurts*."

# 28

## DAMAGE CONTROL

"**H**OW MUCH OF this *Celebrity-Buzz TV* story is true?"

Pablo sat alongside Keisha and Joe who were, if not more, mortified to be sitting across from Broyce Miller answering his questions. Pablo never wanted the Mason story to come out, and since months had gone by with no sign of their incriminating video surfacing on TMZ.com, Pablo thought he was safe. Now the world would find out his embarrassing truth, and Pablo didn't know how to fix it. Where was the real-life *Olivia Pope* (Judy Smith) when you needed her? This was a *scandal,* for sure!

"We need to understand what the sexual assault was. And why you, Joe, didn't come to the network immediately with this situation." Broyce's tone was not to be messed with.

They were seated across the desk from their executive in charge, while a throng of lawyers sat on the side taking notes and listening with intent.

"Well, it was my understanding that no charges were gonna be filed. And, so, ummm…I didn't see the point in involving the network in something that wasn't gonna happen." Joe was clearly lying to cover for Keisha. He was still her *bitch,* after all.

"Regardless of what points you see or don't see, these allegations are serious. And, the network should've been made aware immediately." Sharply turning towards Keisha, Broyce wrinkled his heavy brow. "And what was your role in this, exactly?"

Keisha paused before answering. "Well, Pablo came to me with a *slight* concern, but didn't wanna do anything about it."

"You kiddin' me?" Pablo muttered under his breath.

Keisha shot him an evil side-eye.

"You two have put the network AND the show in serious jeopardy," Broyce said, staring down Keisha and Joe. "And we need to make a—"

"We can get this under control and…"

"You're fired, Joe."

All the sound sucked out of the room. Only the constant hum of traffic beneath the window could be heard. It was a reminder that millions of people were rushing around below, unaware of the bomb that just went off in Broyce's office.

Joe tried to save himself. "But wait! None of this is my fault!"

Two of the attorneys looked up from their legal pads, watching Broyce's physical demeanor. The strapping executive rose from his chair and loomed over his desk like a judge after delivering his verdict. "You were the Showrunner. You didn't come to the network with this issue. You breached your contract and we're cancelling your overall deal."

"But, I was…"

"I think you should leave, Joe."

Vong dropped his chin and slowly slinked out of his chair. Keisha followed his dispirited little body with her squinted eyes. She was clearly disappointed he'd caved so easily. Who was going to be her puppet now? She should've studied her mama better. Keisha needed a plan B. STAT.

Joe exited the office in silence.

"As for you," Broyce said, glaring at Keisha, "ALL creative goes through Pablo. Understood?"

"Got it," she mumbled.

Keisha? Defeated? This was a day Pablo never saw coming.

"Do you want to say anything, Pablo?"

This was his chance to get the Mason story buried, once and for all! "I…ah," he paused. "I really don't need to be the subject of some salacious 24-hour news cycle."

"Fine. We're already in the process of assembling a team to run a full investigation. But in the meantime, we'll craft a statement that will address the TMZ story, that's about to break, as slanderous and based on false accusations. Is that good for you?"

"Perfect." Pablo felt relieved.

"I hope this video that Harvey Levin has isn't a smoking gun I don't know about."

Looking smug, Keisha raised her hand and index finger in defense. "I've got an idea, and I think—"

"I wouldn't say another word, Keisha. You're already skating on thin ice."

"But, I…"

"We can legally pull you off the show, while you retain your 'created by' credit and residuals. I wouldn't push us." Broyce wasn't fucking around. "We're going to need a moment with Pablo alone, so I'd appreciate if you'd leave us with the room."

Without saying another word, Keisha gracefully stood and confidently strutted out of Broyce's office, without looking at Pablo or the team of attorneys.

The door latch clicked. Broyce paused for a few moments before addressing Pablo. "If this story is indeed *true* Pablo, for the record, you have the right to pursue charges. The network will support whatever decision you make."

Pablo took the moment to himself. Looking past Broyce, and now adoring the beautiful view offered through the oversized windows, his eyes glazed over. He finally had the support from someone who cared. However, filing a lawsuit against Mason would surely ruin his career for good. Unfortunately, that's how show business worked. No one wanted to touch the rotten egg. And Keisha? She would probably find some plan to get away unscathed. Pablo would lose everything, again. It was a harmless pass. A fumble on Mason's part. It was not worth flushing his career down the toilet over. The real lesson learned? Seeing Keisha for who she really was, and his eyes were wide open now. He'd have to wait and see the fallout after the video came out, if it ever did. The attorneys stopped writing on their pads. Pablo's phone began vibrating over and over with intermittent text alerts.

"Pablo?" Broyce leaned over looking concerned. "Are you OK? I know this can—"

"Can I just take a moment and look at my phone for a minute? I know it seems odd, but given the circumstances, I just…"

"Take all the time you need. We're here for you."

Pablo made his way over to the far side of Broyce's office and scrolled through several alerts. What called his attention was the new group chat with himself, Keisha, Joe and Rachel. He nervously opened and read the three individual text messages he'd just received from his supervising producer.

**Rachel TEXT:** 911
We got major cast problems at the new model apt.
DISASTER!
I need you all here ASAP!

Pablo's stomach dropped. He was solely responsible for scoring the most expensive apartment to be filmed on a reality TV show, ever. As an executive producer now, his name was riding on everything. This was day, fucking, one. How could so much be going wrong?

He gathered his senses. "I'm sorry, Broyce. I have to go. It's urgent."

"Okay," the exec said, raising his brow. "You sure?"

"Yes." Pablo dashed for the office door. "We can pick this up later on. Tomorrow?"

"Just let us know when you're free."

"For sure." Pablo was tripping over himself to get out. "I need...um...a moment. To ummm...process everything."

Without waiting for a reply, Pablo tore out of the office and down the hall toward the elevators. He accidentally ran into an intern carrying a stack of scripts, fresh from the copier. Yellow and blue pages flew into the air. "Sorry," he said, and kept on running. He was out of breath when he reached the elevators. Pounding the down arrow several times, he began to panic. His adrenaline was kicking in and his heart began to race. He hated 911 texts, now. They only brought more drama into his life. He was convinced he officially had PTSD from seeing those three numbers appear on his phone screen. Pablo had to do damage control. The elevator door opened. He stepped in and continued pressing the lobby button well after he began moving. The forty-eight-floor ride was luckily uninterrupted, but it felt like an eternity. He finally reached the ground floor.

Pablo rushed out of the network lobby only to see Keisha's stretched Escalade still parked out front.

A pinging sound went off in his head.

His anxiety level heightened.

Pablo apprehensively approached the car.

The back window lowered.

Keisha looked angelic, staring at him from her air-conditioned ride. "I figured since we both got the same text, you'd need a lift." She had a soft smile on her face. Disarming.

*Fool me once, shame on you; fool me twice, shame on me!* Pablo's gut screamed at him. He did everything he could to mirror her cool demeanor. "So, we're talking again?" he asked.

Keisha opened her door and moved over on the seat. "The model's apartment is only ten blocks and four avenues over. I think we'll survive."

Reluctantly, Pablo got in the Escalade and carefully closed the door. The two of them sat as far apart as they could. Silence was the only thing shared between them. The car pulled away from the curb and Keisha stared out her window. How could she be so calm after the press attacked her like that today? Pablo wondered. And Broyce basically threatened to pull *Model Muse* from her. Was she delusional? Navigating Manhattan's streets together was bound to be excruciating. It was approaching 4 p.m. and traffic was bumper to bumper. He pulled out his iPhone and typed as fast as he could.

**Pablo TEXT:** KK is up to something. HELP!
I think she knows her mom and I are working together.

The Escalade traveled only a few blocks when congestion enveloped their ride. The silence was eating Pablo alive inside. *Please be there,* he thought. His heart started pounding faster and faster. A sense of foreboding took over his body. Looking down at his screen, Pablo noticed a message was being written in response to his cry for help. Time seemed to slow down as the singular ellipses flashed across his text chain. Abruptly, the car jerked in traffic, but Pablo didn't lose focus. At long last, the text arrived.

> **I.C.E. TEXT:** I'm here!!! First, I've never been a fan of KK. Her behavior is emblematic of the bigger problem in Hollywood - unchecked POWER. You just chose to ignore the truth of who she's always been. Secondly, I saw the Celebrity-Buzz piece. You OK? I wish I knew Harvey Levin or someone at TMZ myself. I'd call on your behalf. Ugh!

Not knowing what to say, Pablo simply replied with one sad faced emoji. Immediately, another text bubble animated and moments later a new text appeared on his screen.

> **I.C.E. TEXT:** You may not want to hear this but ever since you launched this war against KK, you've basically become her. Please know that her actions were only a trigger permitting you to experience a very real side of yourself. You think she's the monster? #YouSpotItYouGotIt #KeepingItReal #Truth

Waves of horror cascaded down Pablo's body while reading the message. Then, another one popped up. He shuddered at the thought of what it would say.

**I.C.E. TEXT:** Getting involved with her mother & trying to take her down was a foolish endeavor. KK will never hold herself accountable or be held accountable by anyone else for that matter. Sorry. I just want the best for you...and this isn't YOU! xo

Jay couldn't have chosen a worse time to play therapist. Pablo put his phone away. He was no longer in the mood for confidences. Keisha remained quiet and the two ex-BFFs spent the rest of their ride gazing out their individual windows, fixating on the traffic jam they were stuck in. As the Escalade approached 432 Park Avenue, Keisha broke the silence and said, "I forgive you."

What? Surely, this was just a glitch in *The Matrix*. "Excuse me?"

She smiled and tilted her head. "I forgive you for everything you've done to me."

Over her shoulder and through the window, Pablo could now see Harper waiting by the oversized glass doors lining the marble drive with Mike, the sound guy, and two PAs. The car slowed down and stopped right in front of Park Avenue's most prestigious address.

Pablo didn't know what to make of Keisha's remarks. "What have I...?"

"I know you've been working with Mama somehow," she said, keeping her cool. "I'd be careful if I were you."

In that moment, both Escalade back doors were abruptly opened by a PA on either side, ready to usher them in the building. Keisha stepped out of the car and waved at the small crowd standing by the curb. Was every moment a red carpet moment? She appeared to gain her strength from public adoration. It was awesome to witness, *and* pathetically sad to see at the same time.

Dread took over Pablo's body now. Keisha wasn't going to rest until she'd torn down every pillar in his life and he came crashing down too. War wasn't pretty, and the first bomb had only just dropped. Stepping out of the car, he forced the tranquil expression on his face as he, too, played the part for the crowd. With onlookers trying to see what was going on and reaching for their cell phones, both Keisha and Pablo were herded into the nearby lobby, like cattle.

# SHITSTORM

B Y THE TIME Pablo and Keisha had pulled up on the pretentious marble exterior drive, Rachel had already begun filming the newbie models' *"move-in"* to a 73rd floor-through apartment owned by an idiosyncratic textile giant at the renowned Park Avenue "Cigarette Building." Production had lucked out with the wealthy uberfan whose fascination with *Model Muse* prompted him to offer his two-floor *mansion in the sky* while abroad in Israel; purely for the bragging rights of seeing one of his homes on television. The network hadn't balked at the pricey insurance they had to shell out, seeing as there was no fee involved in renting the space which could easily go for upwards of two hundred and fifty thousand a week.

432 Park Avenue had forever changed the New York City skyline, and several old New Yorkers regarded the date

of October 10, 2014 as *"the beginning of the end"* to their beloved metropolis. Several media outlets had reported on that day that 432 Park was now officially the second tallest building in New York, next to One World Trade Center. However, with the famous lower Manhattan building being mostly measured with its iconic spire, the new Park Avenue condos would boast the tallest rooftop in the city with incredible views. At the time of its completion on December 23, 2015, 432 Park became the tallest residential in the world. Although, it's association to the growing wealth inequality was also remarked upon by the building's architect himself, Rafael Viñoly. He was quoted as saying, *"There are only two markets, ultraluxury and subsidized housing."*

Other critics had scoffed at 432 Park's slenderness and simplicity. Fashion consultant, Tim Gunn, described the building as, *"[It's] just a thin column. It needs a little cap."* Regardless of what trivial fashion pundits had to say, the now infamous residence had become home to the *Model Muse,* season seven, contestants.

The crew hastily descended on Keisha and Pablo as they walked through the threshold. Like a surprise tornado twisting its dizzying way towards an unsuspecting target, everything seemed to happen at once. Mike started wiring for sound. De La Renta began touching up Keisha's makeup. And Harper handed Pablo a fist full of note cards.

"Things are a complete disaster upstairs," Rachel blurted, seemingly beside herself. "I've got girls tearing the place apart, literally *throwing* expensive art around, while another girl, clearly doped up on some kinda drug, used her suitcase as a bobsled and flew down the stairs." She took a deep breath. "There's a gaping hole in the wall where she crash landed."

Pablo felt discombobulated. "What the…"

"My nerves are already shot—and this is day, *fucking,* one." Rachel stopped to catch her breath. "Joe hasn't answered any of my texts or phone calls, but I think you guys should go in, on camera, and lay the law, ASAP!"

Keisha gently laid her hand on Rachel's shoulder, as Mike tucked in her microphone wire around her waist. "Joe's occupied at the moment. We can take it from here. Don't worry. Hashtag we got this."

She had finally lost her ever-loving mind. Pablo was convinced.

Keisha smiled at Rachel. "You know? If we're gonna play this as a whole new scene, I'll need a wardrobe change."

Crickets.

They were all gobsmacked. No one knew what to say.

It was like Keisha didn't hear one thing Rachel had said.

"De La Renta?" she turned to her glam guru. "I'll also need a remix on this hair and a new lip."

"Copy that, Mommy."

"Where can I go freshen up?" she asked.

"You can use the manager's office," Rachel said, in disbelief. "It's just down that hall, to the left of the concierge desk."

"Perfect," Keisha chirped. "I'll freshen up, and Pablo can go upstairs and get the lay of the land. Cool?"

*Now you wanna be nice to me?* Pablo thought. "It's a plan," he said, taking the high road. "Can you be ready in 15 minutes? Please?"

"I'm *still* a Supermodel, after all. I can change hair, makeup and clothes in 5." She raised her eyebrow at Pablo. "Good for you? Mr. Executive Producer."

*Can't you just fucking faint and accidentally knock yourself out?* Pablo's internal dialogue was starting to sound like Joe Vong. Models fainted regularly on the show, but now he *actually* needed it to happen. Keisha knew exactly how to push his buttons, always had. She repeatedly found ways of winning the battle, no matter what odds were stacked against her. "Fine," he said.

Keisha smirked.

Turning and taking Rachel by the arm, Pablo ushered her towards the elevator banks. "Let's see what's goin' on upstairs." He glanced back and saw Keisha being escorted towards the side hallway. He yelled, "I'll come back downstairs, so we can film our arrival from the lobby. Okay?"

Keisha didn't say anything, but he knew she heard him. She heard everything.

Pablo's ears had popped twice on the rocket launch ride upstairs to the 72$^{nd}$ floor. Perfectly situated in a large utility room, one floor down from the girls' apartment, Rachel had been set up to monitor the contestants on an 85 "screen TV with several camera views laid out in contact sheet form. This satellite control room had become her base of operations, while covering the girls in their new 56-million-dollar abode that had yearly real estate taxes and common charges totaling enough cash to buy a Hollywood actor's offspring entrance into *University of Southern California*. The utility room was stuffy and smelled like feet. Rachel's most likely. Rubber Crocks made your toes sweat. Pablo really had to get over his obsession with smells. Sitting alongside Rachel, Luciana, and Harper, they fixed their eyes on the mammoth screen and watched several scantily clad model contestants walking around in underwear, unpacking their bags, etc.

Prenilla was in the kitchen. The flame-haired model was eating an obscene amount of cantaloupe. She carefully ate each slice without letting the food touch her lips. Pablo thought it looked odd, as he imagined the three other models watching Prenilla with fascination did. Ava, and two other new contestants, made their way over to the asymmetrical monolith where the redhead was gorging.

"God. You really looooove cantaloupe," Ava said.

Prenilla swallowed the last of what was in her hand. "Yeah, I have a delicate stomach. It's pretty much all I can eat."

"Cantaloupe is all you can eat?" Ava snapped, not looking satisfied with the response. "What about rice or mashed potatoes?"

Prenilla began to shake. Her eyes darted around the room. She took off for a nearby bathroom and slammed the door.

Ava turned to the other two and said, "Man, that *is* a sensitive stomach."

"Uh-huh. Lemme count it down," one of the girls chuckled. "In three, two, one. Projectile." She then whispered, "Bulimic."

Prenilla's audio levels thrust into the red zone as she vomited in the bathroom.

"Are you kidding me?" one of the other girls said. Standing in a bra and panty, she started squirming around. "I gotta take a piss so bad right now. Is that the only nearby bathroom?"

"Yup. And there are chicks taking serious dumps in the other ones we're allowed to use." Ava chuckled and then whispered, "Laxatives…"

"I can't hold it." The fidgety model ripped off her white lace Veronika's Privates and, like a gymnast hopping on a balance beam ready to perform, she bounced up on the kitchen counter with her butt down in the kitchen sink, holding herself up with only her arms. The cameraman and Mike, the sound guy, pushed in for a closeup. The able-bodied girl squealed as she let loose a powerful stream of urine.

"At least run the fucking water," Ava yelled, while laughing full out. She then turned to the shocked girl, standing with her mouth open, and whispered, "Diuretics."

One floor down in the makeshift control room, Rachel screamed, "Jesus Christ. What a *shitshow* cast."

"Listen. I plead the fifth on this one." Luciana raised her eyebrows and violently spit her words at Rachel. "Mira. That disrespectful, wig wearing, dumb-as-a-bag-of-rocks *pendeja* is gonna be mentoring these trashy bitches. AND, managing one from under her wing. Didn't you hear her earlier? From under her *fucking* wing. Super-star...*mi chocha!*"

Harper turned to Pablo and whispered, "What's a *chocha?*"

Pollyanna strikes again. Pablo rolled his eyes and quickly typed on his iPhone. He pointed at the screen. The words read: *You're sitting on one!*

The main monitor now showed the *pissing match champion* pulling up her panties as they continued to hear Prenilla's audio of her vomiting in the bathroom.

Rachel sighed and softly spoke into her IFB. "Roll out on this scene and then get someone in there to sterilize the kitchen sink and bathrooms."

"Let's grab Keisha before things really get outta hand," Pablo instructed.

"Outta hand?" Luciana shrieked. "This makes the Fyre Festival look like a baby christening."

When the elevator doors opened in the lobby, Keisha was standing patiently waiting with a new outfit on—yellow Gucci blouse, skinny black jeans and Jimmy Choo heels. Her hair was pulled back in a low ponytail, she wore vamp red lipstick *and* she'd donned a new attitude.

"See? What'd I tell you?" She smiled as if she was going to receive the award for Miss Congeniality.

Ping.

Pablo's ears were ringing now.

He knew the gig was up. She'd been up to something, for sure.

The potent smell of fresh lilacs from the vase atop the round, black marble table next to them should've calmed his nerves, instead he felt like throwing up.

Without warning, De La Renta jumped in front of Pablo's face and powdered his forehead down. "Watch yourself," he whispered under his breath, "She—"

"Okay everyone, clear the area," Rachel barked. "I need them upstairs, ASAP!"

Pablo swallowed hard after hearing his friend's earnest warning. He'd never seen De La Renta so concerned for his wellbeing. The crew moved aside, allowing both Keisha and Pablo to step onto a waiting elevator that had been held for them.

This was one of those times where Pablo imagined a movie soundtrack playing in his head. A disassociation method he'd recently taught himself. It helped him process stressful real-life situations and allowed him to feel as though he were watching a film and not experiencing *reality*. It calmed his nerves. Pablo conjured up the *Avatar* film score. Specifically, the haunting sound of wailing voices, blaring brass instruments and pounding kettle drums as *"Hometree"* was brought to the ground. Man could be such a destructive force. But Keisha? She was a destructive force unto herself.

The Supermodel nonchalantly flipped through images on her iPhone and addressed Pablo without looking at him. "I have a little bit of news that *Celebrity-Buzz TV* didn't have the *'inside scoop'* on this afternoon," she said.

At this point, Pablo didn't even have the energy to panic. His mind, body and soul had been pushed to their limits. He was functioning on what little strength he had left. He sighed. "Okay, let's have it."

Keisha didn't answer. Still looking at her phone, she fluttered her lashes with a childlike smile.

In an attempt to intimidate, like she always did, Pablo tried to stare her down. Instead, his grey contacts fogged up, forcing him to blink rapidly. Thank God she didn't see me flinch, he thought. Well, he hoped. She saw everything too.

"I'm just so excited to finally meet your mother this weekend."

"Huh?" Pablo did a double take. "You met my mom a long time ago? Plus, my parents are on a cruise in Russia."

"Oh, not Helena." Keisha turned her iPhone screen off and was now looking at Pablo. Innocence was her new visage. "I figured since you ran off and stole my mama that you were finally ready, and *desperately* needed time with your *real mama*."

WTF?

Needle scratch.

Boom! An emotional bomb went off in Pablo's head. Keisha had hit the right button, again, and he was no longer in control of his mind and body.

A crooked smirk grew across her face. "You didn't wanna be caught up in a 24-hour news cycle. So, I got better. Your mama and I are sitting down with Robin Roberts on *GMA*. The topic is—"

"ENOUGH!" Pablo shouted, beside himself with fury. He thrust his hand between the elevator doors right before they were about to close, causing them to recoil. It was time to have it out, once and for all.

Rage coursed through his veins.

Forcibly, Pablo hauled Keisha off the elevator, dragging her out into the stark lobby of veined marble and polished wood. He was now under the influence of his surging emotions and wasn't thinking clearly, at all. Coupled together as they walked, he had a firm grip of her arm. The clacking sound of Keisha's Jimmy Choos echoed in the cavernous space as they quickly made their way towards the side hallway near the concierge. The man standing behind the desk was Mason's doppelganger—tall swimmer's frame, Nordic appearance—and had the look of condescension plastered across his face.

Pablo no longer cared what people thought. End of story. Period. She was not going to win, this time.

# I SEE YOU

"**G**UYS. WHAT'S GOING on?" Harper called out. Her saggy jeans, fanny pack and worn out sneakers were the antithesis of 432 Park's sophistication.

The elevator doors closed, and without its famous passengers inside. Halfway across the lobby, Pablo had stopped dead in his tracks. He couldn't speak. Gurgling bile began rising in his throat. Keisha smiled at him like a mentally-ill schizophrenic. *I'll be damned if some throwaway bi-racial baby is gonna crawl outta the gutter and steal my shine!* Her words, he'd heard in the control room, now echoed in his head. Abruptly, Pablo tore off his microphone, then snatched Keisha's mic pack and slid them both along the slick marble floors in the direction of where Mike, the sound guy, and Harper were standing. The disconnected microphone wire dangled between Keisha's legs like a pendulum.

No one else dared to say a word as they watched Pablo haul Keisha by the arm, past the mailroom and to the nearby manager's office. De La Renta was inside packing up his flat-iron and lipstick pallets when Pablo shoved Keisha across the threshold. The thrust of releasing her arm caused her iPhone to fall and shatter on the floor. WHAP.

"What in the hell?" De La Renta hollered. He sized up the situation. "Oh, I see *this* is a wrap. And the only thing better than having plans is, CANCELLED plans. I'm the fuck out." He scurried out, closing the door behind them.

Alone now, Keisha stood quiet and in control. Pablo bent over and picked up her iPhone, waving the destroyed device in her face.

"See? Just like your life. Falling apart."

Keisha smiled. "Oh, is it?" She took a seat in a nearby chair.

The room was bleak and ill-fitted for the prominent address. The banal office furniture didn't match the aesthetic the lobby had to offer. The space felt very backstage and looked more like a Chase Bank manager's cubicle.

Pablo chucked the splintered phone into her lap and turned his back on the Supermodel in an effort to regain his composure.

"You know, David, it's funny what you can dig up about—"

"What did you just call me?" Pablo turned around, glaring at Keisha in contempt. She had picked up her iPhone and was flicking at the glass shards.

"Oh, well, I figured we should use your *real* name from now on, not on camera, of course."

"Pablo Michaels *is* my real name. I told you about *David* in confidence...."

"Marge says hello, by the way."

Boom! Emotional bomb number two went off in Pablo's head. His knees went weak.

"She's such a HUGE fan of the show. She said something like, *always knowing she'd see your name in lights,* or something like that. Anyway, she's been so helpful in connecting me with your mother."

"Wait…I…how? AND STOP calling her my mother." Pablo started fidgeting with the black threaded Apriati bracelet around his wrist, and nearly broke it off. He'd *never* told Keisha about Nurse Marge. Or the fact he'd been in Marge's care for almost four months before his birth mother had finally signed away her rights to him so he could legally be adopted. The nerve-racking process of having to wait and see *if* the Michaels' could bring their son home had been a harrowing experience for both his parents. It had been especially difficult for his mom. Pablo now feared digging up this story, and thrusting it upon his parents thirty years later, would bring all that pain flooding back into their lives. His mom and dad were private people. They wanted nothing to do with the spotlight. Pablo was now facing his worst nightmare and he would do anything to protect his parents. Anything. Keisha had her ways, but how did she know where to start looking for the truth?

The hum of the florescent lights seemed to get louder and louder, the longer he stood in the office. Pablo studied Keisha's body language. Nothing. He couldn't read her. Dumbfounded and at a loss for words, he declared the obvious. "Why are you doing all this? It's gonna tear my family apart."

"Listen. Broyce wouldn't hear me out earlier, but I figured out the perfect solution. I just need you to go to the press and say the whole Mason thing was a lie."

"Ummmmm? Earth to Andromeda. What sci-fi planet are you on right now? I'll give you a hint, it ain't *FIERCE!*"

De La Renta's voice came tumbling out of Pablo's mouth. "How will I explain the video recording, when it comes out? Hello?"

Keisha seemed amused at how he was unravelling. "Oh, that's the easy part. I'll just say I asked you and Mason to have a fake conversation knowing Miss Thing was there."

"What!?" he screamed, raising his voice.

Keisha didn't succumb to his threatening tone and softly said, "We'll just pass it off as an elaborate sting." She spoke slowly and conclusively as if convincing herself it were true. "This is how we trapped the culprit who'd been leaking all this naughty stuff about *Model Muse*."

Her calculations were petrifying. Pablo sighed, wanting nothing more.

"And who cares about Miss Thing, really? You certainly shouldn't. He's fucked all of us over, and it's time he got kicked to the curb. I'm doing you a favor. Really. And payback's a bitch. Remember?" She paused. "Please don't be so naïve; people do this all the time. Someone's gotta take the fall here."

He hated when she condescended to him. "That'll *never* work."

"It *will* work, because I say it will work," she yelled, raising her voice to match his admonishment. And there they were–Gollum eyes were back. Keisha started vigorously rubbing the destroyed iPhone between her hands. What was she doing? Trying to distract him? She continued and said, "You'll tell Broyce this story's *fake news* and I'll make a public statement clearing up the whole mess. Miss Thing? A wrap. And good riddance."

"What?"

"It's either do as I say, or I go on *GMA*. I need you to own this, David." Keisha continued and locked gaze with him. She was hypnotic; he couldn't look away. "Besides, if I go down and get fired over this, like Harvey Weinstein? You'll have sealed your own fate. *Model Muse* is nothing without me." Her toothy grin looked faker than a two-dollar bill. "It won't last. And I'm sure unemployment wasn't fun for you."

Pablo started pacing back and forth. "The public and the media will eat me alive. I won't be able to work in this industry, anymore."

"Oh, don't be so dramatic. We have at least another 10 seasons of *Model Muse* with me at the helm. You'll be fine."

"That's years—of being *your* bitch! And after? Then what?"

"No one will ever remember anything 10 seasons from now. You could easily get your own talk show by then."

"You're fucking delusional."

"Don't EVER call me delusional!" Keisha roared.

The two stared at each other in silence. The energy in the room was now palpable. Pablo's heart had picked up its pace and thumped harder in his chest.

"So yeah, social media will go nuts for a hot minute and come after you. Who cares?" Keisha had regained her composure and spoke with a controlled, softer voice. "After three days, they'll find someone else to shame and persecute. You'll be fine. Miss Thing will get the worst of it. Don't worry."

Pablo simply stared at the deranged Supermodel. He swallowed hard and summoned all his strength. "I'm so done with all your manipulation. You can keep your shitty deal. You wanna do *Good Morning America*? Fine. I welcome the opportunity to meet my birth mother now. How 'bout I join you at the studio for the interview?"

"Really?"

"Yes, really." He was doing his best at faking his confidence. "And good luck trying to thwart the network investigation that'll be looking into all your misconducts. Miss Thing can't hold water, and hashtag real talk? Broyce isn't your biggest fan anymore. I have faith the network will uncover everything you've done, and you'll go down. You deserve to be exposed for who you are." It was time to hit below the belt and take her out. "As for *Model Muse*? I'm sure a more relevant Supermodel, like *Naomi*, would love to take over your hosting duties. The show *will* go on, as they say. Hashtag trust."

Keisha's eyes burned with rage. He knew the N-word would provoke a reaction. Pablo hated the fact he'd stooped to her level, but sometimes you had to get dirty to win the war.

His phone started ringing in his pocket—he'd forgotten to put it on silent.

They immediately stopped arguing. Well, they paused the battle as if a ceasefire had been called. The ex-BFFs continued to stare at each other while listening to Pablo's phone play its melodic tune. Eventually, it stopped. He fished the iPhone out of his pocket and pretended to mute it, but he activated the Voice Memo App instead. Recording the rest of this conversation was essential, and he needed to do it on the down-low. "Receipts are needed," Miss Thing had always said. Pablo needed hard evidence against the shady Supermodel. Placing the device, face down, on the desk to their right, Pablo turned to Keisha and smiled.

The trap was set.

She grinned like *the Grinch* who stole Christmas. "I'm better at this than you are. Remember?" Keisha steadily rose out of her chair. "I can easily call the police after you leave here and say you assaulted me. Who do you think they'll believe?"

"I've never hurt anyone in my life. It'll never stick."

"Oh, really?" She started moving towards him. "*You* just ripped off my mic in front of a group of people who work for ME!" She was yelling now. "Dragged ME down a hall and locked ME alone in here with you."

"That's not enough," Pablo calmly said. He'd found his Zen amidst the insanity.

Keisha reached for him, with her hands now covered in blood! "Looks like the police will have enough, now. And your fresh fingerprints, *all over* my phone."

"What have you done? You're bleeding!" Keisha was twisted, but Pablo never saw this coming. "You're gonna make it look like I hit you with your phone?"

"Why not?" she cackled. "There's no *video* evidence of me cutting myself—so it's my word against yours. Besides, I had no other choice and this is war."

Pablo ran his hands through his silver hair and backed up closer to the wall. It was profoundly disturbing she chose to go this far; however, he needed to record more of her insane accusations. "You're killing me," he cried.

"The hands around your throat are your own, David."

He was sickened by her flagrant disregard for the name his parents had given him.

"You'd be willing to accuse me of a heinous crime? Over what? Because I wouldn't lie to the world for you?"

"It's called power and leverage, and I know how to wield both of them."

Keisha took another step towards Pablo and stood within inches of his face. He could smell her breath. Stale. Sour. Not what anyone would expect standing that close to the Super-model. He instinctively backed off from her advance. He was now pinned against the wall.

She reached forward with her bloodied hands, declaring her words like a mother to a child. "Your fight was never with me, David. You've only been fighting with yourself. Just the thought of what others might think of you, has *always* been enough to terrorize your mind. Why do you think you've been so easy to control? You've never been good enough for You. It's that voice in your head that's the real enemy, not me."

Pablo could barely breathe as he pressed himself against the wall. He was no longer acting. Her words had struck a chord. "You're the devil," he stammered.

"Oh really? Look in the mirror and see what you find."

No. He wasn't like her.

Was it true?

Was *Pablo Michaels* the true antagonist here?

*You think she's the monster? #YouSpotItYouGotIt*—his mentor had just texted him the same thing.

His mind felt like it was splitting open.

"Where's the heroic, innocent *Pablo* I met at Michael Kors?" she said, taking a step back and kicking off one high heel. She untucked her yellow blouse and then tugged at her wig, causing it to sit askew. "You've changed!"

Pablo broke out in a cold sweat.

He was living a nightmare and wanted to wake up.

Keisha grinned and wiped her bloodied hands over her face, looking like a gory soldier in battle. "You're basically me now. And frankly? I'm relieved. I was getting a little bored."

Pablo stared in horror at Keisha's disheveled appearance, with her vacant eyes peering through blood. Television was now full of modern-day cons. They lied when they were on camera, leaked whatever they wanted to the press and lied about their lives when asked about the truth. This was the real person he'd never seen before—the one buried below all her pain. An apparition of the woman he'd once revered. He was now looking at the face that accompanied her demonic voice.

"I think, we're gonna get along a lot better now. You *finally* have the balls to hang with the big boys." The unhinged Supermodel then moved in close to his ear and whispered, "Welcome to the club."

# THE JOURNEY HOME

I N AN OVERWHELMING state of panic, Pablo lunged for the exit. He felt the cold metal of the doorknob in his hand. He was about to turn the handle, when the realization hit. He'd left his iPhone on the desk behind him. He needed the recording—desperately. It was his only proof that Keisha was now blackmailing him.

"If you walk out that door, I'll assume you're ready to start a *full, on, war*." Keisha's voice was shrill and commanded attention.

Pablo had his back to her now. He just needed to get his hands on his phone and he'd be set. Playing her game was the only way out.

Breathe. Be calm, he said to himself.

With a dramatic exhale, he let the tension go out of his body. Pablo turned around and smiled, showing her the kind face she knew and loved. The coldness disappeared from her eyes and she relaxed her aggressive stance. She took on a friendlier disposition.

"Good. At least you see it my way now." Keisha snatched a tissue out of the Kleenex box sitting on the desk, and began wiping the blood from her face. "Every last person who's had any *real* success in this business is a wounded soul. Corrupted by the very pain that allowed them to join this gang of misfits." She continued cleaning her face. "Don't beat yourself up. Becoming one of us isn't easy, and you just passed the test."

Pablo continued to slow his breathing down in an attempt to appear composed. Keisha spat into the tissue and closed her eyes, wiping the blood from her lids.

Now was his chance.

Pablo reached around her waist and felt around on the desk for his iPhone. He kept an eye on his arm, careful not to bump her accidentally. Success. He got it. Slipping it into his front pocket, he looked up to discover her steadily gazing into his eyes, again. Had she seen him? Did she know what he was up to? He couldn't read her expression.

The Supermodel tucked in her blouse, stepped back into her Jimmy Choos and shifted her wig back on straight. "So yes," she continued, "the devil *IS* fierce, you see—"

"Actually, I don't see," he interrupted. She didn't seem aware he'd recorded their conversation.

Now was his chance to be the hero—once and for all.

"I've been led by the wrong set of eyes for too long." Pablo reached up and plucked the individual grey contact lenses out of his eyeballs. His defiance was the first step to absolution. The cloudy halo that had obscured his vision was gone. He clearly saw Keisha for the first time in years. He flicked the contacts at her. "I've spent enough time looking at life through your eyes. Now, it's time for me to do something *good* for a change, and seek paradise through mine."

She chuffed. Clapping her partially bloodied hands together, she mocked his efforts in being brave. "So, that's it? You quit? How noble of you."

"No, I have a contract and I'm a professional. I'm going to, how did you put it, again?" Pablo paused and thought for a moment. "Oh yes, you said, *I'll be just fine and we'll play, on camera, the way the audience expects us to play.*"

"You're a joke. I'll destroy you."

"I can assure you, you absolutely won't," he said, with confidence.

Keisha looked nervous now. Her eyes darted back and forth between his. She seemed to be assessing if he was bluffing. "Why. How do you know?" she said, bluntly.

"You taught me a valuable lesson today. *Power and leverage* are key to success in your world. And I've learned from you how to *wield them both*." Pablo was now holding his iPhone firmly in his right hand. He pressed play on the audio recording and turned up the volume to max. Keisha's voice boomed from the small device.

*"I'm better at this than you are. Remember? I can easily call the police after you leave here and say you assaulted me. Who do you think they'll believe?"*

*"I've never hurt anyone in my life. It'll never stick."*

*"Oh, really? You just ripped off my mic in front of a group of people who work for ME! Dragged ME down a hall and—"*

Pablo hit pause, shut his phone off, and slipped it back into his pocket.

Keisha's face iced over.

"I recorded everything you just said to me in this room. And I'll take this directly to Broyce, the media *and* the police should you step so much as one inch outta line."

Checkmate.

"You'll forever be known for saying, *'There's no video evidence of me cutting myself—so it's my word against yours.'* And no amount of spin will save you from your own confession." Pablo felt a surge of courage. "So, the way I see it? Brenda and I have you on a short leash now. And you're right, payback *is* a bitch."

Keisha remained fixed on his gaze. Any last hint of love or caring, if any of it was even real, drained from her eyes. She was gone. Locked away. They were done.

Grasping the handle firmly, Pablo threw open the door and walked out on her. He walked out on all the bullshit games. And, likewise, he walked out on his own egoistic behavior that had landed him in this mess. As he reached the end of the hall, he could faintly hear Keisha calling him by his real name, "Pablooooooooo...."

He had nothing more to say.

Pablo strutted back into the lobby with a self-assured stride. Walking by Rachel, he smiled and said, "Film this scene with Keisha and the models alone, I'm taking the rest of the day off." He continued past the crew and out of the building, not saying another word to anyone. When he reached the sidewalk, he noticed how oddly fresh the air smelled, and he drank in the sunset that pierced between the buildings.

There was a sudden release of energy like he'd been cut free from an umbilical cord. He was fearless, and ready to set out on life's new journey. Realizing that Keisha was never his true rival, she no longer had any power over him. Yes, he had a damning piece of evidence that could take her down for good, and he'd keep her in check. That wasn't the point, though. With every fiber of his being, Pablo now knew that everything he perceived in the world was just an outer reflection of his inner thoughts. He'd been looking outside himself, vowing to overcome Keisha as his enemy, but the ultimate battle lay within.

Not knowing where he was going exactly, Pablo roamed south on Park Avenue. He just needed to physically get as far away as he possibly could for now.

Sympathy replaced his rage towards Keisha, who had only wanted what she could get out of him. *I was probably the one true friend she'd ever had,* he thought. He would no longer expect anything of substance from her again. However, on camera, they would continue to appear like BFFs for the sake of the show. Their fans would expect it. Plus, Pablo needed his job and looked forward to future opportunities. One day at a time.

Text alerts started going off in his pocket. "Nope. Not doing this," he mumbled. Pablo was ready to take an all too important break for himself. Pulling out his iPhone and getting ready to turn it off, he noticed a voicemail prompt from I.C.E.

He'd *never* spoken to Jay on the phone before. They met in the virtual world of Instagram DMs and eventually exchanged numbers to text offline. *Jay Manuel* was now calling him?

Pablo dug around in his pockets and found his AirPods. He was frustrated he'd missed the call when arguing with Keisha. After popping the white earpieces in, and pressing the notification alert, the message began to play. Jay's familiar voice filled his head and was a welcome sound, drowning out the noisy NYC traffic.

**I.C.E. Voicemail:** "Hey, Pablo, I'm *positive* you're letting me go to voicemail and I wouldn't blame you. I was such a dick sending you those texts earlier, and I'm sorry. I called because I wanted you to hear the intent in my voice and to know that I'm sincere.

I just want you to see the truth behind your relationship with Keisha. You needed her so desperately in order to validate who you were. But when she turned her back on you–betrayed you–it was really you who abandoned yourself. By trying to undermine her you became exactly what you hate! So, I ask you. Who did you really become mad at Pablo?

It's finally time to let go. Time to forgive yourself! You'll be amazed at how magically things fall into place once you let go of everything. One lesson I've learned is, people will never remember the things you've said and done. They'll only remember how you made them feel. What you do next, will ultimately define your future.

I hope we get to speak someday soon. I'm sorry I missed you. Take care. Bye."

Pablo's dark brown eyes glazed over as he stared down the avenue. He felt at peace. He was ready to forgive himself. The inner voice that had guided him, stayed with him, and allowed him to reach success, was there all along, just waiting to be heard. Pablo was now ready to listen to his heart and see through his own eyes. That was *finally* enough for him.

He was enough.

Feeling the sudden rush of true acceptance for himself, gratification filled his body—more love than he could've ever imagined.

He smiled, and knew everything was going to be OK. The ground felt solid beneath his feet. And with each step he took, he felt assured that he was on the path to hope and redemption. Powering down his iPhone, Pablo tucked it in his pocket and continued to wander down Park Avenue.

## END